## THE SECOND GENERATION . . .

*The Oklahomans*, Whitney Stine's 1980 bestseller from Pinnacle Books, established the Heron family in the prairie town of Angel, following the Cherokee Strip land rush of 1893. From the first Discovery Well in 1903, through statehood of Oklahoma, World War I, the Great Depression, to the onset of World War II, the Heron petroleum empire burgeoned into international prominence.

Now, *The Second Generation*—in the continuing saga of the Heron clan, spurred on by the disaster of Pearl Harbor, the patriotism of the war years, and the devastation of the atomic bombings—courageously fights a powerful adversary who plans to wrest control of the giant Heron domain.

**Whitney Stine**, *a native of Garber, Oklahoma, who now lives in Upland, California, has had many best-selling books, including* **Mother Goddam**, *the story of the screen career of actress Bette Davis;* **The Hurrell Style**, *for which he wrote the text accompanying glamour photographer George Hurrell's famous portraits; and* **Stardust**, *the three-generation saga of a famous acting family. He is now writing the third book in* **The Oklahomans'** *series,* **The Third Generation**, *which Pinnacle Books plans to release in the fall of 1982.*

_Phyllis_

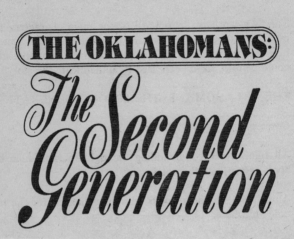

# THE OKLAHOMANS:
# The Second Generation

### Whitney Stine

**PINNACLE BOOKS**                    **NEW YORK**

This is a work of fiction. All of the main characters and events portrayed in this book are fictional. In some instances, however, the names of real people, without whom no history could be told, have been used to authenticate the storyline.

THE OKLAHOMANS: THE SECOND GENERATION

An original Pinnacle Books edition, published for the first time anywhere.

First printing, September 1981

ISBN: 523-41488-9

Cover illustration by Norm Eastman

Printed in the United States of America

PINNACLE BOOKS, INC.
1430 Broadway
New York, New York 10018

*For Max and Hap Simons, Reed and Phyllis Forbes, and Peggy Stine. . . .*

# The Oklahomans:

# THE SECOND GENERATION

# 1

## The Day of Infamy

"... *Last night Japanese forces attacked Hong Kong. Last night Japanese forces attacked Guam. Last night Japanese forces attacked the Philippine Islands. Last night Japanese forces attacked Wake Island.* ..."

*War!* Letty Heron Story Trenton leaned firmly back on the sofa, listening intently to President Roosevelt's voice on the Philco radio console. In her mind's eye she could see him, standing stiffly before the members of Congress as his urgent, insinuating voice rang out in every living room in the land.

*War!* Letty patted her high silver pompadour, examined her veined hands, and then glanced at her children seated around the radio, all solemn and expressionless, as were their own children, clustered on the floor in front of the fireplace. Except for the occasion, it could have been a festive gathering.

Her husband, Bosley, stood behind her, thin, strong hands placed protectively on her shoulders, imparting constant strength through his fingertips to buttress her in what he knew was a supreme ordeal.

Her older son, Luke Heron—whose father had died claiming the very land on which the clapboard house

1

stood, in the Cherokee Strip land rush, before Oklahoma became a state—sat on the hand-carved love seat with his wife, Jeanette, a thin, nervous, menopausal woman of forty-six. He was staring resolutely at a file of papers on his lap. At forty-seven, he was still handsome, although his forehead was prematurely wrinkled—probably, Letty reflected, from looking down those long conference tables where he presided as the president of the Heron Oil Company.

". . . *Hostilities exist. There is no blinking at the fact that our people, our territory, and our interests are in grave danger . . .*" There was no mistaking Roosevelt's pent-up anger, Letty thought, and when he spoke about the surprise attack on Pearl Harbor, and used the phrase "a date that will live in infamy," Bosley grasped her shoulders with such power that she drew in her breath.

As President Roosevelt's voice continued to fill the room, and the import of his words became explicit, Letty gripped the sides of her chair, forcing herself to remain seated. She wanted to rush out of the room and take a quiet walk in the meadow or stroll by Heron Number One, from which oil was still being feebly pumped—anything to get out of the house, away from that artful, disdainful voice that was, with each syllable, changing what had been a horrifying crisis.

Letty smoothed fresh wrinkles from her blue watered-silk dress and changed positions in the wingback chair that her late brother-in-law, Edward Heron, had made by hand. She decided that most furniture, Edward's included, was designed for young people. It seemed that the older one became, the more difficult it was to sit for very long. She sighed and glanced at her granddaughter, Patricia Anne. She was quite pretty—no, Letty corrected herself, she was *beautiful*. How sad it was that George Story was not around to see his granddaughter; he would be doubly pleased because she had inherited his good looks, a creamy olive complexion, electric-blue eyes, and dark, burnished hair the color of molasses.

Patricia Anne smiled at her grandmother. For a moment the light coming in through the window created an illusion: the sun turned Letty's hair from white to yellow, and, with her head centered in the momentary halo, the wrinkles in her face disappeared. Patricia Anne caught her breath; for a moment she had glimpsed what her grandmother must have looked like as a young girl. She felt strangely removed from the voice on the radio. While time did not stand still on the farm, the hours seemed to creep by more slowly than when she was on the road with her father and mother, or at school in Kansas City. She went into the kitchen and filled a glass from the tap; the well water tasted sweet and pure, and as she sipped, she thought that the taste must be somewhat like champagne. She took a deep breath and went back into the living room at the exact time that President Roosevelt's voice faded away.

Bosley, his gray head high, walked slowly to the radio and turned the knob. There was complete silence in the room. He pressed his lips together firmly and let the air out of his lungs all at once. "It's apropos, I suppose," he began gently, "that when we've all gathered here for what was to be a family reunion—the first in many years—we're now all drawn together for another purpose."

The telephone rang insistently, and Hattie, the housekeeper, appeared a moment later. "Mistah Trenton, it's a Mistah Hopkins." She paused importantly, her false teeth clicking momentarily when there was no response, and went on breathlessly. "A Mistah *Harry* Hopkins, from Washington, D.C."

Luke stood up, and the file of papers on his lap fell to the floor. "My God, what do you suppose he wants? I can't stand the man."

Bosley nodded. "I can't either, but I've known him for years. Met him when he was just a pipsqueak in Sioux City." He left the room with a wave of his hand and picked up the receiver. It took a moment to become accustomed to the *zip* and *ping* reverberating over the long-distance wires. "This is Bosley Trenton," he said evenly.

"This is Harry L., and we're on the scrambler," was the acerbic reply. "I hardly think it necessary, since I don't care who listens in, but it's wartime, you know."

"Yes, I just heard the President," Bosley replied. "Damn good speech—not quite up to some of Churchill's, but effective nonetheless."

"Glad that you approve," came the laconic answer. "However, I didn't call you from Pennsylvania Avenue to discuss syntax. We're mustering a meeting of the Seven Sisters, and, while Heron isn't exactly the Eighth—yet—we do expect either you or Luke to be present. We don't want a lot of press attention, so the conference won't be held here, but at some out-of-the-way spot—probably Georgetown. I'd hold week after next open, but we'll let you know in plenty of time." He hung up without saying good-bye.

Bosley felt a fresh charge of adrenalin course through his veins and returned to the living room with a jaunty step; he would have whistled if the occasion had not been so consequential. When, as a young man in 1899, he had discovered the anticline in Letty's water well, which eventually led to the spudding of the first of many oil wells, he had whistled a great deal; it was a time of excitement and discovery and sudden riches. He smiled to himself. Wildcatters in those days poked fun at geologists like himself, and the picture did not change until the beginning of the World War. *That* conflagration, he supposed, would now be referred to as World War Number *One*. His euphoria faded as he came into the room and took his familiar stance by the mantel, the new war very much in mind.

Letty clasped her hands in her lap and marveled at the change that had overtaken her husband: it was as if he had lost ten years in age during the few moments on the telephone. There was a new set to his jaw. His eyes were piercing and luminous as he looked over the group. She had not seen him so much in command since the Governor of Oklahoma had appointed him to the Soil Conservation Program during the Dust Bowl days. Once more, he was obviously in his element.

She sighed and looked about the room. Luke was tense, his brow still furrowed. On the large sofa her younger son, Clement, was examining his long fingers—those same fingers that had thrilled audiences when he had played Grieg and Chopin piano compositions as a teenage boy, and much later as he had raised his baton to conduct the orchestra made up of mixed-blood Cherokee Indians. Sarah, his wife, also of Cherokee extraction, sat primly beside him. Letty looked from one son to the other. Luke, of course, was pure Irish and Scottish, and while he was a brilliant, if somewhat stodgy businessman, he did not possess a native intelligence like Clement. There was something quite ordinary about Luke, she had to admit; and although he was her firstborn, she did not love him more than his brother. She shook herself out of her reverie at Bosley's term "Seven Sisters," which was echoed by Luke Three, aged fifteen.

"The Seven Sisters of petroleum"—Bosley chuckled softly, looking over the top of his glasses at Luke Three—"are Standard Oil, Shell, British Petroleum, Gulf, Texaco, Mobil, and Chevron. We're somewhere down the list, with Sinclair and Union." He pursed his lips. "I should think, by now, that you'd know some of the nomenclature of our business." He glanced reprovingly at Luke and admonished, "You haven't been teaching the boy."

Luke frowned. "What did Harry want?"

"I imagine the meeting will concern gas rationing," Bosley replied, "and I suppose there will also be conferences with Boeing, Cessna, and Northtrop. Aircraft production will be accelerated, and that means production of top priority, one-hundred-percent high-octane airplane gasoline will have to be upped." He looked at his watch and laughed ruefully. "I'm still a bit stunned by the Japs' attack on Pearl Harbor. I'll have to get my thinking cap on, as we used to say." He stole a glance at Letty. "I think Luke and I should go to Tulsa immediately. The phones at headquarters will be ringing off their hooks."

John Dice, their banker friend and a former Republican Senator from Oklahoma, stood up and stretched his back. "I wish I was young enough to enlist," he said in his soft Texas drawl that had stayed with him all of his forty-eight years in Angel. "I'm fighting mad. You'd think that damned Roosevelt and his uppity Cabinet would have known about the attack. My God, they've got intelligence units *somewhere*." He scratched his head, his fine eyes flashing with anger. "Someone in the government had to have gathered data on the Japanese troop buildup, plus their accelerated war effort. And to think we sold them all that pig iron—that's going to come right back to us in weapons and tanks and artillery!" He was white with rage.

"Now, Jaundice," his wife, Fontine, soothed, "don't get so het up. With your high blood pressure, you could have a stroke right here and now." She took hold of his arm with her plump hand and bobbed her platinum blond head up and down like a white leghorn pullet.

"Let go, Fourteen!" he admonished, shaking loose from her grasp. "Let me finish."

"Well, you're not filibustering in the Senate now,

6

Jaundice. You sit down this minute, before you surely enough have an attack!"

Bosley held up his hand. "John, my sentiments are with you exactly. Roosevelt said that he'd keep our boys out of the war, and I wouldn't put it past him to have known about, and condoned, this sneak attack, so that we'd have to get in the fighting."

Letty arose. "Now, gentlemen," she said softly, "that's enough political talk for the moment. I have two freshly baked angel cakes just waiting for the knife, and Hattie has just brewed some good coffee. I think it's time to have a little refreshment from the cares of the day."

"Thank you, Letty dear," Fontine said, "but it's been a hectic day, full of surprises, and if you don't mind, I think Jaundice and I will just trot home. His blood pressure's already up, I'm sure."

"There is nothing wrong with me," John Dice announced. "But if the missus says it's time to go—well, it's time to go."

Sam, Born-Before-Sunrise, stood in the back of the room, his snow-white hair and mustache topped by an equally snow-white turban, the same sort of headgear that his Cherokee forebears had worn on that long sojourn from Georgia, known as *Tsa-L-Gi*, the Trail of Tears. With a heavy heart he had listened to the President's message—brave words in a time of great upheaval—and he knew with a certainty that America would never be the same again, just as his own people had never been the same since that long, bitter trip, when the tribes had been escorted by General Scott from their southern homes to lands beyond the Mississippi—the territory that became the great state of Oklahoma. He had sorrowed anew as he heard the Chief of State relate the treachery of the Japanese in the Hawaiian Islands.

* * *

7

On the next farm over, in the lavishly appointed living room of the splendid Federal Restoration mansion that had cost three-quarters of a million dollars in 1927, Fontine Dice looked up expectantly from the newspaper at her husband. "What does 'infamy' really mean, Jaundice? I've heard the word a dozen times lately."

John Dice looked over his spectacles. "Well, Fourteen, it means—well, how can I explain . . ." He paused and lighted a pipe, then puffed energetically. "Contemptible or disgraceful or dishonored—but it's a stronger word than those."

"Then it's about as bad as you can get, right?" Fontine's plump face shook indignantly. "I declare, Jaundice, if I was young I'd go to work in a bullet factory. It makes me hopping mad to think I have to stay here on this darned old farm and see those boys going off to fight the Japs." She patted the yellow curls that had framed her face in the same style since 1919. "Do you feel old?"

John Dice looked at her again over the top of his glasses. "Not especially. I'm not seventy yet, and the bank's doing well, and we have no worries to speak of, but I suppose this will all change with the war. I don't plan to retire soon, if that's what's worrying you." He blew a circle of smoke into the air. "Why do you ask?"

She sighed and got up and turned off the news on the radio. "Oh, I don't know. I'm antsy for some reason that has nothing to do with this Roosevelt business." She started to pace back and forth in front of the enormous bay window. "I guess it's just come home to me how lonesome you and I really are, which I didn't realize until we came back from Bos and Letty's today. It was wonderful seeing all the children and the grandchildren again, and dear Sam—such a success!"

John Dice nodded. "Yes, who would've thought that the poor orphaned Cherokee Indian boy, left over at

8

The Widows by his mother, would ever amount to anything?" He sucked his pipe. "Well, sure as the sun rises and sets, he was a born baby doctor, and if he made all that money in Barbados, he deserves it."

Fontine stopped pacing and turned to the window, and then giggled like a young girl. "Did you know that he was writing a book about his life?"

"No!"

"Yes, but I don't see how—I mean—he can tell *everything*."

John Dice cleared his throat. "Well, I don't, either. He can't talk about his—mutilation, for instance. Did you notice he's wearing a false mustache? It looks good. I guess he's conscious of the fact he has no beard. Wonder what he'll call the book?"

"Why, Jaundice, what else but his Indian name?"

"Born-Before-Sunrise?"

She nodded. "Darn good title." She began to pace again. "And speaking of titles, I don't suppose our girl will ever get a Mrs. tacked before her name. It seems a pity that Bos and Letty have such a large family with all that love back and forth—and we've only got Charlotte, and she's an old maid."

"That's not a very good way to put it, Fourteen," he said, scratching his thinning gray hair. "She's a bright woman. Thirty-seven isn't old anymore."

"It is when you don't have a husband. I don't know what got into her. She went with practically every boy in Angel when she was young, but none of them ever suited her." Fontine looked up fretfully. "Jaundice, we raised her right, didn't we?"

"Of course," he soothed. "She's independent, that's all." He paused. "Why don't you try to get her on the phone again?"

"I'm sure the lines are still tied up. Everyone's calling everyone else." Fontine picked up the telephone and the operator surprisingly, came on the line at once.

9

"Nellie, is that you? Can you get me Charlotte's number in Dee Cee?"

"I'll try, honey," the voice came back clearly, "but so many calls are coming in and going out, my old switchboard's liable to go up in smoke!" There was a pause, then she came back on the line. "Sorry, my trunks are full."

"Darn!" Fontine cried and placed the receiver back on its hook; then she glanced at her diamond wristwatch and turned the radio to the Blue Network, just in time to hear the sweet-voiced announcer intone: "The following program was transcribed." There was a momentary pause, and then the familiar instrumental "Lady Luck" floated smoothly out over the airwaves. The honeyed voice continued in the foreground: "Ladies and gentlemen, Aunt Bertha's Old-Fashioned Oat Flakes present Clement Story and his Cherokee Swing Band, featuring the Storyettes."

There was an upbeat, and the relentlessly cheerful voices of the three girls, in strict harmony, bleated out provocatively:

> *"What says, 'Good Morning' with a crackle,*
> *    What gives energy to tackle*
> *All workday problems, pains, and aches?*
> *    Yes, Aunt Bertha's old-fashioned, Oat Flakes."*

Fontine settled back on the sofa, closed her eyes, and listened to the first number, a romantic ballad, "Say Good-bye Again." During the commercial she sighed. "Jaundice, isn't science wonderful? Here we are, listening to Clement and his band on the radio, while he's just next door at the Trentons'."

John Dice nodded and lighted his pipe. "I was thinking the same thing, Fourteen."

"There's only one thing that could be improved," Fontine exclaimed petulantly, her platinum curls danc-

10

ing. "It's just too bad that Clement can't have a better sponsor. I mean, Glenn Miller has Chesterfield cigarettes."

"Well, what's wrong with Aunt Bertha?" John Dice replied evenly, puffing on his meerschaum. "Her Oat Flakes are on breakfast tables all over America. Don't like them myself, but only because I prefer hot cereal. Ninety percent of the kids in Angel collect those trinkets in the boxes, and most of them belong to Aunt Bertha's Sky Club." His eyes twinkled. "Those membership rings with the fake emerald aren't bad-looking at all—wouldn't mind wearing one myself!"

"Stop your joshing," Fontine replied, and they spent the rest of the hour in silence, quite carried away by the smooth sounds of Clement's music. When the signature tune was repeated for the sign-off, Fontine switched to another station to pick up Elmer Davis's commentary.

In his apartment in Enid, located over the Heron Furniture Company store, Mitchell Heron was also listening to the broadcast. Davis was saying:

". . . There are some patriotic citizens who sincerely hope that America will win the war—but they also hope that Russia will lose it; and there are some who hope that America will win the war, but that England will lose it; and there are some who hope that America will win the war, but that Roosevelt will lose it. . . ."

Mitchell snapped off the radio and poured a cup of coffee. Damn, just when the business was experiencing an upswing, the world would turn into political chaos. At forty-three, he would not have to be concerned about the draft, but what would happen to the economy of the country? Until five years ago, when he had come back to Angel to help his mother on the farm after

11

being in France for many years, he had wasted his life. He might as well admit it; those years in Europe selling those glass figures had been a bust. But now that she was dead, and his inheritance—profit from the sale of the diamond that she had secreted away all during those terrible years of the depression—had enabled him to open a fine furniture store in the same location and similar to the original Heron Cabinet Shop that his father had founded in 1899, it appeared that another spell of rotten luck was just around the corner. Who in the hell would want expensive handmade furniture with the world in such turmoil?

His chief designer, Harry Alderman, who had more talent in his little finger than most college graduates, was 1-A, draft status. Four journeymen, in their twenties, would no doubt be receiving their "greetings" soon. Mitchell shook his head. He had been born with a jinx—apparently a never-ending jinx. He was in a black mood. He went to the sideboard and poured himself a glass of bootleg whiskey, then sat down by the window that overlooked the courthouse square and got quietly drunk.

After luncheon Luke went upstairs to pack, and Jeanette joined him a moment later. "If you don't mind, I'll stay here with Patricia Anne for a few days."

"That's very kind of you," he replied evenly, folding his pajamas. "In fact, you can stay as long as you like." He did not look at her but concentrated on rearranging four pairs of socks in the suitcase.

"I really don't think you'd mind if I stayed here permanently." Her voice, soft and insinuating, brought back many similar incidents over the years.

"You know that I don't care one way or another," he replied unemotionally. "You can stay here, or you can come back to Tulsa. It's strictly up to you." His voice

12

was flat. He rummaged around in his toilet-article case. "Where is my shaving cream?"

"You probably left it in the bathroom." She looked down at her huge diamond wedding ring, then pushed back a lock of hair that had fallen loose from her chic blond upswept coiffure, and waited until he came back into the room with the jar in his hand. She smiled coldly, "One of these days I just may go away and not come back." It was a statement, pure and simple, delivered quietly.

He looked at her for the first time. "I don't know why you won't give me a divorce." He looked at her obliquely, then packed the accessories bag tightly in the corner of the suitcase. "How long have we been living together as brother and sister?"

"Why bring *that* up at this stage of the game?" She went to the window and looked out at the white landscape, her back erect, her thin hips showing through the beige silk dress. "It's starting to snow again," she murmured. "You'd better drive. Bosley's eyesight isn't so good."

"I will."

"Do you think you'll go to war?"

"And maybe get killed, is that what you're hoping?"

"Oh, Luke, be sensible!"

"If Uncle Bos was my age and could keep control of the company, I'd sign up tomorrow, just to get away from you." He picked up the suitcase and went out into the hall.

Letty was waiting at the foot of the stairs. "Luke, look after Bosley, will you? This Japanese attack has hit him hard. Don't let him overdo."

"I won't, Mama," he replied. "Don't worry. By the way, Jeanette and Patricia Anne are going to stay for a while."

Letty brightened. "Oh, I was hoping they would!" She paused. "You know, I *am* kind of jittery. This war

13

is going to be a lot different than the last one. Everything's mechanized now. I shouldn't be at all surprised if it takes place entirely in the air."

He pressed her arm. "Not entirely, Mother. The Japs may have scuttled some of our fleet, but all of our warships weren't at Pearl Harbor, you know."

She opened her eyes wide. "No?"

He clamped his mouth closed. "I've said too much. I'll telephone later, although I suppose all the trunk lines all over the country will be tied up for days. Take care." He lowered his voice. "I love you, Mama."

"And, I love you, son." She followed him out to the driveway and smiled; while she did not approve of a great show of public affection, it was rather nice, she decided, for a son to kiss his mother's cheek.

Bosley came onto the porch. "Letty, something is wrong with my left eye. My vision is blurred. It's like a curtain has come down."

"Thank God we've got a doctor in the house!" She motioned for Luke to join them, and he ran in from the car.

Five minutes later Bosley was sitting on the bed in Sam's room, staring into a small light. "I'll telephone an ophthalmologist in Enid for an appointment this afternoon." Sam removed the light. "How is your eyesight now, Bosley?"

"Why, I can see perfectly well. The curtain has lifted. Thank you."

"I have done nothing. The condition has cleared up by itself." He removed a small stethoscope from the open bag on the bed, adjusted the earpieces, then placed the small round metal cylinder on the right artery in Bosley's neck. "Don't talk now"—he smiled—"or my head will reverberate like a dozen locomotives going at full speed." He rubbed the artery lightly, listened intently, then switched the instrument to the left side, then nodded. "It always seems that these things

14

happen at the oddest times," he said quietly, replacing the stethoscope in his bag.

"I should be back from Tulsa next week."

Sam shook his white turbaned head. "No, you must go to the doctor as soon as it can be arranged."

"But the condition has cleared up, Sam!"

Sam nodded gravely. "For the moment, but I believe that you've just had an *amaurosis fugax*." He paused solemnly. "You see, Bosley, as we grow older, arteries harden and the blood is pumped with more difficulty through veins that are sometimes heavily lined with fatty tissue—like rust."

Bosley smiled. "You mean, Sam, that my pipes are rusty?"

Sam nodded. "It might be put that way. I believe that a bit of 'rust' came up through the artery and for a moment blocked the passage of blood to your eye, causing a blackout. When this happens in other parts of the body, there is also a temporary loss of strength. If my diagnosis is correct, the doctor will simply prescribe medication that will dissolve this 'rust' in your bloodstream. But you must not wait. The same condition may occur again, but in a more serious manner. As far as I can discern, your arteries are clear."

"Damn!" Bosley exclaimed vehemently. "Do you suppose this was brought on by the war?"

Sam smiled ruefully. "No, Bosley, it's just something men our age often encounter—a warning to slow down."

"Right now, Sam, I feel a hundred and three."

Luke undressed slowly, then hung up his clothes methodically, all the while thinking: *Tomorrow is the day for big decisions, the first official day of the war.*

After Sam had driven Bosley to Enid for the doctor's appointment, Luke had telephoned all twelve members

15

of the board of directors of the Heron Oil Company, a chore which had taken three hours of precious time, because Angel's telephone system was primitive and Nellie, the operator, was asthmatic. The board meeting had been scheduled for Thursday at headquarters in Tulsa, which would, he hoped, allow time for airline and train reservations. He smiled wryly to himself. It was not like the old days, when only two members of the Heron board resided outside the state. Now eight men lived in such far-flung places as Oregon, the District of Columbia, Minnesota, and California; only two made their homes in Oklahoma.

Jeanette came in from the hall bathroom, wearing a long plush robe of electric blue. "I hate to stay here when the house is so crowded," she whispered angrily. "Your mother should have another bathroom put in upstairs. This house is so inconvenient." She sat down on the bed and took off her mules. "And also, you'd think that she'd be lost without a full staff. She and Bosley live so graciously in D.C., but when they're here on the farm, it's scandalous, and Hattie should be fired. She's about as efficient as those men who used to work on W.P.A." She paused. "Oh, God, I'm so sick of making beds!"

"Oh, be quiet," he whispered back. "You're sounding spoiled, and since this is the first time the family's been together in years, I'd think you could be a good sport, especially with Uncle Bos unwell." He sighed. "He should be all right as long as he takes his medicine. You'll have more privacy when we leave tomorrow."

Jeanette got up stiffly, took off her robe, and adjusted the ecru lace nightgown. She shivered and wrapped a length of gauze around her upswept hairdo. "Also, do you think they'll ever install a furnace? I'm freezing." She fluffed the pillows and got into bed.

Luke put on his flannel pajamas, switched off the

16

bedside lamp, and crawled in beside her. "It *is* cold," he said, glancing at the hoarfrosted windows. He moved next to Jeanette, pressing his body close to her back, pushing himself against her buttocks. She sprang away.

"I thought you said you were cold," he whispered.

"Well, I'm not *that* cold," she retorted.

Luke sighed heavily and turned on his side, away from her, the slick sheets imprisoning his body in a cold cocoon. Then, with his eyes closed, and even with the pressures of the day turning his brain into a churning caldron, he was astonished to find that he was becoming physically aroused. He tried to relax as the bed warmed. He thought of a cool, green meadow, but the hills on either side thrust up, creating perfect breasts that turned from green to pink. When had he made love to Jeanette the last time? He finally figured out that they had taken separate rooms a year ago last March. What had they quarreled about? Guilt tugged in the back of his brain. One of the most important milestones in his life—and he could not remember anything about the disagreement! He had successfully blocked out the entire episode, but what he could not block out at the moment, was his growing desire as he pressed himself down into the mattress.

Finally, he turned over and brought himself in line with her body. Again she shook loose. "Luke," she hissed, "for God's sakes!"

Suddenly he was outraged, as angry as he had ever been, and he knew then, as the blood coursed up through his temples, that his current attitude reflected his total mental state. The country was at war. He was at war. The family was gathered together for perhaps the last time. He felt desperately alone, bereft and unloved, revolted at his show of desire in the face of her contempt. Intellectually he analyzed the anguish of the moment, which he could not accept emotionally. Again

17

he drew himself to her and seized her around the waist.

"Let me be!" she exclaimed in as loud a whisper as she dared.

He loosened his grasp and turned away from her, seeking a position at the very edge of the bed, where the sheets were icy cold. His body heat melted away; gradually his turgid member grew limp. Then, with his body totally relaxed at last, he fell into a deep, disturbed sleep.

In his dream, he was walking through a meadow covered with wild white and yellow daisies. Looking down, he saw that he was barefoot, and the green turf springing up between his toes was velvety soft and slightly damp.

The terrain looked primitive and unfamiliar until he saw The Widows' Pond. He walked forward, and although his footprints left deep impressions in the snow, he felt no cold, only a strange, warm comfort. He made his way to the back door of The Widows and was greeted by Sam, his white turban slightly askew. In the dream, it seemed to Luke that he was cognizant of the span of time, and he knew that he was back in the days of his boyhood. An almost overwhelming sense of sweet nostalgia came over him, and he thought: *I must enjoy this experience, because it will not happen again. I am being given a reprieve.* . . .

Leona Barrett, auburn hair piled high, stood at the bottom of the stairs, smiling and holding out her hands to him. After experiencing a brief moment of serene, silent communication, she pointed to the top of the stairs, where the figure of a young blond girl stood. She was clothed in white. Stella made little beckoning motions with her fingers, and suddenly, without any physical effort whatsoever, Luke was at the top of the stairs, kissing her hand.

Her room was as resplendent as he remembered: blue walls, fluffy white curtains, dainty flasks on the dresser. His bare feet pushed down into the soft luxurious nap of the burgundy-and-rose Aubusson carpet. When his eyes came to rest on the pale blue coverlet, he let out a little cry of delight and surprise. Stella lay quite nude; her milk-white skin, without so much as a single blemish, almost melded into the satin counterpane. The window was open, and a slight breeze blew the Priscilla curtains gently to and fro—but it was wind warm from the green meadow, and not an icy blast from the frozen pond. He wondered why he was so conscious of the warm draft; then he saw that he was naked.

In the dream, his mind worked on several levels of awareness. Although a part of his brain acknowledged that he was forty-seven years old, his body told him that he was thirteen. His slight physique was not yet muscular, nor had he grown to adult height; yet his manhood was beautifully and finally formed. He experienced a moment of pure joy and delight in this newly found experience of looking at himself as he once was, and again he was aware of the difference in the requirements of a man and the expectations of a boy. He lay down beside the desirable Stella. It was with a sense of great exultation that he anticipated making love to the very girl who had initiated him into the realm of sexual enjoyment. Stella smiled slightly through parted lips as her hand encircled him. . . .

As if returning from a long mental reverie, Luke roused reluctantly from his dream, realizing that the hand that encircled him was *real*. As Jeanette moved closely beside him, he knew that he was in his mother's front bedroom and not in Stella's aerie at The Widows. "Luke," Jeanette whispered, "I've lain awake thinking about us—the way it used to be. I'm ready for you now."

For the first time in more than eighteen months she desired him, and after his dream with the youthful

Stella, to his surprise, he did not want Jeanette. Luke sought to pull away from her grasp, but she held him with new exciting caresses, and as he rose up stiffly again, he was helpless. Very gently, then, he turned on his side, and she received him fully and eagerly all at once. And, as he moved within her, Stella's fresh beauty, her moist warmth reincarnated from his dream, and he was enveloped in sensuous pleasure so exquisite that he cried out in extreme anxiety and began to make noises in his throat. Fearful that the sounds would travel throughout the upper part of the house, Jeanette held her hand lightly over his mouth. She slowed her own movements; their bodies rocked gently, powerful waves of feeling—lulling and then intensifying, lulling and then intensifying—washed over them until they were both sweetly drained of emotion. They fell asleep in each other's arms.

Luke was awakened by the screech of the guinea hens and knew that it was seven A.M., the time that Hattie always scattered feed for the fowl in the barnyard. Why didn't she feed the birds in the late afternoon like everyone else? Also, were the roosters too lazy to crow at sunup? These were amusing, if unfathomable questions that he preferred not to probe.

He looked at the sleeping Jeanette and felt himself stirring again. The night came back, and he smiled and brushed her cheek with the back of his hand. Perhaps her long phase of not wanting to be touched was over, and their life could resume on the old basis; he still loved her very much. Thankfully, his days during the last eighteen months, had been full of Heron oil business, otherwise he could never have endured the relationship. Everything would be different now. He touched her cheek again, and she awakened. He smiled at her. "Good morning, sweetheart," he said softly.

She fluttered her eyelashes, fighting off sleep, but when she focused on his face, her bland expression

20

changed to loathing. "Stop it, Luke!" she whispered fiercely, turned over, and got out of bed in two movements that could have been choreographed, *one, two*. She disappeared down the hall to the bathroom, leaving him hurt, stunned, and aggravated. What had happened? She was so loving last night. . . .

So that he would not be forced to face her again so soon, he got up, dressed, and went downstairs to the kitchen, where Letty was seated at the table, drinking a cup of coffee and reading *The Angel Wing*. She smiled. "Good morning, son."

"Good morning," he replied and poured himself a cup from the pot on the back of the stove. He sat and stared at the checked oilcloth. "Mama . . ."

"What's wrong, Luke, didn't you sleep well? I bought new mattresses for every bed in the house just before the reunion."

"I slept fine, it's just that . . . Jeanette . . ." He wanted to confide in her, just as he had told her all of his problems when he was a small boy, but he could not find words to describe his feelings. How could he tell her about his marital problems?

"Yes?" Her eyes were troubled.

"Jeanette, he finished lamely, would like to stay on a few more days."

She brightened. "Oh, I think that's splendid, Luke. I was hoping she would keep me company for a bit. With Bosley gone, it's going to be very lonesome around the farm." She pursed her lips. "You know, Luke, I don't think we'll be opening the Connecticut Avenue house in Washington this year. The war is going to change so many things, and then too, Bosley will be traveling, visiting the field offices a great deal of the time. At my age, I think I'll just stay here."

"At your *age*!" he scoffed. "You're not old, Mama."

She laughed, and the lines around her eyes deepened, "No, but I'm slowing down. Seriously, I've talked it

21

over with Bos, and we have a suggestion to make. We know that you and Jeanette haven't been entirely happy with Luke Three's military school in Tulsa, and some of those new friends he's been chumming around with." She held up a finger. "I raised you and Clement here in Angel because living was less complicated and values were more wholesome. I didn't want you boys to put on airs." She paused. "Now, I know times have changed somewhat, but Angel has not changed all that much. Also, if the war goes on and on, he'll learn enough about the military when he has to enlist, and we've got a perfectly good R.O.T.C. unit here at the school. Well, what I'm getting down to, Luke, is why don't you let Luke Three visit us for the summer? Then, if everything goes well, maybe enroll him in school here next fall?"

He took her hand. "Mama, that's very unselfish of you—and Uncle Bos, too, but you've raised your family, and it's not fair to saddle you with Luke Three."

"I don't see why not. Patricia Anne will be going to Phillips University in Enid, and she'll no doubt be out here on weekends. We've got Hattie to help, and you know that Luke Three won't be that much of a problem."

"We'll see, Mama," he said, "we'll see."

The clock struck seven-thirty, and she stirred. "I'll awaken Bos," she said.

With the thread of their emotional tie broken, he knew the time had long passed when he could have discussed Jeanette.

# 2

## Feet of Clay

*Bosley and Luke left for Tulsa immediately after the luncheon prune whip had been served.*

The family stood on the porch and waved good-bye as the cream-colored Rolls-Royce sped out of the barnyard, shooting a trail of red dust in the air, which disturbed a gaggle of geese by the smokehouse. There was a sudden drop in temperature, and the women fled into the warm parlor, but Clement and Luke Three lagged behind.

The boy flexed his shoulders and glanced sideways at his uncle; his handsome face still had the downy look of a child, and his voice had not yet begun to creep into lower registers. "I'm like a fish out of water," he cried. "Want to walk down Main Street, Uncle Clem?"

Clement nodded. "I feel discombobulated, too. I didn't get much sleep last night; I kept thinking about the war."

"Weren't you in France during the last one?"

"Yep. I didn't do front-line duty, except with the doughboy band I'd put together. When I came back, all my civilian buddies said how lucky I'd been, not having to fight. I had to remind them that although we didn't carry firearms, we were right up there at the front, playing for the men going over the trenches into no-man's-land." He sighed, shaking the past away. "Let's get our wraps."

Bundled in warm clothing, Clement and Luke Three let themselves out of the iron gate that faced the building housing the new telegraph office. The town of Angel, Oklahoma, sprawled out before them in the crisp afternoon sun. Clement blinked, realizing suddenly that the town was showing its age. Baker's Mercantile Store needed a new facade, he saw; its weathered clapboard was deeply pitted, and the paint was flaking off onto the sidewalk, which itself was sagging onto the asphalted street. *The Angel Wing,* the town newspaper, located next door, was in a similar condition, and the Packard Automobile Agency across the street sported a crooked sign; even the Blue Moon Theater, where *Abe Lincoln in Illinois* was playing, had a chipped box-office window. The town was dying of old age. Were the residents also so old they did not notice its decline? He shuddered and drew his jacket more closely around his shoulders.

Clement visited his home only sporadically, driving in from nearby play dates, but this was the first time that he had actually walked down Main Street in years. Even the five-storied red-brick Stevens Hotel, where the members of his band had stayed only two days ago, looked shabby and unkempt. Several windows overlooking the street featured net curtains tied in huge knots. His mother had named the town, coming in from the Cherokee Land Rush in 1893, only forty-eight years ago, yet the place looked like a town in a ghostly old Edwardian novel.

Main Street was deserted, furthering the impression of a ghost town. Having walked up one side of the street, Clement and Luke Three crossed over and took the other side down, past the bakery, where the odor of fresh bread wafted out over the sidewalk. At least, he thought, *that* had not changed. Nearing home,

24

he paused. "Let's go up the back way by The Widows," he said.

"Where?" Luke Three asked, a perplexed expression on his face.

Clement flushed and explained, "The Conservatory of Music." As they took the slight incline by the frozen piece of ice formerly known as The Widows' Pond, he could not tell his nephew that the famous university frat house had once been a sexual refuge for the lusty appetities of the men of the territory before Oklahoma became a state. The Widows was probably the most famous whorehouse in the midwest. Of course he had been too young to go there himself, but Luke had told him once, in a moment of weakness, that all of his allowance, between the ages of thirteen and fifteen, had been frittered away in seeking the attentions of one Stella. Nor could he inform the boy that Bosley had first taken Luke there on his thirteenth birthday.

He threw Luke Three a penetrating glance. The boy's innocent face, with its wide, incredibly clear brown eyes, was open and friendly. He had yet to chalk up enough experience to wear a mask of indifference. From the look of his small body, he had yet to climb the pinnacle toward manhood at fifteen, while Luke had apparently been extremely well developed when two years younger. Clement sighed and paused for a moment, looking down at the Victorian clapboard that had once been The Widows, and suddenly he wished that the years would fall away and he could be the same age as Luke Three. Oh, to be on the threshold of a strange, fascinating new world, teeming with forbidden fruits. But now there was a war, a war that would be fought differently than any other war. No, he did not wish to go back.

"You're dreaming, Uncle Clem," Luke Three was saying.

25

"And so I am. Come on, let's head back, I'm so tired, I think I'll lie down."

"Feeling sick?"

Clement shook his head. "No, just fatigued." He could not tell the boy that he was depressed by the sight of Angel, that he was depressed because of the attack on Pearl Harbor, or, most of all, that he was depressed because his thirty-ninth birthday was just around the corner.

By the maple tree, Sarah stood silently, watching their progress up the hill. She stepped directly into the pathway. "Hi, Hotshot," she said. "Where have you two been?"

Clement laughed. "To hell and gone."

"Well, I've just started. Come along?"

"No, Aunt Sarah," Luke Three said, "I'm going in and listen to the news."

"I'll walk with you," Clement replied, "at least for a little way." Unconsciously, as they ambled around a briar patch, he took her hand, and they trudged up the slight incline by Heron Number One well. He smiled at the *swish-pip* sound of the old pump.

"Oh, that's noisy!" Sarah said, making a face.

Clement shook his head. "Never complain—just think about the money being forced up every time that piston slides up and down."

"I hadn't thought about it that way," she replied, then asked, "Clem, when you were a little boy here on the farm, when the wells were coming in all the time, didn't the noise deaden your eardrums?"

He considered her question for a long moment. "No, come to think of it, I was never conscious of disturbing sounds." He squeezed her hand. "But then, you must remember"—he smiled—"that I was born in the worst electrical storm that ever hit the Territory."

"Still, it's a wonder that you've retained your perfect pitch over the years." She stood beside the well, and

26

with her red hair pulled back from her face, spotted from the cold, she was very handsome. She was not beautiful in the sense that his mother, Letty, had been beautiful, because she was not so delicately formed. Her Cherokee ancestry was very evident in her face— more so, Clement thought, as she grew older—but she had a certain feminine grace that many big-boned women did not.

He smiled, knowing that he would never capture a prize for male beauty, either; his features were coarse and plain. He bore no resemblance to his half-brother, Luke, who he always thought was the epitome of masculine splendor, especially in those accouterments most highly esteemed by the feminine gender. He himself was average in that department. He looked at his hands with their long fingers. He had something his brother did not: talent. "I guess I'm just a throwback," he said out loud.

"What brought that on?" Sarah asked, a smile playing around the corners of her mouth, suddenly making her appear girlish.

"Oh, I don't know. I was just thinking." He smiled at a new remembrance. "I don't think I've ever told you, Sarah, but I was about five years old when I heard Bella Chenovick playing the piano at a church social. Now, you've got to remember that she was Catholic, but she and her husband, Torgo—you remember, he plays the violin—went to the Methodist church because it took one whole day to get to the Catholic church at Perry and a whole day to get back. Anyway, Bella struck a wrong chord, and it grated on my nerves. When she had finished the piece, I went up to the piano and piped, in what I'm certain was a superior tone of voice, 'You made a mistake, Mrs. Chenovick; *this* is the way it should sound. And I placed my hands on the keyboard and struck A Major correctly. She had played A-C-E- instead of A-C-sharp-E. Of course, I didn't know what was wrong then, technically, but I knew how to correct it. She looked at me as if I was a person possessed of an evil spirit, but she moved over on the piano seat, dismissed the group, and gave me my first piano lesson." He laughed out loud. "That was the beginning."

Sarah gave him a long look. "How in the world did you know where A Major was located on the keyboard?"

He shook his head. "I don't know. I just did, that's all. I've thought about it often. It seemed a natural thing. That chord seemed to *glow* on the piano, Sarah. When I began, I didn't play 'Chopsticks' or 'Nola' or 'Playmates,' or any other of those pieces that I've always called 'baby teeth.' For me it was the classics from the beginning. I only took up jazz during the big war."

Sarah paused by the old maple tree, her eyes wide and intense. "I read somewhere a long time ago, maybe when I was a little girl, that our Cherokee ancestors believed that spirits traveled from one body to another in different lives, and what was learned in one life was passed on in the next. It sounded farfetched, and I've never given it much thought, but with your natural gifts . . ." She looked into his eyes. "How could you have known about that chord?"

He laughed self-consciously. "Oh, you're getting in real deep today, Squaw!"

She grinned. "Now don't make fun of me." She said, turning serious again, "Doesn't reincarnation make sense?"

"What?"

"*Reincarnation.*"

"Nope!" he exclaimed quickly. "I don't believe any of that stuff."

She shivered. "I'm getting cold."

As they strolled back to the house through the snow, making a game of retracing their exact footsteps, Sarah shook her head. "Oh, Clem, with this war and all, I'm afraid. I've never been frightened about the future before."

Suddenly his eyes smarted. "We've had a good life together and a happy marriage. You've been a good wife."

She was silent for a moment, then glanced at him shyly. "There's never been anyone but you, you must know that, and there never will be."

He paused and looked at her solemnly. "Sarah, promise me something?"

"Of course."

"If something . . . should ever happen, I don't want you to grieve. Remember Dad taught us children not to mourn, and when he passed away, we didn't carry on. He always said that death was a *transition*." His voice was very remote. "Maybe that reincarnation business that our forefathers went for is the answer. Who knows?" He looked straight ahead, his homely face pale under the flush of the cold. "You and I have always had a special mental rapport, as if we always knew what each other was thinking."

She faced him, her eyes dark and troubled. "Clem, why are you suddenly talking this way? All the time that we've been married, I've never known you to be— well, so . . . morbid."

He shook his head. "I'm *not* morbid. It just seems like a good time to talk about such things, with the war and all."

"You're not thinking of enlisting, are you?"

He grinned. "I did my duty in the last war, Squaw." He paused thoughtfully, then went on gently, "They called me 'Breedy,' you know, the doughboys. That was the first time I'd ever run into racial discrimination, but I got used to it. It wasn't a vicious thing, and when I formed the band, I became a kind of mascot. I was that 'funny half-breed Indian guy, the one with the goofy grin.' " He snapped his fingers. "I'm talking too much today about the past." He snapped his fingers again. "One thing I've got to do, and that's call Max at Music Corporation of America." He frowned. "What worries me, Sarah—will the public still want to cut a rug with the war on? What's going to happen to the big bands? Are we all going to be out in the cold—like we are right now? Come on, let's go home."

"Okay, Hotshot, but I thought you wanted to check the ice in The Widows' Pond."

"No, suddenly I'm not in the mood for skating."

Clement picked up the telephone. "Nellie, is that you? I need a number in Chicago, it's collect."

Nellie's voice was shrill. "Now, Clem, why'd you be calling anyone *collect*?"

He had known the telephone operator since he was a small boy and took no affront at her inquisitiveness. Everyone knew that Nellie Drack was the best-informed woman in town. "In show business, a client always calls his agent collect," he explained patiently. "It's absorbed in the agent's commission of ten percent."

"You mean that man gets ten percent of your entire salary?"

"Yes," he replied quietly, "he does. Now will you get the number?"

"Oh, of course," she answered. "Imagine him making all that money. . . ." Her voice faded away and a moment later was replaced by Max Rabinovich's. "Howdy, Clem," he drawled.

"Max, please don't be folksy."

"Well, you're calling from the farm, aren't you?"

"Yes." He could see the big man leaning back in his swivel chair, feet propped up on his desk, a big Havana protruding from the center of his face. "What about the gig at the Wyandotte?"

"Well, what about it?"

"Max, don't be funny. With the war—"

"Oh, yes."

"Do we open or not?"

"Of course you open."

"Do you suppose we'll have a big crowd?"

"What has that got to do with it, Clem? You and the boys are on straight salary, not a percentage of the gross." He was becoming irritated.

"Max, *please* stop being a comedian." Clement's voice dropped an octave. "What's the war going to do to our business?"

Max grew serious. "It's too early to tell, Clem, but I think the music business is going to be okay. People want to escape. You give them great swing music to forget. If you were the conductor of a symphony orchestra scheduled to play a heavy Wagnerian concert in Carnegie Hall, or had planned a couple of performances of *Madame Butterfly*, I'd say you were in trouble." He paused meaningfully. "So far, nightclub café business hasn't been hurt all that much. Of course, it's only been a couple of days. . . . I've gotta go now, there's a call from the Coast."

The phone went dead, and at once Nellie's voice came back on the line. "I'm going to take my vacation during the first week in March in K.C.," she trilled. "Will you still be at the Wyandotte?"

"No, I think I'll be at Café Society Uptown in New York City—that is, if our country isn't blown to smithereens by then." He hung up abruptly; mentally, he could hear Nellie say, "Well, I *swan*. Wonder what's got into that boy?"

Luke left Bosley at the seven-story Heron Oil Company building on Peoria Avenue near Woodward Park in Tulsa. "I'll be back in an hour or so," Luke said gravely. "I've got to check something at the house."

31

Bosley nodded and, before going into the foyer, noted that, although Luke lived on Memorial Drive in the south part of town, he turned west on 23rd Street.

Five minutes later Luke parked in front of the Gladstone Apartments, and let himself into 1-A with his own key. The radio was turned to a news broadcast. "Jorja!" he called loudly.

The familiar voice of H. J. Kaltenborn was switched off in midsentence, and a moment later Jorja came in from the bedroom and rushed into his arms. Oh, Luke, how I've missed you!"

He kissed her tenderly on the mouth, sighed, and smoothed the long dark hair that hung halfway down her back. "I tried to call, but there was so much hubbub at Angel I couldn't get near the telephone. I kept thinking of you here, huddled over the radio."

"It was awful," she said, her eyes filling with tears. "I was so upset. Oh God, Luke, what's going to become of us?"

He held her close. "We'll go on somehow, of course. I'll have to spend more time in Washington, but somehow we'll get ourselves straightened out. Now that we're in it with the Japs, Germany's sure 'n hell going to declare war—or we will. All the major powers are going to be involved. What we're going to be doing at Heron Oil is anybody's guess." He paused. "I know that I'll be wearing a dozen hats and away a great deal. We've got to play it close to the ground. No major decisions right now."

She wiped her eyes and broke away from him gently. "I feel so lost," she replied, and her small, compact body shook as she kissed his hand, "and so darned insignificant." She paused. "How long can you stay?"

"An hour maybe. Bos is at the office, probably on the phone. He'll be tearing his hair out—he's an old man, and he gets grumpy. Decisions have to be made now, and there's so much new business that he doesn't know anything about. But, I just had to see you."

He followed Jorja into the bedroom, sat in the wing-back chair in front of the fireplace, and removed his shoes. "Undress for me, honey?"

She was wearing the soft pink chiffon peignoir from Paris that had cost more than double the amount of monthly rent he paid for the Gladstone apartment, but seeing her looking so seductive, he thought the garment was well worth the price. At thirty, she was very beautiful.

Jorja gazed intently into his eyes and slowly undid the long bow at her throat, then, turning sideways, slipped the sleeve down over her right shoulder, the soft material caressing the flesh of her arm with a sensuous whisper. He drew in his breath as she turned her back to him and, looking back over her shoulder, let the tissue-thin material glide down her soft, velvety back until it dropped in a pink cloud at her ankles.

She paused a moment and took a step backward, toward him. He brought his hands up to feel the soft silkiness of her dark waist-length hair. She threw back her head and turned around so that her small, firm breasts were level with his lips. He kissed the delicate area between the mounds. She leaned down, grasped him around the neck, and parted his lips with her tongue. He leaned back, and she knelt and, taking each pant leg in turn, pulled off his trousers. He raised himself upward, and she slid his boxer shorts down over his thighs and calves with a slow, tantalizing gesture that left him shaken and trembling. She looked at his middle and smiled impishly. "I see that Robert Taylor is ready to go."

He laughed and also looked down. "It would seem," he replied, with a grin still hovering around the corners of his mouth, "that he is as infatuated with you as I am."

33

He leaned back in the chair with his legs stretched out before him, and she gently lowered herself over him until he could feel the insistent pressure of her body enveloping him like a soft, moist vise. Astonished at the depths of feeling she aroused in him, he sighed again and again as she maneuvered over him, until all was forgotten except the tenuous sensations that were threading out from his solar plexus. Oh, if he could only sustain the pleasure; oh, if it could last into eternity! He was lost somewhere between pain and pleasure as he closed his eyes. The air went out of his lungs all at once. She was shuddering over him and sighing and shaking with abandonment. Breathlessly they clung together; then she relaxed and cuddled him in her arms, sheltered by the enormous comfort of the big chair.

He savored the feeling of closeness for a long moment and then whispered, "I must leave, Jorja. I don't want to, God knows, but I must." She slowly unwound herself from his embrace. He rose. "Don't know when I'll be back—hopefully, sometime next week. Jeanette and Luke Three will be coming back from Angel on Friday. Then I have to go to Washington for a meeting with Harry Hopkins about the Seven Sisters." His brow furrowed, he dressed quickly.

Jorja laughed softly and, coming up behind him, placed her body against his buttocks. He turned and, taking her in his arms, kissed her lightly on the lips. He knew that she was ready for him again. Sometimes, when he was not required to account for his actions, when he was supposed to be out of town or he could take an afternoon off, he would draw out their love-making to agonizing lengths, but he dare not tarry today, no matter how Robert Taylor reacted. "Honey, I can't."

She stood back and nodded. "I know." She went to the desk in the living room and took out a manila folder. "Here are the statistics on the Lend-Lease shipments to Britain from Desmond Oil, which I got from my girlfriend in their accounting department." She laughed tonelessly. "A lot of good they will do you now that war's been declared!"

Luke finished dressing. "Thank you. With the mess the country's in, will Roosevelt live up to the Lend-Lease agreements or not? It seems to me some of that equipment should be used now for our own troops." He kissed her on the cheek and took the envelope. He grinned. "What would I do without my favorite spy?"

She tweaked his ear. "I've always wondered if you love me because I handle the advertising account for your biggest rival and have access to private data, or because of my body." She laughed. "I suppose I'll never know the answer to that question."

For an answer, he kissed her full on the lips.

"If you can't get away this week, Luke, call at the usual time, because I'm certain there'll be lots of off-the-record memos flying in and out of the office." She patted his gray head, ran her fingers down his cheek, and caressed the lobe of his ear, taking care to lightly massage an erogenous zone.

He shivered and laughed. "Oh, don't do that, Jorja, or Robert Taylor will be stirring again, and we don't have time."

"Were the Herons always Republican?"

Her question startled him. "Why, yes. My stepfather, George Story, and Mama were in and out of the White House all the time when Hoover was President. They had all met in London during the World War, when the old boy was in charge of American Relief. Hoover will eventually be vindicated, I think, and will be regarded in future history books as a good President. Most people—because of the New Deal—think that he personally caused the depression. That's the implication that Roosevelt always maintains, but the crash was the result of many factors that have yet to come to light. The

President, for all of his breeding and charm, can be a pretty cold cookie inside—particularly if you're not on his side of the fence."

She grinned and was suddenly very beautiful. "It would have been so much easier," she replied, "if you had been born a Democrat."

The next morning Jorja arrived at the offices of Desmond Oil Company a half-hour earlier than her usual nine A.M. schedule, and knocked twice on the solid mahogany door. "Come in," a clipped Oxford voice called.

She entered the huge, magnificently decorated office with its high wood-shuttered windows; acres of beautifully bound books, placed carefully by color and binding in floor-to-ceiling handmade bookcases; oxblood leather sofas with matching chairs; brass lamps with shades of tooled suede; and two matching maroon-and-tan oriental carpets that had been imported from Iran in 1915.

The sleek black haired young man dressed in a superbly tailored gray pin-striped suit, with a blue tie, looked up from his polished glass-topped desk. "Yes, Jorja?" His blue eyes softened as he pursed his thin lips.

She placed a manila envelope on his desk. "Not much information here, Robert dear, but Luke Heron's visit was very brief. He'll be going to Washington next week for an important meeting, which he assumes will have to do with gas rationing."

"Did you pass along those phony Lend-Lease figures?"

She smiled. "Yes indeed."

"Good." Robert Desmond picked up the envelope. "What's in here?"

"Just boring statistics that I was able to get during his visit two weeks ago—having to do mainly with oil

36

production in the Maracaibo Basin field in Venezuela."

"Good! I daresay they won't be boring to me." He swiveled his chair around to the window that overlooked the park; the skyline of Tulsa glistened in the morning sun, sending out orange reflections from the windows in the downtown buildings. When he turned back to her, he was smiling softly. "They are all hicks," he said quietly in his impeccable Oxford accent, "every last one of them. The Herons and the Trentons and the Storys are little people. Involved in their little family rituals, they don't know anything about big business. They've been operating Heron Oil like a roadside fruit-stand for far too long. Old Bosley Trenton is senile, and Luke Heron has seen better days." His voice grew hard and echoed in the richly appointed room like a well-rehearsed litany. "And, with your help, my dear Jorja, we will eventually take them over—lock, stock and barrel!"

Luke and Bosley returned to Angel at the end of the week and, seeking relaxation, saddled up horses for a ride over the snowy pasture. On the east side of the pecan orchard, beyond a line of old cottonwood trees, lay a long, flat piece of land. "I think that's the best spot to put in the runway." Bosley indicated. "Not that I want to spoil the farm, but we're going to be using the company plane more than ever."

"Can't you see Currier and Ives landing here in the dead of winter?"

Bosley nodded. "I get a kick hearing those names. Where did you ever find them?"

"John Carrier worked for American Airlines until I offered him more money. Robert Ives came to us from Boeing, where he was a test pilot. It wasn't until they had flown together several times that Jeanette tabbed them Currier and Ives. She's been a collector of the original Currier and Ives prints since college days."

"I'm pleased about this strip, Luke. Time is precious. I don't want to spend all my time on trains between here, Tulsa, and Washington."

"We should have put in the landing strip a long time ago, Uncle Bos, but now it's necessary, no matter what Mama says. We're *not* despoiling the land."

Bosley looked up with a squint. "You know how she is, Luke." He paused meaningfully. "I understand, in a way. She feels this earth is special—and it is. It's made a fortune in oil, and with the wells redrilled, crude production is way up again. But that's underground; now, she says, we're cutting up the topsoil. But with a runway here, maybe some of the well-to-do farmers will make use of it"—he laughed—"although I can't see putting in a shuttle service to Enid."

They heard the neigh of a horse and the sound of hooves before Sam rode up, astraddle old Gertrude. He was riding without a saddle, and his bottom on the gentle old mare was so relaxed it was as if human and horse were one.

"Sam," Bosley said lightly, "the next time you visit, maybe you can make use of the company plane."

"Oh," Sam replied, adjusting his white turban in the small wind that had just sprung up over the prairie, "I won't be back for a long time." He sniffed the wind and looked at the sky. "We better be heading back," he announced. "More snow is on the way."

They turned their mounts toward home and rode on in silence for a moment, the horses kicking up powdered snow as fine as cornstarch. "There is something that I am curious about. How old is Luke Three?"

"Fifteen," Luke replied. "Be sixteen in April. Why?"

"He doesn't seem to be developing physically. He should have some of his growth by now."

"Well, I never thought much about it," Luke replied. "I've been so damned busy, running between Tulsa and the field offices. I haven't spent as much time with him as I should have, and frankly I feel guilty about it. I guess I'm not much of a father to the boy." He frowned.

"How has he been progressing at school?" Sam asked.

"Not well. He hates swimming and track. Mama and I were just talking about that last week. I'm thinking of enrolling him in school here in Angel next fall. He doesn't seem to like military school very much, and I can't say I blame him. That was Jeanette's idea in the first place, and the major runs the premises like a concentration camp, as far as I can see."

Sam nodded. "Naturally he wouldn't like athletics, because he has to undress before other boys that are more physically developed than he is."

Luke turned to Sam. "My God, do you suppose that's the reason he's been doing so badly? It never occurred to me that he'd be so sensitive—and then, of course, I didn't think about his age, either."

"Perhaps, you should examine him, Sam," Bosley said. "I haven't paid that much attention to the sprout either, with him not visiting us very often."

"I have helped a few other cases of arrested development, where the prepubertal growth spurt has been delayed."

"What do you mean?" Luke asked."

"If the boy's glands have not yet begun to function, a couple of injections may speed up the process a bit."

Luke exchanged glances with Bosley. "What kind of injections?"

"Hormonal." Sam drew in his breath. "Without giving a long lecture," he went on quietly, "breasts in girls start developing at about ten and one-half, and there is a growth-in-height spurt about a year later, with the menarche beginning at about thirteen. Boys usually show an increase in genital size a little before their twelfth birthday, the voice changes at thirteen or a little

39

later, and they are capable of ejaculating soon after that. Growth accelerates and the penis reaches adult size at fifteen or so."

"I had everything I have now at thirteen," Luke said slowly. "Such as it is."

Sam nodded. "You were a bit early all the way around. I remember Stella saying that you were a man—in all respects."

Luke grew uncomfortable. "Do you mean she discussed intimate details?"

"Surely," Sam replied evenly. "The girls always spoke about their customers. It was just part of the business."

Luke shook his head. "Do you know, after all these years, I'm embarrassed?"

"Don't know why you should be, Luke," Bosley countered. "I knew you were a full-grown man; that's why I took you to The Widows in the first place." He paused. "Wish I'd been paying more attention to Luke Three."

"Well, don't you be hunting for a place like that to send him," Luke retorted. "I'll not have him patronizing—"

"How easy you forget! Besides, my boy, I don't know if there's any houses around anymore, and I'd be afraid, anyway, with all the diseases. The Widows were clean. Dr. Schaeffer dropped by regularly." He paused. "But we must not ignore Luke Three anymore. This could be serious. What do you think, Sam?"

"I'll look him over, and then we'll have a consultation. If he needs attention, I'll be staying at the old Stevens Hotel for a few months, finishing my autobiography, and I could look after him. Of course, I am not licensed to practice medicine in Oklahoma, but"—he smiled broadly—"I have been a consultant to the family for—how long?"

40

"Well, at least forty-seven years." Luke laughed. "You brought me into the world."

"Then I'll work with young Dr. Hanson." Sam drew in his breath. "It would be my suggestion, Luke, that, if he's doing poorly in school, take him out after this semester and let him go here. The change of atmosphere will be good for him. Do you want me to speak to Jeanette?"

"No, I'll do it." Luke sighed. "She's so peculiar these days."

"Most women are, in the menopause."

Luke turned his horse into the wind. "Do you think that's it, Sam?"

Sam nodded. "You must be very understanding, because it's a most difficult phase in a woman's life. Aside from the physical symptoms, irregular menses, sensitiveness to heat and cold, dizziness, and so forth, she has to come to terms with the fact that she is no longer young—and she may feel less desirable or think that you find her less attractive. She looks for every wrinkle in her face and sees her breast tissues losing elasticity." He sighed. "I'm sure you know what I mean."

"I've been on the road so much, the last two years . . ." Luke muttered. "I've probably been very lax."

Sam nodded. "It's difficult for most men. That's why they often turn to younger women."

Luke blushed to the roots of his hair and turned his horse southward, taking a shortcut to the farmhouse. Sam and Bosley followed. As they reached the maple trees, a flurry of snow was carried by the wind out of the north, and Sam looked back at the dark gray clouds and, knowing that more snow was on the way, smiled to himself. The winter, he knew, would be long and severe.

# 3

## A Feast of Pleasure

*Patricia Anne, dressed in pale green silk with a matching snood, stood at the long buffet.*

Bella Chenovick had recently enlarged the living room, which now included a massive fireplace and a new sitting area stocked with antiques. Patricia Anne sniffed at the bowl of lemonade, and tasted the spiked punch, comprised of orange juice and a puree of Bella's famous peaches, along with ginger ale, and what she knew to be gin. It was unexpectedly delicious. She turned to her hostess. "Mrs. Chenovick, you should patent this recipe."

Bella smoothed her hand-embroidered red-and-white lace apron that reached around and over her generous buttocks and smiled widely. "Thank you, child," she replied kindly, and Patricia Anne thought that she looked like a plump little doll in her black silk skirt and heavily starched headdress brought from Prague fifty years before. A wave of affection swept over her, and she hugged Bella.

"What was that for, child?"

"Oh," Patricia Anne replied, "you haven't changed at all since I was a little girl."

Bella flushed with pride. "Thank you," she said. She knew the girl was Clement's daughter, but she could not recall her given name. That was what getting old did to the memory bank. She could remember everyone from the old days, but it was the children, who were not around every day, whose names escaped her. Then she heard a violin being tuned, and she turned to Patricia Anne. "Ah!" she exclaimed. "My husband's going to play."

Torgo very carefully climbed up on the sturdy old footstool that Edward Heron had designed and made, and looked over the group. The people in the community who meant most to him were gathered for the usual Christmas party: the Herons, the Storys, the Trentons, the Trunes, the Bakers . . .

He cleared his throat as he placed his red bandanna over his shoulder. "Friends, dear friends"—his voice cracking as much from age as emotion—he said, "our party this year is a little quiet because of the war." He glanced over the group. "Some of you were here during those holidays of nineteen seventeen, 'eighteen, 'nineteen. We won that war, and we'll win this one too!" There was scattered applause.

"I've been limbering up my fingers, and if I make more mistakes than usual, it's just my arthritis." He laughed deep down in his throat. "I'm going to play a number I haven't played in a long while." He placed the violin under his chin and played very softly, "It's a Long, Long Way to Tipperary."

Bella reached for her tambourine, and when the music swelled she shook the instrument lightly, adding a haunting note to the melody. Bosley put his arm around Letty, and other couples in the room drew together. To the older generation, the old song had a nostalgic meaning; to the younger generation, it was the melody itself that caught their imagination, then the words, as Bosley's rich baritone rang out in the living room:

John Dice put his arm around Fontine, who looked
up at him and whispered, "Jaundice, where's Temporary?"

He laughed. "It's *Tipperary*, and I think it's in Ireland somewhere."

"But why is Bos singing an *Irish* song?"

"Oh, Fourteen," John Dice replied impatiently, "it's
an old World War One song that the troops sang as
they went to battle."

Fontine shrugged. "Well, that might have been all
good and well, but I still can't see why they'd be marching against the Huns and singing about Ireland." She
toe-tapped out the beat. "Now we're fighting the Huns
again, I suppose they'll be singing another crazy song."

Across the room, Patricia Anne was conscious of a
certain stimulating pressure on her shoulder, and she
realized the man next to her had moved closer. The
feeling that spread between them was so intense, almost
like an electric flash, that she moved away instinctively.
As Bosley finished the song and Torgo bowed, she applauded along with the others, still not daring to look at
the man with such potent sexuality who was standing
beside her.

"That was really something, wasn't it?" a husky
voice asked.

"Yes," Patricia Anne replied softly, counted to ten,
attached a polite smile to her face, and looked into the
warmest pair of brown eyes that she had ever seen. The
man was very tall, with extremely broad shoulders. His
blond hair—which looked as if it had been bleached by
the sun, and yet in winter Patricia Anne knew that was
impossible—was combed back from a wide, intelligent
forehead. But it was his air of masculinity, rather than

his physique, that was so shattering. Her knees felt weak. She had heard other girls describe meetings like this, and she had scoffed at their vulnerability. Now that it was happening to her, she felt embarrassed at her former naiveté.

"I don't think we've met," he said. "My name is Lars Hanson. I'm taking over Dr. Schaeffer's practice."

She held out her hand. "I'm Patricia Anne Story. How do you do." The clinging warmth of his handshake was so unnerving, she had difficulty taking her eyes off his face. She was afraid for a moment that she was behaving like a pre-teen, but she could see that he was also evaluating her. It was the first time that she had been appraised in quite that bemused way, as if he were examining her sans clothing. And while she was pleased to a certain degree, there was an element of danger that was equally exhilarating.

"I've heard the name of Story a dozen times," the doctor was saying, "although I've been in Angel less than a month. Whose relative are you?" His eyes bored into hers.

"Clement Story is my father," she said thoughtfully, waiting for the pleasantly surprised reaction that the name always brought.

He looked at her blankly. "I don't think I've met him," he said.

"He's an orchestra leader."

"Oh?" He paused self-consciously. "I've just finished my residency, and I've been out of touch with current musical trends." He smiled shyly and smoothed his blond hair back from his forehead. "It's been very tough financially, so I have had more work than play. I'd like to meet your father." His eyes searched the room. "Is he here?"

"No, he's on the road."

Lars Hanson opened his eyes wide and looked embarrassed. "Oh, of course, your father has the Cherokee

45

Swing Band—right? I don't know what I must have been thinking about. Will you ever forgive me?" Again his brown eyes bored into hers, and she felt a shiver of fire and ice travel down her spine.

She laughed. "It's kind of refreshing, meeting someone who isn't a fan of Dad's. He'd be very amused."

Lars Hanson examined her face. "To which tribe of Indians do you belong?" he asked seriously, and she burst out laughing.

"Saying it that way, 'tribe' sounds awfully primitive. "I'm Cherokee, like my father."

He was flustered. "It must be obvious that I don't know anything about Indians either." He looked extremely uncomfortable. "We've only been talking three minutes, and I've put my foot in my mouth twice."

She grinned at him. "Don't feel too badly, Doctor, but it would behoove you to study the relationships between families in the community. You see, there are only a few new people in Angel. Most of the residents made the Cherokee Strip Land Rush, and their children were born on farms or oil leases." She paused. "Some originally came from Europe. Bella and Torgo Chenovick are Bohemians, for instance."

"Oh?" Lars Hanson shook his head. "Nationalities have never made any difference to me. I can't tell one from the other. Our family, of course, was Swedish, back about a hundred years or so."

Now that they were chatting easily and not forcing conversation, Patricia Anne was more relaxed. There was still the same compelling sense of attraction, but she was able to look him casually in the eye, without the danger of her heart jumping out of her chest.

Bella put a record on the machine, and as music filled the room, couples started to dance.

"What are they doing?" he asked, watching the intricate steps.

"A schottische."

"It looks very complicated."

"Not at all. I'll show you the steps." She took his hand and began to count.

Bosley and Letty looked over the dancers. "Bos, who is that dancing with Patricia Anne?" Letty asked.

"Search me," he said and turned to Fontine. "Who's Patricia Anne's partner?"

Fontine peered nearsightedly into the crowd. "Oh"— she brightened— "that's the new medico, Lars Hanson. He took over Dr. Schaeffer's practice. He's a good man, but kind of dull." She looked up at Bosley. "He's one of those new pill doctors. Schaeffer always gave shots."

"Yes, yes," Bosley said hurriedly, "but I hope Larson's a better doctor than he is a dancer."

Fontine giggled. "It took me six months to learn the schottische when I came up from Santone. Why, Bos, even today I have two left feet."

Bosley snorted. "And so, apparently, does the doctor."

During the next number, "Lady Luck," Lars Hanson held Patricia Anne firmly around the waist and gracefully whirled her to the left. "I'm more at home now," he whispered in her ear. "I learned to waltz when I was twelve." He paused. "The music is surely smooth."

"That's Dad's signature tune." She laughed. "It's been transposed dozens of times. The original was a jazz piece that he played in the Twenties when he first formed the band. He reorchestrated it as a blues number in the early Thirties—then a fox-trot, a two-step— but the rumba, I think, is the funniest." Her feet followed his exactly, and she began to enjoy herself.

In the afternoon Bella had taken up the rugs and sprinkled Dreft soap powder over the solid oak hardwood, so that the dancers would glide effortlessly over the polished floor. Now older couples drew closer together, and Patricia Anne felt Lars Hanson bring her body forward slowly until his chest was touching her breasts. In other circumstances she would have drawn back instantly, but, with the other dancers closing up, she allowed herself to luxuriously float along in his arms. At the last phrase, Torgo played along with the recording, and then, as the music stopped, he went on sweetly, embellishing and repeating the last phrase, ending on a low, throaty note that had more than a touch of gypsy flavor.

The crowd applauded, and Torgo threw back his head and laughed, and his new gold tooth in front flashed, reflecting all of the lights on the Christmas tree in the corner. "The next number will be the 'Laughing Polka'," he announced.

"Come on, Fourteen, let's do our stuff." John Dice took Fontine's plump hand.

"You'll wear me out," Fontine replied, "but I'll love it!"

Darlene Trune danced by with Bobby Baker, whose broken-out chin, Patricia Anne thought, looked rather like the top crust of a cherry pie that had boiled over during baking. Thank heavens her own complexion had survived adolescence without a blemish; perhaps, she reflected, it was her Cherokee blood. She looked up at Lars Hanson; his jutting chin, directly above, gave him a well-sculptured look. He *was* handsome, although, for a doctor, he was somewhat awkward on his feet; but his long, lean spatulate fingers, which held her hand so lightly, were extremely graceful without being effeminate. How marvelous it was to be held so strongly in a man's arms—so different from boys her own age, who were so tentative about everything, including dancing.

Darlene circled by again and looked heavenward, indicating that she was bored *in extremis*. The girls had known each other casually since they were five, and while they had never been competitive, Patricia Anne could tell by Darlene's expression that she was covetous of the doctor. When Lars Hanson twirled her around the rim of the dance floor for the third time, Darlene leaned over and whispered loudly, "Let's start a conga line!"

Patricia Anne laughed and nodded. When the record finished, she excused herself. "I've got to find a number Dad just recorded. It's a whiz." She thumbed through the stack of disks that were piled on the top of the Capehart, and finally located the record. "Mrs. Chenovick, will you play this one next?"

"Of course. Is it special?"

"You bet," she replied, and whispered in Bella's ear before going back to Lars Hanson.

Bella clapped her hands for silence. "Listen, folks, this is the new Clement Story recording. I'm supposed to tell you that it's called a *conga*." There were laughter and applause from the younger set and stony, uncomprehending silence from the oldsters.

Darlene stepped forward, blond hair dancing, hands outstretched, her pale face and large gray eyes filled with excitement. At that moment, Letty thought, the girl was extremely beautiful and resembled her mother at the same age. Belle Trune had been the most popular girl in school, although to the other girls the reason had not been clear. It was only later, during the depression, when Belle earned extra money by entertaining men in her bedroom, that it was obvious why she had been showered with so much attention when in high school. Letty had not been overly shocked when she found out that Mitchell made weekly visits to Belle's shack on the other side of town. Now here was Belle's daughter, as vivacious as her mother ever was, leading a demonstration of this new dance craze. Letty hoped fervently that history would not repeat itself.

Darlene, flushed at being the center of attention, raised her voice. "The steps are very simple," she cried. "All you do is count. *One, two, three, kick. One, two, three, kick.*" She turned her back to the crowd. "Line up behind me."

The moving queue, stepping first to the left side, then to the right, to the left again, then kicking out with the right foot, in unison, snaked into the living room, around the oak table, into the kitchen, onto the back porch, down the steps, around the side terrace, and into the solarium.

When the line came through the living room again, Bella started the record over and laughed until her generous jowls shook. "This is better than the schottische any day, Torgo," she cried, and joined the end of the line, her plump legs following the Latin beat as if she had been intimately acquainted with the steps since childhood. "Come on, everybody," she shouted, losing her composure completely. "Get hep!"

"Yes, my pigeon," Torgo said, lining up behind her.

Letty, caught up in the wild beat of the music as well as Bella's enthusiasm, tugged at Bosley's arm. "Let's join."

"Not me," Bosley replied, backing away.

"Party pooper!" Fontine cried, grabbing John Dice around the waist. "C'mon, Jaundice, let's do it!"

"Before God and everybody?" He laughed and, placing his hands around Bella's plump waist, started to kick as energetically as he could with a bad back.

Darlene opened the front door and started down the snowy front steps. Now, with the music fading, the revelers took up the chant again to keep in step: *"One, two, three, kick."*

The queue was halfway through the living room for the third time when the needle flew off the record and everyone stopped, laughed, and applauded. The perspiring dancers, flushed and panting, lined up around the punch bowls, and Bella, wiping her face with a bandanna, noticed that the punch spiked with gin was

50

almost gone, while the plain lemonade bowl was still almost full.

Panting and fanning her face, she turned to Torgo. "It's the . . . changing . . . times," she said breathlessly, remembering when, in the 1920s, the only alcoholic beverage in the house had been a bottle of Virginia Dare wine which Dr. Schaeffer had recommended as a spring tonic. She still felt slightly wicked at the thought of patronizing a bootlegger, but after all, George Starger was a friend. He obviously did not make a decent living out of running *The Angel Wing*, and the few extra dollars his avocation brought in helped raise his family of seven children.

Fontine was still breathing fast. "I don't know when I've had so much fun!" she exclaimed to her husband. "This party is just like a Bohunk wake." Then she glanced at John Dice again. "I'm sorry, dear"— correcting herself. "This is just like a *Bohemian* wake." She grew serious. "If I make another social error, you've got my full permission to slap me silly."

In the solarium, Lars Hanson handed Patricia Anne a cup of punch. "I'm already exhausted, and I've a tonsillectomy at seven in the morning." He laughed, then suddenly quieted and reached down and kissed her quickly on the lips, then kissed her again with more pressure. He could feel warmth emanate from her body. She broke away from him gently. Her heart thumped wildly, and she did not know if it was the aftermath of the dance or the reaction to the kiss.

He looked at her in wonder. "I like you very much, Patricia Anne, very much indeed," he said softly. "I've got to go now. It's already eleven, and I must be at the hospital at six to scrub up." He paused and gazed intently into her eyes. "Is it too early for me to take you home?"

She nodded her head. "I came with Grandma and Grandpa, and I'd better go back with them."

He took her hand. "You know," he said solemnly, "I don't know anything about you. Do you live in Angel?"

She shook her head. "No, Kansas City, but I'll be staying over the Christmas holidays at the farm, and I start the new semester at Phillips University in Enid."

"May I see you again? Can I telephone?"

She nodded. "If you like."

He grinned and bent down and kissed her lips lightly, this time taking her in his arms. She had not felt so safeguarded since her father had hugged her in his coming-home ritual, which he had always observed when returning from a long trek on the road. She luxuriated in this new feeling of security and protection. She broke away from him. "Good luck with the tonsillectomy," she said as lightly as she could.

Letty looked into the solarium and then back, and took Bosley's arm. "Look!" she whispered.

He recognized the two figures silhouetted by the moon and sighed. "It's the young doctor, isn't it?"

Letty nodded. "I suppose," she said quietly, "we have a winter romance on our hands. I wonder what Clement and Sarah will say."

"Perhaps, my dear, we should send her home."

She faced him. "Let's not be rash, Bos. She's very young, and they've just met." She colored. "Of course, kissing on what isn't even a first date . . . Well, I suppose we're just old-fashioned. Young people today . . ."

"Well," Bosley said humorously, "she could do worse. At least he's a professional man."

Outside, Luke Three crouched down behind the privet hedge. He had been at the hospital undergoing tests all afternoon and evening—routine stuff, according to Dr. Hanson, who had scheduled the workup. He had told the new intern to drive Luke Three to the Chenovick farm when the last test was completed—a chore that the intern, who was dating a girl in Garber, was not overjoyed about. "You may get there in time for the last dance," he had told Luke Three as he let him out of the Buick at the section road that ran by the Chenovick place, "but I wouldn't count on it."

Luke Three was about to walk up the side steps when he saw Patricia Anne kissing Lars Hanson. Boy, did they look hot! He watched them for a moment. It had looked like they were doing it French style, because their mouths had been pressed tightly together. Jerrard had said that when two people exchanged tongues, it was the way the Frogs did it—but how could people do that when their own tongues were attached to the back of their mouths? He shook his head in wonder. There was so damned much he didn't know!

Luke Three went around to the back door and paused a moment before going into the kitchen, took a deep breath, and entered the room. Darlene Trune was dancing with Bobby Baker, but she looked bored. He poured himself a glass of punch and smacked his lips. Boy, that lemonade was good! He finished the glass and poured himself another, which he drank down all at once; then, as the record changed, he heard the first few strains of "Tangerine," and the ultrasweet voice of Helen O'Connell sing:

> And I've seen toasts to Tangerine
>   Raised in every bar across the Argentine.
> Yes, she has them all on the run,
>   But her heart belongs to just one.
> Her heart belongs to Tan-ge-rine. . . .

He tapped Bobby Baker on the shoulder and whispered, "Let a real man cut in," and, without waiting for permission, swept Darlene into his arms. She was a foot taller than he, and she looked down at him with a bemused expression on her face.

When he held her close, she drew back. "Mind your

53

manners!" she exclaimed, but not too convincingly, he thought. Suddenly he felt very good, very much alive. The other couples in the background grew misty as he caught a heady whiff of her perfume—Evening in Paris. She was a superb dancer and followed his steps easily and in exact rhythm.

He felt himself stiffening and moved back slightly. What a time for *that* to happen! he thought to himself. It seemed that any little movement made him hard these days. He wondered what grown men did when this happened. He sighed. He supposed it was just one other thing that he'd have to get used to, along with everything else about growing up.

When the number was finished, everyone applauded. "Would you like some lemonade?" he asked, and Darlene flashed a smile.

"I surely would," she said, fanning her forehead with the soft, sweet-smelling handkerchief. "I'm still all worn out from the conga."

Bella lowered the lights, and Torgo put on the last record, "Good Night, Sweetheart," and couples pulled magnetically together. Luke Three had guided Darlene to the edge of the dance floor when he felt a tap on his shoulder, and when he turned, Bobby Baker had swept her away, and they disappeared quickly into the mix of dancers. "Damn!" he muttered under his breath and headed toward the punch bowl.

"Luke Three," Letty admonished, "kindly use the other bowl. This is for grown-ups only."

He threw her a long look. So that was why he felt so good! Earlier, he had dipped into the spiked punch.

As the recording ended, the lights came up and the guests started prolonged farewells. In the hubbub of men matching up coats with wives and dates, and everyone saying good-bye, Luke Three managed to wave good night to Darlene Trune, who was being escorted out the front door by Bobby Baker. He shook his head; some guys had all the luck.

In the back seat of the Packard on the way home, Patricia Anne nudged Luke Three. "How come you were so late getting to the party?"

"Oh, I just had some things to do," he said casually. He did not want to tell her that he had been at the hospital undergoing tests and that Sam and Lars Hanson were going to make him into a man.

# 4

## *The Sound of Distant Drums*

*The new Heron service station in Angel was located on hallowed ground.*

Bosley told Luke Three, "That's where Edward Heron, your grandfather's brother, built his first cabinet shop." He explained, "Which later became the site of the Heron Filling Up Station before World War One. It was torn down to make a parking lot." He surveyed the new premises with pleasure. "Now, after all these years, it's being utilized again. I think you're going to enjoy working here after school."

"Yeah." Luke Three grimaced, the world on his shoulders.

The compact building housed an office on one side, a grease rack in the middle, and a merchandising center on the other side, which featured a full line of recapped tires. In front, installed in a wide expanse of blacktop, were two gasoline pumps—one for ethyl and one for tractor gas. The famous blue Heron logo was emblazoned on the sides of the white building and again on the double sign out front.

Jerrard Jones, who had joyously celebrated his eighteenth birthday with a broken eardrum that disqualified him from military service, was appointed manager. He was a likable, lanky lad with a thatch of unruly brown hair and a mouth too small for his large teeth. He had worked as a summer mechanic for his uncle, who managed a Heron station in Enid, and was considered somewhat of a genius with tools. "Hell," he told Luke Three on his first day of work, "I ain't clever with much, but I've got two things I was born with that I'm real proud of. One is the ability to listen to a motor and know exactly what's wrong with it, and the other is my big thing, which leads me to the best broads in town." Jerrard then detailed some of his more recent sexual experiences with the opposite sex.

Luke Three grinned knowingly but didn't reply. He didn't have mechanic's hands in the first place, and in the second place he hadn't had any sexual experiences. Furthermore, he thought, even with Lars Hanson's shots, if he didn't start growing down there pretty soon, he might not ever have any stories to tell. God, it was hell being almost sixteen and still a shrimp in the ways that counted most.

Luke Three hated the starched white uniforms, trimmed in blue, provided by the company, and he especially disliked the white cap with the big blue bill, which made Heron gas attendants look like hotel doormen. The blue serge outer coats, worn in winter, spotted badly, too.

At first he felt foolish bending over the windshields, gazing into the faces of the occupants, while he swabbed the glass with a wet towel. But after a while he discovered that it was not at all necessary to be cognizant of the driver or the passenger as he performed his duties. Later he also discovered an extra bonus: with the straight, tight skirts women wore because of the fabric shortage, rather interesting glimpses of dimpled knees could be obtained, or sometimes, if it was a lucky day, a great deal more could be seen. Soon he became an expert on which ladies of the town wore panties and which did not. If the view was good-to-excellent, he tarried rather long with his water and towels, scrubbing away at nonexistent spots while rubbing himself by leaning firmly against the fender of the car.

Luke Three was somewhat less drawn to measuring the air in the tires with a gauge, or checking the oil with a dipstick. He was even more remiss with side work around the station, but was seldom in error in totaling the day's receipts. Mathematics came easily, and more than once he caught Jerrard in small mistakes in addition and subtraction.

When Luke stopped overnight at the farm on his way from Wichita to Tulsa, he surveyed the station with approval. "The place looks good, son," he said. "Jerrard tells me you're doing a good job, now that you've settled down into routine after school and on weekends."

"Well, Dad," Luke Three replied, "we'd do a much better job if we didn't have to run around so much. With the rack on the left side, it's difficult for Jerrard, if he's doing a grease job, to hear a car driving into the lane where the gas pumps are located. Also, customers have a difficult time finding the restrooms."

Luke threw back his gray head and laughed. "You've been working here for six weeks, and you want to redesign the building! Why, we've had one of the most famous industrial architects in the United States draw up these plans. We haven't had any complaints and we've been building this particular model since nineteen-forty."

"Maybe the other station managers aren't very well organized, or it never occurred to them to complain." Luke Three paused, and went on heatedly, "But I'm telling you, Dad, guys could work far more efficiently if you had *three* designs. One would be for corner locations, with a grease rack in the center; the second, with a grease rack on the left, when the station is situated on the left side of the street; and third, with the rack on the right side when the building's on the right side. Also, I don't see why the customers should traipse through the office to use the restrooms. They go right by the cash registers, and it seems to me that would invite robberies in the big cities. Why can't there be outside doors to the latrines?"

Luke looked at the boy in amazement. "Go on."

"Well, Hattie has been complaining that she can't use bleach because it'll fade the blue trim. It seems to me, if the uniform itself was blue, it wouldn't show dirt so much."

Luke frowned. "Any other ideas, young man?"

Luke Three grinned. "Only that the profit margin for a Heron manager is really lousy. You don't give very good discounts—"

"Whoa!" Luke exclaimed. "Let's take one thing at a time. Money isn't so plentiful, with the war."

"Yeah, every time anything difficult comes up, that's what everyone says." Luke Three shook his head. "It seems to me that people have more money to spend and less to spend it on than they ever did before. Even the oilers in the refinery make a lot more than Jerrard does." He paused, face flushed. "Remember, that boy works nine hours a day, six days a week, and he doesn't even get a lunch hour—just eats catch-as-catch-can. If we were union—"

"Look, boy," Luke replied angrily, "unionization is the ruination of this country. Don't talk to me about that!"

Luke Three knew that he had gone too far. "Yes, sir," he said. "By the way, the reporter from *The Angel Wing* was in yesterday for an oil change and thought there might be a story in me working at the station. I think it would be good publicity."

"For you or the company?" Luke replied quickly. "Well, I don't! I didn't put you in the station here in Angel to get your name in the paper. You're here to learn something about the business—firsthand. You tell him that, will you?"

59

"It's a she," Luke Three said and suddenly blushed. "Darlene Trune."

Luke gave him a long look. "Belle Trune's daughter?"

"Yes, she's so . . . pretty."

"So was her mother," Luke said distractedly, and for a long moment he could see Belle at fifteen, flying high on one of the swings on the school playground, showing her white cottom bloomers to all the boys with glittery eyes and expectant faces gathered in a circle below. This recollection conjured up another memory. Returning from a Halloween party at the Dices', he was passing the feed barns on Uncle Edward's homestead when he heard the sound of giggling, which he finally traced to a nearby haystack. There, under the full October moon, lay Belle Trune, spread-eagled. All he had been able to discern at first was naked buttocks lodged between the upturned soles of a pair of Mary Jane shoes. He watched, fascinated at the sight, and when the bare form rolled into the hay, he had dropped his pants and assumed the same position. . . .

"What're you thinking about, Dad?" Luke Three asked. "You're a million miles away."

"Oh, not as far as all that." Luke smiled sheepishly, facing his son. "How come . . . Darlene came back to Angel? Didn't she live with her grandparents in Oklahoma City?"

Luke Three shrugged his shoulders. "When her mother took over the Red Bird Café and started to make some money, she sent for Darlene."

"How old of a girl is she?"

"Eighteen, I guess. She took journalism in high school." He paused thoughtfully. "Did you know her father?"

Luke nodded. "I went to school with both of them."

"I heard he died awfully young."

"Yes," Luke replied. "He died of a heart attack."

60

But he did not add, "in bed with Belle." He placed his hands on Luke Three's shoulders. "Son, I wouldn't have any truck with the Trunes. They're not our kind of people."

The boy looked at his father reproachfully. "I've always liked old Belle. She's nice."

Luke thought: *Yes, and so did every man in town, including Mitchell*. Aloud, he said, "Besides, Darlene's too old for you."

Luke Three looked up in surprise. "Holy cow, Dad, she wouldn't look at me twice. I'm still a kid to her."

Luke grinned. "For a moment I'd forgotten." He cleared his throat. "I'll go back home now." He glanced at Luke Three's soiled white uniform. "I've got some questions to ask our general manager over the telephone."

A blue 1939 Chevrolet coupe slid to a fast stop in front of the pumps. Luke Three nodded politely. "Aft-'noon, Mrs. Blake. Want a fill-up?" He edged closer to see if it was a lucky day, and he smiled broadly because her tight flowered skirt was very, very short, and she had a pair of gams that looked at least as good, he figured, as Betty Grable's did in *Moon over Miami*.

She smiled; her flaming red hair made a halo around her freckled face. "The works."

Cissie Blake, her husband, Felix, and their small girl, Gretchen, had recently moved to Angel from Los Angeles, and Mrs. Blake was the most sophisticated woman he had ever met. She occasionally wore trousers, and she smoked cigarettes, which were unheard of for a woman in Angel, and she spoke wonderful English in a lilting, musical voice minus the low, nasal twang to which he was accustomed.

Luke Three took his time to wash the windshield, wondering, as he gazed through the glass at those long, beautifully shaped gams, if her entire body was covered with freckles or if those exciting little brown spots were confined only to her face, arms, and legs. He rubbed himself up against the fender of the car and sighed gently.

He forcefully plunged the nozzle of the gas hose deep into the tank, then stood back, leisurely working the lever back and forth, back and forth. He remained physically excited, hearing the gurgle of the gas as it gushed out of the hose. He was disturbed every time he performed this little ritual—which was several dozen times a day.

At last, with the tank full, he could hardly wait until he had taken Mrs. Blake's money, counted out her change, and waved her out of the station, before he rushed, still tumescent, into the washroom to unbutton his pants. He took a tape measure out of his pocket and grinned broadly at the results: he had grown seven-eights of an inch in only one week! Last Thursday he had measured only four and a half inches. God bless those shots that Doc Hanson had given him. Already hair was sprouting on his upper lip. Triumphantly he stuffed himself back into his trousers, and whistled "Chattanooga Choo Choo" all the way back to the pumps.

Luke snapped his blue cummerbund into place and pulled on his tuxedo coat, then glanced in the mirror. Yes, this was the same face that he shaved every morning; yet, clothed in evening clothes, his figure took on an added dimension, but his hair was definitely thinning out and also getting grayer. The process of aging was inevitable, he supposed, although inside he still felt the vigor of youth.

"Jeanette," he called, "aren't you ready yet? We've got to be there early. The head table is supposed to assemble in that little alcove off the ballroom, and we're to go up to the dais as we're introduced." There was no reply. He lighted a cigarette and went into the dressing room that separated their bedrooms. Where was that woman? He glanced into her room. Perfectly made up, with a piece of netting wrapped around her coiffure, she was lying on her side on the bedspread, her long satin slip pulled down over her ankles. "What's the matter?" he asked.

"Just a little dizzy," she replied weakly. "I don't think the catfish I had for lunch agreed with me."

"Well," he said sullenly, "we're due at the banquet in half an hour. We don't dare be late."

She placed a hand on her head and got up very slowly. "I'm better," she said at last. He sat at her dressing table while she slipped the form-fitting high-necked, long-sleeved mauve crepe-de-chine dress over her head. The purple sequins scattered over the bodice glittered as she backed up to him. "Zip me up, please," she asked and shivered as she felt his fingers go up her spine. Carefully she unwrapped her head, put on her diamond earrings, and reached for her silver fox jacket. "I'm ready," she said without a backward glance in the mirror.

He did not retort, "It's about time," which was on the tip of his tongue, because he knew that after his speech to the dealers she would appear at his side, smiling and shaking hands obligingly, holding up her part of their public image as a "most admired couple."

Luke's speech to Heron dealers gathered from all over the Midwest, was short and to the point and ended with a plea: "I ask your support as we go into America's first year of war. There will be many changes in the months ahead. Gas rationing is expected to go into effect sometime in May, but rationing will not necessarily mean lower profits for all of you. But it does mean that you must give better service. It's imperative to increase your own personal standing in individual communities." He paused dramatically, his face pale. "Because of future foreseeable transportation problems, we have started to build a pipeline from the Eastern Seaboard to the Midwest. Also, the four tankers ordered last year are due for a spring delivery, which should help alleviate the gasoline shortage that we expect. And, while we must, out of necessity, increase our production of hundred-octane aircraft fuel, Heron is continuing experiments with certain alkylation and polymerization processes. Also, with many dealers going into the armed services, we will shortly begin a training program for women as service-station attendants. There's much to be accomplished, and I most humbly ask for your help and continued support. In turn, Heron Oil Company, as always, will stand behind you one hundred percent."

There was a quick, scattered round of applause. Before the lights went up to full in the ballroom, Jeanette whispered, "I wouldn't call *that* an ovation."

"What did you expect?" he whispered back, stone-faced. "Cheers and confetti? They know damn well, as soon as rationing goes into effect, business is going to fall about forty percent, and they don't like the idea of women conning their jobs while they are off to the South Pacific engaging in hand-to-hand combat, either." He noticed that the dealers and their wives were getting up from their tables. "Come on," he said, "put a smile on your face. We've got a duty to perform."

Luke and Jeanette took their places at the door and shook hands with the subdued banqueters. He had turned to speak cordially to the aged banker Everts, from Enid, who had once been on the Heron board of directors, when he heard a murmur and turned to find Jeanette crumpled on the floor.

He knelt by her side and held her head in his lap, panic rising in his throat. "Will someone please call the hotel doctor?"

A few moments later a large florid-faced man in a tuxedo too small for his frame hurried into the ballroom. "I'm Dr. Townsend. I was next door at a wedding reception." His hand found Jeanette's wrist. He paused a moment. "Pulse normal," he muttered, "breathing normal, color good. Let's move her to the settee by the door." He paused. "Just a moment, I think she's coming around."

Jeanette's eyelashes fluttered. She opened her eyes, and the room came into focus. The doctor smiled. "You'll be all right." He took a glass of water from one of the tables. "Take a sip."

She shook her head. "Can't. Nauseated."

Looking at her drawn, pinched face, Luke suddenly remembered that his Uncle Edward had been stricken with food poisoning at a picnic and lived only a few hours. "Could something have been the matter with the food?" he asked.

The doctor looked up. "Anyone else taken ill?"

Luke shook his head. "Not that I know of."

"Fish on the menu?"

"No," Luke replied, "the main course was medallions of beef."

"Olives?"

"No," he replied, "but she did have catfish for lunch."

"Will everyone leave, please? I'd like a word with the patient."

Luke waited in the foyer, smoking cigarette after cigarette. Finally the door opened and Jeanette came out, holding the doctor's arm. "She'll be all right now," he said to Luke, "but she should see her own physician tomorrow."

Luke shook the doctor's hand. "Thank you. Please send me the bill. Here is my card."

The doctor shook his head, smiled, and was about to rejoin the wedding party next door, when he turned back. "I almost forgot to offer my congratulations. I understand, Mr. Heron, that you have a teenage son. Let's hope the new baby is a girl."

"Pregnant!" Letty exclaimed on the telephone. "Jeanette, are you *positive*?"

"Well," Jeanette replied darkly, "as positive as anyone can be!"

"But, at your time of life, dear—"

"Oh, Mother, stop harping about my age," Jeanette snapped. "Don't you think I'm not well aware of the difficulties? Do you think for one moment that I want to have a baby at forty-seven?"

Letty sighed gently. "The child may be quite gifted—"

"Yes," Jeanette interrupted with a hollow laugh, "or a complete imbecile. I've been told by those who know that babies born during change of life usually have something wrong with them."

"Nonsense, that's an old wives' tale." Letty paused. "There's only one thing that's terribly important: You must do exactly what the doctor tells you—"

"Mother, I am not a child!" Jeanette hung up the telephone angrily.

Letty placed the instrument in its cradle and turned to Bosley. "I assume you heard the conversation?"

Bosley nodded. "My grandmother had a baby girl at forty-five."

"Was she healthy?"

He nodded. "Turned out to be my mother, a brilliant woman. I'll bet her I.Q. was a hundred and eighty. If she'd been born during a later period—like during the Twenties, for instance—she'd probably have ended up as the president of a bank." He paused. "You know, Letty, if you have second thoughts about the kind of care that Jeanette will be getting in Tulsa, why don't you call Sam? If I remember rightly, he conducted a seminar in Vienna, before the war, that had to do with menopausal babies."

66

"You're right, Bos," Letty replied. "I'd forgotten that. I think I will see what he has to say." She paused thoughtfully. "Do you suppose he'll tell the truth in his autobiography?"

Jeanette had paced the floor all morning, and by the time Luke returned from lunch at one o'clock she was on the private line, her hysterical voice pitched so high he had difficulty understanding what she was trying to say. "I said," she screamed, "You'd . . . better . . .come home *right now*."

"All right," he soothed, "I'll be there in ten minutes." He hung up and called his secretary on the intercom. "Bernice," he explained calmly, "I've got to be out of the office for a bit. Would you call Barshin, Raskon and Murray, and see if Mr. Raskon can come at three instead of two?"

"I'll try, Mr. Heron," Bernice replied, "but I know he's very busy."

"He'll make it," Luke said evenly. "Other stockbrokers in town would give their eyeteeth for the Heron account."

"Is your wife all right?" Bernice asked. "She called at least five or six times while you were out to lunch."

"Yes, she's fine." He paused. "I'll be back by three."

Jeanette greeted him at the door in a state of anxiety. Her eyes were red-rimmed from crying. For a moment Luke thought that she had been drinking: her pale face, minus makeup, was flushed, her hair was pushed up under a snood, and she still wore a nightgown. "You might as well know," she blurted, "I'm not having the baby! Mame Hollis had an abortion last month at a place in Kansas City. I just got an appointment. Can Currier and Ives fly me up? Sarah will put me up for a few days—"

Luke took her roughly by the shoulders. "What nonsense is this?" he exclaimed angrily. "Of course you're going to have the baby."

"But this place in K.C. is run by a doctor; it's like a hospital. There's absolutely no danger. Mame Hollis—"

"To hell with Mame Hollis. She's a tramp. She's had two abortions that even I know about. You'd take her word? No danger! Do you think that I want you to put yourself through that? And furthermore, I want that baby!"

"You want the baby! Luke, you must be out of your mind. We're too old to raise a child. It was difficult enough with Luke Three. We'd be sixty-five years old before the child would be out of high school—talk about *fair*! And besides all that, who knows if you and I are still going to be together!"

"If you think there's going to be a divorce in the family, you're badly mistaken, Jeanette, he replied furiously. "You and I are going to stick together whether you like it or not."

"I wouldn't be too sure about that," she cried. "I could leave you—flat."

He looked at her quietly. "A legal separation is not a *divorce*. But, with the baby—"

"I'm not having a baby! If you don't let me go to K.C. I'll kill myself."

He shook his head. "You like yourself too much for that, baby. Jumping off pianos or using a knitting needle is simply not your style."

She began to cry. "Don't make fun of me."

He tried to take her in his arms, and she backed away furiously. "Don't touch me. If it hadn't been for you—"

"Don't give me *that*, Jeanette," he replied quietly; his heartbeat was back to normal. "You wanted *it*, you didn't mant *me*. You were so hot you'd have let *any* man make love to you. Don't place the blame on me."

She lighted a cigarette nervously. "I'm going to

K.C.," she said defiantly, "and you can't stop me. It's my body!"

"It may be your body, but it's my child!" he exclaimed. "And furthermore, if you don't behave I'll hire around-the-clock nurses and keep you tied in bed. You're going to have that baby, whether you like it or not!"

She snubbed the cigarette out on a tray. She had not heard him use that tone of voice with her in many years, and she knew he meant what he said.

"Now." His voice still had a stinging edge. "You have your choice: you can go home to Angel for a week or so until you calm down, or you can stay here and behave yourself. There is one other alternative. Do you want a nurse?"

"No," she said, backing down from her former position, "I don't want a nurse. As it is, I can't stand to have a stranger in the house, that's why I have Mrs. Reynolds come in every day to do housework. I won't have anyone underfoot."

He was tired, very tired, and after their altercation he felt weak as well, and he still had to go back to the office and meet with Raskon. He checked his watch. "I'll stay home for a little while longer," he said more gently, "if you need me."

She shook her head. "No, Luke," she replied quietly, "go on back to the office. I'll be all right. Only sometimes, I feel like I'm going out of my mind." She placed her hands over her stomach and then over her breasts. "No, I can't kill the baby. That's not right. It should have a chance to live." She was quiet, beaten. She eased herself down onto the sofa. "Go on back, I know you've got a lot on your mind." She looked up, trying to concentrate on problems other than her own. "Have you found out who's been buying up Heron stock?"

He shook his head. "Mostly large purchases from small companies that we've never heard of. We can't understand it; the stock isn't a good buy right now. The dividends are way down, and the price is up. Our second quarter will be better, but it takes time to gear up for wartime production." He took her face in his hands; her cheeks had lost their pinched look, and she appeared to be more relaxed. "Are you going to be okay?"

She nodded numbly. "I promise I'll be better. By the time you get home tonight, I'll be back to normal." He wanted to bend down and kiss her cheek, but it had been so long since any affection had passed between them that he hesitated, and then the moment was gone. "I'll be home for dinner at six," he said.

After Luke had left, she called Sarah in Kansas City. "I won't be coming to visit," she said. "I've changed my mind. I'm going to have the baby after all."


Luke came back to Angel for a meeting with Bosley concerning the Heron trucking firm, which had been formed to augment the short supply of railroad tank cars, some of which were being placed in service after being warehoused for many years. It was an important issue, and Luke was not pleased when his son, who was sitting on the porch swing, ask him to sit down for a moment.

"Dad, there's a couple of things I want to ask you. I would have talked with Sam, but he's busy finishing his book, and Doc Hanson has so many patients . . ."

"Yes?" Luke had a feeling that the questions the boy had in mind should be tackled on a bright sunny day, very early in the morning, when his mind was functioning at full speed, and not on a day when he had to remember figures and be prepared for a barrage of inquiries from Bos, who could turn devil's advocate at the toss of a matchstick. "Yes, what is it, Luke Three? I haven't got all day."

The boy looked down at his feet. "Never mind, Dad, it's not really all that important."

Luke sat down in the porch swing beside him and summoned a kinder tone. "Okay, come on, what's eating you, son?"

"Jerrard said that he heard an old-timer who used to go to The Widows say that he used to see you over there regularly and that your sweetheart was a girl named Stella."

Luke wished that he was anywhere in the world but Angel, Oklahoma, at that very moment. "Yes," he said carefully, "I did 'go with' Stella."

"You mean you went steady?"

"Ah—no, I visited her, Luke Three." He paused uncomfortably. "You are aware of the sort of place that The Widows was, aren't you?"

Luke Three continued to examine his shoes. "Jerrard said it was"—his voice was very low—"a whorehouse."

Luke could feel the blush start above his collar. "It was more than that; it was a place where a man could go when business and family pressures were getting to be too much and he had to have relaxation. You could play cards there, or have dinner or a drink. Stella was a girl who was very nice to me, and just a few years older." He had to make Luke Three understand that he had not been a delinquent.

"Were you in love with Stella, Dad?" For the first time during the conversation, Luke Three looked at his father.

In his mind's eye, Luke could see Stella's lovely form encased in white dimity, and feel her warm and clinging skin next to his body, through the light material. Her lips had been so cool and yet had set him on fire that

71

first time, when she had given him the confidence to be a man. And all of the times afterward had been so fulfilling, each experience memorable, so that through the years that part of his life had grown more lovely. . . .

He realized that the boy was waiting for an answer. He cleared his throat. "I did not feel toward Stella the same way that I felt for your mother before we married. Each man is different and looks at the sexual part of his life differently." *Oh, God,* he thought, *I'm sounding pompous.* The words were not following each other properly. "I was truly in love with your mother, but I was not truly in love with Stella. I felt passion for her."

Luke Three regarded him soberly. "What's the difference between love and passion, Dad?"

Why was the boy placing him in such an awkward position? "Passion," he continued quietly, "is more of a powerful, sexual feeling, while love, in its purest form, is a feeling of affection and warmth toward someone you truly desire." How could he discuss a man's sexual feelings with a boy who was too immature to understand what he was talking about?

"But isn't that the same thing, Dad?"

Luke shook his head and thought about Jeanette and Jorja, the two J's in his life. If he couldn't differentiate what he felt for each woman, how could he explain the difference between love and desire? He decided to be blunt. "Before I met your mother, I had a relationship with Stella, which was not continued after marriage. I fell in love with your mother, and she became my lover, my wife, my companion, and my complete mate. I didn't need anyone else." He paused. "Do you know what I mean?"

"Yes. But you never thought about marrying Stella?"

Luke sighed and pondered how to answer the question. "Luke, men didn't marry the women who worked at The Widows." Of course that was a lie, because Mary Darth had given up the profession and became the wife of Senator Reginald T. Savor. Well, he obviously couldn't dwell on *that*! "Some men's needs—that way, sexually—are more intense than others'," he added lamely.

"Oh," Luke Three asked, "you mean *coming*, and all of that?"

"Y-yes," Luke stammered. "The whole business is rather complicated." He searched his mind for the right words. "Your body is going through many changes, which Sam told you about, and I explained to you a long time ago, more or less, what you'd be experiencing. Boys your age, when they are growing up so quickly, feel passion rather than love. In the meantime, just remember that what you're going through is not unique; it's every man's trial." He cleared his throat meaningfully and got up from the swing. "When you want to know more, just ask me, or, if I'm not here, Dr. Larson will be glad to talk with you. Understand?"

"Yes, sir."

As Luke walked down the path to the gate, he realized that his shirt was damp with perspiration. How difficult it was to explain sexual matters to a boy who was armed with details about his father's teenage exploits! Damn Jerrard for telling him about Stella! He thought back to that first time at the Widows, when Uncle Bos had introduced him to Leona Barrett. Bos was a wise man; knowing that he could not discuss such intimate topics in those cavalier days before Oklahoma had become a state, he had done the next best thing—he had simply taken Luke to The Widows for his first sexual experience. Could he himself do the same thing for Luke Three if The Widows were still in operation? No, Luke thought, he couldn't. He examined his own feelings for a moment. Was it because his son's growing into manhood was somehow a threat to his own masculinity? It was a question that he dare not answer.

# 5

## The Inward Cry

*Jeanette carefully removed the fine black wool evening jacket, sprinkled with red sequins, from the tissue-paper-lined box.*

How she loved beautiful, expensive clothing! It was the most beautiful ensemble that she had ever owned—and the most expensive, five hundred and seventy-five dollars. She held the sparkling material up to her face and, a smile playing about her lips, turned to the full-length pier glass. She burst into tears; facing her reflection, she recoiled. She saw a tall woman with an upswept hairdo, breasts enlarged because of pregnancy but no longer firm, and a ridiculously distended stomach that made her look like a grotesquely drawn figure in a cartoon. "Luke," she screamed, "I can't go, I can't go!" She lay down on the bed and sobbed as if her heart would break.

Luke came into the bedroom, tying his bow tie, and looked down at the pathetic figure. He sat down on the edge of the bed and reached out his hand. "Don't paw me!" she cried. "I just look awful. Go to the party and leave me alone."

"Jeanette"—his hand was still in the air—"come on,

now, you'll look . . . fine. You've got to go; it's an important event. We can come home early if you like."

"I don't want people making fun of me." She wept. "A funny old lady with a baby in her belly."

He placed his hand on her shoulder, but she moved away from him. "I don't want your pity!" she said savagely and dried her tears on the sheet, leaving streaks of mascara on the counterpane.

"Oh, come on, Jeanette," he coaxed. "You'll be fine. Everyone will expect you to be there. After all, it's the thirty-ninth anniversary of the Discovery Well at Angel. I can't go alone."

She got up from the bed, with some difficulty with balance, but refused his assistance. "It should be perfectly clear to you by this time, Luke, that I don't want to be touched." She was dry-eyed, and her mood had changed. "Besides, next year's anniversary will be the fortieth—that one's really a milestone. Remember when we were forty, Luke?" she asked plaintively. "That wasn't so long ago. If I only knew then what I know now, I'd have had a hysterectomy. No one in their right minds should have a baby after thirty-five."

"Jeanette," he pleaded, "please."

"Well, you got me this way!" Her mercurial mood changed again. Now she was vindictive. "I don't know why in the hell you're so smug. What are you trying to prove—that you're still virile, that you've still got what it takes, that you're not impotent? Every time I go out in public, people point to me and say, 'There she goes, that's Luke Heron's wife. Good to know that he was able to knock her up at his age!' "

"Jeanette, for God's sake, be sensible. You're carrying on like a—"

"Like a what?" she interrupted. "A hysterical bitch-wife-mother?" Her mouth curled. "Why not? That's what I am—all three combined in one fabulous package!" She began to cry again. "Look at these breasts—

75

do you think there'll be any nourishment for the baby? Look at these hips—are they wide enough for the baby?" She brushed the tears from her eyes with the backs of her hands.

"You know damn well that the doctor says you'll be fine," he replied tersely.

"What does he know? I'm just a statistic to him. What if I bleed to death?"

"Jeanette, for God's sake, calm down." He got up and patiently removed his tie and took off his cummerbund.

"What are you doing?" she cried, eyes wide and staring.

"I'm not going to the party alone. I'll stay home. In your condition—"

"My *condition*! All we've been talking about is my condition, and I'm sick and tired of it!"

"But," he replied lamely, "you brought up the subject."

"So you're turning it around as you always do." She paced up and down. "It's always *me*, never *you*,—the triumphant male on a white charger."

He unbuttoned his shirt. "Oh," he replied wearily, "I wish I could help you, Jeanette."

She squinted at him. "You could have helped me before it was too late, but you wouldn't let me go to Kansas City."

"Now, don't start that up again. My God, Jeanette."

"It would have been the best solution all the way around."

"I'll be in the study," he said quietly. "You better tell Mrs. Reynolds that we're having dinner in, although I'm not very hungry. I'll call Uncle Bos at the hotel and tell him we're not coming."

"What are you going to say?"

"I'm going to tell him the truth, that you're not well and that I don't want to leave you alone."

"Make up your own excuse. Don't blame this little fiasco on me."

"What can I say?" He looked at her helplessly. "One minute you're one way, and the next you're another. You're beyond dealing with, that's all."

"Oh, you're so used to 'dealing' with people every day of your life that you don't even know how to treat your wife."

"You're right, Jeanette, I don't." He left the room, and a few moments later she heard him on the telephone. She sighed and went into the bathroom. The beveled glass mirror above the washbasin showed only the upper portion of her torso. Cut off above the waist, she was surprised that she looked so well, considering what she had just been through. She peered closer into the glass. Her face was smooth and unlined. She wiped away the mascara under her eyes with a tissue, then reached for the eyebrow pencil. Her eyes done, she then applied lipstick. Her cheeks were naturally pink and did not need the blush of rouge.

She smoothed her upswept hairdo; the latest fashion was very becoming to her heart-shaped face. She snapped on the new brassiere that raised her breasts into a remarkably youthful line, slipped into the red blouse and skirt, then, putting on the jacket, stood back and looked at herself critically in the mirror. The transformation was amazing. The slightly bouffant jacket covered her stomach, and the long tight skirt, slit to the knee, was very complimentary to her figure. Her legs, she decided, were still good. Red pumps corrected her posture, and, as the last touch, she picked up a red-sequined evening bag and long black gloves, then went into the hall and stood for a moment in the doorway of the study. "I'm ready whenever you are, Luke," she said quietly.

A half-hour later they came into the ballroom of the hotel, and Letty, dressed in pale blue chiffon, came forward to meet them. "I'm so glad to see you, dear," she said, kissing Jeanette's cheek, "glad you've recovered. You look absolutely stunning."

"Thank you, Mother, I should. This outfit cost an arm and a leg."

"One would never guess you were in the family way," Letty whispered.

"Well, *I* know. At this very moment the little beast is kicking up a storm."

Bosley touched Luke's shoulder. "Thank God you're here, Luke. I thought I was going to be forced into giving the opening speech." He lowered his voice. "How is she?"

Luke shook his head. "Honestly, Uncle Bos, why my hair is not all white is beyond me. It'll be the greatest day of my life when that baby is safely delivered. I'll really deserve the Purple Heart."

Bosley laughed gently. "I think the *Croix de Guerre* would be more appropriate."

Luke nodded. "Amen."


Mrs. Reynolds surveyed Jeanette's figure several days later and nodded her hennaed head. "Thank your lucky stars, Mrs. Heron, that you've got big bones. It's those sweet little women who look like balloons during pregnancy."

"I'll be staying home during the last two months," Jeanette replied. "I think women in my condition on the streets are ridiculous, especially when they look like a grandmother."

Mrs. Reynolds smiled softly. "A change-of-life baby always comforts the mother in her old age." Too late, she realized what she had said, and went on quickly, "I mean—"

"I *know* what you meant," Jeanette retorted. "I am not blind, deaf, or dumb, but with my luck the kid will be sickly and I'll end up taking care of it until I'm seventy." She laughed then and decided not to fire Mrs. Reynolds after all. "Would you teach me petit point?"

"Of course!" Mrs. Reynolds replied enthusiastically, trying to make up for her earlier gaffe, and soon Jeanette was working on a cover for the footstool which Mitchell Heron had given them for a Christmas present. The piece was based upon an old Pennsylvania Dutch pattern discovered among his father's old drawings.

When the company plane was free, Currier and Ives flew Luke and Jeanette to Angel, before heading back to Washington with Bosley.

Luke Three's grades had improved. "A's and B's," he announced proudly. "Not one C in the bunch!" Then he handed in a list of suggestions about how to improve service at the Heron station. Luke was pleased, but he did not want the boy to get a big head, so he did not reply.

Early on a foggy Saturday, Sam tendered Jeanette an invitation for tea in his suite at the Stevens Hotel. As was his custom, he immediately launched into the subject of the visit. "Jeanette," he said in his high-pitched voice, "this business of becoming a mother at your age has very special joys."

"Name one," she replied laconically. "It's a terrible responsibility."

"Of course it is," he answered quickly. "Having a baby at any age is a responsibility, but the child will bring you much happiness," he promised. "I telephoned your personal physician in Tulsa this morning, and he assures me that your physical condition is excellent. We also spoke of other matters." He looked down at his long spatulate fingers. "After the baby is born, and your uterus returns to normal, he will give you a series

79

of tests and probably recommend certain medication—"

"Medication? I never take anything if I'm not ill," she announced firmly, her eyes questioning.

He nodded. "I am in agreement. But I am not speaking about self-dosage. We are only now learning about menopause and its effect on both the body and the psyche." He went on earnestly, "A woman's body must become accustomed to doing without certain hormones that begin to be manufactured by the body during adolescence and menarche. In middle age, glands cease to secrete certain hormones, and the body rebels. It goes into a prolonged withdrawal, almost, in a way, like a narcotic addict or an alcoholic withdraws when drugs or liquor are taken away. Your doctor will replace these hormones, which you will take orally, so that your body adjusts more easily to the changes taking place."

"Why, Sam!" she exclaimed. "I've never heard of such a thing!"

He smiled. "This treatment is new and, as yet, somewhat controversial. In many cases it has been proven that replacing the estrogen in a system that no longer manufactures the substance in the necessary quantities is most helpful, not only physically but, more importantly, mentally."

"Mentally?"

"Yes." He gazed at her impassively a moment, this dignified elderly man whom she trusted so implicitly. "Much of the discomfort of menopause is actually psychological, the feeling of aging. Men go through very much the same sort of mental strain at the climacteric." He smiled softly. "The male condition is usually referred to as 'the seven-year itch.' " He paused meaningfully.

"I always thought that was an old wives' tale," she retorted. "But I haven't noticed much change in my own deportment."

"An interesting word, 'deportment,' " he replied easily. "Did not you notice a change of attitude a year or so before your pregnancy?"

She looked uncomfortable. "Sam, life doesn't exactly begin at forty. I suppose I did alter some of my views."

"Your physical relationship with Luke, for instance?" His voice was gentle.

She colored and minutely examined her charm bracelet, "We hadn't been getting along—that way—for some time, but I don't think that's unusual, is it? Most of my women friends say their husbands aren't very demanding, and other things seemed to have replaced . . ."

Sam shook his head slowly. "Again you use an interesting word—'demanding.' As we grow older, of course, everything achieves a different look. That is what maturity is all about. But the physical relationship between a man and a woman should take on new meaning, and certainly not cease altogether. After all, Jeanette, you do love Luke."

"I wonder." She sighed. "He has been the only man in my life, and yet we have a very full schedule. He's away a good deal of the time, as you know, and with the war and—and my pregnancy, it seems . . ." She rubbed the back of her neck. "Oh, I don't know, Sam, what I mean. It's not that I want to be any younger—who would want to go through all of that again? It's just that everything is so uncertain today, and having a baby at my age and bringing it up in a world where values are—I don't know. It all seems so futile."

"It is not at all futile, lady," Sam replied with conviction. "You have a proud heritage and a famous name." He leaned forward. "Think about the baby's future! The second generation of the Heron family was actually very small. Mitchell has never married. Patricia Anne is Clement and Sarah's only child, and you and Luke have only Luke Three. There is room for a new baby. If it is a boy, there is a fabulous future with Heron Oil.

81

If it is a girl, new blood through marriage will be incorporated into the family constellation." He adjusted his white turban. "I do not know why you are so concerned. Could it be," he asked gently, "you are reviewing this part of your life from a purely selfish point of view?"

"Selfish, Sam? *Selfish?*" She frowned and considered the question before answering, "I have to think further about that."

"Having a baby has many far-reaching effects beyond the mother's point of view," he countered. "You will be raising a *person*, one who has rights, desires, dreams, and, hopefully, talent. Having a baby is where selfishness ends."

She looked directly into his eyes. "Sam, here I've been thinking about my own problems, and I hadn't really thought of the baby as an individual human being before."

"That is only natural, Jeanette," he replied quietly, "because the baby isn't a person with whom you can identify yet. It's only a little form inside; you know it is alive, because you feel it kick and move; but once it's in your arms and you see its face and you are acknowledged as a person too, your outlook will change, because that is the way of life. Do you understand what I am saying?"

She nodded. "Yes, Sam, I see."

He looked at his watch. "I must go, or I will miss my train." He paused and smiled. "I was only able to get a reservation because of Luke's influence. It is nice, very nice, to have friends in power."

She looked him in the eyes. "Sam, this so-called power sometimes frightens me. Luke is a good man, a fair man, yet he so often must deal with types of people that misuse their positions. There are some days when it seems he's going on nervous energy alone, and I'd like to help him, yet it's as if he's untouchable. Do you know what I mean?"

He nodded, adjusting his white turban, and he suddenly looked like a very old man. "Jeanette, we all change as we grow older, more on the inside than the outside. You must try to be more understanding, I feel, even with what you are going through. War changes men's feelings and the way that they do business and the way they treat their families."

"I know that intellectually, Sam, but emotionally it's quite different." She placed her hands awkwardly over her stomach. "My fears are different than his."

He raised his eyebrows. "Do not be too sure of that." Then he glanced at his watch. "I really must leave." He took her hand. "Good-bye. Keep in touch with me."

She kissed his cheek and hurried out the door.

Later, on the way to the station, he thought of the Heron family and Angel and all of the yesterdays that crowded in upon him, and he smiled softly in the gathering dusk. He had two important goals left in life before he made his "transition": one was to see his adopted family through the troublesome time ahead, and the other was to properly launch his book, *Born-Before-Sunrise*.

That night Luke called from Washington. "Mama!" He laughed. "Guess what? I just purchased a new Cadillac for you, the last one off the assembly line in Detroit. It's been customized for a socialite here who's just gone on to her reward. I got rather a good deal on it— the only thing, it'll have to be repainted. The old gal had it painted *pink*."

Letty drew in her breath, then smiled crookedly. "Son, don't you dare change the color."

"You mean, you'd drive a pink car?" he asked incredulously.

"Why not? It'll be the last pretty thing I'll be getting for the duration."

Nellie broke in. "Letty, you're either losing your mind or getting senile—or both. It's completely out of character for you to scandalize the town."

"What's so terrible about a pastel-colored automobile?" Letty asked heatedly. "I've never understood why cars always have to be dark blue or black. Why, George Story once had a cream-colored roadster that was the sharpest-looking thing on the road."

"Nellie," Luke put in quickly, "will you please get off the line?" There was no answer, but the crackling sound in the background ceased abruptly. "You'd better ask Uncle Bos, Mama," he said, making his voice gentle.

"I will not. After all, it's my car." Now that she was having second thoughts about her decision, she asked plaintively, "What's the exact color? Would you say it's—like strawberry ice cream?"

"Not really." He fought for the right word to describe the color. "I'd call it—well—it's *shocking*."

Letty's mind was filled with doubt. She wasn't all that fond of pink, truthfully, and the town was so conservative, and she had always behaved so decorously. It was on the tip of her tongue to say, "Better have it painted black." Then she thought that perhaps the town needed shaking up a bit. "Send it," she said quickly, before she changed her mind.

By late afternoon everyone in Angel, through the courtesy of Nellie, knew that Letty would soon be getting delivery on a new Cadillac—a new shocking-pink Cadillac.

The tree-lined street where Darlene Trune lived was no longer located on the outskirts of town.

A new subdivision of twelve acres of land was situated beyond the house, where fat Holstein cows used to

84

wander. Belle's old house, which had been neglected during the depression, now sported a new coat of yellow paint, and the dilapidated front porch was restored with new clapboard. Gleaming brass screening material, stretched taut in pine frames, added a pristine touch to the facade.

As Luke Three escorted her up the walk, after they had seen *Now, Voyager* at the Blue Moon, Darlene sighed, looking at the dark house. "Mama hasn't come back from Enid yet, I guess," she said. "She went over to attend the revival of *Gone with the Wind*. She's seen it four times. Would you like to sit on the front porch for a while, Luke Three?"

"Yeah, I guess so, although it's kind of cold," he replied. His head was still spinning from the romantic movie and all the kissing engaged in by Bette Davis and Paul Henreid. They sat down on the porch swing in the semidarkness and looked at the moon through the screen. "Look, you can see Ursa Major!" Darlene said, pointing to the sky.

"It's pretty awesome, isn't it?" he replied, still trying to see Ursa Major and not succeeding, and at the same time not wanting Darlene to know that it always took him a good fifteen minutes to find the Big Dipper, even when he was vaguely aware of its location. He placed his arm around her. She snuggled down against his windbreaker, but she could hear his heart beating through the thick material. She was warm, yet her forehead, resting against his chin, felt strangely cool and somewhat clinging. "Darlene?"

As she looked up, he kissed her on the lips twice in rapid succession and then paused, savoring the moment. She reached up and, pressing her lips to his, boldly inserted her tongue in his mouth. He sighed at the unexpected pleasure, and he felt himself hardening.

"Why, Luke," she said, breaking away, "you don't even know how to kiss!"

His face burned in the darkness. "Let's try again," he said gruffly. He took her awkwardly in his arms, bent his mouth down again, and touched her lips. Then, as their tongues met, he kissed her and found that the experience was absolutely shattering. So *this* was what Jerrard was always talking about! This was what caused all that passion in the movie! It felt tingling. Again he gave her a long kiss, which she anticipated and returned. As she nestled down into his arms, her elbow brushed his groin. At that moment Belle's old Model A Ford drove into the driveway, headlights throwing a wide arc over the front of the house. Darlene and Luke Three hastily pulled apart, and by the time Belle opened the screen door they were sitting sedately in the swing, three feet of space between them.

"How was the movie, Mama?" Darlene asked casually.

Belle cleared her throat. "Fine." She peered into the semidarkness. "Is that you, Luke Three?"

"Yes, ma'am."

"I think it best you be starting home."

"Yes, ma'am."

Belle waited until he was out of earshot; then she turned to her daughter. "What do you mean, lollygagging out here on the porch?"

"Well," Darlene replied sullenly, "we could have gone *inside*."

"I'll not have you smarting off at me, young lady," Belle retorted. "You know that you shouldn't entertain boys here alone."

"Oh, Mama," Darlene said, getting up slowly, "I'm eighteen years old, and Luke Three is only a kid."

"Maybe so, but he can still make you pregnant."

"Pregnant?" Darlene opened the door to the living room and switched on the light. "I don't know what gets into you, Mama. I'm not going to get pregnant."

Belle followed her into the house. "Just remember, he's a Heron and you're a Trune."

"What does that mean?"

"It means, young lady," Belle replied crossly, "that although he can give you a baby, he won't marry you."

"I think this conversation is juvenile, Mama. I have no intention of getting either pregnant or married."

Belle gave her daughter a long look. "You don't know this town like I do. Conditions here are a lot different than Oklahoma City. Angel is owned by the Herons, lock, stock, and barrel—even if it doesn't seem that way to outsiders. You grew up differently than I did. I want you to listen, because I know from experience."

"What do you mean, Mama?" Darlene's eyes were large and questioning.

Belle knew that in the heat of the moment she had said too much. "Oh, nothing." She tried to make her voice sound casual.

Darlene frowned. "*How* do you know so much about the Herons?"

Belle sighed. "Well, I suppose there's no harm telling you." She went to the mirror and smoothed her hair back from her forehead, and noticed that the lines about her eyes were deepening; her eyes were sunken hollows. "Well," she murmured, "what do you expect at forty-seven?"

"What?"

"Nothing." She turned and looked her daughter in the face. "I wanted to marry Mitchell Heron once, Darlene."

"So that's it, Mama. Well, why didn't you?"

"He didn't want to marry me." Now that she had said the words, the air was clear, and the air had not been clear in the house for a long time.

"Was it because of his money?"

Belle shook her head. "He didn't have any then. We were both broke. He was farming his mother's place." She sat down in the big chair by the door. "I was on relief."

"Mama, why didn't I know any of this?" Darlene sat down on the arm of the chair.

"You were too little and living with your grandparents. Why do you think I always came to visit you, instead of you coming here much? Your grandpa always had work in the oil fields and could support you well."

"Mama, you were so pretty. I remember that pink hat that you always wore when you came to see me."

"Yes," Belle replied laconically, "it was the only one I owned. Oh, I don't want to go back over those days, Darlene." She paused. "But there's one thing I want you to remember: the Herons are peculiar people. They stick together through thick and thin." She pointed a finger in the air. "Now, it's not that I don't like them. Letty's a good woman, and she's done a lot besides naming this town, but I'd hate to be a woman marrying into that family."

Darlene stood up. "Why do you keep harping on *that*, Mama? I'm not interested in Luke Three!"

"Oh," Belle said, getting up and placing her arm around Darlene, "I know you're not, honey. You're going to get a college education at Phillips University and meet some nice bright boy who has a real future ahead of him, someone who'll make a success on his own and not tied to old family money." She hugged her. "I'm going to be very proud of you someday."

Darlene laughed tonelessly. "Does that mean you're not proud of me *now*, Mama?"

"No, goose." Belle hugged her again. "But you've got gumption. Ambition is the most important thing a woman can have." She paused. "I never had any get-up-and-go, and neither did your grandma and grandpa. Otherwise," she finished wryly, "they'd have got up a town like Letty, or discovered oil like Bosley Trenton, or opened a general store like the Bakers. Instead, they claimed a piece of land that didn't even have a creek. No, honey, it's all going to rest with you—what you make of your life, how you're going to live it. And with your ambition, you may never be rich, but you won't be running a jerkwater café in a town that's seen better days, either."

Later that night, Darlene lay in bed, looking through the open window at Ursa Major, and thought about the conversation with her mother, then thought about Luke Three. She had kissed a great many boys during high school, but none of the boys ever made her feel like Luke Three did when he kissed her—and he was an amateur, too. His lips were so strange, hard and soft at the same time. There was a kind of electric spark when they kissed, that she had never experienced before. And, thinking about those kisses that she had shared, she began to shake inside. It was a long time before she could go to sleep.


Luke Three stretched himself out in the long bed and dozed. Half asleep, between reality and unreality, he felt a warm form next to his. The skin, warm and clinging, was slowly creeping over his body, and as he grew harder the new skin encircled him and moved slowly and deliciously back and forth. Suddenly he gave a little gasp and awakened fully. It had happened again. Now he was cold, moist, and sticky. He reached for the handkerchief under his pillow.

When he turned on his side, away from the window and the sky with the constellation of Ursa Major that he could never find, he closed his eyes, thinking about Darlene Trune and how wonderful her lips felt as she had kissed him so deeply, just before her mother had driven into the driveway in the old Model A.

Apparently this business of trying to find someone to fuck with was more complicated than he had thought. Of course, before he could proceed to that important step, he would have to know more about how to do it. He knew that he would be a good lover if he only got the chance. His desires were so strong lately. Didn't women want men as much as men did women? He could hardly wait until the right opportunity came along. He also wanted to satisfy a woman completely, like Jerrard said *he* did.

"Oh, Lord." He closed his eyes and prayed. "Oh, Lord, please, oh, please, give me a big one!"

With the swift turning of the leaves during a severe cold spell in the first week of September, a calm sort of detachment came over Jeanette. She had always disliked autumn before, because, as she looked at nature gone wild, she knew it was a death dance before a barren winter. But this year, bundled up in heavy clothing that made her more gargantuan in size, she strolled in the park both morning and afternoon. And as the leaves leisurely drifted down from the red-and-gold maples and the fiery oaks, and with the crisp crunch of leaves underfoot, her serenity increased. Her forehead lost tiny frown lines, and the corners of her mouth, which had been pulled down for so long, gradually relaxed. She smiled often at absurd occurrences—the cat returning with grease on its fur, a wrong number on the telephone, a cake in the oven rising only on one side—that would have tried her patience before.

One Wednesday afternoon she even attended a matinee performance of the National Touring Company production of *Life with Father*, and laughed so much that the mascara ran down her cheeks. And that night, after supper, she delineated the plot to Luke between peals of laughter.

He looked at her quizzically, amazed at the change in her personality. She was exhibiting all of her old flair for storytelling, and she seemed more like her old self than in the previous three-year time span. And that night, when he kissed her on the cheek, she held him awkwardly in her arms, then stood back, smiled, and looked down at her enormous stomach. "Our little boy is getting in the way, isn't he?"

He looked at her tenderly. "I want you to know that a girl would please me just as much."

She nodded. "Me too, but it's going to be a boy." She placed her hands on her stomach. "Here," she said, "feel right *here*." She guided his hands to the lower part of her abdomen.

A look of wonder came over his face. "Yes, I can feel it moving."

"And this is mild. Sometimes, Luke, I have to sit down, he kicks so much."

"Did Luke Three cause so much trouble?" he asked, a concerned look on his face.

"Yes."

"But why didn't you tell me—or at least let me feel him inside you?"

"It didn't seem so important then, Luke. Of course, I was younger too, and I guess I just took it as a matter of course." She sighed gently. "But now—well, this baby is going to be very special." She took off her loose dress and slipped a lace nightgown over her shoulders. "Luke, I don't want to be alone. Would you sleep with me tonight?"

"Why, yes—if you want me to." He was silent as he undressed, surprised at her invitation.

"I want to know that you're near."

Momentarily he felt a pang of guilt about Jorja, but later, when the lights were out, he gingerly placed himself around her back, and they went to sleep holding hands.

September 18, 1942, at four-fifteen in the afternoon, Murdock Edward Heron was born, after ten minutes of intense labor. Arousing from twilight sleep, Jeanette looked down at the tiny orange form cradled in her arms, then smiled at Luke, who was standing at the foot of the hospital bed. "I told you it was going to be a boy. Isn't he beautiful?"

"He looks awfully dark and mottled," he replied.

"Oh, he'll be pink tomorrow!" she exclaimed. "All babies look like that when they're born." Then she pressed the tiny form to her breast and sighed gently as she heard the milk gurgle into his mouth. The room went out of focus, and she lapsed into a gentle, undisturbed sleep.

When Jeanette awakened, the room was dark; only a pale night light near the door illuminated the sleeping baby in her arms. She flushed with pleasure; the nurse had left him with her. Being a mother at her age did not seem so strange now. He would be a comfort to her as the years passed, and if she attended his college graduation looking like a sixty-year-old lady, so be it! She would be the sharpest, most well-groomed grandmother in the whole wide world!

# 6

## A Web of Lies

*Jorja poured the special blend of Chinese tea from the tall, graceful Spode teapot into the thin, fragile cup.*

"Do you want a biscuit?" she asked, looking up at Robert Desmond.

He swiveled his chair from the window overlooking Tulsa's skyline and shook his head. "No, I've got to watch my weight." He took a sip of tea, nodded, smiled thinly, and sighed gently. "What is the latest from Heron?" He lighted a long oval Turkish cigarette and blew a discreet volume of smoke in her direction.

She fanned the air in front of her and busied herself with the portfolio on her lap. "Production of one-hundred-percent high-octane airplane gasoline is up thirty percent. . . ." And she went on and on, quoting figures and prices in a bored tone of voice, occasionally wetting her lips. "Here's something rather interesting. Do you know how many B-17 bombers are scheduled to be turned out this year? Two hundred and seventy-nine."

He looked up, pursed his lips, and snapped, "Where did you get that figure?"

She patted her upswept hairdo. "An old friend in the aircraft industry gave the data to Luke last week."

"Strange," he mused. "That's twenty percent over the figure that I have. I wonder which is right."

"Luke's information came from the lion's mouth, so to speak," she answered smoothly.

Robert Desmond flecked an imaginary bit of lint from his immaculate gray serge suit and, going to a large gilt-framed landscape of rural Belgium on the wall, pushed a button. The painting turned over automatically, revealing a world map littered with colored stickpins. "We can keep the figures current," he said, "by checking the newspapers every day and subtracting the Allied losses in destroyers, aircraft carriers, B-17's. . . ." He pushed the button again, and the painting was returned to its original position. "Jorja, anything else?"

"Not at the moment. However, I have volunteered my services—for a fee, of course—for any weekend work that Luke has in mind."

Robert Desmond maintained a blank face and replied, "Don't most ceilings look alike?"

"Not really!" Jorja laughed. "Actually, Luke has assured me that any confidential secretarial duties will be fulfilled by me. Now, I've been short of information to feed him. Do you have some figures about Desmond oil production? That seems to be what he's interested in most."

Robert Desmond pushed a manila envelope across the glass-topped desk. "This data has been altered considerably. It shows our profit margin for the quarter to be down twenty-five percent." He chuckled. "With a gross so embarrassing, Luke would never dream that our little, apparently almost bankrupt company is steadily buying his stock. As far as he's concerned, we're out of the running."

"But won't everyone on Wall Street know that Desmond's buying Heron?" Jorja asked, leaning forward and placing her hands on the front of his desk.

"Don't do that," he said. "I hate fingerprints." He removed a spotless white handkerchief from his breast pocket and meticulously polished the glass top. "As to your question, naturally we're not scooping up whole blocks of Heron under our own name. Not by a long shot. About twenty-five men—good men in the industry, too—are making rather large purchases." He smiled, but his dark eyes held no amusement. "No one can pin the deals on us—not until the time is right to strike."

It was dawn, five-thirty in the morning, October 28, 1942.

The Heron DC-6, recently camouflaged with three shades of green paint, which looked as if it had been applied by preschoolers in finger-painting class, and with even its blue logo obscured, slid into the landing pattern above Burbank airport.

John Carrier and Robert Ives looked at each other in complete surprise. Familiar with the facility, having landed and taken off numerous times, they were locked firmly into the radio landing pattern. Carrier shook his head. "Something's wrong. Look, Bob, that drive-in theater is supposed to be over *there*, and the runways here, and that track of houses— Say, everything appears reversed. Get the tower back."

The copilot nodded and called the controller. "What's wrong? We're coming in ass-backwards."

The controller chuckled. "You boys haven't been into Burbank lately, have you? Proceed as directed."

"But—"

*"Proceed as directed."*

Now that they were comfortably close to the ground, Carrier whistled softly. "Keerist, Bob, look!" The entire area had been so expertly camouflaged that it was only apparent now that the original drive-in theater had been painted to look as if it were the airport, and vice versa, and the track of houses, small structures complete with lights, had been erected over chicken wire draped with tiny bits of green-and-blue cloth. The same material, placed on enormously high beams, was stretched over the entire field.

A moment later, the DC-6 touched down under the camouflage net and came to a stop by the tower, which was treated identically. "My God, John, this is incredible. Whoever did this job must have been a special-effects expert at one of the Hollywood studios before the war."

They taxied the DC-6 to the terminal, and Carrier got up stiffly, stretched his back, and opened the hatch, then awakened Clement, who was sleeping, strapped in his seat. "Mr. Story, we're here."

Clement roused, yawned, and turned to the window, expecting to see the familiar airport, but a heavy drape obscured his vision. He had forgotten the rule about windows being blacked out.

He came down the steps and looked up in wonder. "Are we in the right place?" he asked.

Carrier nodded. "Isn't this the pizzazz?"

The long black studio limousine was waiting a discreet distance away. "Good morning, sir," the driver said, opening the door. "You'll find a thermos of hot coffee on the seat."

Clement leaned back luxuriously in the plush seat and took a sip of the coffee as the machine sped toward Universal Studios. He mentally thanked Luke, who had told him over the phone, "Clem, if you're going from Denver to Hollywood, might as well take the company plane. It will be deadheading from Tulsa to the coast anyway, to pick up some of the board. Take advantage!"

Clement hated private planes almost as much as he did commercial airliners; he felt uncomfortable in the air. He sighed softly. But, there were times—like now—when it was certainly advantageous to be a member of a famous and influential family. As the limousine turned onto Hollywood Way, he saw four huge gasoline trucks pull into the airport drive, and as the bold blue Heron logo on the trucks flashed by, a sense of pride welled in his breast. His family was helping to win the war, as the poster said, "in the air, on the land, and on the sea."

The huge production number which was to comprise the finale of *Boys Up Front* was being shot on Stage Nine at Universal Studios. As Clement arrived on the set, all the male extra players in Hollywood, dressed as soldiers, sailors, and Marines, seemed to be gathered en masse.

"It's an open cattle call," the assistant director told Clement. "With so many regular extras in the service, we got a dispensation from the Guild to advertise in the papers for bodies—nine hundred, to be exact. They each get five bucks and their lunch"—he laughed,—"and four cigarettes if they behave."

The set for the picture consisted of an enormous sky backdrop with fleecy white clouds, hung behind a wooden structure, built in forced perspective, that looked far more real than the tower and airfield at Burbank airport, which it was supposed to resemble. Directly in the foreground were a series of huge, flat belts, built into the floor of the set, which was set in motion by the property man. While the assistant director conducted a disastrous dress rehearsal, the extras complained bitterly at being asked to stand, and then walk in strict formation, on the moving belts.

Clement addressed the band, which had arrived the day before from the Denver personal appearance. "While we were in Colorado, I saw the orchestra short subject that we filmed last August and I hid my head in shame. The audience in the theater howled. I didn't realize there were so many hammy Indians in the band. Remember, we're not Spike Jones and His City Slickers!" He paused. "I think if we were *really* playing, you'd all look more natural with your instruments. But as it is, when the cameras start and the playback machine is turned on and our own music starts blaring out of the speakers, you boys *fake* too much. Your playing has to match the music—and it does—but you're all uncomfortable, and it shows. Why, I've never seen so much eye-rolling in all my born days." He finished gruffly, "So, let's tone it down."

At eleven o'clock the band was called to take positions in the foreground, in front of the hundreds of extras marching on the moving belts. The assistant director shouted, "Quiet. Quiet on the set."

The director turned to the cameraman and whispered, "Roll 'em." Then he raised his voice and exclaimed, "Action!"

Miraculously, the extras, who had been rehearsed for four days, kept in perfect step to "The Battle Hymn of the Republic," which Clement and the band had previously recorded. The scene was repeated once more—then lunch break was called—and four times that afternoon, before the director was satisfied.

At five o'clock Clement addressed the band, "David Yarrow, the director, will be filming close-ups of all of you playing instruments. Now, he's a week over schedule on the picture, and he won't be devoting a lot of time to your facial expressions, so watch it. After he finishes with us, everything will be in the can. Don't mug too much."

That evening, as the studio limousine sped over the Cahuenga Pass toward the Beverly Wilshire Hotel, Clement spoke to the driver. "Turn down Hollywood Boulevard at Cahuenga."

The sight that greeted his eyes was very similar to the

set he had just left. The streets were teeming with soldiers, sailors, and Marines, and a variety of women of all ages, shapes, and sizes, dipping in and out of the many bars that spotted Hollywood Boulevard and lining up in front of restaurants and theaters—all with a light-hearted, carefree spirit of camaraderie, servicemen on a last holiday before going overseas. He was filled with a certain sadness that he could not at once explain, and his own experiences during World War I came back to him with a sudden clarity. Oh, if he were only fifteen again!

After a bath and dinner in the Heron Suite, which was kept year-round by the company, he waited a moment in the lobby for the limousine to pick him up at the front door. There was a long queue of people lined up at the front desk, inquiring about rooms from the polite but harried clerk. "Sorry, nothing. . . . Please inquire later. . . . Sorry, all booked up. . . ." The clerk occasionally pointed to the large sign in back of the information counter that read: RESERVATIONS LIMITED TO FIVE DAYS. Clement sighed, knowing that there were a number of persons, unable to find apartments or houses, who had established a set, endless routine of moving from one hotel to another every five days.

The band played at the Hollywood Canteen that evening; it was an off night, and not many celebrities were in attendance, yet the place teamed with servicemen. Clement recognized Betty Grable, Linda Darnell, Lana Turner, and Bette Davis, either dancing or signing autographs. Again, as the band played the last number, "Good Night, Sweetheart," he felt a momentary feeling of regret for being typecast as a civilian orchestra leader when he really wanted to be of more service to his country.

That night, on his way back to the hotel, he asked the driver to take Hollywood Boulevard again. It was two-thirty in the morning, and sleeping servicemen were stretched out on the bus benches from Vine Street west. Here and there in doorways, an occasional soldier or sailor embraced a prostitute, who quickly rearranged clothing as Military Policemen made their rounds. Cabs filled with service personnel were headed toward Point Mugu, March Air Force Base or El Toro Marine Base. And the wind, sweeping down the boulevard, was warm, carrying on its breezes the fetid fumes from the ever-passing cars. As the limousine headed down La Brea Avenue toward Wilshire, Clement felt a sadness slip over him like a heavy cloak. He felt displaced, an alien form in a town he knew so well.

Sarah ran a comb through her red hair and retied the soft blue bow at her throat. The peignoir, which she had ordered from Saks Fifth Avenue on her last trip to New York, was as flattering, her mirror told her, as she had known it would be when she first glimpsed the design on the mannequin in the window. It was the most expensive clothing purchase she had ever made: two hundred dollars. But she wanted to be especially beautiful for Clement. This was their wedding anniversary. She was in the foyer when she heard his car in the driveway on Signal Hill, and when he opened the door his face was suffused with pleasure as he took her in his arms. "Happy anniversary, darling," he said.

She felt her eyes tear. "Happy anniversary. Come on, I've got your bath ready," she replied softly as she pressed his hand.

He grinned and patted her derriere. "Great. After thirteen hours in the air, and four stops for refueling, I feel like one of the Brothers Grimm." He started through the hallway toward the bathroom, turned, searched in the pocket of his overcoat, and thrust a tiny blue foil package toward her. "I almost forgot."

"What's this?" she asked.

100

"Oh, just something for putting up with a guy who's on the road all the time," he replied casually and turned back toward the hall.

She grasped him by the shoulders. "You're not getting off that easily!" she exclaimed, then handed him an identical small blue-foil-wrapped package. "Happy Anniversary, Clem."

Wordlessly they both opened the jewel boxes; each gave a little cry, then they hugged each other, laughing until their eyes smarted. They had given each other Tiffany watches—hers in rose gold and diamonds, his in yellow gold and onyx.

"Who says that we don't think alike?" she said humorously, touched at the gift.

He shook his head. "You're really something, Squaw, and as soon as I take a warm bath— It *is* warm, isn't it?"

"Well, Hotshot"—she grinned—"it was when I drew it, but it's probably lukewarm now."

"As soon as I take my lukewarm bath, I'll show you exactly how I treat a wife whom I don't see as often as I'd like." He gave her a long look, and they both paused and shared the moment; their camaraderie, their love for each other, was very precious then.

Later, when he came in from the bathroom with a towel draped around his middle, he sat on the foot of the bed and caressed her instep. She felt the chill of metal and looked down. He was attaching a tiny gold chain around her ankle. "To keep you in slavery"—he laughed—"just in case someone wants to know who you belong to." He kissed the tiny heart-shaped diamond that dangled on the chain.

She giggled. "Oh, that tickles."

He kissed her knees, the outside of her thighs, her stomach, and the cleft between her breasts, then her neck, and finally his tongue dove into her mouth. He

101

kissed her deeply. "It seems like I've been gone for six years," he said, "instead of six weeks."

Her body was warm, the flesh clinging and sweet-smelling. He luxuriated a long moment in the tactile pleasure of skin upon skin. "Oh, I love you, Sarah," he said at last.

She moved up to meet him as she felt the extension of his body touch her thighs. He lay still a long moment, and she covered his cheekbones with kisses. Looking up at his face, she thought him quite handsome. Maturity had filled out the sharply sculptured planes inherited from his Cherokee father, and had softened the thrust of his jaw, but time had not altered his passionate response. If anything, he was a better lover now than when younger. That was one of the beatitudes of growing older, she mused, when experience—knowing what was expected and how to achieve complete fulfillment—took precedence over ardor.

Their bodies swayed with intimate rhythms now. They moved together, closely engaged, responsive, again and again, bringing each other to supreme heights of delicate feeling. Tremors spread out from their midsections, which held fluttery, deep sensation; then he launched his slow, thrusting, caressing motions again.

As he moved within her to that sweet and fulfilling final echo of passion, he spent copiously. It seemed that they were both floating above the counterpane, and, as the trembling gradually receded, they finally lay quietly in each other's arms, slightly drowsy, completely satisfied. He sighed as his strong heartbeats became gentle palpitations. "I love you so much," he whispered contentedly.

"Oh, and I love you too, Clement. Isn't it wonderful that after all these years it keeps getting better and better?"

He nodded, then buried his face in her hair. "Hush, now," he murmured, "let's go to sleep."

102

Clement awakened at six o'clock in the morning, as the room was becoming filled with light. He discovered that they had not changed positions but were still entwined in each other's arms. He began the slow machinations of love once more.

Clement and Sarah, dressed in robes, having consumed an enormous breakfast, listened to the eight-o'clock news on the radio. The Japanese were gaining in the South Pacific, and the reports on the home front were not encouraging. President Roosevelt had advocated a belt-tightening program, and strikes were rumored.

Clement looked up from his second cup of coffee and made a face. "I hate chicory mixed in coffee. And I hate one-night stands and the war and being away from you and taking midnight planes and—"

Sarah nodded. "I know. It's all so defeating, somehow. I always try to put on a cool, composed face for the boys at the U.S.O., but sometimes I have to go into the kitchen and cry, looking at those young, boyish faces—kids just out of high school and basic training, not dry behind the ears yet, with no life experience, going out there, maybe to die. I wonder how many will be coming back? Every time I walk down the street and see all those stars in everyone's window, I think: *What can it be like to have four or five boys in military service?*"

Clement folded the paper carefully and fastened his eyes on a headline as he spoke in a quiet, strained voice. "You might as well know, my dear, that I've applied for a commission in the Army."

She took his hand. "I was waiting for you to tell me," she replied softly.

"You *know?*"

She nodded. "Brigadier General Hopper was seated

next to Luke on the dais of a fund-raiser in Washington last Monday, and he mentioned . . ."

Clement got up and went to the window. "God Damn!" he exclaimed. "I've never been able to do anything in secret without my crappy family finding out." He whirled around. "Did old Hopper indicate that my request was going through?"

"According to Luke, he didn't say, but I would assume so."

"Don't be too sure. Glenn Miller got turned down by the U.S. Naval Reserve."

She looked at him incredulously. "You're kidding!"

He shook his head. "Would you believe that they told him in so many words that they didn't know how he'd fit into the Navy?"

"That's absurd."

"I know," Clement retorted bitterly. "I suppose they thought he wanted a desk job or some such thing. Jesus Christ, as musicians we're not exactly unknown. So Glenn applied for the Air Force, and if he doesn't make it, he's going to be the unhappiest guy in music. He told me all about it last week in Hollywood."

"I didn't realize that you two were so friendly," Sarah said, placing the coffeepot on the stove.

"He has his niche, and I have mine," Clement said slowly. "I've never felt any animosity just because he's gotten better breaks than I have. He's riding a special curve now, with *Orchestra Wives*, a big hit movie, and his string of record successes." He looked up. "I've never envied anyone in my life, Sarah. But if the Air Force doesn't take *him*, the Army may not want *me* either." He peered at her. "What else did old Hopper tell Luke?"

Sarah shrugged her shoulders. "Nothing, really. Your name came up in conversation. The general naturally thought that your half brother would know that you'd applied, that's all." She paused, then glanced at him expectantly. "If you do get taken, what are you going to do about the boys in the band?"

He glared at her. "What do you mean? I'll take as many with me as I can. Many of them are draft age anyhow." He paused. "Apparently it works like this: they enlist too, then after basic training I request that they be transferred to my company. Oh, I'll probably lose a few to other bands, and that's okay too, because hopefully there'll be other musicians that I can transfer over until I have the band up to capacity. Of course, they may not all have Cherokee blood, but I'll do what I can." He hit his palms together lightly. "That is, if they decide to take an old man my age." He paused. "Playing for the U.S.O. and the boys at the camps is great, but I want to tour the war zones, too." A light came into his eyes. "I'll never forget the expressions on those guys' faces in the hospitals during World War One." He shook his head. "Boy, that band was lousy! Hell, I was only a kid myself, but we'd come into a ward and entertain, and it was as if it were the second coming of Christ. When we played from the back of an old truck just back of the front lines, you'd have thought we were the London Symphony Orchestra."

"Don't you think all that's changed?" Sarah ventured, giving him a long look. He shook his head. "As far as protocol goes—but the boys on the battlefield haven't changed. Guys are still out there to get killed." He paused. "You see, Sarah, I've got to *contribute*, and if old Hopper turns me down—well, I suppose there's still the Marines."

On November 19, Jeanette and Luke brought Murdock, aged two months, back to Angel for Thanksgiving. Letty and Bosley met the entourage at the landing strip, then invited Currier and Ives back to the clapboard for dinner. "It's not much." Letty grinned. "Hattie's Spanish rice isn't very Spanish."

105

Murdock was very alert and seemingly appraised the dark plowed fields on either side of the pink Cadillac with appreciation, because he cooed, pointed his little plump fingers, and performed various bodily functions in what appeared to be a state of ecstasy.

"He's just like his Uncle Clement," Jeanette said, laughing. "Pure ham." She turned to Bosley. "Which side of the family makes him crave attention?"

"I wouldn't rightly know. Remember, I married late in life. So you can't say that I had anything to do with it. The only one that I knew really was your grandmother, Luke. Lavenia was a corker. Lots of spunk. I first met her on the train coming down from Wichita in eighteen ninety-four. She thought I resembled the original Luke." He glanced at Letty. "Is that true?"

"Yes—you did, in those days." She turned pink. "It was all I could do to look at you. It was like Luke had been raised from the dead." She paused. "Do we have to talk about all this?" And she almost added, "in front of the children," but caught herself just in time, remembering the children were grown.

"Mother, why don't you want to talk about the old days?" Luke asked seriously.

"Oh, that's all water under the bridge. When Sam's book comes out, you can study it to your heart's content. It'll all be there. I gave him the family records."

"You did?" Luke's forehead settled itself into the usual frown. "Why? That seems like an invasion of privacy."

"I don't look at it that way at all," she replied softly. "All of our lives were so entwined then, because we'd all made The Run together and shared an experience that has still kept all of us close. There's no one dearer than John and Fontine, or Bella and Torgo, or the Stevens and the Bakers. Why, the story of The Widows would make an entire book."

106

Luke clicked his teeth. "I've got enough to do keeping the Heron image up to snuff as it is."

"There's nothing wrong with a little family history, Luke," Bosley put in as they drove up before the house.

But Luke was bothered the rest of the day. Sam knew a great deal about his young adulthood, but surely he wouldn't detail his trips to The Widows to see Stella. . . . He remembered her fresh beauty and once more could feel the exquisite touch of her warm embrace.

"Luke," Jeanette called, "are you going to stay in there all day?"

It was only then that he realized that everyone had gone into the house and he was still in the back seat of the Cadillac. "Sorry," he said, and to make up for his lack of attention took Murdock into his arms. "I'll carry him into the house."

Letty met him in the hall. "You're in your old room at the top of the stairs."

"Oh, Mother." Luke shifted Murdock from one arm to the other. "Could I sleep in Clem's old room?"

"Why, yes, of course." Embarrassed, Letty looked away.

Luke went on quickly, "With no crib for the baby, he'll be sleeping with Jeanette, and I wouldn't want to roll over on him during the night." He had neatly solved the question of them sleeping apart, something which his mother would not understand.

Luke Three came into the house only two minutes before supper was served. "Hi, Dad," he said with a smile and held out his hand.

Luke looked at the boy in surprise. "Well, you've come up in the world since I saw you last!" He could look him directly in the eyes.

Luke Three grinned. "Better late than never. I was afraid I was going to be a little squirt for the rest of my life."

107

"Are you still going to Dr. Larson?"

"The last time I was in the office, he said that I didn't need to come back for two months."

"How's the station going?"

"Fine. Averaging a hundred and ten a day."

"That's good, son. How's the goofball doing?"

"Jerrard? Great. He's the best mechanic I've ever seen."

"Yes?" Luke replied skeptically. "And of course you've known *so many*!"

"No, I mean it. He has a way with his hands. He works on a car the way that Uncle Clem conducts his orchestra."

"Just don't be double-dating with him," Luke cautioned. "He's got a fast reputation."

"Aw, Dad, he wouldn't take me along. After all, he's nineteen. I'm still a kid to him."

Luke looked at his son with new eyes: he was a *man*. When Luke had seen him three and a half months ago, he was still a boy. "Do you like school?"

Luke Three grinned. "I'm happy here, Dad. Living with Grandma and Grandpa is the best of all, and with school and my job, what more could a guy ask for?"

"Ever see Belle Trune's daughter?" Luke put in conversationally.

"Yeah, once in a while." And, afraid that he would be questioned more thoroughly, Luke Three went on quickly, "I don't date, Dad, don't have time. To keep my grades up, I've got to burn a lot of midnight oil." He glanced sideways at his father to see if he had succeeded in distracting him from the subject of Darlene Trune and saw that his father was thinking about something else. He smiled to himself. Truthfully, Darlene was on his mind much more these days than he liked to admit. If he closed his eyes, he could still feel her soft, warm, moist mouth and her darting little tongue. . . .

# 7

## *An Alien Cry*

*Sarah waited until she heard the car in the driveway; then she went out on the porch and handed Clement the yellow envelope, that had arrived that morning. He read out loud:*

CAPT CLEMENT STORY
77643 LARAMIE STREET
KANSAS CITY MISSOURI

YOUR APPOINTMENT ANNOUNCED STOP REPORT DATE
APRIL FIFTEEN FOR BASIC TRAINING FORT MEADE MARY-
LAND STOP FULL DETAILS ON WAY STOP CONGRATULA-
TIONS AND ALL MY BEST.

JAMES COCHRAN, MUSIC OFFICER

Bella Chenovick opened *The Angel Wing*, took one look at the front page, and cried, "Torgo! Torgo! Come here." She held out the paper, and he looked down at a photograph of Clement in his captain's uniform, coming out of the Mason Street Induction Center in Kansas City, Missouri.

109

"Well, my pigeon"—he laughed—"doesn't he look handsome? And to think that it was you who gave him his first piano lesson at the age of—what?"

"Five." Bella beamed, and then her eyes grew misty. "You know, Torgo, I was just thinking the other day while I was out in the peach orchard, seeing all those bare branches, I thought to myself, these trees are like me and you—old and funny-looking."

"Ah," he replied, his own eyes bright, "but in the spring they'll leaf out and bloom again—just like we will."

She nodded. "Yes, and it's like that boy, Clement— he'll be blooming with a whole new career."

"Yes," he agreed. "Now maybe we'll have some *class* to our service bands." He went to his old violin, hanging on the wall, which he could not play anymore because of his arthritis, and stroked the bow. "He'll put in a lot of strings, so there'll be some sweetness, and I hope he cuts out the tuba altogether. Noisy instrument! Old Sousa had a fine marching band, but so stiff and staid, and every other military band has always copied him. I'm sure they use the same orchestrations. But now, with our own Clement in service, there'll be a new sound!"

Major Schultze, in charge of Music Services, was a gray-haired, tall, thin man with erect posture, who nevertheless always gave the impression of stooping— probably, reflected Clement, because he adopted a condescending air. He peered over his glasses and tapped the motion picture screen. "Watch the bouncing ball," he intoned, as if he were a professor teaching midgets how to play Jew's Harps. "Keep the beat!"

After the film was over, Clement stood up. "Sir, I know forming a band is difficult because we lack a trombone section, and—"

"It is of no consequence," snapped the major. "Musicians will come drifting in by and by. In fact, I have the transfer for a trombonist from the Hal McIntyre civilian band on my desk now."

"But the violin section—"

The major took a long breath. "When you have been in the military as long as I have, Captain Story, you'll realize that nothing is ever accomplished overnight. As far as violins go, we could do without them entirely. This is a *marching* band." He paused and went on blandly, "I don't think you'll be playing the Café Rouge of the Hotel Pennsylvania this season."

The sarcastic bastard! Clement bit his lower lip at the rebuff. It was well known to every musician in the room that one of his biggest play dates every year, aside from the Hotel Wyandotte in Kansas City, was the Pennsylvania. "I think that was an unfair statement, sir." He kept his voice low.

The major smiled mirthlessly, showing all of his rather yellow teeth. "I was merely making a statement, Captain, nothing personal. Your current gig will last for the duration, which may be some years in the future, unless we make the Krauts and the Japs heel fairly soon. Who was it said that the words 'military service' should be translated 'conformity'?" He paused. "Shall we take another look at the bouncing ball?"

The lights were lowered once more, and as the strip of film was projected on the screen, Clement's face burned in the darkness. That son of a bitch! It was rumored—and Clement thought it highly likely—that Major Schultze had given flute lessons when he had led a high school band in the early Thirties. Any military man of any experience whatsoever could elaborate on the reputation of flute-players—acts that had nothing to do with music.

\* \* \*

111

Clement wrote a long letter to Glenn Miller, who had been transferred from the regular Army to the Army Air Force and was presently stationed at Knollwood Field, North Carolina, where he had been named Director of Bands Training for the Army Air Forces Technical Training Command.

"Dear Sir:" he scribbled (knowing Glenn would get a kick out of that epithet).

I suppose that you've been through the same routines as I have here. I find that getting up at six o'clock in the morning is very difficult after not getting to bed before two or three in the morning, and not even knowing my name until noon, for so many years. Making a bed so tight that it will bounce a quarter in the air is a real bitch, to say nothing of marching in formation, and I haven't shined my own shoes since I was twenty. Rifle practice has restored my self-respect, though. More than once I've thanked God that Uncle Bos taught me how to shoot when I was a boy. But, I really got a thrill when I placed third as an "expert" in the entire battalion! The man who scored highest is a tough old bird, a former Resistance fighter from Norway, and the second guy worked in the circus as a professional sharpshooter. My medal, which I wear proudly on my chest, does my ego as much good as a hit record. We're instructed (as I'm sure you were) to keep the beat no matter what happens and to hell with modern harmony. I'm going to fight this thing out, though. Can you give me any thoughts?"

And he signed the letter "Capt. Clem."

Glenn Miller wrote back that he was having the same sort of difficulty and that he was fighting constantly with the traditionalists who wanted the music played as Sousa wrote it, without any modernization whatsoever. He advised Clem to continue to keep up the good fight.

Clement folded the letter, which he placed in his footlocker before reporting to Major Schultze, who announced with a very grave face that he was being transferred to Knollwood Field. He introduced his replacement, a Major Ray Cornwallis, formerly of the music department of Universal Studios in Hollywood.

Clement smiled broadly as the major singled him out from the group. "Good to see you, Clement, welcome aboard!" he exclaimed happily, pumping his hand.

"Corny!" Clement shouted, then hurriedly covered his tracks. "Sorry—Major Cornwallis."

Everyone laughed except Major Schultze, who was gazing out the window, a faraway look in his eye.

That night, with some difficulty, Clement reached Glenn Miller by telephone at his barracks. After the usual exchange of greetings, he inquired, "Did you have anything to do with Schultze's transfer?"

There was a low laugh on the other end of the line. "That bastard almost drove me nuts, too, when I was at Fort Meade. I pulled some strings and had him shipped up here."

"Do you think that's wise?"

Glenn laughed. "Why not, Clem? For the duration, all he's going to be doing is copying orchestrations."


After the harvest in June, 1943, the newly plowed fields of red Oklahoma soil turned into a fine powder from the drought and covered every tree and bush. Horses, returning from the fields, took on strawberry colors, while automobiles, traveling down the dirt roads, shot up clouds of pink—the same shade as the Trentons' Cadilliac. Then, the winds came, and for two days parched Angel was surrounded by a red mist so thick that it obliterated the sun.

Townspeople hung wet sheets at doors and windows, but the farmers went one step further and put up winter storm windows, then stayed inside and performed such winter work as mending harnesses, repairing tools, oil-ing equipment, and completing other chores most usually scheduled for the cold months. With all schools closed, both farm and town children, unable to play outside, were assigned alternate periods of drawing and coloring between household job assignments—all the while complaining bitterly about being slaves to their parents.

Everyone listened to the news programs on the radio, but the bored announcers could promise no letup in wind conditions. This particular red blizzard, pains were taken to point out, did not orginate in the Dust Bowl, but incorporated a wider area. The choking onslaught was the worst dry spell in many years. Housewives made gauze masks to cover the faces of family members who had business to transact on the outside.

All merchants closed up shop, with the exception of grocery stores. Luke Three and Jerrard opened the Heron service station only three hours a day: eleven A.M. to two P.M. Between serving the few customers, they played indolent games of Chinese Checkers and drank coffee from a thermos prepared by Hattie.

Jerrard looked out at the red fog and shook his head. "One thing sure 'n hell, we're going to be busy as beavers when this lets up. Everyone's going to have dust in gas tanks and radiators, and Lord knows what will happen to engines. We better rest when we can, Luke Three, 'cause all hell'll break loose when the sky clears up."

He then made a fast move on the board, skipped over six of Luke Three's men, and, scooping up the remaining marbles, declared himself grand winner. He poured more coffee while relating the story of the girl in Pond Creek who had unwillingly forfeited her virginity and then kept pestering him for more attention. She had called him four times—collect—before he had told Nellie to refuse her calls. He explained in minute detail their most intimate moments in the back of the car, in the hayloft, and in the front-porch swing.

Hearing such graphic details made Luke Three's heart beat rapidly and his crotch burn deliciously. He excused himself and, going into the lavatory, unfolded his tape measure and opened his trousers. He beamed with pleasure: he was exactly seven and one-quarter inches! Humming a few phrases of "I Hear a Rhapsody," he stuffed himself back into his tight jockey shorts. Jerrard was right; the briefs were much more comfortable than loose B.V.D.'s.

At three o'clock in the morning, the third night of the terrible dust storms, crashes of thunder were heard, and flashes of lightning illuminated the countryside; a torrent of rain, which lasted five minutes, splashed mercilessly out of the heavens. Then quiet was restored, and the sky sparkled like stardust thrown on a piece of black velvet.

Angel awakened to a world of clear air, but the sidewalks of Main Street and the roofs of the houses were plastered with red mud. On the farms, Holstein heifers left in feed pens were stained pink and black, and white leghorn roosters left out during the deluge were as rusty-colored as Rhode Island reds. Red speckled pigs were a common sight, and clothes hanging on lines through Garfield County were the palest magenta hue.

The sun rose in the cloudless sky, and heat poured down from above. Then, at ten o'clock in the morning, dark, menacing clouds again appeared over the horizon, and in half an hour the sky was purple-black. The wind rose to gale strength, swirling the now-dried earth heavenward in pinkish puffs that turned northwest Oklahoma into a surrealistic canvas that Salvador Dali might have been proud to sign.

This eerie phenomenon lasted only twenty minutes; exactly as the clock tower on the train depot climbed to ten-thirty, the heavens opened up once more. Sheets of rain came down with such unearthly force that it seemed as if a kettle had been turned upside down over a miniature town. It rained steadily for three and one-half hours, and as pink rivers ran down the dirt streets of Angel, covering Main Street with a deep red sea, houses became white again and livestock regained their former identity.

"Well, Jaundice!" Fontine Dice exclaimed, looking out over the wide expanse of dried yellow lawn shimmering with droplets of water caught by the sun. "If that wasn't a sight! If old Reverend Haskell was still alive, he'd have likened this deluge to Armageddon."

"Maybe so," John Dice agreed, "but it reminds me of one of those Technicolor movies where all the colors are far too bright to be real."

"Hey, looky there, Luke Three's going home to lunch from the Heron station." She paused meaningfully. "You know, he doesn't look or act like a Heron. Imagine him throwing a fit to stay here in Angel to work and go to school, instead of going to that high-falutin military school in Tulsa."

"I don't think it's strange at all, Fourteen," John Dice replied. "Folks, even kids, are getting back to the simple things since the war. And besides, Angel's scholastic standing is damn good, even if I'm going to be on the school board come September. Maybe with young men leaving high school to go into the service, teachers have more time to spend with their students. I'm glad Luke and Jeanette had the sense to let him stay with Letty and Bos."

Fontine frowned. "Here they've raised their own family, and taking on another. I don't think it's fair at all."

"Oh, I don't know," he replied philosophically. "You and I will never get that opportunity—not with Charlotte being an old maid."

116

Fontine swallowed. "I think I'll fix a cup of tea." She went into the kitchen, put water on to boil, then opened the refrigerator. There was still one piece of cherry pie left from last night. The thought of their only daughter living in Washington, D.C., and never coming home, was too painful to bear without a little caloric nourishment.

The orchestra was bused to the large service club at Fort Meade fifteen minutes early.

Clement waved to the band. "Okay, settle down, boys, it's true the civilian gravy train's over, but we're all professionals. We'll play this like a regular date and hope we have a few fans out there." He sighed. "I wish the Storyettes were here—it would sure help to have a little glamour—but, since they're recording that commercial for Aunt Bertha in New York, I guess we'll just do our usual gig."

"Who else is on the program?" Tracy Newcomb, the pianist, asked.

Clement laughed ruefully. "Us—just *us*!" He referred to his notes. "After 'Lady Luck,' we'll go into our new hit single; without the girls, it'll sound crappy, but the boys will expect it. From then on, we'll follow the lineup we did last Sunday on the air. I suppose we should add 'Roll Me Over in the Clover' for an encore; we've got to do something extra for the boys. I sure as hell wish we had some special material." He tapped his baton on a music stand. "Okay, let's rehearse the new ending for 'Red Sails in the Sunset'—"

"Far be it from me to give an opinion," the drummer interrupted, "but it seems to me we should finish with that. With the guys going overseas, it might be a nice note—"

"No!" Clement shot back. "These kids are homesick enough without that sentimental old thing to end the

117

night." He brightened. "Let's pull a switch and finish with a few bars of 'Good Night, Ladies.' That'll leave them laughing."

But it did not leave them laughing. The show, from start to finish, was dreary and uninspired. Nothing the musicians could do raised the dark caliber of the evening. "It's not that they weren't appreciative," Clement told Max later over the telephone. "They were so respectful it turned my stomach. We did everything but stand on our heads. They just sat there—enjoying the music, all right, but they weren't having any *fun*." He sighed. "Of course, the Storyettes would have added bosoms and legs, and that never hurts, but they can't join the service just to give us some pizzazz. We've got to do something special. I'm not used to bombing."

"What was the M.C. like? A hot wire?" Max asked, and Clement could see him chomping on his cigar, sitting in his big overstuffed chair in the window that overlooked Lake Shore Drive, trying to evaluate a performance that had taken place fifteen hundred miles away.

"We didn't have one."

"You mean you did the show *cold,* without a warm-up?"

"Sure. We can't take a whole troupe with us. It was just me and the band."

"That was the trouble," Max said authoritatively.

"Thanks!"

"No, Clem, you know the spirit in which I made that comment. Hell, you've been in show business long enough to know that you've got to have someone break the ice. If there isn't anyone else, then it's got to be *you*."

"You're kidding, Max. I'm not an M.C. I can't make with the jokes."

There was a long pause at the end of the line. "It

doesn't have to be a polished routine. I mean, let's be square with each other, you're no Bob Hope. But you've got to come up with some kind of material that will make the boys relax." He paused. "I think the trouble is that you're so damned famous, and they're so in awe of you, that they're afraid to really unwind. Clem, you can judge your nightclub and radio audiences like the back of your hand, but you don't know one damned thing about the G.I. audience."

"Hell, Max, they're the same people."

"Not by a long shot. The uniform has made the change. It's a one-hundred-percent male audience out there now—no women to soften them up, no booze, no cigarettes that have to be lighted, no toasts to make, no dinner to eat. The G.I.'s are just *sitting out there*, exclaiming, 'Here I am, *entertain me!*' "

Clement paused. "You're right, Max. I hadn't thought about that aspect. Everything is so new. Here I've been in the business for twenty-five years, and it's like starting all over."

"What did you do in World War One?"

"That was different. I was just a kid, playing the piano for Elsie Janis in the hospitals. Later, when I formed a band, we played in the back of trucks at the front lines. Amateur stuff, even in those days. Everything is so sophisticated now . . ."

"I think that may be your trouble, Clem," Max replied thoughtfully. "I don't mean to play down to the boys, but it seems to me that you've got to choose more upbeat numbers, work in more comedy, and use the old dance standards very minimally. Go easy on sentiment, because they don't have anyone to moon over." He paused. "Say, that may be the key right there. You've got to *amuse* rather than *entertain*, if you get my meaning."

"I think you're right, Max."

"Well," Max replied modestly, "I always am."

"Yes, you son of a bitch!" Clement said affectionately.

"When am I going to see you?" Max asked.

Clement sighed. "Whenever the damned war is over, I suppose." He paused. "Seriously, though, how long do you think I'll be able to work in pictures and radio?"

There was a long pause at the other end of the line, and Clement knew that Max was puffing energetically on his cigar, trying to come up with a lucid answer. "Let's put it this way: special appearances are great publicity for the Army—The Clement Story Army Band! As far as radio goes, you'll be recording several shows in quick succession, to be aired when you're not available." He laughed. "Don't worry, you'll still be making a hundred grand a year for the foreseeable future."

"I wasn't thinking particularly about the money, Max, I just don't want my career to nosedive."

Max laughed. "When the war's over, you'll still be on top, don't worry about that. The clients that I'm really concerned about are big-name movie guys who won't be having any pictures in the theaters for a long, long time. They may lose their audience—but not you." He paused. "Besides, at this point you're an institution."

"Well"—Clement laughed—"this is one institution that's feeling pretty crappy." He paused. "Now, before I do my next show at March Air Force Base in California, I've got to work up some kind of an M.C. act."

"Well, just don't hesitate to be irreverent."

"I don't get you. What do you mean?"

"I mean, make a little fun of yourself. Remember, Clem, you're in the service too."

Suddenly a new, controversial approach filled Clement's mind. "Thanks, Max, I think you've just saved my life."

"What did I say?"

Clement laughed. "Never mind." He paused and turned serious. "Max, I want you to know that I sure 'n hell think a lot of you."

"I hate cheap sentiment," Max replied gruffly, but Clement knew that he was touched. "Now, I'm going to hang up. This call is costing me a fortune. You called me collect, didn't you?"

"I sure as hell did, Max. With you taking ten percent of my earnings, you don't think I'd pay for the call, do you?"

"Cheap Indian crapshooter!" Max exclaimed, and the line went dead. Clement grinned. Max was one of the best friends he had ever had.

It seemed to Clement that every enlisted man in California had crowded into the huge hangar at March Air Force Base near Riverside, California. The flight from Los Angeles had been delayed twice, and the soldiers had been waiting for over an hour when he and the boys in the band arrived. They could have driven inland from Los Angeles in less time. He longed to have back the old bus that had taken them all over the country. He looked down at his new uniform and black shoes and smiled; for a moment he had half expected to see his usual sky-blue tux and patent-leathers.

He stood behind the hastily set-up partition and took a deep breath, waiting for the G.I. who was handling the spotlight to get his bearings. Finally he was rewarded with a bright flicker and stepped out on the makeshift stage, waving his right hand, which was holding a baton. This informal, strictly civilian gesture somehow established the necessary camaraderie at the outset.

A huge wave of applause wafted through the hangar, and he grinned and bowed once. For an hour he wanted the G.I.'s to forget they were soldiers who might have no future.

He went leisurely to the microphone and drawled, "Thank you, ladies and gentlemen—oh! Sorry!" He got his laugh and went on quickly, "I've not been in this chickenshit outfit long enough to remember that I'm not in the beautiful Blue Room high atop the Cherry Pit Hotel, overlooking the beautiful Titacaca River in downtown Intercourse, Pa." The soldiers laughed, whistled, and stomped, and the applause deepened.

"Now, ladies and gentlemen—oh, sorry again—I wish to hell there were some ladies present. On the other hand, maybe it's a good thing they're not, with all you horny guys out there. Hubba, hubba!" Again he received whistling, stomping, and heavy applause.

"I know you guys are fed up with training," he continued. "I just got out of basic myself. I'm one of those ninety-day wonders that all you enlisted men have been cussing lately!" He waited for the shouts of laughter and catcalls to quiet. "Well, I'm just as misplaced as you guys are, haven't had a woman in"—he checked his watch—"ninety days, three hours and . . . four minutes." He paused, secretly proud of his timing. "It took me four minutes to button up my pants!" There was more laughter; then he held up his hands for silence. "Now, I know you all didn't come down here to listen to this half-breed Indian tell jokes, and now we're going to get down to some sweet music."

There was such a roar of approval from the soldiers that Clement thought the entire ceiling of the hangar would lift up two feet before it settled back down again.

He held up his hand. "Now, I'd like you to meet the boys in the band." One by one, he introduced the men, who loped down the center aisle from the back of the hangar. The first, Tracy Newcomb, waved to the crowd, accepted the applause, then sat down at the piano and softly began to play "Lady Luck." He was

122

followed by Jim Knotts, who picked up the second phrase of the tune with his steel brushes. After being introduced, each member joined the band, until Tiny Little, who doubled on all the subsidiary instruments, picked up the glockenspiel just in time to sound the last note. Their timing, so carefully rehearsed, was perfection itself.

Clement turned and made a great show of counting the orchestra, then turned to the audience. "I swear we're missing some people somewhere." He paused, and the audience was so quiet that he could hear his own breath feed back in the microphone. At that moment a platoon sergeant down front, who had been cued, shouted, "Where in the hell are the Storyettes?"

Clement, hand behind his back, gave the downbeat, and the band broke into a rowdy, jazzed-up version of "A Pretty Girl Is Like a Melody," as the three girls, dressed in black silk opera hose and short pink skirts, danced out from behind the screen. The band then segued into "Hold That Tiger," which the girls breathlessly sang in harmonic, little-girl voices.

When the Storyettes finished the last song, the soldiers were on their feet, applauding wildly, whistling, and stomping their boots. When order was restored a few moments later, Clement swung into "Moonlight Cocktail," and all of his other famous swing numbers. Then, wet from perspiration, he held up his hands. "We gotta beg off now, fellas. We've got to take the White Knuckle Airline up to Travis Air Force Base and do another show for the poor sons of bitches up there!"

A sergeant in the second row stood up. "Captain Story," he shouted, and Clement placed his hand over the microphone and leaned forward so that he could hear "Yes?"

"I'm a quarter Cherokee from Enid, Oklahoma, and I know you're in a big hurry, but could you sing a little bit of 'The Old Chisholm Trail?' "

Clement smiled widely. "Sure thing," he said, and turned to the pianist. "Tracy, will you bring out my guitar?" He turned to the Storyettes, seated in front of the bandstand behind him, and loudly whispered, "How about a little harmony, girls?"

The band struck up "Tumbling Tumbleweed" as Tracy swaggered onstage with the guitar, and the soldiers howled with glee. Clement took the instrument, eased down on his haunches, and, as the spotlight zeroed in on his slight figure, sang a capella:

*"Come along, boys, and listen to my tale.*
*I'll tell you of my troubles on the old Chisholm Trail. . . ."*

The Storyettes, in the background, hummed along with him. It was one of those rare moments when lyrics, music, and voices became a litany.

*"Coma ti yi youpy, youpy ya, youpy ya . . ."*

As he sang the plaintive old cowboy song, he decided to close every show with the number. The last stanza was particularly moving, and he brought a new simplicity to the lyrics, which might prove to be an epitaph to the men out front.

*"I won't punch cattle for no damned man.*
*Goin' back to town to draw my money,*
*Goin' back home to see my honey.*
*With my knees in the saddle and my seat in the sky,*
*I'll quit punchin' cows in the sweet by and by."*

He paused and lowered his head as the Storyettes softly sang:

*"Coma ti yi youpy, youpy ya, youpy ya,*
*Coma ti yi youpy, youpy ya."*

124

There was a deep, all-pervading silence in the crowded hangar. It seemed to Clement that he had been squatting on the stage for hours, his legs were so numb; yet he held his position, savoring the moment. He heard a quiet rustling out front. His throat caught. He was being given the most supreme compliment of his life, a silent standing ovation. By this time, although he had no feeling in the lower portion of his body, he got to his feet; the movement broke the spell. There was heavy, prolonged applause, but no whistles or stomping. "Give the Axis hell!" he shouted with tears in his eyes, as the spotlight switched off and he left the stage in darkness.

Clement arrived in Washington, D.C., bone-weary, after having slept very little on the all-night flight. He dozed for three hours at the radio station, then recorded four spots pitching war bonds, picked up a new tailored suntan uniform, and was driven to nearby Fort Belvoir, Virginia, where he met the boys in the band. The camp, besides preparing engineers for overseas duties, was also a training center for civil service hostesses who would eventually preside over the many service clubs abroad. It would be a decided change of pace to look out over an audience scattered with members of the opposite sex. They rehearsed; then he told the band to knock off for lunch.

Major Harney, his immediate superior, whom he always referred to mentally as "Horny," had telephoned him earlier at the radio station. "Sorry to bother you, Captain, but I've a favor to ask," he said in a voice that always reminded Clement of shoofly pie and cornbread. "I ran into an old college buddy of mine yesterday, who thinks you've got the greatest band in the world." He paused, "And I have to agree. Anyway, he wants to meet you. Since we're having lunch today at the officers' club, can you come along for an hour?"

Clement laughed. "Sure."

"Thanks. I hate to put you through this. . . ."

Clement was becoming irritated at Horny's patronizing attitude, but he controlled his voice. "See you at twelve-thirty." At least, he reasoned, a middle-aged fan was still preferable to being stuck with some gushy, starry-eyed menopausal woman who might faint. That little episode had taken place twice.

The officers' club at Fort Belvoir was more crowded than usual, and as Clement came into the dining room from the bar, a little flurry of excitement accompanied his entrance. It was strange being a celebrity in the service. Thank God he was performing instead of attending tail-gunner's school like Clark Gable, or learning to fly like Jimmy Stewart. He had heard that their cohorts were making their lives miserable because they had to keep proving that they were ordinary guys. Of course, he reasoned, they were *not* ordinary guys but accomplished actors whose very special ambience set them apart. That creative glow could not be dulled by adopting a different profession for the duration. Gable, Stewart, and others, instead of taking the easy way out at some desk job at Fort Roach in Culver City, were actually fighting for their country.

It was a peculiar life he was now leading, he concluded, and he was fortunate to be able to continue making films and recording a weekly radio show. He and his band, like other service orchestras, were helping the war effort—or so the boys in the Pentagon kept saying. He hoped they were right, because he was working twice as hard as he had as a civilian.

Horny was seated at a window overlooking the parade grounds, where an inspection of troops was being conducted for the benefit of Washington brass—one bad aspect about Fort Belvoir being located so near the nation's capital. The personnel had to endure frequent visits by dignitaries, which sometimes interfered with actual training programs.

Horny's companion, a nondescript, round-faced civilian with thick pop-bottle glasses, was introduced as Mr. H. R. Leary, and he passed over one of the weakest handshakes that Clement had ever encountered. Leary, who had an unlined face—at least, that part not magnified by the glasses—had prematurely white hair and a sickly smile.

Fifteen minutes of boring small talk followed the introductions, chatter that even Horny did not bother to maintain, once the roast chicken was served. Just before the coffee arrived, Horny searched the table for his package of Lucky Strike cigarettes, which Clement remembered because of the new white background. "Lucky Strike green has gone to war," the ads proclaimed. The package had been propped up against the sugar bowl.

"Excuse me, I must have left my Luckies in the jeep," Horny said. "Be right back."

The moment he left the table, Leary took off his pop-bottle glasses. "Can't see a damn thing with these," he remarked with a laugh. His personality changed abruptly. Gone was the awestricken, painfully shy man. He leaned over confidentially and continued brusquely, "I don't have much time. I'm not going to give you my title because that's not important. Suffice it to say, I'm in a branch of the government involved in work that no one knows very much about." He grinned, and Clement began to warm up to the man. "You don't read about what we do in the papers until it's a *fait accompli*; then someone else gets the credit—or the blame. What I'm getting at, Captain Story—you can *perform* a great service for your country."

Clement laughed. "When I signed up, it was with the understanding, of course, that I would *perform*."

Leary did not smile. "Perhaps I chose an unfortunate term. I probably should have said 'render.' " He paused meaningfully, then went on quickly, his round face suddenly not quite so soft; there was an unmistakable hard line around the jaw. "Occasionally it's very necessary to speed certain documents from one area to another. Naturally, we have specific people in our employ to perform these jobs—people who, shall we say, blend into the woodwork. But now it's becoming increasingly difficult to bring these people into certain zones without raising questions about their identity." He paused and allowed a small smile to play around the corners of his thin mouth. His voice became soft and persuasive. "I think you'd make an excellent courier. Logically, you can be booked into any area, under the pretext of entertaining troops."

Clement gave him a long look. "You mean you want me to be a . . . kind of . . . spy?"

Leary shrugged his shoulders. "Nothing quite so dramatic, I'm afraid." He smiled wryly. "All that will be required of you, shall we say, is to deliver papers to a designated person."

"I saw a film once," Clement replied quickly, "about foreign intrigue. I remember the diplomat carried a briefcase strapped to his wrist." He frowned. "He didn't have a key, but the 'receiver' on the other end did." He paused. "Is it to be like that?"

Leary shook his head sadly. "Not at all. Certainly nothing as conspicuous as an orchestra leader carrying a locked portfolio."

"Could I conceal the papers in the lining of my saxophone case?"

"First, you must forget about that sort of image." Leary sighed gently. "It's simply not done that way anymore—if, indeed, it ever was." He removed an envelope from his inner pocket. "Read this, please."

Clement looked at his service address on a familiar

128

blue envelope and gasped as he recognized Sarah's handwriting. "Where did you get this, Mr. Leary?"

"Read the letter, please."

Clement glanced at the large, vague scrawl:

August 12, 1943

Dear Hotshot:

This note is going to be shorter than usual, because I've got to prepare dinner. I stood in the line at the butcher's all morning for one lousy pound of bacon. The chops that I'd hoped to buy were all gone by the time I got up to the counter, so don't let me hear you complain about the "slumgullion" you get in the mess hall! Ha, ha.

I'm looking forward to you being home for Xmas. I'll write later when my mind is not filled with a hundred and one details. Remember, I love you, Clem, and I wish you could be near me.

Squaw

Clement looked up indignantly. "How did you come by this letter? I've never seen it before." He was suddenly very angry. "I want you to know that I don't appreciate my mail being tampered with!"

"Hold on, Captain Story," Leary replied quietly. "Who said anything about your mail being confiscated? The letter is a fake."

"What? Don't you think I know my own wife's handwriting?"

"I said it's a *fake*."

Clement could feel the blood pounding in his temples. "Look, dammit, it's the real thing. No one but Sarah ever calls me Hotshot. No one knows about that, and not even my mother knows that I occasionally call her Squaw."

Leary drummed his fingers on the table. "Captain, if

this letter could fool you, it would certainly pull the wool over the enemy's eyes." He paused and enunciated very clearly. "This letter contains a coded message, written by a forgery expert in our employ, who studied examples of your wife's script. 'Hotshot' and all the rest were carefully researched. And, of course, we had her blue stationery duplicated." He paused again, and his voice was very persuasive. "All you have to do, Captain, is carry this letter, and others like it, with you, and, at a given time and location, merely discard the letter along with a paper or magazine."

"You mean," Clement asked incredulously, "that's *all*?"

Leary nodded his white head. "That's about it. In most cases you will never even meet your contact." He paused, and a cautionary tone crept into his voice. "There is only one thing: I am the only person who will ever contact you; I am your only connection. If my calls should ever cease, then it means that there is no more work for you. You are *never* to try and contact anyone else. You won't even have so much as a telephone number to call." He paused. "Is that understood?"

Clement nodded. "Yes, sir."

"Go about your normal routine duties. I may be in touch with you often, or months may go by between calls, but you should never be apprehensive. Understand?"

"Yes, sir."

Leary looked up. "Another thing—Horny doesn't know anything about this. Remember, I asked to meet you because I'm a fan."

Clement laughed. "You call him Horny too?"

Leary looked up guiltily. "I did? We went to college together, that's where he picked up the nickname, and I guess it's second nature by now." He paused and looked worried. "Nevertheless, it was a bad slip of the lip." He paused and looked Clement straight in the eye. "That could have gotten me in trouble if I'd been on an assignment. It's snafus like that that give people away." He glanced toward the bar. "Ah, here's the major." He replaced his pop-bottle spectacles and became the mouse once more.

"Damnedest thing," Major Harney said, sitting down and lighting a cigarette. "On my way back to the table, I ran into a lieutenant who said we knew each other years ago and insisted on recounting a couple of stories in which I was supposed to be involved. I didn't want to be rude to the man, but I've never seen him before in my life."

Clement exchanged looks with Leary. Obviously the man was a plant to delay the major from returning to the table until the "all clear" was given.

As they got up to leave, Leary held out his hand. "Thank you, M-Mr. Story," he stammered "I—mean, Captain Story, for your autograph." Then he turned to Major Harney. "You're a good guy, Bill, for introducing us."

After he had gone, Harney turned to Clement. "Thanks for putting up with him. He's a terrible bore. I don't know what's gotten into him. He was such a live wire in college, but apparently he's in some badly paying kind of work in Georgetown." He rubbed his jaw and shook his head. "He had such promise, too. Edited the yearbook, was on the debating team, and greatly loved politics." He laughed ruefully. "Now, I'd be surprised if he makes five grand a year." He paused. "But the strangest thing—I never figured him for being interested in music. Hell, he always had two left feet and couldn't tell one note from another."

Clement nodded. "Oh, once in a while," he said offhandedly, "I meet people who may not be musically inclined themselves, but, thank God, they buy my records."

131

"You mean they worship from afar?"

Clement blushed, and it was the effect of honest emotion. "You might say that, Major Harney." Then he smiled to himself. What was the word in circles of intrigue when one assumed a certain identity? "Cover"—that was the word. Well, apparently H. R. Leary had assumed a cover that suited both the moment and the occasion. If he liked music at all, he was probably deeply involved with the classics. Clement could see him in a semidarkened room, his white head resting on a pillow on the floor, while the phonograph played something like "In a Monastery Garden." Very definitely he was not the "Beer Barrel Polka" type of guy.

# 8

## *Seven-League Boots*

*There was a long queue, formed in an orderly fashion, in front of the Blue Moon Theater on Main Street in Angel on Sunday, October 2, 1943.*

The manager, ignoring the all-star cast of the film, had spelled out on the marquee:

CAPT. CLEMENT STORY

in

THE BOYS UP FRONT

Patricia Anne and Lars Hanson were near the end of the line, which was mainly composed of teenagers; the older folk had arrived earlier and were, consequently, nearer the box office.

After the newsreel (four B-17s lost over Germany; women's skirts get higher; Hollywood bond rally nets $150,000 in defense bonds; Frank Sinatra mobbed by bobby-soxers in New York) and the cartoon (Porky Pig), the main feature started; behind the title, Clement and the Air Force Band played "Lady Luck."

The plot of the picture concerned a G.I. and his buddies on leave in Hollywood, and during a romantic

133

scene on Mulholland Drive, with the soldier kissing his girl in a jeep, silhouetted by the moon, Lars placed his arm around Patricia Anne's shoulders. As she snuggled up against him, a flickering current of excitement passed between them—a continuing experience that they were both beginning to enjoy tremendously when together, but which left them both extremely frustrated after saying good night.

Since Patricia Anne attended Phillips University in Enid during the week, and studied at the dormitory Saturday and Sunday, she did not often have a chance to visit Angel, and since Lars Hanson's office was open Monday through Saturday, and he had frequent house calls on Sunday, he seldom had the opportunity to drive to Enid to see her.

Just before the film's finale, when Clement and the band were scheduled to appear, the usher tapped Lars Hanson on the shoulder. "Telephone, Doctor."

"I'll be right back," he whispered to Patricia Anne.

He was back a moment later. "I've got to leave. Cissie Blake's little girl has a temperature of a hundred and four. Will you wait for me in front of the theater?"

"No," she murmured, "I'll be at the Sugar Bowl. Sorry you've got to miss Dad."

"I'll catch the end of the movie later in the week," he whispered. "The manager is very understanding about my calls." He kissed her cheek and hurried out of the theater. She placed her hand on her cheekbone, where the imprint of his lips still burned, and was so distracted that she almost missed the first glimpse of Clement as he lifted his baton for the downbeat.

His appearance on the screen brought loud applause, and Patricia Anne thought that her father photographed as much less handsome than he was in person. On film, he looked very foreign, and his Cherokee Indian features stood out distinctly: wide forehead and high cheekbones. Although she was certain that he was

134

wearing the same light shade of screen makeup as the band, he nevertheless appeared two shades darker. But his smile, which he flashed often, was the same; his geniality, sincerity, and supreme goodwill came over exactly as in real life. It occurred to her then that he was a *good* man and for the first time as an adult, observing him in closeup, she thought: *He stands for something that is totally American; his music is a way of life.*

His first number, "What Do You Do on a Saturday?" was greeted with cheers, and the rhythmic beat of the music was so infectious that the teenagers in the audience stood up en masse to crowd into the aisles to jitterbug, much to the consternation of the older people in the audience, who could not see the screen for the dancers. A chorus of "Down in front" and "Sit down" brought the usher back into the theater, but he could do nothing to disperse the jiggling bodies.

The fast swing number segued into "The Battle Hymn of the Republic," which, although melodic, was not conducive to dancing. And even though the teenagers returned promptly to their seats, order was not to be restored. They took up the chant, clapping rhythmically to the beat of the famous old number that had sent soldiers into the front lines since the Civil War. As the beat of the music rose to a crescendo, and the hundreds of uniformed men on the screen threatened to march right down onto the stage of the Blue Moon Theater and into the audience and thence out into the street, the ending title flashed on the screen. A covey of doves was released on the mock airfield, and the camera followed as the white birds flew off into the distance.

Applause rent the theater once more as the lights came up, and there was a little flurry of excitement that marked a special occasion. Patricia Anne edged her way into the aisle and was greeted by Bella Chenovick, who had tears in her eyes. "Wasn't he wonderful!" she exclaimed. "He looked so real—just as if we could reach out and touch him!" She wiped her eyes with a lace handkerchief and looked around. "Where's Doc Hanson?"

"He had to make a house call," Patricia Anne replied evenly.

Bella shook her head. "You could do worse than marry him," she advised, "but of course you'll be home all the time while he's out catering to the sick. That's the only trouble about marrying up with either a doctor or a lawyer. Their mistresses are the world at large."

Patricia Anne thought that perhaps Bella was being overly dramatic, but she did see the point. She nodded numbly. "I'm not going to marry anyone, Mrs. Chenovick, until I graduate from college."

"Good for you!" Bella exclaimed, her eyes twinkling like two diamonds in a lump of pastry dough. She glanced over her shoulder and lowered her voice so that her husband could not hear. "Torgo asked me the other day what you were taking in school—home economics and cheerleading?" She laughed. "He was actually *serious*." She looked worried. "Just what *are* you taking, dear?"

"Journalism."

"Is your daddy going to buy *The Angel Wing*?"

Patricia Anne smiled. "No, Mrs. Chenovick. Newspaper reporting is not my cup of java. I want to be a *novelist*."

Bella raised her eyebrows. "Like that wonderful Grace Livingston Hill?"

"Yes." Patricia Anne smiled. She could not tell Bella that it was Katherine Anne Porter whom she most admired, because she knew that the library in Angel didn't have any of her books, and she wasn't at all certain that Bella had even heard of the little woman who had written *Pale Horse, Pale Rider*.

Patricia Anne felt a twinge of regret every time she visited the library. On the left side of the little area, no bigger than a playpen, tucked away in the basement of the City Hall, was the children's book department; on the other was the adult section, with one wall devoted to Zane Grey, Agatha Christie, and Grace Livingston Hill. The only classic set of books that the library owned was *The Complete Works of William Shakespeare*, published in 1896 and donated by Rochelle Patterson. The books—except for *Hamlet*—had yet to be opened. She had noticed the last time she was in the library that someone had scrawled on the outside of the volume: HAMLET IS A NAZI.

Captain Clement Story bowed to the audience after the ON THE AIR sign flashed off. The hour had sped by without incident, and after finishing an extra commercial message for war bonds he wiped the perspiration from his forehead and retired to his dressing room. As always after a live performance, he was at a high emotional pitch, and it took at least a half-hour to regain his usual relaxed demeanor. Actually, whenever possible he preferred to transcribe his weekly radio show, because the waxing seemed to proceed more smoothly and with less physical strain. But the advertising agency handling the Aunt Bertha account only permitted the show to be recorded when he went on duty with the band. Even then, the executives complained about the background noise that always seemed to be present on the British recordings when Clement utilized the London studio. In fact, one broadcast was totally ruined when a bomb exploded in the street, which rendered the equipment inoperable for a day and a half.

The limousine was waiting at the studio door to take him to the airport, but it took fifteen minutes of autograph-signing before he placated his fans. Once he was settled in the back seat, the chauffeur handed him a blue envelope. Clement did not know to whom the communication was addressed, nor from whom it came; he only knew that he must pass on the envelope to a man wearing a blue overcoat, carrying a bird cage. He smiled to himself. It was like one of those old Charlie Chan movies, where intrigue was a way of life. He would be meeting the band in London. They were taking a separate flight. In the old days they had always traveled together. He did not like to travel alone.

After the exceedingly long and uncomfortably crowded flight to England, he felt cramped and out-of-sorts coming down the steep flight of steps at the airport landing field. He would have liked nothing better than to crawl into bed at the hotel. Apprehensively, he looked about at the little group awaiting the disembarkation of the passengers, cautiously watching for a small, furtive little man with a hawk face and darting eyes, carrying an enormous bird cage with a splendid white cockatoo inside. No one in the crowded waiting room looked the least suspicious, nor was he recognized. He was just another officer. The older man lurking near the water fountain certainly looked like a gangster from Kansas City, Missouri, but it turned out that he was the driver of a lorry parked at the curb.

Clement was quickly passed through the queue at the customs stand. He paused a moment with his luggage, biding time, feeling edgy and strange. Again he seemed like a character in a movie—play-acting. Where *was* the contact? A young man, blond and no more than eighteen, jiggled his elbow. "May I 'elp with your baggage, Capt'n?" he asked in an almost incomprehensible Cockney accent.

Still searching the throng, Clement shook his head. "No, thank you," he replied curtly, looking past the young man. What would he do with the envelope if no one such as described showed up?

"I'd be mor'n 'appy to 'elp you, Capt'n," the young-

138

ster persisted. "In fact, me hack is just outside. I'll even take you to your 'otel."

Clement was becoming annoyed. "I said, 'No thank you'!" It was then he saw that the boy was wearing a blue overcoat and was carrying a book entitled *The Birdcage*. Feeling guilty and somewhat deflated, he flashed a weak smile. "Thank you. Now that I think about it, I could do with a lift."


It was a wondrous time of life for Luke Three.

He was growing so fast that Bosley had to take him to Enid twice to purchase new clothing. His shirt size grew from medium to large, and the length of his trousers, although his waist size remained at 28, elongated from 30 to 34, causing his grandfather to remark, "If you shoot up any more, you're not going to be able to get ready-mades."

Luke Three was pleased. "Dad has a tailor in Tulsa that I plan to see, after I get the *rest* of my growth." But what delighted him most of all, as he gazed at his naked figure in the mirror each night before going to bed, was his midsection, which had kept up a steady pace with the rest of his body.

At the station, he no longer pressed himself against his female customers' fenders when washing windshields, because, while his hands were busy on the glass, he was so tall that he had to bend down to catch a glimpse of their legs. Each night he took his new blue uniform with the white trim home to Hattie to be laundered, and he visited the barber once a week and occasionally stopped by Lars Hanson's office for cream for his face, which was red from a slight acne condition.

But the greatest change of all was his attitude. Some of the excitement he had at first felt when working at the station was gone; in its place was a sense of new responsibility. He became more punctual and added the day's receipts more carefully, checking and rechecking his figures. And he also found that he made more sales when he greeted customers with an easy smile and a cheerful greeting. The small two column interview, written by Darlene Trune in *The Angel Wing*, with a photo of him at the gas pump, hadn't hurt his reputation either!

During lunch at the Red Bird Café, Belle would gaze at him fondly. "You're looking more and more like your dad every day," she remarked frequently. "But of course you're taller—and just a mite better looking!" And she would laugh at his embarrassment.

Now that he was shaving every day, Luke Three had to rise a half-hour early, which he did without complaint, and when he enrolled as a junior in high school, he went out for track and football. No longer did he turn his backside to his classmates, as he had in military school. He displayed himself shamelessly and soon became accustomed to his trackmates' envious glances. He was the best-developed boy in his class.

His marks in school soared. He found it was easier to concentrate on his work, especially when teachers spoke on abstract subjects, to which he had always turned a deaf ear in the past. He often understood the theory before they finished speaking. Communication, he decided was the key, and as he became an A student he also gained the respect of the class.

Luke Three decided that sixteen and a half was the perfect age, and at night in his bed, with his hands roaming over his chest and thighs, he was pleased that he was a "late bloomer," as his grandfather had remarked. He was not a little kid experimenting with himself; he was a grown man, ushering himself into a delightful new world of feeling and release.

\* \* \*

Jerrard hosed down the sidewalk in front of the Heron service station, then called to Luke Three, who was adding up the day's receipts, "How much did we take in today?"

Luke Three looked up from the adding machine. "Four hundred dollars, which is good for a Saturday, but that includes Mrs. Steven's lube job and the two recaps you palmed off on Stinky Snodgrass."

Jerrard shut off the water and grinned. "Pretty good for Halloween," he said and removed a large can of Crisco from the bottom drawer of the desk. "Come on, you take the right window, and I'll take the left."

Each took handfuls of shortening, which they rubbed over the windows. "God, this is a mess." Luke Three grimaced.

Jerrard nodded. "Yep, but it's easier to wipe off in the morning than crayon marks and soap." He finished the job, then rubbed his hands on a towel. "Going to be doing a little window-soaping yourself tonight?"

Luke shrugged. "I'm supposed to go to a party at Darlene's, but I don't have a costume."

Jerrard laughed. "Well, you could go out with the older guys and push over a few privies."

"Naw. If word ever got back to Grandpa, I'd never hear the end of it."

Jerrard lowered the grease rack. "You know, Luke Three, I never thought of it before, but I guess you've got a lot of responsibilities for a guy your age."

"What do you mean?"

"Bein' a Heron and all."

"It's not so bad."

"I didn't mean it was *bad*," Jerrard retorted. "But with having to work here in this crappy station, and not having any fun, and worrying about what people think about you, and all that money . . ."

Luke Three cleaned his hands on a towel and considered the questions. "Well, Jerrard, in the first place, I never think about having a lot of money, because *I* don't; and in the second place, I'll be in charge of the company one day, and Dad says that I've got to get practical experience somewhere." He checked his new blue uniform and adjusted his sleek air-force-type cap. "After all, if I hadn't been working here, we wouldn't have these new outfits, would we? Dad's also made some other changes based on my suggestions." He paused thoughtfully. "You see, Jerrard, Dad mostly conducts meetings now, and I think he's lost touch with the station guys. It's not his fault, because this retail operation is just one of the company's interests." He grimaced again. "You see, Jerrard, old guys—high up, like Dad—fcrget what it's like to be a grease monkey—" He was interrupted by the sharp sound of a certain horn in the driveway. His eyes gleamed. "That's Darlene."

She rolled down the window of the Chevrolet coupe. "Fill her up!" She looked up at him with wide eyes, and he could see that she was pleased to see him.

"Hi," Luke Three said, and, looking into the car, saw that her red skirt was pulled up halfway above her knees. There was also a deep valley between her breasts, which rose above the low-cut blouse. "How much gas do you have?" he asked.

"About a quarter of a tank."

"Could you come in tomorrow? I've already added up the day's receipts, and we're about to close up."

She considered the question with the same gravity as if he had asked her opinion about who was a better actor, Clark Gable or James Stewart. "I suppose I could come by in the morning." She was reluctant; then she sighed. "Are you coming to the party?"

He shrugged. "I tried to get to Enid to get a costume; tomorrow's my morning to open the station."

She frowned. "Are you trying to say, Luke Three,

that you aren't coming?" Her voice held an edge of anger.

"I don't like being put on the spot," he replied defensively. "I don't like that at all."

She set her mouth in a hard line, started the motor, and sped out of the driveway with a loud screech of tires, leaving him with a bewildered expression on his face.

Jerrard leaned an arm on his shoulder. "What got into her?"

"Search me," Luke Three replied innocently.

Jerrard laughed. "I wish I had a young hot piece like Darlene Trune running after me all the time." He sighed. "It's too bad my last name's not Heron."

Luke Three whirled around, suddenly angry. "What in the hell has my name got to do with it?"

Jerrard stood his ground. "Well, don't think for one minute that she's interested in that thing in your pants. No siree." He laughed. "Every time she looks at you, there's dollar signs whirling in her eyes."

The station suddenly went out of focus, and Luke Three was only conscious of Jerrard's leering face and the contemptuous expression around his sullen mouth. Doubling up his fist, he lunged at Jerrard and hit him smartly on the side of the jaw. As Jerrard staggered backward, Luke Three flew at him again and, in the split second that Jerrard was off balance, landed another punch under his chin. Jerrard's lower teeth bit into his upper lip, and he yelped in pain.

Luke Three had doubled up his fist again, but as Jerrard hit the door behind him he used the frame for leverage and swung back, hitting Luke Three's jaw twice in rapid succession. The blow caught Luke Three off guard, and he staggered backward and fell against the left gas pump, hitting his head against an oil-can spout. He was momentarily stunned. His head throbbed.

When he looked up, all he saw was a pinkish haze. Jerrard towered over him, ten stories high.

Then a giant hand came into his line of vision. Jerrard helped him up. "Sorry, Luke Three," he said slowly, all anger spent. "I sure hope I didn't hurt you bad."

His equilibrium gradually returned to normal. "Your face is a mess, Jerrard," he said with no animosity. "Better get cleaned up."

Jerrard grinned and brushed the blood from his lip. "Yeah, and you better take care of that eye." He paused. "I want to apologize," he finished awkwardly. "My big mouth—I didn't mean to slur either Darlene or you."

"I know you didn't, Jerrard."

He turned at the washroom door. "Luke Three?"

"Yeah?"

"I'm not . . . fired, am I?"

Luke Three looked at him as if he had lost his reason. "Why—no."

"Thanks." He closed the washroom door softly, and Luke Three eased himself down on the edge of the desk. Did he really have the power to fire? As far as he was concerned, Jerrard, being the mechanic, gave the orders. After all, he'd worked in filling stations all of his life. Suddenly his eye began to throb. "Jerrard," he called, "close up the station. I'm going home."

"Yes, boss," came the muffled, polite reply.

Luke Three pulled on his jacket and grinned. Jerrard had called him "boss"!

He parked the bicycle alongside the back porch, carefully opened the screen door, and was halfway up the stairs when he heard his grandmother's voice. "Hurry and wash up, because we're going to have an early dinner."

"I'll be down in a minute, Grandma," he replied.

144

Upstairs, he surveyed his face in the bathroom mirror; his jaw had swollen, and the back of his neck, where he had fallen, was sore. Peering closely at his reflection, he had to admit that there was a slight purpling under the right eye. "Damn!" he muttered angrily, and carefully threw cold water on his face.

Later, over apple pie and cheese, Bosley examined Luke Three's face. "Are you getting a shiner?"

"I feel foolish, Grandpa." He grinned sheepishly. "I ran into one of the gasoline pumps this afternoon."

"Oh!" Letty exclaimed. "Did you go to the doctor?"

"Naw. I didn't really hit my eye—just my cheek. I didn't think it would turn black."

Bosley grinned. "With it being Halloween, you'd better make up a better story than that. No one will believe you."

"Yeah, it is kind of silly, isn't it?"

"Are you going to Darlene's party?" Letty asked.

"Naw, I think I'll go down and protect the station."

A moment later the doorbell clanged persistently. Hattie came out of the kitchen, wiping her hands on her apron, and scurried across the hall runner. "Hold on, I'm coming," she called loudly. There was a long pause, and then Hattie's voice reverberated from the hall into the dining room. "Miz Trenton, you better come out here."

Letty looked helplessly from Bosley to Luke Three, shrugged her thin shoulders, and joined Hattie at the door. On the threshold stood a small child wearing an obviously homemade witch costume and carrying a large purple department-store bag. "Twick or tweet!" lisped the tiny voice.

Letty exchanged looks with Hattie. "What did you say, dear?" she asked gently.

"I said," came the impatient retort, "*twick or tweet*!" The wraith stamped its little foot.

A dark form separated itself from the evergreen

bushes that lined the porch. "Why, hello, Mrs. Blake," Letty said graciously. "We can't make out what Gretchen is saying."

Cissie Blake threw back her flaming red head and laughed. "I know she don't talk very well, but what she said was 'Trick or treat.' "

Letty looked at her blankly. "But what does it *mean*?"

"Well, in California"—Cissie Blake stared at Letty—"it means that if you give the kids a treat, like a piece of candy, they won't trick you—do any damage." She was becoming embarrassed. "I thought this was a universal Halloween tradition."

Letty ran her hand nervously over her gray hair. "Well, we've never heard of it in Oklahoma. But you know, Mrs. Blake, I think it's a good idea. We'll find something for Gretchen." She looked up apologetically. "I'm afraid she'll have slim pickings elsewhere tonight, with no one prepared." A thought struck her. "You know what? I'm going to call *The Angel Wing*. George Starger should do a story on this trick-or-treat business. It's a wonderful custom. Not that there's much vandalism hereabouts, but there is *some*, and if the kids can be bribed to behave themselves, everyone will breathe easier. Come on in and have a cup of coffee, Mrs. Blake."

"Thank you. Please call me Cissie."

"I've got some orange chocolate sticks *somewhere*," Hattie said to Gretchen. "Wouldn't you be more comfortable without your mask?"

Cissie Blake looked at the hand-carved furniture in the living room and smiled. "I've always wanted to see the inside of your house, Mrs. Trenton. I've always loved antiques."

Letty glanced at Edward Heron's heavy oak and mahogany pieces. "Oh, these?" She laughed. "I wouldn't

146

call any of my furniture *antiques*. Nothing came from the old country."

Cissie looked at her in wonderment. "But these are *American* antiques, Mrs. Trenton!"

Bosley stepped forward. "Speaking of antiques"—he laughed—"Mrs. Blake, I'm Bosley Trenton, and I think you know Luke Three."

"Hi, Mrs. Blake," Luke Three said. "I've got those windshield wipers you ordered."

"Good," she replied, accepting the cup of coffee that Bosley poured.

"Now, if you'll excuse me," Letty said, "I'll call *The Wing*."

"My husband and I didn't think we'd make Tucumcari, let alone Angel, when we started out from California. Everything has been replaced on our Buick, as your grandson will tell you." Cissie Blake laughed. "Our old car is about as bad as those old rattletraps the Okies pushed across the deserts before the war."

There was a long silence, and then she flushed. "I'm sorry. I guess I put my foot into it. Didn't mean to degrade those poor people who came to California to find jobs." She nervously took a sip of the coffee and then explained, "We're originally from Bakersfield, and we had a lot of camps set up for the Ok-la-ho-man"—she pronounced the word carefully—"fruit-pickers."

Bosley nodded gravely and noted that she was wearing trousers. "What brought your family to Angel, of all places?" he asked kindly.

"Oh, Felix—that's my husband—heard through the Bakers that the John Deere franchise was up for grabs, and we thought it would be safer to live here."

"Pardon?" Bosley leaned forward.

She sighed, and her large bosom moved up and down, causing her white blouse to separate slightly from the belt, revealing an inch or so of very white skin. "Well, if the Japs bomb the coast—"

147

Letty came in from the hall. "George Starger is coming right over with his camera. He wants us to recreate the scene with Gretchen at the door." She paused meaningfully. "He's going to do a feature article supporting this trick-or-treat idea."

Cissie Blake nodded. "That's a good idea." She looked up. "May I smoke?"

"Certainly," Letty said. "I'll fetch an ashtray. We don't have many around nowadays," she explained as she hunted in the buffet, "since Bosley stopped smoking cigars." She finally found a crystal dish. "Will this serve? Lord knows what Hattie did with the trays."

"Thank you," Cissie replied and lighted a small, fragrant white shaft. She inhaled deeply and blew the smoke out all at once. "Smoking helps my asthma."

Letty exchanged looks with Bosley as Gretchen skipped in from the kitchen, her mouth smeared with chocolate. "Oh, this is good, Mummy," she said, holding out a stick of partially consumed candied orange peel.

"You must give me the recipe sometime," Cissie Blake said, and at that moment the bell rang.

Letty answered herself. "Trick or treat!" George Starger shouted, then laughed. "This is really a break, Letty. Thank you for giving me a lead story for tomorrow afternoon's edition."


After Letty and Bosley waved good-bye to George Starger and Cissie and Gretchen Blake, Luke Three shuffled into the living room and switched on the radio. "I guess I'll listen to 'Baby Snooks,'" he said. "I don't feel like going out after all."

"All right, dear," Letty replied. "How about another cup of coffee, Bos?" They sat down at the table.

"I don't know why," Bosley said, waving his hand in

the air, "but ever since I left off cigars I just can't stand the smell of smoke—especially *woman* smoke."

"Yes, and I'm repelled by women in pants." Letty rearranged the white bow at her throat. "Now, it doesn't bother me so much to see women in pants in the big cities like Washington, where they're taking over men's jobs, or in Wichita, where they have to climb all over those planes, riveting and such, but to have a woman in my home, even if she is from California, smoking and—"

Bosley sighed gently. "Letty, it's refreshing to see that you're still capable of being shocked, at your age."

"Shocked, Bos? I don't think that's quite the right word." Letty set her mouth. "And it has nothing to do with age." She brushed a strand of silver hair back from her brow and pursed her lips. "It's just that—well, modern women sometimes leave me cold. Maybe I'm just not sophisticated, dear. Maybe the world is passing me by and I don't know it."

He took her hand. "There is one thing that *I'd* like to know, and that is, where Luke Three got that shiner."

"Did you see his jaw? The knot is as big as a doorknob." She nodded philosophically. "Let's just hope that the subject that caused the altercation was worth it!"

The next day, *The Angel Wing* carried two feature stories, side by side. One featured the headline "TRICK OR TREAT" IDEA MAKES GOOD SENSE, but the second was more succinct: PRANKSTERS RELOCATE PATTERSON COUPE, and related:

Unexplained is the mystery of how former school teacher Rochelle Patterson's 1937 Buick coupe was placed atop the ladies' changing room of the swimming pool last night. Miss Patterson, in an exclusive interview with

149

*The Wing*, stated that she had parked the car in her garage just before nightfall, and had gone to bed at nine o'clock. "I absolutely heard nothing at all," she remarked, when told of the outrage early this morning. "Whomever pulled the prank were as quiet as the proverbial mice."

Several Halloween parties, given by local citizens, broke up about midnight, and there were no reports of gangs of youths out after that time. Chief of Police Ed Brooder speculated: "The only way that anyone could get that coupe up there on the pool house was to disengage the chassis from the frame and reassemble it on the roof, which would take a dozen men." Jerrard Jones, manager of the Heron Service Station on Main Street, who spent the night in Pond Creek, said: "The job would be impossible from a mechanical point of view outside of twelve to fifteen hours of work, with a team of professionals." Could it be a real witch's brew? Were goblins really at work? Or, has a local citizen learned something about spiritual levitation? No one knows, least of all Miss Patterson, who plans to hire a crane from Enid to bring her automobile back to earth. Anyone wishing to help with the expense is advised to telephone 827 before nine P.M. tomorrow.

Luke Three folded the paper precisely in fourths and poured a second cup of coffee from the thermos for Jerrard and himself. "Why did you do it?" he asked suddenly.

"What?"

"Put old Miss Patterson's coupe up there."

Jerrard frowned. "Don't accuse me, Boss. I spent the night in Pond Creek, and I can prove it." He turned his neck to the light to reveal a large red hickey.

Luke Three laughed. "You know darned well that you're the only mechanic in Garfield County who has the know-how to break down and reassemble that car. I figure if you worked straight through, starting out at one o'clock in the morning, you could have had it finished by five A.M." He wheeled around in the desk chair. "I just want you to know that *I* know, and I don't care who helped you." He stopped the chair in front of Jerrard. "And I just want to add that if I ever get into an executive position with this company, you'll always have a job."

He went to the window and looked plaintively out on Main Street. Without turning around, he continued, "But if Dad were here, you can bet your bottom dollar you'd get the ax." He turned dramatically. "You see, Jerrard, the only thing wrong with Dad is that he doesn't *evaluate* actions properly. He'd figure that a guy who would go to all that trouble would have a heart full of sin. It would never occur to him that the guy maybe would maybe be a mechanical genius."

# 9

## Night Music

*Mac's bar was located next to a pawnshop on one side and an old B movie theater on the other, and, even from the sidewalk, reeked of Lysol disinfectant.*

A sign was posted on the front, proclaiming in large letters: OFF LIMITS TO MILITARY PERSONNEL.

Clement looked down at his apparel and then remembered that he was not in uniform. H. R. Leary had told him to wear civilian clothes for the meeting in what was perhaps Washington's most disreputable bar, a place where even enemy agents did not care to be seen. It was two o'clock in the afternoon. He looked around for the expected M.P., who usually stood at the door of such places, but the street was empty. The only occupants, Clement saw, were two men engaged in an intimate, eyeball-to-eyeball conversation at the bar. The decor, he saw with amusement, reminded him of a dozen old movies: rattan tables, with matching chairs, were scattered over skimpy, soiled raffia rugs, which were, in turn, guarded by dusty, ragged artificial palm trees complete with motheaten monkeys. A ceiling fan moved lazily over the bar. Leary, whom he had not seen when entering the bar, waved from a back table. They ordered rum and Coca-Colas from a tall, willowy person with bleached hair who could be a member of either sex.

"Sorry about the place," Leary said, taking in the room at a glance, "but it's safe." He cleared his throat and handed Clement a familiar blue envelope. "When you land at Prestwick, Scotland, purchase a copy of *Punch*, then go into the telephone booth next to the magazine stand and fake making a telephone call. A woman in a green hat with a red feather will wait outside the booth. Leave the letter in the magazine, and be certain that she gets into the booth when you leave."

"Is that all?"

"That's it." Leary wearily took a sip of the rum and Coca-Cola.

"You look tired, H.R."

"I am. I've been in conference all day. I had cold turkey for Thanksgiving yesterday. Up all night working. I'm dead. Right now I need a man, about forty, who knows France like the back of his hand. Someone who's fluent in the language, or at least understands it well." He sighed and wearily passed a hand over his head. "And someone with those qualifications isn't going to be easy to find."

Clement shrugged his shoulders. "Wish I could help, but I don't even know anyone who speaks French, for that matter." A bell rang somewhere in his brain, and he looked up quickly. "Is this a dangerous mission?"

"Not really."

Clement chose his words very carefully. "I know a man in that age group who worked all over the Continent before the war. He does know French, but I don't know how well. I think he was some type of a salesman." He paused. "I don't know the whole story, but he was in some kind of trouble, and couldn't come back to the States for a long time."

Leary's eyes narrowed. "He sounds interesting. Does he have a big family?"

Clement shook his head. "He never married."

Leary began to drum on the table with his long, spatulate fingers. "Tell me more, my boy, tell me more."

His name is Mitchell Heron, and he owns the Heron Furniture Company in Enid, Oklahoma."

Mitchell Heron stood on the sidewalk and glued a large sign to the front window that read: CHRISTMAS LAY-AWAY PLANS AVAILABLE NOW. It was the day after Thanksgiving. He did not want to get into the business of charge accounts, but reserving certain merchandise, like end tables, footstools, or lamps, made sense for wage-earners who did not have much ready cash but who were willing to make frequent payments. He was more fortunate than other merchants, who depended on shipments from Eastern locations. There was a warehouse full of excellent wood in back of the store, the shop equipment was comparatively new, and he had hired an excellent over-the-draft-age manager and a talented cabinetmaker who had flat feet. Luck had finally come his way.

The store was turning a good profit for wartime, and even some of the wealthy Enid matrons, who had postponed purchasing larger pieces of furniture because of the depression, were now ordering nine-piece bedroom suites and dining room tables with pull-out leaves that would seat twelve. The only shop items difficult to obtain were certain varnishes and a type of linseed oil that his craftsmen preferred.

"You're wanted on the phone, Mr. Heron," Georgette, his plump little office manager, called from the doorway. "It's some frog. I can hardly understand him. You speak French, don't you?"

Mitchell shrugged his shoulders. "Not very much anymore." He followed her into the back of the store and picked up the receiver. "*Oui?*" The word rolled off his tongue with surprising alacrity. He was surprised that he could converse so well after so many years. The man's patois was even familiar. He was a Monsieur Darlan from Lyon, and he wanted a Queen Anne chair.

H.R. Leary leaned back on the divan in the cheap Washington hotel. "What's his accent like, Pierre?"

The plump little man tugged at his mustaches and shrugged. "At lease he does not speak with an Oklahoma twang, and he seems fairly fluent. I think, with a little work, he will do—at least from a language point of view."

Leary rummaged through the file on his lap. "The dossier the boys came up with is quite complete, but filled with trivia, as usual." He glanced at a page. "For instance, who would give a tinker's damn that he worked for a dollar and a quarter a day in the harvest fields in nineteen thirty-nine?" He wrinkled his forehead. "Wild teenager; fast cars; an active sex life: two girls in trouble in his home town; kicked out of Stanford for poor grades; enlisted as a private in the infantry in World War One." He squinted. "That's not bad, Pierre, it shows some character. At least he didn't use the Heron name to get a commission." He pored over the sheets for a moment and then looked up. "Damn! We can wipe all that off, because he deserted in the Army in nineteen eighteen in France."

"Court martialed?"

Leary shook his head. "No, probably because of the conditions at the time. Of course, the military was run a lot differently then—not that he could get away with it today. At any rate, he stayed in Europe after the Armistice, obviously with some sort of forged identification, because he was later able to get a passport in his own name." He consulted the papers again. "From nineteen nineteen to nineteen twenty-nine he worked for Brel

Ceramics, which, if memory serves, used to be fairly well known as a merchandiser of knickknacks and gewgaws. It couldn't have been very lucrative. From 'twenty-nine to 'thirty-six, he was employed by Schlosser and Company, manufacturers of glass paperweights and bud vases." He looked up. "I wonder if he speaks German."

"That would be an advantage." Pierre worked his mustaches.

"He came back to the States in 'thirty-seven and bummed around the country, like so many unemployed did, and ended up back in Angel, where he farmed his mother's homestead." He continued to read, then smiled. "That's when the big change occurred. He picked up the pieces of his life then and settled down. When his mother died four years ago, she left him a valuable ring, which he sold to open the furniture store." He placed the file on the coffee table. "That's when he really got respectable and showed his métier." He leaned forward. "You see, Pierre, Heron Furniture used to be one of the finest lines in the country, but when his dad died in the Twenties, his mother married the general manager of the company, a Manford Pederson, a sharpie, who stopped production on the good line and started to manufacture cheap veneers. Then the crash wiped out everything. The loss of reputation must have bothered Mitchell, because he's bringing the fine line back. The name is beginning to mean something other than oil."

Leary took a deep breath and expelled the air in his lungs all at once, and went on, his voice barely above a whisper, "The question is, Pierre, should we pursue this particular issue any further? I hate to take a chance on a man with such an undependable background."

Pierre smiled without humor and calmly replied, "Yet we have agents who have killed dozens of people

156

without a thought, and who have connived and lied and cheated—but that's part of the game. And with Roosevelt, Churchill and Stalin meeting in Teheran, we must move now." He shrugged. "I have a good feeling about this fellow; certainly he learned to handle himself 'on the dole.' Sound him out; agree to wipe out his military records and give him a clean bill of goods. It might work."

Leary grunted. "Officially, his records were lost years ago."

"He does not know that, does he?"

Leary smiled. "Probably not. But, on the other hand, I don't want to blackmail."

Pierre eyed him with amusement. "Why not, if it will work?"

"Either Mitchell Heron will willingly work for us, or he won't. He's got to enter into this business with his whole mind." Leary paused. "After all, Pierre, he's putting his life on the line."

"So is every other man in service, H.R."

Leary nodded. "Of course, but dying for one's country on the battlefield is one thing," he replied flatly, "but being knocked off in an alley in Bordeaux without even being acknowledged as missing is something else again. It's that damned family I'm worried about. If something happens, I don't want an investigation that might prove embarrassing to my superiors. With Clement Story also working for us—"

"But what has he to do with Mitchell Heron?"

Leary looked up in surprise. "Oh, it's the same family," he explained patiently. "Mitchell Heron's Uncle Luke married a woman by the name of Letty White. When Luke was killed, she married George Story, a mixed-blood Cherokee lawyer, and bore Clement. Bosley Trenton, Letty's current husband, is a stepfather to both boys."

157

"Sounds very complicated, I must say," Pierre replied, with a sigh. "This family business must be handled with great delicacy, H.R."

Leary smiled mirthlessly, showing all of his teeth. "That is why, Pierre Darlan, I'm giving you the assignment of conscripting Mitchell Heron."

Mitchell Heron lounged in the comfortable booth situated by the window in the restaurant of the Youngblood Hotel. He was a few moments early for his appointment, which gave him a few moments to look over the old drawings that had been brought down from Minneapolis by his Grandmother Heron on one of her trips to the Territory before 1900. The only Queen Anne chair in his father's portfolio was transitional; he hoped Monsieur Darlan was not a purist. Queen Anne designs were not popular in Enid.

"Mr. Heron?" The voice startled him. "I am Pierre Darlan."

He glanced up into the face of a moustachioed little man who looked like a typical French civil servant or department-store clerk. He had seen hundreds of these little mice in the old days on the streets of France, and they all wore the same dark suits and carried the same harried expressions. Even when they smiled—as this man was doing now—it was with a certain benign air of quaint distraction.

"Do sit down," Mitchell said with more enthusiasm than he felt; somehow this man did not look like a furniture connoisseur. Instinctively, Mitchell was on guard. How strange, he thought; it was as if he were back on the road again, living by his wits, and had encountered a man whom he instantly distrusted. In those days, riding the rails with starving 'bos all around, he had learned to be wary. During the last years, when he

158

had worked on the farm for his mother, and even when he had opened the furniture store, there was no need to be constantly suspicious, because he was surrounded by his own people. But now an alarm sounded repeatedly in his brain.

Mitchell looked out of the window at the passersby: a woman pushing a baby stroller, a farmer in overalls, a businessman with a briefcase, a school child going home for lunch. This was all ordinary activity, innocent people going about daily routine, but here in the restaurant he sensed danger. He was careful to keep his face masked, and looked up pleasantly. "What would you like for lunch? I can recommend the Spanish omelet, or, if you care for *offal*, the special of the day is giblets and rice."

Pierre Durlan smiled. "The Spanish omelet will do very well," he replied. "Ah!" He glanced at the roll of drawings. "I'm pleased that you brought these along." Mitchell had the feeling that he was not at all pleased. Something was wrong.

Pierre looked at the man with the troubled eyes sitting opposite. He had not expected Mitchell Heron to be so chary; he had expected a more friendly, outgoing sort, perhaps wearing cowboy boots instead of oxfords. On paper, Mitchell Heron was exactly the psychological type they were searching for so intently; in person, however, he was very distinctive-looking. In a crowd, could he pass for a Frenchman? "Monsieur," Pierre said, relapsing easily into his native language, "your father's early pieces of furniture are very valuable now. It is certainly commendable that you are carrying on the tradition."

Mitchell smiled, but he felt no warmth for the man. "Thank you." He pointed to the drawing, which he unrolled carefully. "About this chair—you want only *one*?"

Pierre looked down at the design on the table in front of him. He made his voice sound interested. "Yes, only one."

"This is a transitional design, not pure Queen Anne." Mitchell saw that Pierre was distracted, watching a child on a tricycle on the sidewalk. He leaned forward and whispered, "Monsieur, what do you *really* want?"

Pierre sighed gently and waited a moment until the omelets were placed before them, then studied Mitchell with a very concerned expression. "I was just thinking that here in this peaceful, quiet town, the war seems very far away."

"Yet we have an airfield here, a training center for pilots," Mitchell replied. "On a Saturday night it is overrun with soldiers. The town is not so tranquil then."

"That is not what I mean," Pierre replied. "Living here, it must be difficult to realize that thousands of men are dying on battlefields all over the world, and that there are other men, not in uniform, who are seeking to prevent more bloodshed. Those men are a crucial link in a network that spans oceans, defies color barriers, and overcomes language difficulties. They are men with special talents, far more difficult to recruit than soldiers." His words were electrifying, yet he gazed at Mitchell casually, almost as if they were discussing various aspects of the weather.

"I take it, then, Monsieur, that you are not really interested in furniture?"

Pierre's eyes narrowed, and he allowed himself a small, dry laugh. "I know almost nothing about it. My wife inherited some rather delicate Louis Seize pieces— which is the only style that I can identify with some measure of accuracy."

"I have a copy of a commode of that period that I should like very much for her to see."

Pierre looked out the window and replied quietly,

"She was murdered by the Nazis." It was a flat statement. He might have been casually asking the waitress for tea instead of coffee.

Mitchell stared at him. "I am sorry."

Pierre nodded. "Yet I escaped with my life—an irony. You see, I had some important papers to deliver. We were in the street. The bullet that was meant for me, she took. I started to run. I could not stop. She died in the street—alone—without me to even hold her head, or say good-bye, or kiss her cheek."

For the first time Mitchell felt there was something warm and human about the man; the air of a poseur was gone. Pierre Darlan was vulnerable after all.

"Shortly thereafter, I came to this country," Pierre continued. "My days of working with the French Resistance were over—as far as making personal contacts with my countrymen was concerned." He paused meaningfully. "Now I work here in America for those same men and women." He took a bite of the omelet. "Ah, this is cold," he said.

"I shall have it reheated," Mitchell offered. He was growing tired of speaking in French when he was still thinking in English.

"I am not hungry now, anyway," Pierre replied, lighting a brown cigarette. "I am aware that you lived in southern France for many years and are familiar with the small villages that cluster around Plaisance-du-Gers."

Mitchell nodded. "I was what we Americans call a traveling salesman." He laughed derisively. "Frankly, more travel than sales."

"Had you ever thought of going back?" Pierre's tone was casual; he might have been asking if Mitchell had intended to visit Oklahoma City again.

Mitchell nodded. "Often—at least for a vacation. I could afford to go first class now, which would be a new experience. In those days I rode a bicycle." He laughed awkwardly. "Now I am speaking as if there was no war. It is easy to forget."

"It is entirely possible to go back."

Mitchell stared at him. "What are you saying, Monsieur?"

*"I am saying that, under certain circumstances . . ."*

"But why would anyone in their right mind want to . . ." A light came into Mitchell's eyes. "You mean, if there was a *purpose . . . ?*"

"Exactly." Pierre closed his eyes for a moment and suddenly looked incredibly weary. "As I said before, I work for my countrymen on this side of the ocean." He went on carefully, "Occasionally, like now, certain information must be passed along. Most operatives can only be used for a short time because, even with disguises, they are discovered, and, of course, a great many die or are placed in concentration camps."

Pierre paused and looked out of the window at the empty street. A cold drizzle made the buildings across the street appear to be photographed through distorted glass. "From time to time, we introduce new faces. It occurred to me that you might think such a job worthy of consideration. But it is very dangerous, Monsieur." He sighed. "When we send a man through the network, he knows and we know that we may not see each other again. Life hangs on such trivialities as a tone of voice, an unfamiliar gesture, a direct glance. Anything out of the ordinary can bring a sudden—or, more plausibly, a protracted—death." He looked out of the window again. "It is so tranquil out there on the street, yet in here we are speaking of terrible ways of dying."

Mitchell nodded, and he was glad of his maturity. He could be objective. "How many people die in their sleep in bed," he asked, "go peacefully into that great good night?"

Pierre nodded and studied his stubby fingernails. "Not many, *mon cher*, not many," he replied sadly. "If you still want a 'vacation' in France, knowing what I have just told you, it can be arranged."

"You have just sprung this idea," Mitchell answered; yet the idea was stimulating. *To get away*, to be useful, to contribute . . . He looked up. "Monsieur Darlan, I will be candid with you. Until a few years ago, my life had no real purpose. I was never ambitious like other members of the Heron family. I was a black sheep. I only found myself when I opened the store to reinstate my father's name."

"Then you must, by all means, stay here in Enid," Pierre replied casually, although his heart was beating very fast.

Mitchell held up his hand. "You misunderstand. All those years in France, I had nothing to uphold. I was not talented like Luke, who has had such success with Heron Oil, or Clement Story, who is a famous bandleader—I had no *talent*." He shook his head. "So I do not know if I would have talent in this area you speak about." His French was becoming fluent and easy. "I might be like one of those bombs that fails to detonate."

"Yes, it is true, you might," Pierre agreed, "but instinct is really talent of a peculiar sort." He snubbed out his brown cigarette. "The job is not long—we think, a total of six weeks. Could you arrange to be away for that length of time without suspicion?"

"Yes, I could take a vacation." Mitchell rubbed his fingers together. "How do we go about this thing?"

Pierre looked up apologetically. "You must have extensive training over a short period. If during this time either we or you feel that you are not responding, then we—how do you say it?" He lapsed into English. "Call it quits."

"By the way, Monsieur," Mitchell needled, smiling slowly, showing all of his teeth, "how do I know you are not a Nazi, or a fifth columnist?"

163

Pierre removed a wallet from his inner pocket and flashed a card, and Mitchell nodded briefly. "Of course, that could be forged. I once met a man on a freight train to Nashville who faked a chauffeur's license for me for fifty cents that fooled everyone for years."

Pierre shrugged. "Beyond this, you will have to trust me. The network all over Europe and the Middle East is based on *trust*."

"How long do I have to make up my mind, Monsieur Darlan?"

"I am embarrassed to tell you that we must leave tomorrow morning."

Mitchell looked relieved and switched back to English. "I thought you would say half an hour. Actually, there are only three things that I'd like to do before we go. I must tell my manager that I'm taking a holiday; number two, I'll make out a will—"

"What else?" Pierre asked. "I must warn you not to inform relatives."

"I am not a dunce, Monsieur Darlan!" Mitchell replied impatiently. "To them, I'm just taking off, wherever my flight of fancy guides me." He paused. "The other thing that I was thinking about, if you don't have any objection, is getting a piece of ass."

Bosley looked down the long conference table at the men who comprised the Heron board of directors. "I have called this special meeting," he said crisply, "to discuss Secretary Harold Ickes' new plan involving tank-car shipments. The Office of Defense Transportation plans to dictate the route of all tank cars—ours included."

"But," Hightower exclaimed, "that's unconstitutional!"

Bosley laughed dryly. "It's for *defense*. There's no real comeback." He paused. "What will upset our apple

164

cart is the fact that no longer can we send certain shipments via the railroads to our special customers who buy Heron products."

"True," Hightower acknowledged, "but then, neither can the other oil companies, either. We'll all be in the same boat."

"Also," Luke put in, "this new directive may work in our favor. As it is, when we send shipments to a given destination, the cars sometimes stay on the sidings for weeks, empty, before they can be rerouted back to where needed. It seems to me that the railroads could perform a great service if they'd organize complete trains carrying crude from the oil-producing areas to the Atlantic seaboard—or wherever needed. Also, if the cars were coded so that it would be apparent whether they were full or empty, they could route the trains in a more efficient manner." He paused. "Let's not fight this maneuver. Transporting crude by rail is the only answer until the Big Inch pipeline is finished, and Lord knows when that will be!"

"Yes, gentlemen," Bosley agreed, "and also let's not forget that there may be other advantages that even old Ickes hasn't thought about. It's ridiculous to use cars to transport crude less than a couple of hundred miles; let oil trucks do that, and save the cars for long hauls. While we're talking about that, if the railroads start scheduling our cars, they've also got to haul them in for repair when needed. They can't expect us to send ours back to our own shops for repair. We're going to save a bundle. Of course, they'll bill us for the overhauling, but they've got repair shops all over the country, while we have two, one here in Tulsa and the other in Dallas."

The next night, when Luke had supper with Jorja, he told her about the Ickes proposal. "Hasn't word come down to Desmond yet?"

"No, but I suppose it's because he doesn't have many tank cars." And later, when Luke had left after making love, Jorja called Robert Desmond at home.

"Why can't you wait until tomorrow?" he asked crossly. "I'm in the middle of a Beethoven concert."

"Well, dear heart," she replied jubilantly, "take the record off the machine. What I have to tell you will make up for any interruption. The Office of Defense Transportation has decreed that the railroads will take-over the routing of *all* tank cars, no matter if they're owned by Standard Oil or Heron or any of the other companies."

"So?" His voice was very distant. "How does that affect Desmond?"

Her voice rose. "Because there will be many small hauls that will fall to trucks."

"Ha!" he exclaimed. "I will start making agreements tomorrow. I thought Dad was twittering in his eaves when he bought that old trucking firm, J and D, in Memphis in nineteen forty. It's been a losing proposition from the beginning, and I almost dumped it twice."

"Thank heavens you didn't," Jorja replied, "because someone has to get those contracts, and it might as well be Desmond."

He was jubilant. "You have just performed a major service, my dear, and you shall be rewarded."

"There is a white gown in the window at Dorn's—"

"You can have it."

"You didn't let me finish. It comes with a white mink jacket."

"Blackmail!" He laughed. "But go ahead, it's yours. Charge it to my account, as usual. Now get off the phone. I want to listen to the last movement of the Ninth Symphony and think about all of the money that's going to be coming in from our fleet of trucks."

# 10

## The Rumble of Heaven

*Luke Three sat down on a counter stool at the Red Bird Café.*

He read the menu written on the blackboard above the Nehi soft-drink sign, and grinned. "I'll have the Blue Plate Special, Belle," he said.

She gave him a tired smile. She once must have been pretty, he thought, and she still had an interesting-looking face, with her soft hennaed hair and large gray eyes, but she was fat around the hips. She ladled out a large portion of ham and lima beans and added a two-inch-high baking-powder biscuit.

"Glad you got here early," she said pleasantly. "Yesterday I was swamped with all those truckers who ate me out of house and home before my regular customers dropped in for dinner. By the way, save some room for lemon meringue pie."

"This sure is good, Belle," he said, chewing on a large cube of ham.

She laughed. "Thanks." She smoothed her apron over her wide hips. "By the way, Luke Three"—she made her voice sound casual—"have you seen your Uncle Mitchell lately?"

"Naw." He brushed his dark hair out of his eyes. "He's taking a vacation."

"So," she said, "he's gone off again. He always had itchy feet. He should have been born in the old days of the vagabonds."

"He's okay, for a bachelor." Luke Three's voice cracked. He tried to keep it even and did not succeed. Doc Larson had told him it might take as much as three months to switch over. "Did you know, Belle, Uncle Mitch used to hitch rides on boxcars?"

Belle smiled sadly. "So did a lot of other men during the depression, Luke Three, when there wasn't any work anywhere. They were glad enough to pick up odd jobs here and there." She paused and thought of Mitchell knocking on her door on hot summer nights, and how his strong body had felt, pressed up against hers. She wiped the grill with a soft cloth. If they had married, she would be living in a fine house in Enid right now, instead of working twelve hours a day as chief cook and bottle-washer at the Red Bird. "He was a nice man," she said softly. "I'm just surprised that he never married."

Luke Three's voice was shrill. "I don't think that I ever will, either." All of his friends had sounded the same way when they were growing big down there.

He finished the Blue Plate Special, then walked into the restroom at the back of the kitchen. When he finished, he removed the tape measure from his pocket. He heard Darlene's voice saying, "Mama, I thought I saw Luke Three come in?"—which was enough to make him stiff. He could not believe his eyes: he was seven and three-quarter inches! Darlene had a place to put it, but the important thing was, would she let him?

He buttoned up his trousers and came back into the dining room, whistling, then pretended to discover Darlene. "Hi," he said, thankfully sounding like his old self again. He had not seen her for a week, and he thought his heart would thump out of his chest.

She gave him a smile, pushed a number on the juke-box, and then turned so that her back was pressed up against the machine. Her reddish-blond hair was drawn back in a pompadour, held by a white rose. He tried not to stare at the two mounds that swelled her pale green sweater until it looked as if it would burst like a balloon. The room was suddenly filled with Clement Story's recording of "Red Sails in the Sunset." Darlene sighed. "Why don't you get some new tunes, Mama?"

"I will," Belle replied, "one of these days when I get some money together. I still think that's the greatest record he ever made, though. It's so *smooth*."

Darlene sat down beside Luke Three, and he could feel the warmth of her body, even though their elbows were not even touching. He looked down at his empty plate and ordered a chocolate malt, which he didn't want, but he had to prolong his stay because of that wonderful feeling of Darlene being next to him. He was hard in his pants.

"How's your dad?" Belle asked, as she placed the tall, brown concoction in front of him.

Luke Three shrugged. "Fine, I guess. He's just as critical as he always was. You'd think that the Heron station here in Angel was the only one in the whole operation, from his nasty memos."

Belle laughed hoarsely. "Your daddy knows what he's doing, all right. He didn't become president of the Heron Oil Company for nothing. He was bright even when we were going to grade school, and he was valedictorian in high school."

He wondered why Belle was being so defensive. He also resented her familiarity with his family affairs; yet Angel was a small town, and he supposed that everyone knew everyone else's business. Angel wasn't like Tulsa, where no one gave a person the time of day. He really preferred the impersonal aspect of city life. He glanced at his watch and paid the bill. "Save some of the special for Jerrard, Belle, he'll be late today. He's draining the crankcase on Mr. Baker's Chevvie."

Watching him walk across the street, Belle sighed slowly. "He's a good boy, honey," she said thoughtfully. "He's going to be nice-looking, I think, when he grows up. With his money, he'll probably marry a college girl from Tulsa, wouldn't you say?"

Darlene didn't reply but pushed down two more levers on the machine. The first number was Peggy Lee's "Why Don't You Do Right?" and Belle felt a strange stirring in her breast. Was the selection a coincidence, or did the words to the song describe Darlene's feelings at the moment?


Mitchell Heron, followed by Pierre Darlan, got off the plane at National Airport in Washington, and pulled his overcoat around his shoulders. It was a cold day. He was filled with an excitement he had not experienced in years. Even as a boy, he had never felt destined for a staid lifestyle; he had always hated the orthodox, the commonplace, the narrow attitudes of his schoolmates in Angel, and later on felt stifled by the snobbery at Stanford. If Clement Story was a throwback to his Cherokee ancestors, then he, Mitchell Heron, was a throwback to some earlier generation where professional adventurers, vagabonds, roamed the world in search of romance, excitement, and challenge. He was on the threshold of a new beginning; even if he was not chosen for the job, he would be in the running, and that's what counted. It had been a long time indeed since he had been in the running for anything.

"We'll be going up into Maryland," Pierre said conversationally as they picked up their luggage. Once they were outside again the cold sun came out, causing a haze to form over the damp street.

They got into a 1938 Packard that looked as if it had seen better days, but the engine was tuned to a whistle. Pierre drove the car into the midst of traffic and was silent until the cars had thinned out on the road. "By the way, from now on we will speak only French, and your name is Michel Bayard." He paused. "The big building to your left is the Pentagon. We will be driving right *through* it." He smiled and added, "In fact, there is even a bus stop in the middle."

Mitchell glanced at the huge structure. "It's not as big as I thought it would be, somehow."

Pierre laughed. "It was the same way with me when I saw the Lincoln Memorial, which I thought would be as tall as the Eiffel Tower."

"How long has it been since you were in Paris?" Mitchell asked.

"Too long," Pierre replied quickly, and then went on in the same tone. "When we get over the bridge, you will see the Botanical Gardens. The Mall is to the left, and, beyond that, the White House."

The sun had gone under a cloud and mist was rolling in fiercely as Pierre took a side street that eventually led into New York Avenue, and from there he headed north once more. After about twenty miles, during which the bad weather was discussed and landmarks pointed out, he turned down a dirt road that wound around a small pond and finally snaked by a faded two-story clapboard farmhouse, complete with cupola.

Mitchell sighed appreciatively. "This looks very much like the old family homestead in Oklahoma," he said, then frowned. "This is your headquarters?"

"No, but this is where you are going to be stationed for the next ten days."

Pierre let Mitchell out of the car and parked in the

barn, disturbing a mother hen and her brood and a goat tethered outside the back door of the house. The bucolic scene was serene and peaceful, yet Mitchell sensed a wrong note. A man dressed in overalls, and wearing a mackinaw and heavy cap was repairing a fence. Another man in work clothes, and sporting a carpenter's apron, was putting up storm windows, and from the back porch wafted the sounds of an announcer on the *Farm and Home Show*, giving a weather report. A plump little gray-haired woman with pink cheeks and a basket of eggs rounded the wash house, smiled, and said, "Aft'noon."

Pierre opened the back door ceremoniously. "Welcome to Rocky Gorge," he announced pleasantly.

Mitchell coughed. "All you need, Pierre, is the smell of homemade bread. How come you slipped up?"

"What do you mean?"

"It's all storybook out there." He indicated the barnyard with his thumb.

"I do not understand."

Mitchell smiled coldly. "Of course you do. You set me up."

Pierre laughed out loud. "Not only you—everyone else, too. Congratulations. Your potting instincts are still working."

"Potting?"

"You know. People who transplant—potters—have green thumbs, a born instinct about gardening." He paused. "You have a similar instinct that is much more valuable. You, and men like you, can *smell* when something is wrong. You have passed the first test."

Mitchell followed Pierre into the kitchen, then the living room, which was filled with an assortment of old farm appliances and furniture. They trod up the worn, carpeted stairs. Mitchell expected the usual front bedroom. Instead, the place featured a 16mm projector, a motion-picture screen, and a few chrome chairs. Heavy plush carpeting muffled footfalls. The other room contained communications equipment, including a short-wave radio, a teletypewriter, a ticker-tape machine, and a crytograph. Three young men dressed in overalls, heads bowed over small desks, were too busy to acknowledge them. The attic contained four army cots, and there was a modern bathroom off an alcove.

Mitchell went to the window and looked below. The plump lady was pruning rosebushes, and the man who had previously been mending the fence was opening an umbrella over a tractor seat. The fog had lifted, and there was hazy sunshine. "It all looks so innocent out there," he said.

Pierre studied a chart and did not look up as he spoke. "Anyone driving by would not take a second look, because everything appears normal."

"But aren't the neighbors suspicious, with so many people coming and going?"

"Oh, we do not entertain many guests. Some arrive after nightfall and leave before sunrise."

"Who's the fat lady?"

"She looks like the perfect farmer's wife, eh?" He pulled his mustaches. "Behind that gray wig, she has a photographic memory, and she also takes shorthand at an unbelievable rate."

"The two men?"

"Guards. There is another in the loft over the barn." Pierre nodded his gray head, then went on apologetically. "They are not really needed, but"—he shrugged—"let us say they make us feel more secure." He took off his coat. "By the way, the first thing on the agenda is a mug shot. In the closet is a change of clothing. When you have completed your toilette"—he grinned—"come into the comm. room."

The old tweed suit Mitchell hung on his frame im-

173

parted a gaunt look. He looked as if he had lost ten pounds. The shirt had been patched in two places, and the underwear and socks had been worn smooth.

When he returned to the communications room, the camera had been set up and Pierre was testing the camera bulb. "Are you circumcised?" he asked without turning around.

"Why, no," Mitchell replied.

"Good. Most Frenchmen are uncut. Do you have any marks on your body? Any scars from operations? Birthmarks?"

Mitchell shook his head. "None, but I have a double little toe—a family abnormality."

Pierre continued to test the release mechanism on the camera. "Are you heterosexual?"

Mitchell looked at him strangely. "I've never been asked that before," he answered quietly, "but the answer is yes."

"Just checking. After all, you're a bachelor. We had a gifted young man who was with us for four years in Germany before the war. He was a respected businessman, very adroit at passing along important statistics about troop movements. But at a party one night he had too much to drink, passed out, and just happened to awaken in the apartment of one of Hitler's elite guard. A dangerous liaison was established." Pierre shrugged his shoulders. "Someone informed the SS. The guard was excused, but our man was tortured until he confessed to spying. He was hanged." He paused dramatically. "I've told you this story for two reasons. One, there is jeopardy in any sexual encounter; use your hand." He glanced at Mitchell stoically. "Also, there is danger, and remember that danger is a relative thing, having mainly to do with luck. If you are lucky, you will get in and out of France without too much trouble. Anything unexpected must be handled quickly, carefully, and expertly. One thing in your favor is that you are a survivor. Do you drink?"

"Oklahoma has always been dry, so we didn't grow up with liquor in the house. It has to be an unusual occasion for me to take a drink. When I was abroad, I sometimes had a glass of wine—an acquired taste."

"You know the wines of France?"

"Well"—Mitchell grinned—"I can tell the difference between a Clos de Vougeot and a Monthélie, if that's what you mean."

"All wine in France is bad just now, because the Nazis took over all of the best cellars." Pierre smoothed his mustaches. "Your accent is passable, but you will have to watch it when you are very tired. We also lost a man because, with his second cognac, his Texas drawl became very apparent. One thing you do not need is to speak French with an Okie twang." He turned to the door. "Ah, Felicia, do come in and meet Michel Bayard."

The plump lady from below stood in the doorway. Without her gray wig, she looked about thirty. "Hi," she said. "If you sit down, I'll cut your hair."

She draped his shoulders with a white cloth and took a pair of scissors from her apron pocket. "The front is all wrong. Let your sideburns grow about an inch, too. Also, start a mustache, which I'll show you how to trim."

Mitchell laughed. "I feel like a puppet."

"And so you should," Pierre replied. "This is just a beginning, *mon cher*." He handed him a sheet of paper. "You've been away from France for ten years. Memorize these new slang phrases."

Felicia ran a comb through his hair, snipped a few strands over his forehead, then attached a small, clipped false mustache to his upper lip, stood back, and exclaimed, *"Voilà!* That is what you will look like when you've grown your own."

175

Pierre stationed himself behind the camera. "Now, Michel, look at me. No expression, please." He pushed the bulb in his hand, then changed plates. "Once more. Now, again!" He then handed Mitchell a notebook. "Identify these sketches, please."

"A Louis Seize commode."

"And this?"

"A seventeenth-century side chair, Dutch origin, probably walnut."

"This?"

"An oak cupboard. It's German, I think. There's a lot of Gothic tracery. The fifteenth-century Krauts liked a lot of carving." He glanced at the next drawing. "This one's an oddity. It's a French pearwood side table, early nineteen hundreds. My grandmother owned one, but it was made of oak." He smiled at the next design. "What's this one doing here? My stepfather, Manford Pederson, introduced this veneer bird's-eye maple bedroom suite in nineteen thirty."

"Can you identify this piece?"

Mitchell examined the strange tubular chair with a suspended fabric seat, back, and armrests. "I've never seen anything like it, looks uncomfortable as hell."

Pierre laughed. "Not at all. It was designed by Marcel Breuer in Germany in the middle Twenties, a fact which you should know."

"It's still an abomination. My dad would turn over in his grave. Why are you giving me the third degree about identifying these pieces of furniture?"

"Because you'll be employed for a short while in what used to be a furniture factory."

"Where?"

"We'll get into that later," Pierre replied languidly. "The place has been converted to manufacturing gunstocks now, but the employees are the same—some very fine craftsmen. One never knows when talk will get around to the old days."

"I am not a *finisher*," Mitchell put in quickly.

"But you are, no doubt, familiar with the basic tools?"

"Yes, but I couldn't be called a craftsman by any means."

"But you are well versed in—ah—theory?"

Mitchell nodded. "But I know absolutely nothing about gunstocks."

"Neither did the employees at the factory at first. You will be performing an assembly-line job— balancing stocks, a simple task. The thing that is important is the feel of the wood, to know immediately if there is a flaw, an imbalance." He glanced at Mitchell's hands. "Let your fingernails grow. Next week Felicia will show you how to cut them in European style." He paused. "And, I suppose, your toenails as well." He looked up. "Michel, how long has it been since you've seen a dentist?"

"About a year and a half."

"Any work you need will be done here. I do not want you to develop a toothache and have American filling technique discovered. Now we shall have dinner."

Mitchell accompanied him downstairs to a beautifully arranged table. Pierre sat at one end of the table and Mitchell at the other. Felicia served the first course, a bowl of *potage St. Germain*. "This is delicious," Mitchell said. "I haven't had pea soup like this since I left France."

The next course was a small poached white fish. Pierre watched carefully as Mitchell picked up his knife and fork. He cut a small bite, placed his knife on the plate, and had the fork in his right hand, tines halfway up to his mouth, when he paused, placed the bite back on his plate; then he began to eat in the European manner, and Pierre laughed. "Good, you remembered." He paused. "Small details like this may save your life."

177

"You people are certainly thorough."

Pierre smiled wryly. "This is only the beginning. For the next ten days you are in our hands—and safe. Then you will be on your own. Then if you make a mistake and forget some of the things we have taught you— well, then *you* are responsible." He took a sip of wine. "If you get cold feet anytime during the next few days, you can always back out."

"No, I'm going to be putting to use everything I have ever learned in my life."

"What it all boils down to, in our business, is *guts*."

Mitchell laughed as he was served a tiny rack of lamb. "And if I continue to eat like this for the next ten days, I may add a few more."

"Eat well," Pierre answered grimly, "because when you get to France you will be staying with some very poor people and consuming only ragout and cheese and bread and wine."

Mitchell smiled suddenly. "What more could a man want?"

"Ah, yes, *mon cher*, but the ragout is horsemeat, the cheese is rotten, the bread is sawdust, and the wine is watered." He paused. "Don't you know that France is *starving*?"

In the comfortable farmhouse in the rolling Maryland hills, as he ate a gourmet dinner, it was difficult for Mitchell Heron to realize that he would shortly be walking down a dusty French street, smelling the awful stench of war, wishing fervently that he were pacing up and down on the sidewalk in front of his furniture store in Enid, Oklahoma.

H. R. Leary leaned back in the easy chair in his office in Langley, Virginia, and took a cautious sip of bourbon. "Well, Pierre, what do you think? Do we have a star or a supporting player?"

The Frenchman laughed softly. "There is star *quality* in Mitchell Heron, but beyond that, I do not know."

Leary leaned over the coffee table and picked up two file folders. "The psychiatrist's report is extraordinary. All tests, including the Rorschach, indicate that psychologically he's a true mercenary."

Pierre's eyes brightened. "That means, of course, that the violence hidden beneath could come out at any time. Under pressure, he could fall apart." He studied his fingernails. "Yet, in all of our time together, I have never seen a resentment or a fear buildup, no animosity, no aggressive tendencies. If I did not know that our sainted doctor from Vienna knew what he was talking about, I would say that he has made a mistake with this one."

"I have always been schooled not to employ violent men," Leary countered.

Pierre gave him a quick, automatic smile. "All men are violent—sometimes. I have found Mitchell Heron to be ordinary in ways that he should be clever, and clever in ways that he should be ordinary. But for this particular mission I think that he fills the bill better than anyone we have in our command at present. A year ago, I would not have recommended him for the job; too much could happen to him because of his naiveté in the field." He sighed and picked nervously at his forefinger. "But the good ones that we used so often are dead or have been captured. I often think of Lature, who was so brilliant, standing up before the firing squad, or Madame C, who was captured by the SS and brutally tortured, yet revealed nothing."

"Patriots all, I agree." Leary nodded wearily. "It's easier for us in America to train men to be sent to help the Resistance, because we do not see the suffering over there." He grew pensive. "Would you go back, Pierre?"

"At my age? No. Even Mitchell Heron is really too old. I am only a few years his senior, but with all that shrapnel still in my legs, I cannot run any more." He smoothed his mustaches. "You would not return, would you, H.R.?"

"I might," Leary conceded crisply, "on a special mission. They wouldn't let me, of course. I would like to feel the slipstream once more as I deplane, and experience the marvelous relief as the parachute opens overhead, and then the firm, solid earth under my feet. The feeling is very close to an orgasm. It is called the *cremasteric reflex,* and it happens to many who parachute." He stared off into space a moment and then snapped back to reality. "But that feeling of a sudden fall will never happen again."

"I would sleep better," Pierre said, burrowing down in the chair with his drink, "if I could have him one more week."

"Impossible."

"Still, he is perfect in many ways. Single, a loner, French resident for many years. Good accent. Passable German. Intelligent. Quick mind. Expert marksman. Only drawback: a famous name."

Leary leaned forward. "But you are wrong. His name is Michel Bayard."

Pierre laughed uneasily. "Oh, yes, of course." He paused. "What do we do if we lose him?"

"Michel Bayard is dead," Leary announced flatly, "One Mitchell Heron is killed in a car crash, B.B.B.R.—body burned beyond recognition."

"If they catch him and he talks?"

Leary tapped his fingers together. "He has worked in a former furniture factory, balancing gunstocks. He has made one contact in one office, using one password. That is all they can get out of him." His face was a mask. "He might tell them about a man named Pierre, who does not really exist, or a farmhouse in Maryland that we will have deactivated." His eyes took on a yellow cast. "You see, my dear Pierre, that is the most beautiful part of it all. He can tell nothing because he knows nothing!"

It was very late at night, and Mitchell was very tired. His feet ached from the heavy wooden shoes which had inflamed his soles for a week. He still felt awkward, especially when climbing stairs, but he was becoming accustomed to the unnatural weight. Now, he could walk across a plowed field without shuffling. He tried unsuccessfully to focus on a map of Southern France and the Low Countries to which Pierre was pointing.

"You know this area very well, having traveled extensively from St.-Laurent-de-la-Salangue on the Mediterranean to Mimizan on the Bay of Biscay, eh?"

Mitchell's eyes drooped, and the map swung around and around under his eyelids. He was so exhausted, Pierre's rapid French was becoming difficult to understand. His head nodded.

"Wake up, Monsieur Bayard, wake up!" Pierre exclaimed, shaking his arm. "Repeat what I have just said."

". . . Bay of Biscay . . ." Mitchell passed his hands over his eyes and tried to muster his thoughts. "Can't we continue in the morning, Pierre?" He forced his eyes open. "My mind is fuzzy."

"Fuzzy!" Pierre shouted, switching suddenly to English and jarring Mitchell out of his lethargy. "Why, you stupid son of a bitch, I'm trying to save your ass!"

Dumbfounded, Mitchell stared at the little man, who before had always been so soft-spoken. His face was now a mottled red, and his eyes bulged out of their sockets. "You ignorant Okie bastard, you miserable shit of a man!"

Mitchell felt hot blood course to his head. He was wide awake now, and he clenched his fists. He would punch the little man's pudgy face until it was bloody

181

pulp. He was about to rise, when it suddenly occurred to him that Pierre had cursed him in English. He calmly replied in French, *"Pardon, Monsieur?"* He smiled innocently. "I speak only *français*."

Pierre laughed out loud and clapped his hands and reverted to French once more. "Sorry to insult you, Monsieur Bayard, but I had to discover how you would react. We once lost an Englishman posing as a Belgian, when a terrified old woman ran up to him on the street and whispered in English that she was being stalked by the Gestapo. Without thinking, he replied in English that he could do nothing. Of course she was working for *les Boches*, and he was arrested at once. He was shot—but not, of course, before they pulled out his fingernails—and he talked." Pierre got up slowly and rubbed his back. "It is time for bed, *mon cher*. Have a good night's rest." He paused. "Have you had much association with Catholics?"

"No, we always went to the Methodist church in Angel. I went to a Catholic furneral once in Lyon."

"We will go to Mass tomorrow morning at six-thirty, then." Pierre handed him a piece of paper. "You know, of course, the Lord's Prayer, also memorize the Hail Mary, which might come in handy sometime. As far as Mass goes, it will be in Latin, but do pay special attention when to stand, sit, and kneel. Churches can be very useful occasionally as places not only to worship but to rest, and, more importantly, to hide."

Mitchell shivered involuntarily. Suddenly the journey seemed impossibly difficult. A strong sense of foreboding took hold of him. He was afraid.

"Ah, yes," Pierre was saying. "Take this packet, in which you will find a dozen postcards from such places as Pine Bluff, Arkansas, and Troy, Alabama. There are also sheets of stationery from hotels located in the southern part of the United States. You will also find the supposed itinerary for your vacation, with appropriate dates attached. Write a few lines to your family, which we'll mail later from those places. Include brief allusions to local attractions, which you will find listed in the proper order."

"You think of everything, don't you?" Mitchell said bitterly.

"We try." Pierre shuffled the papers and yawned. "I'm tired," he said. "Say in the last letter that you are enjoying your vacation so much that you are taking a few more weeks." He smiled wryly. "This is in case we can't bring you back precisely on schedule. About eight o'clock Friday morning, three days from now, I will drive you to Hightstown, New Jersey, where you will learn to parachute from an airplane."

Mitchell looked at him in amzement. "I assumed that I was to be *smuggled* into France."

"You are—by air. Other routes are too dangerous just now—not that dropping out of the sky is foolproof either, but you have already said that you have no fear of heights."

Mitchell stiffened. "A friend in service told me that his paratrooper training lasted several weeks."

"And you have only one week. Does that bother you? Allay your fears, Monsieur Bayard. You will only be trained to jump and to land safely—all you need to know for the present. You will not even be schooled in packing your chute." He smiled. "Obviously our techniques have vastly improved since your friend took his training. Do you have hemorrhoids?"

"Why, no," Mitchell said.

"Good. See you in the morning."

"Good night."

"Monsieur Bayard, Here is something to wear around your neck."

Mitchell examined the tiny gold medal on a chain. "What is this?"

"Saint Chrisopher"—Pierre looked up soberly—"the

patron saint of the traveler, especially the traveler in jeopardy."

The fog had cleared above the airfield. Pierre and Mitchell were seated in an old Chevrolet parked beside the darkened runway at the airbase, drinking coffee from a thermos. "Briefly, Monsieur Bayard," Pierre was saying in French, "you will be landing near Glasgow at a small military airport. After chow, you will be taken to a barracks to rest. It is doubtful if you will get much sleep on the plane. Bucket seats are not the most comfortable."

"I learned a long time ago to rest when I can," Mitchell replied earnestly. "I don't think the ride will throw me off routine." He sighed. "What am I to do for money?"

"Glad you reminded me." Pierre reached in his pocket and brought out a stack of French banknotes. "Try not to carry these around. Hide the bulk in a safe place and put a few extra francs in your shoe." He looked at him intently. "We hope to drop you the next night, if good weather conditions prevail. There can be no wind. It is essential to drop you precisely, within a kilometer of the target site. Instructions, via short wave, will be sent to our friend Paul. He will meet you, God willing." He removed a four-inch silver tube from his coat pocket, a tube that resembled a miniature cigar flask. He handed Mitchell a small vial filled with pale amber paste. "When you get on the plane," he said conversationally, "insert this tube in your anus. It contains the information that you are to transmit."

"What?" Mitchell looked at Pierre as if he had lost his reason. He thought for a moment that he had misunderstood the meaning of the French sentences. "Eh?"

"You heard me correctly. The vial of lubricant contains a form of petroleum jelly." Pierre smiled mirth-

184

lessly. "A by-product so kindly manufactured by the Heron Oil Company." He paused. "I thought that was rather an ironic, but nice, touch."

"I can do without snide remarks, Pierre!" Mitchell exclaimed. "I don't think that's funny." He exhaled all at once. "How long do I have to wear this damned thing?"

"Hopefully, not long. You will receive instructions."

Mitchell glared at him. "Do you mean to tell me that all I have to do is carry this thing up my ass halfway around the world? *That* is my mission?"

Pierre nodded. "*Oui, Monsieur Bayard.*"

"I do not believe this," Mitchell replied angrily, hitting his palms together. "You brought me all the way from Oklahoma, put me through all of that training—for *this*? I feel like a fool."

"What do you think your crash course cost us in time and money, and, as Mr. Churchill so kindly stated in 'blood, sweat, and tears'?" Pierre was as irascible as Mitchell had ever seen him; he thought he knew all of the Frenchman's mercurial moods.

Mitchell realized that he was also deeply and personally offended, and the thought enraged him even more. He spoke in English. "You play your little scenario like a game, Pierre," he shouted, "and I'm sick of your duplicity! My God, no matter what I've endured in my life—and it's been no bed of roses, let me assure you—I've never been forced to undergo both physical and psychological tests—" He was so furious that he was shaking.

Pierre shook his head, then went on calmly in French. "Quiet down, *mon cher*, the road has been difficult." When he continued, his voice was low and soothing, almost a verbal caress. "And do you know something? Of all of my pupils, and there have been many, you have absorbed more knowledge in a short space of time than all of the others combined."

185

Mitchell lowered his head. "Yes, Pierre," he replied in French, "and if a German sympathizer had made me angry the way you just did unintentionally, I would be a dead man. I answered in English even before I thought."

Pierre held up his forefinger. "You have learned a valuable lesson, I hope. I assure you, if there was any other way to deliver this capsule . . ."

Mitchell was immediately contrite. "All I can say, then," he replied helplessly, "is that its contents must certainly be very valuable."

Pierre shrugged. "Who knows? Not I." He gestured feebly. "They tell me nothing."

"What?"

"I know very little more than you do, *mon cher.*" He lit a cigarette thoughtfully. "One of these days I am going to divorce myself from this dirty business, before I am too old and scarred to lead a normal life."

Mitchell put in quickly, "What if someone finds the tube?"

"I doubt that an ordinary soldier or even a member of the Gestapo would search an obvious workingman for such a receptacle. This mode of transportation is somewhat new in our field. Of course, convicts and drug smugglers have used this method of concealment for many years; it is an established practice, I understand."

Pierre looked out of the car windows as the camouflaged runway lights, with their protective hoods, were switched on, filling the landing field with ghostly, pale lights and deep gray shadows. From above, no detail of the terrain would be visible to an enemy plane. "It is time," he said simply and opened the door.

They both took deep breaths of air. Pierre held out his pudgy hand. "I've become fond of you, Monsieur Bayard. Do not disappoint your old teacher. Do a good job. And, who knows, we might meet socially somewhere after the war." His mustache moved in the slight wind, creating a moving shadow on his face.

"You mean you are going to desert me now?"

Pierre nodded and smiled softly. "My job with you is over as soon as you get on that plane."

Mitchell shook his hand and said in English, "Thank you, Pierre, for all you've done. I'm sorry I blew up back there in the car. You didn't deserve that. You'll be in my thoughts, my friend." He swallowed hard and then smiled. "Especially every time Mother Nature calls."

Pierre grinned. "Adieu."

Without glancing behind him, Mitchell walked swiftly to the plane, which had taxied down the runway and was now a hundred feet ahead. He thought: *I can turn around, get back into the car, and no one will reproach me. I can take the train back to Enid. . . .* But of course he knew that ploy was not possible. He was in too deep now to back out.

# 11

## The Flight of the Dove

*Letty and Bosley had flown in from Washington on the afternoon of December 23, 1943.*

Fontine Dice knew their exact moment of arrival, because the noise of the DC-6 distracted her from her favorite afternoon radio program. The silver-voiced announcer was finishing his introduction: "We all know couples like lovable, impractical Lorenzo Jones and his devoted wife, Belle. Lorenzo's inventions have made him a character to the town, but not to Belle, who loves him."

Fontine raised herself up from her armchair, rubbed her swollen legs, and reached the window just in time to see the corporate plane with its strange camouflaged paint gracefully disappear behind the cottonwoods to land on the cemented runway that cut through the pastureland. She smiled and shook her head. Imagine the Trentons flying back and forth to Angel as if Washington, D.C., were no further than Enid!

She listened to her program, then turned off the radio and went into the kitchen, where the new cook was kneading yeast dough. "Here, Helen," she said

188

brusquely, "let me do that. It's good for my arthritis. Why don't you go out and gather the eggs?"

Helen, the last of a long succession of cooks during the wartime years, nodded and replied, "Yessiree, Miz Dice," and turned her gaunt form in the direction of the service porch. Fontine looked after her with compassion and thought about family feelings. When Helen's second husband, Jeremiah, was crushed by a tractor the year before, it was discovered that he had left a handwritten will leaving the farm to the children. The document was dated the day after his first wife had died, long before he had met Helen. Although they had weathered the depression together, and she had worked beside Jeremiah in the fields, the children had taken over the farm immediately after his death, leaving her with nothing. White-faced and trembling, she had come to Fontine and announced, "They've turned me out, Miz Dice, turned me out!" Fontine's heart had gone out to her.

As Fontine worked the dough into a smooth, satiny mound, she thought about what children sometimes did to their folks. Poor Charlotte in far-off Washington, a dried-up shell of a woman with no man of her own and no children! A tear escaped Fontine's eye and fell on the shiny loaf that she was forming.

At that moment John Dice came in the back door. "Aft'noon, honey," he said and kissed her cheek—a ritual he had performed every morning and evening for the last fifty years. He gave her a long look. "You've been tearing up?" he asked kindly. "What's it this time?"

"Oh, nothing, Jaundice," she replied slowly. "I'm just a little blue, I guess. It all started when I heard the Heron plane come down, and it came to me how much we've all gone through since the opening of the Strip."

He grinned. "It's not like you, Fourteen, to go back

189

and study like that. Still and all, we've all come a long way from Santone and that little house we had." He laughed. "Who'd have thought then that we'd have so much now?"

She looked questioningly at him. "You know I don't know anything about money. Are we millionaires yet, Jaundice?"

He gave her a guarded look. "I suppose, if all our holdings were put together. Why?"

She sighed. "Who're we going to leave it to?"

"Well, come to think about it, I've never considered."

She tested the heat of the oven with her hand and placed the loaves on the middle rack. "Well, if we leave half of it to Charlotte, that's plenty, with her being single and all. Even if she does get married, she's too old to have babies, and I don't think it's right for us to leave it to some glamour boy or other." She went to the sink and washed her hands, carefully working the soap under her fingernails and into her diamond rings. "Jaundice, with us not having a proper education or good upbringing, I think we should do something for the younger generation. I don't mean after our deaths, either. I mean right now. I'm going to call Letty and Bos."

On the next farm over, Hattie Fulks came into the sewing room, smoothing her apron over her wide hips, her false teeth clacking. "Mrs. Trenton, Mrs. Dice is on the phone."

Letty took her shoe off the pedal of the sewing machine and disengaged the foot, then went to the instrument in the hall. "Yes, Fontine?" She really wanted to finish repairing her favorite blue skirt, which she had just torn on the door of the plane. She would have to cut the conversation short; Fontine was apt to go on and on. She listened a moment and then replied, "Yes, we'll come at four tomorrow."

She hung up and smiled crookedly. If they were being asked to tea—and Fontine never served tea—it meant that something important was about to be discussed. The last time that the Dices had invited them over, Letty had agreed to knit three dozen pair of booties for the English war orphans. Eight months later, by the time she had finished two dozen—the project being delayed because they had been in Washington—Fontine had sent a note thanking her for the package but saying that heavy mufflers were needed now, and for heaven's sake not to send any more booties!

Letty grinned as she sat back down at the machine. It would be best to leave her purse at home, in case Fontine was selling tickets to some impossible charity affair or collecting money for some wartime fund-raising scheme that would come to naught.

The next afternoon Fontine surveyed the tea cart and nodded appreciatively. Letty had told her that in England buttered bread, jam tarts, and sometimes even little sandwiches made out of watercress or fish paste, were served along with something called crumpets. But, deciding to prepare something special, she had made cream puffs. She looked at the pastry with hungry eyes. She had eaten one of the shells—hot from the oven, and another freshly filled with custard, and a third as she had taken the golden mounds from the refrigerator. The puffs, she decided, were so good and rich that they would soften the stone heart of the most confirmed miser. It being Christmastime and all, it might not be a bad idea to mention that old skinflint Scrooge if her proposal was turned down.

The door chime, which John Dice had imported from Germany's Black Forest in 1929, played the first four bars of "*Ach, du Lieber Augustine,*" and Helen, dressed in black, with her little white lace cap slightly askew, answered the door. "*She's* in the drawin' room," she said, rolling her eyes, and Letty had to smile. No matter how many servants the Dices employed over the years, they all seemed to be cut from one piece of cloth. Fontine was always too busy to supervise help properly, was known to overpay scandalously, and on one or two occasions, when the Dices had first come into money, had treated servants like guests. Helen had always been dirt-poor and didn't even know how to serve. Her cotton stockings were always wrapped around her legs, which looked like wooden screws.

Fontine was dressed in a soft pink hostess gown, which went perfectly with the heavy, ornate oak furniture that Edward Heron had copied from his father's 1840 designs.

"So good of you all to come," Fontine said, stretching out her plump arms. "I've just been listening to the news on the Philco, and the Japs are being scattered all over the South Pacific!" She clapped her hands.

"That *is* good news," Bosley replied, kissing her on the cheek.

"What do you hear from Clement?" Fontine asked.

"Very little," Letty replied. "Over half of his last letter was censored—so cut up with a scissors that there wasn't much information left. Apparently he's playing for the troops in England." She looked over the tea cart. "My heavens, Fontine, you've outdone yourself. How many people are you expecting?"

Fontine smiled. "Not many."

The doorbell chimed again, and Letty pursed her lips. "Really, Fontine, you've got to have that changed. It's not very patriotic to have a door chime playing a German tune."

"I know." Fontine sighed. "Everyone tells me that, but I like the melody. It's so cheerful." She excused herself and greeted Bella and Torgo Chenovick. "Do come in and rest." She glanced at Bella. "Have you lost weight? You look kind of peaked."

Bella patted her thick waist and announced, "Haven't lost a pound and don't intend to. But, truthfully, I've not been getting much exercise lately, with keeping the fruit stand open only a month. When the fresh peaches were gone, I had to close. I'm usually able to keep open another six weeks, because everyone wants my preserves, but with the sugar shortage I can't put the fruit up properly anymore, and it's almost impossible to get pectin." She turned to Bosley. "It looks like to me"—she waved a plump finger—"that with you people formulating new by-products from cracking the crude, you'd come up with a sugar replacement that would at least be fit for canning."

He laughed. "My dear Bella, I would like nothing better. But, as versatile as hydrocarbons are, it's doubtful if we can come up with anything like an artificial sweetner. Besides," he chided, "with all your money, what are you doing peddling fruit at your age?"

She laughed, her pink cheeks shaking. "Tell him, my husband."

Torgo grinned. "It keeps us both young." He gestured vaguely. "And money? It's just cash that slips between your fingers." He was showing his eighty years, and he had difficulty hiding emotions. His eyes grew misty. "When we hit the first well, I went back to Prague and set my people up in the business of exporting little dolls in native costumes. When that failed, I sent more money. This time, my brother and his wife exported lace by the yard, making contracts with village lacemakers. They went broke again, and I put more money into a music shop, which also failed. I then gave them ten thousand dollars for a new venture and told them I was through." He smiled ruefully. "That was the last I heard of them. They knew they'd bled me."

Fontine rang for Helen, who appeared a moment later, looking more disheveled than ever. "Yiss'm?"

"You may serve the tea now."

"Yiss'm." She poured the pale liquid into the cups, her hand shaking.

After the cream puffs had been consumed, Fontine stood up. "We were talking about money just now, and I'm glad, because that's why I've asked you all to come over today."

Letty closed her eyes and counted to ten. What charity was making Fontine feel guilty this time? Letty thought that she looked like nothing so much as a poutter pigeon.

"I've got to wait until Jaundice gets here, and he's already late. He'll slap me silly if I go on without him."

At that moment a car horn sounded in the barnyard, and then the stomping of heavy boots was heard in the hallway. "Howdy, everyone," John Dice said jovially, throwing his ten-gallon hat on the bust of Buffalo Bill. "I'm much obliged to you all for showing up." He sat down in his big leather armchair and eyed the one remaining pastry. "Have Helen get me some coffee, Fourteen, you know I can't abide tea, and have her put that puff in the ice chest." He looked over the group. "The doctor says I have to watch my sweets; otherwise I'll be pumping insulin." He sucked his teeth for a moment. "Now, I've got a proposal to make. We've all known each other since we were young, and we've all accumulated a lot of money—primarily because of the Heron leases." He nodded to Letty and Bosley. "And for that, we're all more than grateful."

John Dice took a sip of the coffee that Helen had brought, and smacked his lips. "That's good. Nothing like good old boiled coffee. These new pots don't make a cup of java worth a tinker's damn." He took another sip. "Now, Fourteen and I have been talking about what we're going to do with our money when we die. Charlotte's an old maid, and there won't be any grandchildren from that quarter, so we're going to be stuck with a lot of cash and property." He turned to Torgo,

"What are you folks going to do with your wherewithal?"

Torgo shrugged. "It's a problem we haven't solved yet."

"How about you, Bos?" John Dice paused eloquently and then went on quickly. "I know you've got the family, of course, and you've naturally got to take care of them, but there must be quite a bit invested here and there. What's going to happen to it after the Grim Reaper?"

Bosley took Letty's hand. "What do you think, my dear? After all, it's essentially your money Jaundice is talking about. You've got a private fortune, you know."

Letty smiled crookedly. "You've always taken care of everything, Bos. I haven't even looked at my bank statements or investment reports since way before the war."

Fontine laughed. "No one could ever call you extravagant, Letty. But I suppose Uncle Sam takes quite a bite. You know, Jaundice and I were thinking that, even with the prosperity that the war's brought, Angel is a fairly poor town. The kids are leaving right after high school and going on to New York or California. Now, when the boys come back from overseas, what do we have to offer? Angel's going to end up to be a big old folks' home unless we do something about it right now." She eyed Letty. "You still own most of the business section, so some of the responsibility rests with you."

John Dice got up and thrust his hands in his pockets. "Look at us," he said quietly. "We're all in our late sixties and seventies—a pretty bunch of old people." He swallowed hard. "What I think we should do is help the youngsters of the community. Many of our kids don't even want to go to college, and I think one reason is that they aren't encouraged in that direction." He paused. "Now, all of you know I'm not educated, and neither is Fourteen. If you remember, we didn't even

195

learn to read and write until we were in our twenties."

Bosley held up his hand. "What are you getting at, Jaundice? How are you going to part us from our money?" He laughed. "If you're going into all that ancient history"—his eyes twinkled—"it's got to be more than a two-dollar bill."

"You're right, Bos." John Dice placed his hands in his vest pockets. "I propose, folks, that we build—and endow—a library for the town of Angel."

"I think that's a marvelous idea, Jaundice!" Letty exclaimed. "A marvelous idea!" She flushed. "I wish I'd have thought of it myself. That's one thing about getting older—we all go inside too much and don't pay attention to what's going on right on our doorsteps. It's as if we were blind. I don't like that. Come to think of it, I don't like that at all."

Bosley frowned. "How much money are we talking about, Jaundice?"

John Dice made a little motion with his hands. "I don't know. But before I scratch the surface, I want permission to go ahead."

Torgo stood up and flexed his fingers. "When I came over here to this country, I was broke. Even when I made The Run, I only had one twenty-dollar gold piece in my sock." He placed his hand on Bella's shoulder. "We'll go along. Garfield County and the Herons have been good to us."

Bella nodded. "Whatever you say, Jaundice, it's good enough for us."

Bosley fingered a little Spode ashtray on the coffee table. "I might mention now—I'll have to look it up to be certain—but I believe that we can take off some of this library funding from our income taxes."

Fontine laughed. "That's good news. I have to sign the checks along with Jaundice"—she rolled her eyes—"and we pay so much that I don't even look at the amount anymore. I just scrawl my name." She paused.

"You know, besides everything else, I think it will be wonderful to know that we've contributed something to the town." She hit her palms on both sides of the chair. "Something just occurred to me! Do you suppose that's why Leona Barrett gave The Widows over to being a university? Did she get a good rake-off on her taxes?" Then Fontine blushed to the roots of her very blond hair. "What's come over me? Thinking about *that woman*!" She considered her statement for a moment. "Maybe she wasn't so bad after all."

John Dice sighed gently. "Fourteen, it's taken you long enough to come around. My God, she gave the house and grounds to the university right after Statehood, and that was in nineteen seven."

"Well," Fontine said grudgingly, "I'm an old woman now, and things do seem different when I look back. But it must have given her great pleasure to see her name on that building." She paused. "What gets me still, however, is the amount of money she must have taken in from her—ah—profession. After all, the Conservatory is still going strong, and as far as I know, no one's ever asked for a penny."

Bosley laughed. "And why should they, with a fabulous income filtering in every day?" He shook his head and did not catch Letty's warning look. "Leona was clever, because when she died a few years ago—" He stopped and clamped his lips together. For a moment he had forgotten where he was and whom he was with.

Fontine looked as if she had seen a ghost. "Died?" She turned to Bosley suspiciously. "I thought no one had ever heard hide nor hair from her since she left Oklahoma. How come you were in touch, Bos?"

"Fourteen, hush your mouth. Don't be asking fool questions." John Dice got up and went on loudly, "It's after five o'clock, and I'd like to have a glass of beer before dinner. Anyone join me?"

"Oh, Jaundice, sit down," Letty said kindly. "I sup-

197

pose at this point in all of our lives it doesn't hurt to admit that Leona Barrett had an interest in the Heron Oil Company. When she died, she left her shares to the Conservatory, making it the richest university in the United States."

Fontine's mouth flew open. "Something's wrong with my hearing. I know I can't be getting everything."

"You don't need a hearing aid, dear," Letty replied, "It's true."

Bella leaned forward. "But how did this come about, Letty? We were all here at that time, and I don't remember anything . . ."

Letty pushed a strand of gray hair back from her forehead. "When we were down and out, just before we finally struck oil, George needed five thousand dollars to bail us out. Everyone in the Territory was poorer than church mice. People hardly had enough to eat. Well, I only knew one person who might have that much cash."

Fontine looked at her incredulously. "You humbled yourself before *that* woman?"

Letty looked her straight in the eyes. "No, I offered her a business proposition. A quarter of Heron stock for five thousand dollars."

"What a bargain!" Fontine exclaimed.

Bosley's voice was very low. "It was no bargain. It was problematical whether we'd strike oil or not."

Torgo roused suddenly. "But, Bos, *you* knew that there was oil *there*. After all, you're a geologist."

Bosley laughed feebly. "My friend, my profession was very young in those days. I only knew, from climbing down water wells, that there was an anticline—but the oil dome could have been very minuscule, perhaps not even enough to pay back the original investment. Or we could have hit a duster, too. We didn't have very sophisticated equipment, couldn't drill down more than three or four hundred feet."

"Then Leona Barrett was really taking a chance?" Bella asked.

"Yes," John Dice put in unexpectedly, "but don't forget the drillers were regular customers, and she heard them speak about hitting oil sands."

Fontine whirled around. "Jaundice, how do you know these things? Were you ever over there?"

Humorously, he held out his hand as if to ward off a blow. "You know better than that, Fourteen, you kept me so busy at home that—" He looked around the group and blushed. "After all, Poppa Dice worked over there."

Bosley suppressed a chuckle. "That's water long over the dam. Suffice it to say that the investment paid off handsomely, and when Leona went to New York and married that industrialist and became a famous hostess, she was wealthy in her own right."

"Why, I never knew any of this," Fontine fumed.

"Well, it wasn't any of your business, Fourteen."

"I suppose you knew all about it?"

John Dice smiled blandly. "Of course. As you know, I've handled all the Conservatory of Music funds since the beginning. How do you think the Dice Bank weathered the depression? It was Leona's funds that kept us solvent. The interest alone . . ."

Fontine went to the window and looked out over the pastureland in the direction of the university, her plump arms at her sides. She turned and smiled softly. "Hell," she said slowly, "what am I upset about? My stars! Here we are, all old and dear friends, and it wouldn't be fitting if we couldn't discuss private things together."

She nodded her platinum head. "And this all leads up to saying that if Leona, moldy in her grave, can have the satisfaction of knowing that she helped thousands of young people write and compose and sing and carry on, all of us should be able to endow one little library." She sighed contentedly. "Shall we all have a

199

wing named for ourselves? After all, if Andrew Carnegie can do it, why can't we?"

H. R. Leary, at Royal Gorge, answered the telephone and immediately knew from the peculiarly dead silence that he was on the scrambling system, "Magic." He listened a few moments and forcibly controlled his anger.

He took a deep breath and made his voice dry and emotionless. "General," he countered smoothly, "I'm aware of your problem. But please try to see our side of the situation. We delivered one extremely capable operative to you in the time scheduled, fully briefed and ready to perform. How you get him to his destination is your problem. The guy upstairs says that Monsieur Bayard must be there either Wednesday or Thursday night, preferably Wednesday."

Leary closed his eyes and listened intently to the rising one-sided argument; then he went on grimly. "Also, don't forget you've also got to bring him back. You can't leave him too long, because he's only trained to a certain point. For instance, he has no survival experience whatsoever." He listened to the diatribe once more and then replied, "Thank you for returning my call, General." He took a deep breath and shook his head, thanking the powers that be for the four-thousandth time that he was not a general in the Army Air Force.

The general, in Washington, threw the instrument into its cradle and angrily paced to the wall map. He consulted a current list of airplanes, made a quick decision, and called for his aide de camp to prepare a coded radio message to the colonel in Prestwick: PREPARE A BIG-ASS BIRD. . . .

The colonel at Prestwick swore softly as he looked at the yellow scrap of paper placed on his desk by the newly-arrived-from-the-States buck sergeant. "For

Christ's sake," he said indignantly, hitting the desk with his fist and wishing the old yellow pine piece were the general's face, "it isn't as if we haven't got enough on our hands, without ferrying some jackass into southern France in a B-17." He fumed. "Get me the major."

The sergeant called out a moment later, "He's on the wire, sir."

The colonel cleared his throat. "Major, a directive has just come in from HQ Wash. to get a B-17 ready for a no-bomb run tonight—weather permitting—to Plaisance-du-Gers." Since he had been a French teacher prior to the war, he gave the town the full Gallic pronunciation and paused a moment in anticipated pleasure, biting his cigarette holder, waiting for the expected "Where?" And when it came he repeated the name with a little less accent. "That's near Toulouse, if memory serves. You have a Frog civvie to drop."

There was a pause while the major digested the information; then he asked tactfully, "Sir, do you think that we need a full crew? If it's just a plain drop, I'd rather save the bombardier and the gunners for another operation. We're sending a squadron of B-17's over Essen tomorrow to hit the munitions factories again, and—"

The colonel wrinkled his brow a moment. "No, better send an entire complement of men, in case they run into some Kraut fighters unexpectedly."

"Very well, sir," the major replied quietly. He hung up the telephone. "That miserable bastard!" he said to the sergeant, "He knows damn well it's Christmas and we're short of manpower. He also knows we lost twelve planes yesterday over Berlin, and three limped back, and that I've got seven men in the hospital." He consulted the manifold on his desk. "Get me the line chief," he said curtly.

"Yes, sir?" The line chief said over the intercom.

"What do you have on the lineup that you're not using tomorrow?"

The line chief checked statistics on the wall chart. "I've got four B-17-G's but the ball turret on one needs to be replaced, and the electric system is shot on another, and—"

"Anything operable?"

"Now, sir?"

"Yes!" the major snapped. "Of course *now*. Clean out your ears."

"Yes, sir." The line chief paused a moment, keeping anger out of his voice. "*Sylvia Sue* has seventy-eight missions behind her, sir, but she's a fine ole broad; however, I wouldn't want to push her into a long flight. Lately we've used her mostly for training purposes."

"What I have in mind isn't a bombing mission, Chief," the major snapped. "We've got to drop a Frog civvie."

"Alone?"

"Of course."

"Where's the target site?"

"South of Toulouse."

The line chief whistled and studied the question. "She'll make it as long as she's not flown down the Berlin corridor. Deviate around the coast, over water, and stay clear of flak batteries. I'd feel better if she had a solid crew, sir. The boys may be just going along for the ride, but I figure if you're willing to spare a big-assed bird, then the mission is crucial. Also, the risk of losing the Frog civvie is less." He hung up and turned to a corporal. "Son of a bitch! This isn't our day. That old fart wants *Sylvia Sue* for some private job. I hate to send her out on a wild goose chase, but—"

"Well, Chief, we've got tons of propaganda sheets in the storeroom. How about dumping a few?"

202

"What's on hand now?"

The corporal summoned a bored voice and recited: "*Free French, We Support You,* and *Band Together, Frenchmen.*"

"*Free French,* I guess."

"Okay, Chief!" The corporal went back into the storehouse and confronted the private. "You better get your ass in gear, Private. We're gonna drop about fifty thousand leaflets over France tonight. Load up *Sylvia Sue.*"

"That old crate?" the private asked.

"Don't be snotty. If you'd been on as many missions as she has, you'd be creaking too!"

"Okay, okay!" The private shrugged his shoulders and spat into the fern pot. The corporal sure could get testy, he thought. The Air Force should send the fucker back to the mountains of Kentucky, where he belonged.

The line chief checked Mitchell's gear. "I suggest you carry your parachute, sir," he said politely. "No sense putting it on now. You don't want this thing strapped to your back for five hours. Here's your oxygen mask. The engineer'll show you how to plug it into the ship's system." He visually checked Mitchell's clothing once more: a one-piece coverall, similar to a flight suit in that it was electrically heated, was worn over an old tweed coat. Dark trousers were tucked into heavy boots. A wool cap, pulled down over his ears, was lightly secured under his chin by a soft movable strap. "You'll do," the line chief said dryly and accompanied him out to the airfield. "Do you have everything?" he asked as they approached the gray and olive-drab camouflaged bomber.

Mitchell, thinking about the silver tube he was accommodating, shrugged his shoulders. "I'm not taking a briefcase, if that's what you mean." The dimly lighted field was illuminated now by a green signal from the

203

tower. An ambulance, which Pierre had told him was referred to as a meat wagon, and a red fire truck were parked nearby.

It occurred to him, as he walked out to the field and felt a chill creep up from the asphalt, that he might not be returning home. He could get *his* in a comparatively peaceful little French village, or on a dark road in the middle of the night, or again, in the air, if the Flying Fortress was attacked by enemy night fighters. It was not the best policy—he smiled grimly to himself—to dwell upon such possibilities. Yet underneath the apprehension there was also a provocative sense of daring that he had not experienced in a very long time. A dangerous journey lay before him. He savored the growing conviction that he was *not afraid*.

Mitchell had occasionally glimpsed, as he drove by the airfield on the outskirts of Enid, planes lined up in battle formation, like grasshoppers on a broad leaf; but in comparison to the giant B-17 that loomed above him, the small Army planes back home seemed like impotent gliders.

The ten crew members about to enplane assembled under the wing, fresh from an evening briefing. The line chief introduced Mitchell casually to the captain, a rosy-faced stick of twenty-one or -two, known as the old man; the copilot, a lanky six-foot-three lieutenant with an easy grin; and the bombardier, a chubby, cheerful sandy-haired lieutenant. Next came the flight engineer, the radio operator, and the gunners: two waist, one tail, and an upper and lower ball.

Lieutenant Hal Beldon, the navigator, ambled up. He wore a perpetual frown on his sunburned face. He was twenty-five, going on ninety. "*Sylvia Sue* looks big from down here," he remarked, "but you'll see how cramped we get inside. It's like a sardine factory, without the sardines. Hubba, hubba!" He yawned elaborately. "I could sure do with more sack time. I just got back from a mission over Berlin this afternoon, a real bitch if there ever was one. We limped back on two engines, a shot-away horizontal stabilizer, a frozen landing gear; to top it all off, the ground crew found a live cannon shell in the right wing. We had to land at the emergency field over at Woodbridge. Our old man was a genius, though, made a belly landing that should have been filmed for Roosevelt and the Combined Chiefs of Staff. Only after we skidded to a smoky stop, shooting sparks, did the captain realize that his legs were peppered with flak." He raised his brows. "But that's typical. Something happens up there," he mused. "I dunno, you go outside yourself somehow—you almost become someone else—or you'd go Section Eight."

Mitchell nodded. "I know what you mean. I have a Cherokee Indian friend who maintains that during particular stress we're *all* capable of tuning in to some universal force that gives us additional power to rise above the condition that we're undergoing at the particular time."

"Yeah." Beldon passed a hand over weary eyes. "It's like that in a way. Sometimes you're tuned in to the enemy. You know what he's thinking and what maneuver he'll try next." Beldon clicked his teeth. "Come on, let's climb into my station; you'll be sitting with me," he said, gesturing to the rear of the bomb-bay doors. "Let me get one more look at *Sylvia Sue*." He backed off and looked over the curvaceous blonde painted on the fuselage. That's the old man's dream girl, copied out of *Esquire* magazine." The whistled through his teeth. "He says the real *Sylvia Sue* has better tits, but I don't see how. Hubba, hubba!"

Looking at the painting of the bronzed, long-legged beauty wearing the scantiest two-piece bathing suit that he had ever seen, Mitchell had to agree. Her nipples stood out like diamond nailheads.

Once inside the B-17, Mitchell could see that the interior was indeed extremely compact. Plywood doors, open to bulkheads separated each station. Up ahead, the radio operator, who was also assigned to check the German fighter frequencies, slid into his swivel seat. Above his head rested a flexible-point fifty-caliber machine gun, to be utilized in case of necessity, although he was usually busy with his headset and dials. Farther along, Mitchell could see the huge closed bomb-bay doors, and behind them, the engineer in the upper turret, then the small cockpit, crowded with instruments.

When Beldon sat down at his table, there was no extra room beside Mitchell's seat, which had been hastily bolted to the flooring. He was shown where to secure his parachute pack and how to strap himself into the low bucket seat. Once settled, Beldon murmured, "By the way, our facilities are on the primitive side. If you have to take a leak, use the condom attached to the funnel over there. Hubba, hubba!"

"Condom?" Mitchell laughed. "Didn't the guy who designed this plane understand anything about toilets?"

Beldon frowned even more than usual. "Believe me, sir, this is a big improvement over what we used to contend with. We had a hose that ran from that funnel to the outside. But at twenty-five thousand feet it's fifty below zero out there, and of course the damned line would freeze up. At lower altitudes it was okay, except the stuff would fly all over the plexiglas ball turret underneath the fuselage. You can imagine what effect this had on the disposition of the ball gunner inside! All he could see was a thick slick of yellow. Someone, bless 'em, came up with this arrangement, and it works."

In the cockpit, the pilot and copilot meticulously finished their preflight checks; then the pilot barked, "*Mesh one start one.*"

The copilot repeated the first routine operation, then continued as instructed, until all four engines were turning over. The plane throbbed, oscillated, shook, and groaned. The blasé crew was accustomed to the violent vibrations, but Mitchell was forced to close his mouth to keep his teeth from chattering.

*"Release parking brake."*

The copilot released tail wheel control locks to allow the pilot to turn the plane down the taxiway and onto the runway.

"There's no crosswind!" the pilot exclaimed with relief. Two missions back, a B-17-G had been literally blown off the runway.

The copilot called off the airspeeds, a task he would continue to perform until the plane was airborne. Even without bomb tonnage, it took the concentrated efforts of both pilot and copilot to maneuver a smooth, carefree takeoff.

The two inboard motors were set to idle at 800 R.P.M.'s, while the pilot lined the plane up on the runway. The copilot locked the tail wheel, all the while eyeing the instrument panel and paying special attention to the boost, rev, pressure, and temperature gauges. The pilot advanced the four throttle, over which the copilot would assume control as soon as maximum power was reached at 2500 R.P.M.'s. The pilot headed for the far end of the runway and lifted off at 150 m.p.h.

Once airborne, the pilot called, *"Gear up!"* and the copilot braked the pedals gently, enabling the wheels to stop spinning so that the landing gear would slide methodically into position in the wheel wells. When the temperature gauge reached 200 degrees, the copilot opened the cowl flaps to prevent further rise, and once the plane was climbing, brought the engine revs back to 2200. The pilot synchronized the props to 150 m.p.h. and 500 feet per minute rate of climb, and began a wide left-hand turn over the airfield below.

With Beldon bending over his charts, Mitchell relaxed, now that the vibrations had leveled off to a steady pace. He chortled as he read a poem laboriously inked above Beldon's table:

> Don't back the attack
>   By attacking a Wac
> Or riding the breast of a Wave.
>   But sit in the sand,
> And do it by hand.
>   Then buy bonds with the money you save!

Twenty minutes out, as the Channel Islands came into view over the right side of the plane, a bored, studied voice crackled over the intercom. "Pilot to navigator. Over."

"Navigator to pilot. Over."

"Pilot to navigator, we're going to be hitting the cold in about twenty min. Over."

"Roger." Beldon turned to Mitchell. "It's time to plug in your suit. When we shoot up to ten thousand feet, you'll need more warmth. When you finish, might as well snap in your oxygen equipment; we'll be going up to twenty-five thousand. The mask will be tight, but you'll get used to it."

"How long will we be up so high?" Mitchell asked, feeling a spurt of exhilaration from the pure oxygen.

"Until we're past Brest, a town on the outer tip of Brittany. After that, we'll be over safe water. We don't expect flak, but in case you do see puffs of black smoke out there, don't panic. A few cannon will be firing from below. The Krauts are accustomed to huge formations flying over, and eight hundred Forts sound like the Battle of Armageddon compared to only one pipsqueak." Beldon grinned over his habitual frown. "Flak don't pepper just the *sides* of a plane; it comes from all directions. So snap the two pieces of your overalls together like I'm doing with my suit—that is, if you ever want to

208

be a daddy. I've known guys whose balls looked like hamburger when we got back to base." Mitchell hastily complied.

The crew had been on oxygen for well over an hour when the pilot announced he was taking *Sylvia Sue* down to six thousand feet. They were safely over the Bay of Biscay, headed south toward the jutting-out coast of Spain.

When the lower altitude was reached, the crew took off the masks, which left strange oval marks around their eyes, over their cheeks, and down under their chins. Beldon shared a thermos of hot cocoa with Mitchell. When he was not peering over his charts or making notations in his logbook—which he was required to do every four minutes—he told shaggy dog jokes from his high-school days. The pair avoided serious conversation, and from their polite attitudes might have been sharing space in a commercial airliner.

The radio operator stretched his back and buzzed the intercom. "R.O. to navigator. Over."

"Navigator. Over."

"R.O. to navigator. Pretty smooth trip. The old man's a good pilot, but I can't wait to get back. This is my twenty-fifth mission, and my tour of duty is finished. It'll be London tomorrow—that is, if London is still there!"

Beldon laughed wryly. "You stupid son of a bitch," he said affectionately to his best friend. "You'll be in Piccadilly Circus, and I'll be over Berlin again. I still have four more missions before I can get laid properly."

A voice interrupted. "Pilot to R.O. Over."

"R.O. to pilot. Over."

"Cut the crap! Record the drop, Beldon. We should have documentation to prove we've carried out this mission."

"Yes, sir. Roger." Beldon pushed a switch that activated the K-24 British camera—pointed through the buttom of the fuselage—which automatically took photographs at ten-second intervals. Satisfied that the camera was working perfectly, he pushed the button to await further instructions.

"Pilot to all gunners: On command, test fire. We're almost over the Gascony coast. Over."

"Roger."

Each station received the same instructions. On count, there was a simultaneous burst of fire from above, from below, and from the sides, causing the aircraft to vibrate wildly again. Mitchell shivered. "What's the purpose of the test, if we don't have bombs?" he asked.

Beldon laughed when he looked at Mitchell's stricken face. "Routine. If we *do* run into night fighters, we know we're operable."

From the lower ball turret, the gunner studied the dark terrain below. The run had been carefully scheduled when the moon was new, yet the sky gave off a faint glow as the plane gently dipped lower and lower. It was difficult to believe that the world was at war, the gunner thought, the countryside looked so serene. The trip now almost seemed like a pleasure tour. He crossed himself. "Holy Mary, Mother of God," he prayed, "let the Frog civvie land safely." Then he smiled and added, "Also, please let us get home in one piece!"

The pilot looked below. "Pilot to navigator. Over."

"Navigator to pilot. Over."

"Aren't we about at target? Over."

"Yes, sir. I'll get the Frog civvie ready. Roger." Beldon realized what he had said and blushed a furious shade of purple. He looked at Mitchell apologetically. "I'm sorry, sir, I didn't mean to be disrespectful."

Mitchell was amused. "I've been called a lot worse things than a Frog civvie," he quipped.

Beldon assumed the role of dispatcher, got up

quickly, and opened the hatch, letting in a blast of chilled night air. "Better secure your 'chute," he advised, as Mitchell ran his hands over the pack on his lower back, which was—thankfully—buckled tight and secure. "Drop clean when you bail out, delay as long as possible, count to ten, then pull your ripcord handle," he admonished, then bent over his charts again, making a last-minute calculation. He rasped into the intercom, "Navigator to pilot. Over."

"Pilot to navigator. Over."

"Ready for primary target. Over."

"Roger."

Mitchell leaned over the navigator's seat. "What's the primary target?"

Beldon grinned. "You, sir. The secondary target is the leaflet clusters." He held out his hand. "By the way, Merry Christmas."

Mitchell placed his forefinger through the big ripcord handle. "Merry Christmas."

"Get ready," Beldon croaked, checking his location for the last time. "Set." He counted to five. *"Go!"*

Mitchell jumped wide to avoid contact with the hatch frame and braced himself for the violent slipstream that emanated from the aircraft; the sudden impact was more intense than he had been trained to expect. The icy wind hit his face, and he felt as if he had been slapped by some giant hand.

He began to count. *"One."*

When he felt the indescribable sensation of free-fall, he corrected his position to keep himself from somersaulting willy-nilly through space.

*"Two."*

His instructor's voice came back to him. "It's at this point that some guys go off in their pants. It all has to do with the rush of air, the anxiety of the moment, and the curious awareness of falling." Mitchell smiled and, for some reason, thought of Belle Trune.

*"Three."*

Now, with the wind whistling eerily about him, he was surrounded by complete darkness as the sliver of a moon, which had provided luminescence, was obscured by a cloud.

*"Four."*

He looked up, half expecting to see the girders of the 125-foot practice tower; a familiar sight at Hightstown.

*"Five."*

His forefinger was still clamped through the ripcord handle.

*"Six. Seven."*

He knew one moment of sudden, terrible panic; then, as perspiration soaked his armpits, his instructor's voice came back again. "Don't make the mistake of judging time. Remember, time is accelerated during free fall. It can easily seem like five minutes when it's really only a couple of seconds. Keep your bearings."

*"Eight. Nine."*

One more count to go. He held his breath.

*"Ten."*

Still looking upward, Mitchell was conscious of the sudden glorious flare of camouflaged silk, and a moment later his body was jerked violently upward. There was a flash of pain in the groin area, and his arms felt as if they had been pulled from their sockets. But the huge canopy opened like a fantastic gray-and-green surrealistic flower with giant scalloped petals. He began to sway gently back and forth as he floated majestically downward.

An enormous sense of relief almost overpowered him. His eyes smarted. The air was warmer now, and he was taken aback by the utter silence that surrounded him. It was as if he were the last man on earth, completely alone, gliding gently downward, downward, until his feet disappeared in white mist. Encased in an opaque world, he felt moisture from the clouds condense on his face.

His heart returned to normal rhythm now that the enormous silk mushroom had opened, but then became erratic again when he could not see the earth below. What if fog covered the ground and he could not see to break his fall? Both legs could easily be broken. He could, at the very least, crack an ankle. What if he landed in a tree and could not detach himself from his parachute rigging? What if he landed in the village square or on a rooftop? Landing strategy was included in Exercise Six. He had only taken five lessons.

He was slipping wetly through the mist now, and he fervently pressed a glove against the St. Christopher medal. Although it was very dark below, he could discern different shades of gray that marked various fields. A black square lay directly below. He searched his memory. Ah, yes, a black field meant newly plowed earth. About a mile to the right he saw a momentary glimmer of light; three flashes meant that Paul was waiting. It seemed like an eternity before he saw the light glow again: one-two-three, pause, one-two-three. God bless that navigator; he had dropped him exactly on target!

# 12

## No Place to Go

*Mitchell took a deep breath, his senses sharpened, and he was ready to roll on impact.*

The plowed field loomed up, and as he descended the last fifty feet he relaxed his body as he had been taught at Hightstown. Miraculously, he was on his feet a second later. He was prepared to be dragged a few feet by the wind, until the parachute completely collapsed, but impact was so gentle that the giant white flower had already collapsed behind him. Quickly he unbuckled the parachute and gathered up the rigging lines, then, reaching the deflated canopy, swept up the voluminous smooth silk awkwardly in his arms. From the middle of the field, he slowly made his way to a nearby tree.

His heartbeat was returning to normal now, but he was still apprehensive, nervous, agitated. Should he start to walk? Pierre's soft voice came back: "If there is a signal, Paul will find you. If there is no signal, bury the chute, take an azimuth on your compass, and walk north about a mile to a farmhouse with a green light in the window."

214

He stood under the tree, feeling very much alone. There was no sound. What if the flashes of light concerned another operation, not his? He leaned back against the rough bark of the tree, sensing despair. Alone, he was vulnerable to outside forces. If *les Boches* had seen his parachute, a platoon of soldiers would already be on their way to the area.

He had taken out his compass and held it up to the moon, when he heard a low voice out of the darkness mutter, "*Carmen.*"

He automatically whispered back, "*Don Jose.*" How ridiculous the passwords sounded in the stillness of the field!

A black form separated itself from the darkness and hugged him. "My name is Paul. We are glad to see you, Michel Bayard. Take off your coveralls." Paul started to fold the parachute, and after he had stuffed the acres of soft silk into the coveralls and placed the bundle beside a rough stone fence, he hissed, "I will retrieve this tomorrow, but now we must leave very quickly. Follow me."

They came out into a clearing. The ground fog was lifting as Paul wheeled a tandem bicycle onto a nearby dirt road. Mitchell claimed the rear seat. "We must go only by back roads," Paul murmured. "It is after curfew."

Memories flooded over Mitchell. The last time that he had ridden a double bike was many years ago, when he had taken Belle Trune for a ride on a Sunday. Taking the section road that led by the Chenovicks', they had finally strolled hand-in-hand under Bella's blooming peach trees and made love in a haystack in the shadow of the old windmill.

"We have only two kilometers to travel," Paul interjected, disturbing Mitchell's reverie. "Permit me to pedal; you must be exhausted."

"I am not tired," Mitchell replied.

"I am trying to place your patois," Paul said thoughtfully.

"It is rather difficult," Mitchell replied smoothly. "Because of my small speech impediment, I sometimes chew my words." That was what Pierre had told him to say if questioned about his accent.

"So, that explains it," Paul replied. "I am very conscious of regional brogues because I was a speech teacher before the war. After the occupation, I had to come back to my father's farm."

"You will teach again, Paul."

"God—and France—willing!" He steered the bicycle down a small path, which led near a cottage where a dim light illuminated the luxuriant thatch that grew down over the eaves. "*Entrez,*" he said warmly, pushing the door open. The men examined each other. The Frenchman was about thirty-five, Mitchell judged, and he had dark hair, green eyes, and an enormous square lantern jaw that just kept him from being handsome. He had great personal warmth, which Mitchell had sensed in the darkness. Paul shook his head and grinned, showing bad teeth, which he tried to hide with his hand. "It is good to have you here at last. With you arriving at Christmas, it is an omen."

"*Merci, mon ami,* I hope so. A *good* omen!"

The cottage contained two rooms, with an enormous kitchen taking up two-thirds of the space. Walls were whitewashed below a heavy-timbered ceiling, and a welcome heat emanated from a large baking oven built into a blackened chimney. A rough-hewn table, two benches, and a rocking chair—all worn with age—and a few wooden crates completed the furnishings. One red candle burned.

"Madeleine!" Paul called.

"*Oui?*" The voice came from the bedroom, and a moment later a pleasant, round-faced woman of ample girth appeared. Her wooden shoes clacked across the kitchen as she held out her hand, slowly appraising Mitchell all the while. "Welcome to this poor house," she said formally. "Have you eaten?"

Mitchell nodded. "Very early."

"At least, then," she replied softly, "have some bread and cheese. We have nothing else. We could not even find a pidgeon for Christmas." She spread a bit of gray homespun on the table, and, while Paul fetched a huge loaf of bread, longer and thicker than his arm, she removed a pail from a cupboard and set the table.

Mitchell bowed his head a moment and made the sign of the cross, then ate a spoonful of the soft white cheese and grinned. "Ah, Madame, the *fromage blanc* is excellent." He had not tasted this sweet mixture in ten years, and, looking at the kitchen and Paul and Madeleine, he felt a fresh rush of nostalgia. In a way, it was almost as if he had never left France; old habits came back to him. He fished in his pocket for a penknife and cut a chunk of bread from the huge golden loaf in the middle of the table, then helped himself to sweet butter and berry jam.

"The bread is not so good." Madeleine grimaced. "Wheat flour is precious. Since the Occupation, the government has decreed that millers must add two percent rye flour to the white."

Paul shook his head. "I think it is more like six percent."

Madeleine nodded. "Before Hitler, black bread was only for convicts."

Paul opened a bottle without ceremony and poured a glass of red wine for Mitchell, then reached into the back of the bread oven and removed a small, compact short-wave radio receiver-transmitter. He set his pocket watch on the table, placed the earphones over his head, then connected the batteries. Pierre had schooled Mitchell in the use of a similar model.

Paul wheeled the dial and leaned forward. "The BBC

is coming in clear as a bell tonight." He began to print letters on a pad of foolscap. After a few moments he put aside the pad. "The rest," he said, "is news." He listened intently, and a smile broke over his face. "Ah, the Red Army is gaining strength. They will liberate the Ukraine and Crimea yet!" He listened a few more moments, switched off the set, removed the earphones, and replaced the radio in the oven. "I wish I could have been a mouse at the Teheran Conference. Roosevelt, Churchill and Stalin must have agreed on establishing many new fronts to crush the enemy from all sides."

"Perfect!" Madeleine exclaimed. "And their war machine annihilated. Never again can they make war. Germany first, then Japan." She looked up. "My father fought for France during the First World War and died at Château-Thierry."

Mitchell was about to reply that he had also been a part of that operation, but a note of caution intervened. Certainly some Frenchmen had perished there, but the main action had come from the United States Marines. He had no intention of raising doubts in their minds. Besides, it was at Château-Thierry that he had left his regiment and had gone AWOL to Paris and met Françoise, and that was not the proudest episode of his life. "I am very tired," he said at last.

"Of course!" Paul sympathized. "Madeleine has made your bed. I hope you don't mind sleeping in the stable. At least there will be privacy."

Madeline gathered up a quilt. "You could sleep here by the oven, but we rise at four. You would get little sleep, because it is past one in the morning."

Paul laughed. "Besides, the horse, Estelle, is a pleasant soul, old and very gentle. She has been with us for so many years, she is family."

Paul picked up the kerosene lantern, and Madeleine took a pillow from the cupboard, and they guided Mitchell to the rear of the house. Estelle, a high wooden trundle bed situated at her feet, was sleeping on her side. She did not open an eye as they came into the stable. Paul lighted another kerosene lantern and, shaking Mitchell's hand briefly, said good night. Madeleine repeated the ritual.

Mitchell was awakened at dawn by a series of rude thumps that shook his bed. Estelle was staring at him intently; then, as if turning exhibitionistic, she answered a call of nature. Mitchell laughed. It was all so incongruous; here he was, deep in France, sharing a bedroom with a very rude horse. This would make a great story to tell, if he lived long enough to tell about it. Before he went to sleep, he thought of the huge, decorated tree that woud be standing in the living room at the Trenton clapboard in Angel.

After a simple breakfast prepared by Madeleine, Paul came in from the fields, his wooden shoes rattling over the floor. "I have notified London that the Otter has arrived safely."

"Otter?" Mitchell frowned.

"Your code name."

"Any further instructions?"

"*Non.* In a few days instructions will be transmitted by short wave." Paul smiled encouragingly. "I must go to the grist mill in the village this morning to bring back some flour. I could use some help. Do you have an identity card?"

Mitchell fished in his pockets and handed the paper to Paul. "A fine job," the latter said. "First-rate work. Have another cup of tea while I hitch up Estelle."

Plaisance-du-Gers had changed not at all from Mitchell's memory. The stone houses with moldy tiled roofs, and the winding streets like mazes, seemed like detailed photographs taken by a tourist. And he knew that Paul and he, perched high on the cart that featured wheels six feet high, were part of the picturesque townscape.

He peered at his hands. Although his fingernails had been suitably broken by Felicia at Royal Gorge, he had no calluses. But he doubted that he would be asked to turn his palms upward for inspection.

Paul halted Estelle at a small intersection. "I'll go on to the grist mill, Michel," he said easily. "You have a doctor's appointment in a few moments. The office is at the rear of the courtyard. I'll pick you up in half an hour."

"You could have told me," Mitchell said under his breath.

"*Pardon.* I forgot."

Mitchell knew, of course, that Paul had not forgotten—another precaution. He could hear Pierre say: "Keep all information to yourself. Never give your plans out to anyone in advance." He climbed down from his seat and ambled into the courtyard of the old red stone building, which had been dexterously fashioned.

Mitchell found a door, simply marked PHYSICIAN, and found himself in a small foyer that held only one short bench, upon which rested an old woman and a baby in a wicker basket. She wore a shapeless maroon dress. A white, starched lace cap was pulled down over her forehead. She did not look up as he came into the room, but continued to crochet. The baby was sleeping, its thumb stuck securely into its pursed mouth. But there was something strange about the old lady that bothered Mitchell. All was not as it appeared to be; his instincts told him to be wary. A few moments later a woman in white opened a little window. "Monsieur Bayard?"

"*Oui.*"

"*Entrez.*"

He went into a small office. The woman, he saw at once, was very beautiful. She was tiny, but perfectly proportioned, from the top of her shiny hair, which was

220

drawn back severely from her face, to her neatly leather-shod feet. He looked down at his clumsy wooden shoes and felt inferior.

Her eyes were a cold, pale blue. "I was listening to the radio just before you came in, Monsieur. They were playing the overture to *Carmen*."

He nodded. "Her lover, Don Jose, is my favorite operatic character."

She relaxed somewhat, although her back was still erect. "You have something for me, Monsieur Bayard?" She glanced at an adjoining door. "I will excuse you."

He returned a few moments later with the silver tube wrapped in a handkerchief. She smiled slightly for the first time. *"Merci, Monsieur Bayard."*

"Whom do I have the pleasure of addressing?"

"They call me Lise." She paused. "You should not keep Paul waiting."

Although her French was faultless, instinct told him that she belonged to another nationality. Wouldn't it be ironic if she also, was an American? They could be two people in an alien land, pretending to be someone else.

*"Adieu,"* she said.

*"Adieu."* He went into the foyer. The old woman did not look up from her fancy-work. He examined her again, noticing the placement of her long skirts, and suddenly he knew what had bothered him from the beginning. She was holding a Sten gun firmly between her legs.

He waited inside the door until he heard the clomp of Estelle's hooves and the rattle of the cart; then he rejoined Paul, whose jacket was dusted with flour.

"How did you like the doctor?"

"She's very beautiful. Is she a general practioner, or is she a specialist?"

Paul shrugged his shoulders. "I only know that she is not a medical doctor but a metallurgist."

Mitchell sighed. A *metallurgist*? It was no use trying to unravel the threads of a story in which he was only a minor character. He had come to France to accomplish a mission. His work was over. "What do we do now, Paul?"

His companion smiled, hiding his bad teeth with his hand. "Unload the flour for Madeleine's bread, then go to the fields to work. The millet is ready for harvesting."

"I am ready to help, of course," Mitchell replied slowly, "but—when can I leave?"

"That I do not know." Paul shook his head. "Each night I will listen to the BBC. Certainly a message will come soon."

Suddenly Mitchell felt afraid. "I hope so, *mon cher*," he said with much more enthusiasm than he felt.

That night, his back aching from unaccustomed field work, Mitchell ate generous portions of meatless stew and bread, washed down with raw-tasting burgundy. Then he got up and stretched his arms to the ceiling. "May I take the bicycle into the village? I am very restless."

"Have one drink at The Golden Apple, and return well before curfew," Paul replied, admonishingly.

Mitchell sauntered into the crowded bistro and ordered a cognac, knowing, of course, that it would be diluted—and, he reasoned, it was better not to know with what. Still, as he sipped the brandy, a warm glow suffused his stomach, not as warm a glow as he had remembered, but a glow nonetheless. He glanced casually around the small room crowded with the working class, and was pleased because he blended with the milieu so well. He felt very much at home. In a peculiar way, it was as if the furniture store and Enid, Oklahoma, had never existed.

He rolled a cigarette with one hand, the way Pierre had taught him to do, lighted the ruffled end, and puffed a moment as he became oriented to the room. Hunched forms, all with weatherbeaten, stoic faces showing wan traces of malnutrition, lined the bar. There was a vaguely familiar face among the group—the bareheaded man at the end of the bar, who was dreamily looking into space. He spoke, nodded to a companion, then laughed and turned back to his beer, a thin smile still playing around his lips. A scene from childhood came back to Mitchell: Luke and he both sixteen were tossing a ball back and forth in the little clearing near the pecan orchard. Then a later scene, almost duplicating the first, flashed into his brain: they were again tossing the ball back and forth during a Christmas holiday; but this time, they were twenty-five. He glimpsed Luke's profile as he reached high up in the air for the ball, which he triumphantly grasped in his catcher's mitt, and then turned, laughing. He carried the same expression on his face that the man at the end of the bar had displayed when he had turned back from his friend.

Mitchell felt the skin on the back of his neck prickle, and involuntarily shivered. The man looked to be in his mid-twenties, and his resemblance to Luke at the same age was unmistakable. It was like going back in time. Mentally, Mitchell reconstructed his Heron family tree. The senior Luke and his brother, Edward, who had participated in the Cherokee Strip Run, were Grandmother Lavenia's only children, he knew that. Could there be another branch of Herons in Minneapolis, some cousin, perhaps, on his grandfather's side, who had a boy who carried the family resemblance? But what would he be doing in Plaisance-du-Gers?

Mitchell shook his head. How ridiculous! This man was a Frenchman: his clothes; his dialect, which Mitchell had heard vaguely when he had spoken to his friend,

223

were pure Gallic. He stood up and nonchalantly ambled to the lavatory and, as he passed the young man, jolted his back slightly with his arm. "*Pardon,*" he apologized.

"*Oui, Monsieur,*" the man growled, and continued in French, "Watch where you're going."

Mitchell controlled his expression and looked quickly into the man's face. It was exactly as if he were looking into the young Luke's face. He went into the lavatory and washed his hands carefully, his mind going back twenty-five years. Both Luke and he had been in the service in France in 1918, and had chanced upon each other at Château-Thierry. He remembered that Luke had laughingly told him that the French fillies were much more passionate than the girls back home, and had related some intimate details of his sex life that he referred to as "the French technique"—which to Mitchell did not seem all that different from the experiences that he had encountered back in Angel. But Luke was notoriously sexual—at least, liked to give that impression—in those days when he was just out of his teens.

Mitchell took his place back in the bar, and now and again stole surreptitious glances at the man, with whom he now felt a strange kinship. Was it possible that one of the girls that Luke had bedded had conceived his child? The age would be about right, he figured. Or was this man the product of some genetic trick? He had heard that certain people resembled each other so closely that they could be taken for relatives, and everyone was supposed to have a counterpart, a twin, somewhere in the world. An old wives' tale, he had always thought, but now, with proof positive almost at his very elbow . . .

The bartender took a dinner of turnips and carrots to the back table, and his wife, a gaunt-faced wraith with dark, stringy hair, took his place behind the bar. Starting at the rear, she checked each man's glass, refilling

224

several on the way, and humorously nudged the slackers into ordering another watered drink. Now and then she threw her husband a penetrating, chastising look that plainly said that if he did not look after business they would be out in the street. When she reached Mitchell, she looked into his face, frowned, and then glanced quickly down the bar at the man, then back to Mitchell, then shrugged. The thought struck him that, of course, if the man resembled Luke, then he must also resemble *him*.

A sudden hush fell over the habitués of the café, and Mitchell swung around easily on the bar stool. A German lieutenant, accompanied by an aide, a sergeant with a cruel face, stood at the front door.

"Identity cards—out!" the sergeant exclaimed in a hoarse voice; to a trained ear, the thick patois proclaimed that he hailed from Berlin.

Everyone in the café stood up, and Mitchell felt a strange composure settle over him; he was not nervous, and even his heartbeat was peculiarly steadfast. He could have held out his hands in front of his face, and there would not have been the slightest tremor. Pierre would have congratulated him on his poise.

Mitchell nonchalantly checked the exits with his eyes. A soldier, holding a rifle, was positioned at each entrance. The ritual began. The sergeant stood briefly before each man, took his card, and, in turn, handed it to the lieutenant, who compared the photograph to the subject and checked the official stamps. Occasionally he would ask a man to remove a cap, or, in one case, the sergeant shone a flashlight into a unshaven face. Scant attention was paid to elderly men; the younger the man, the closer the scrutiny.

With slow determination, the little procession made its way down the bar, until at last the lieutenant was standing in front of Mitchell, who found himself gazing into the eyes of the most handsome man he had ever

225

seen. He could have been what women in America called a "matinee idol." But the most surprising quality about his male beauty was the fact that he seemed completely unaware of it; it was as if he put on his face every morning the same way that he donned his uniform. The lieutenant took the card from the sergeant, perused the photograph a long moment, searched Mitchell's face, seemingly going over every pore, then flipped the document back to him.

In that instant Mitchell's heart skipped a beat, and as they moved down the bar he felt a slow blush start up from his neck. His face flamed until he thought the skin would sizzle. Had he flushed so guiltily while the officer was looking him in the eye, he would have been pulled out of the line; an innocent man would not have colored.

Having finished scrutinizing identity cards, the sergeant held the door open for the lieutenant; the habitués resumed their former positions, while the hubbub of voices took up interrupted conversations once more.

The proprietress shook her head. "Twice tonight they have come," she murmured to an old man next to Mitchell, "and it is still early."

The old man nodded. "They are looking for someone special, then, perhaps a sky man."

She filled his glass quickly. "Shut up!" she whispered, then stood back and lighted a black cigarette, now and then looking up and down the bar with a practiced eye. Mitchell saw the man at the end of the bar get up from his stool and wave. "Good night, Jean," the proprietress called as he left by the rear door.

Mitchell wanted desperately to follow the man, to catch up with him in the street and start a conversation, just to hear his voice. The idea was preposterous, of course; the man might take him for a member of the Gestapo, and he could end up a corpse in an alley. Strangers, these days, could not be trusted.

In his mind's eye, Mitchell tried to remember what Françoise had looked like. He recalled a fluff of reddish-blond hair. The slimness of her figure had suggested malnutrition. She had a gamin quality, or at least he had thought so then. He remembered something else: she was from Alsace. This brought back a funny story that she had told him about the force-fed Strasbourg geese producing the best pâté de foie gras in the world. Funny how little incidents came back. She was ashamed of her lingerie, which was faded and torn, and one day he had bartered two tins of corned beef in his knapsack for a pale pink silk chemise. She had cried with delight at this luxury and had thrown her arms around him, promising him a fabulous Sunday in bed. Had he loved her? Or was his blood so hot in those days of his youth that only her body held attraction?

He thought of the little room—an attic, really—and the eiderdown mattress, so worn in places that, with their strenuous lovemaking one day, the feather stuffing literally flew out into the room. He smiled, recollecting how the feathers had settled down on their naked bodies until they were covered with a white snowlike mantle. How moist and warm her body had seemed, and how she left him gasping and trembling all over. Closing his eyes, he could feel once more her fingers tracing butterfly wings over his back as he made love to her with all of his young strength and breathless virility.

He sighed and opened his eyes. He was back in the noisy café, sitting at the bar, looking at his own reflection in the glass. Where was Françoise now? Was she still slender, or had middle age added poundage around her waist, causing her glorious breasts to drop? Was her hair gray, or had she dyed it red? Did she have all of her teeth? He shuddered. It was no use going back. Speculation was dangerous; the past was too close. He had to get out of the bar. He shrugged his shoulders carelessly, downed the drink, threw a five-franc note on the top of the bar, and left abruptly, hoping that the proprietress would not think it strange that a working-man had left so large a tip. But he could not stay in the place one moment longer, or he would lose control.

By the time he reached the street, he was trembling. He slouched into an alley, then held his back erect against a brick wall until he was once more himself. He suspected, in that moment of sudden revelation, thinking about Françoise, with the mists of the past so near, that the man who had been drinking beer so calmly at the bar was his own son!

Why had he not tried to find Françoise after the war was over? He was confused. It was painful going back a quarter of a century to the vagabond he was then. Suddenly he remembered that he *had* tried to find the address once afterward; it was in the rue de Boulogne, which was undergoing restoration. She had moved. Yes, that was it. The concierge said that she had moved. Why had he not tried to trace her further? He could not now remember; it was probably only a momentary desire to see her. He might have been broke and hungry—there were many lean periods in those days—and, truthfully, he was probably horny as well. She had been marvelous in bed. What would have happened had he found her with a baby?

Mitchell shook his head. Perhaps he was hallucinating and had only imagined the resemblance between the man at the bar and himself; yet the proprietress had also noticed the similarity of their features.

He hesitated in the middle of the sidewalk, debating on whether to turn back; then he shook his head and continued slowly down the street. For a long moment he had forgotten that he was in an enemy-occupied country.

He found his bicycle where he had left it, in back of the café, then glanced at his pocket watch. There was plenty of time to get home before curfew. He headed down the meandering dirt road to the farm, pedaling leisurely, thinking of that striking-looking man back in the café.

To the right, far in the distance, he noticed a rosy glow which startled him. Sometimes in Oklahoma, when atmospheric conditions were right, the Northern Lights could be seen playing over a huge expanse of sky. How his mother had laughed when she had told him, as a boy, that he was seeing a rainbow at night, a rainbow that played over the horizon near Ponca City! He knew where Ponca City was because the family had gone to rodeos at the 101 Ranch, owned by old Bill Cody, Buffalo Bill. Once, too, he had tried to hide under the bronze skirts of the statue of "The Pioneer Woman."

But in all of the years spent in France, Mitchell had never seen or heard of the aurora borealis. *How very peculiar!* he thought, watching the glow; then, as he followed a twist in the road and rounded an apple orchard, he saw that it was the roof and stables of Paul's farm, flaming up into the sky, that had caused the glow. At that moment he heard an automobile motor behind him and skittered off the road, hiding his bike among the apple trees. The car zoomed past, but he recognized four German uniforms. He knew with a terrible certainty that he did not belong anywhere in the vicinity.

Feeling calmer than he had ever felt before, he pushed the bicycle onto the road and pedaled to the nearby crossroad and took a little-used path over a rising hill. At the apex, he could see the farmland below. Four automobiles were parked in the clearing by Paul's barn, and flames were shooting from the windows of the house. He collected his thoughts. Pierre had given no instructions about how to proceed if he lost contact with Paul. He knew that there was a "friendly farmhouse" a kilometer or so from his landing site, but, since Paul had met him, he could not ascertain the correct direction. Damn Pierre! He had apparently thought of everything, and yet . . . Lise was the only other contact left.

Below, and to the right, lay a mow of freshly gathered hay. He buried his bicycle, then slumped down into the fragrant, sweet-sour-smelling stuff. The cognac that he had consumed at the café came to his aid, dulling his senses, and he slept.

He dreamed that he was back on the threshing crew in the old days, going from field to field under the relentless June Oklahoma sun. His mouth was parched, and he was very, very hungry. Then he saw his mother, Priscilla, peering at him from the screen door at the Heron clapboard, old and half out of her mind, and he began to cry and could not stop. . . .

He was awakened by the throaty grumble of a bevy of doves, and he saw that the sun was situated well above the horizon. His face felt strangely tight, and when he looked at his reflection in the timepiece glass he saw that his cheeks were stained with the damp chaff that had adhered to his face. He must have cried in his sleep. He was ravenously hungry. He climbed the slight hill and saw that the farmhouse below still smoldered under the gaze of two German soldiers. His skin grew clammy as he wondered what had happened to Paul and Madeleine. He touched his breast and felt the comforting St. Christopher medal. "Help me," he murmured. "Help me."

Mitchell tied his wooden shoes on the handlebars of the bicycle and, as nonchalantly as if he made the trip every day, took the road into the village, pedaling slowly. He half expected to run into a platoon of Germans at every twist in the road. The sky was as blue as a piece of thin chambray; yellow and purple nettles were scattered by the roadside; and here and there in the pastures, snow-white cows with peculiarly twisted horns chewed soft cuds.

The village looked at peace—yet underneath, he knew, a foment of emotion smoldered. He was not alone; there were perhaps ten or twelve other cyclists on the streets—some, like himself, pedaling in their stocking feet, their heavy wooden shoes tied over the handlebars. Along with two other cyclists, he wheeled calmly by the Prefecture of Police—now German—headquarters. Through the open double door, he saw his coveralls, bulging out at the seams, and the white silk parachute, resting half on the table and half on the floor. So Paul had neglected to retrieve the package from the field. Stupidity, utter stupidity! Also, out of the corner of his eye, he had glimpsed a small black box—Paul's short-wave radio/transmitter? He turned into the street that led by the doctor's office and parked his bicycle by a small rose-covered arbor. The rear door at the end of the courtyard, marked PHYSICIAN, was locked. He knocked lightly once, twice, thrice.

A woman with a bouffant hairdo peeked out of the open window next door. "The doctor went away yesterday," she said in a voice with a touch of Alsace. "A death in the family."

"When will she return?"

"*She*?" the woman questioned. "Oh, you mean the nurse, Lise?" She looked guardedly about, and pursed her lips. "She was only hired by the doctor a few days ago; now she has taken off—some way to Toulouse, with a man." She winked. "I hope so. In these times there is so little romance."

"*Merci, Madame*," Mitchell replied carelessly. "I was only going to say hello to her from an old schoolmate." He waved cheerfully and went out of the courtyard the same way that he had entered.

What would he do now? He was certain that in the

village there were many members of the Resistance, but how could they be reached? Apparently everyone covered his tracks very well indeed. Mitchell needed to reconnoiter; obviously, he could not continue to pedal aimlessly about the village, and the café would not open for several hours.

Then he remembered Pierre's instructions, and he pointed his bicycle toward the church. Although it was early in the morning, there was a Requiem Mass; evidently a village father had passed away, because the pews were filled to overflowing. Mitchell patiently followed the ritual, then, knowing that there was safety in numbers, joined the mourners in the funeral procession. He blended in perfectly with the other working-class men erratically queued up behind the glass-enclosed hearse pulled by two gaunt white horses.

Footsore, he returned from the cemetery, retrieved his bicycle at the rectory, and bought some hard rolls at a bakery. He was on his way back to the haystack when he heard the scratchy strains of Bizet's *Carmen* emanating from a watchmaker's shop. He sauntered into the store, where a twelve-year-old boy was winding a portable Victrola. In the rear, the proprietor, a heavy-set man with several sets of jowls, was machine-rolling cigarettes. He got up slowly. "Good morn," he said gravely.

Mitchell nodded. "Hearing the music in the street," he said evenly, "brought back many memories. I love opera."

The man nodded with sudden interest. "My favorite character is Carmen."

"I'm fond of Don Jose."

"Etienne," the man said, "go into the back room." When the boy left, his attitude changed and he rushed forward. "We thought we had lost you in the fire."

"What of Paul and Madeleine?"

"*They* got them!" His jowls shook with fury. "An informer found the parachute, and all the farms in the area were searched. They might still have escaped, but Paul was repairing the radio. Madeleine barely had time to set fire to the house as a signal for you not to return." He looked out the window. "This shop may not be safe much longer. We must get you far away. In a few hours the hunt will intensify. There is already a price on your head."

Mitchell smiled wanly. "Such as it is."

The man held out his hand. "My name is Georges," he said quickly, and went on as if he himself was being pursued. "Luck rides on your coattail, Michel Bayard. I saw you in the café and recognized your face from a photograph that Lisa had shown me. Thank God I had the old Bizet recording, and thank God, you were wandering around on the bicycle. Upon such things as this, lives hang. By now I would have had to go looking for you, which would have been a great risk. There are many collaborators. We could have both ended up—and still may, unless we are careful—strung up by our . . . thumbs." He sighed. "Now we will start the alternative plan in motion."

"Where are Paul and Madeleine now?" Mitchell asked suddenly.

"I only know they have been taken for questioning. They *know* Lise, and that is why she left, but they do not know about my being connected with the Underground. I have known them all of their lives, but they think of me only as Georges the watchmaker." He shook his head. "It is so complicated. Each of us knows a little; none of us know much. If we are taken, we cannot betray what we do not know."

"What of Lise?" Mitchell asked.

Georges smiled. "I do not know her very well. She came here a few days ago to assist the orthopedist, who is, incidentally, a collaborator."

"But isn't it dangerous for her to be in the same office with a German sympathizer?"

233

*"Non, non!"* Georges exclaimed. "A perfect cover. Who would suspect her? That is very clever. If Paul and Madeleine inform about Lise, which they will probably be forced to do, the Germans will believe that the good doctor is also in the Resistance"—he smiled suddenly—"and he will be carted away for interrogation. He will never be able to convince them that he is innocent." He chuckled. "So it will work out, it will work out!" He paused and picked up a sign that read SHUT, which he placed in the window front. "Etienne has the cart ready in the rear street. We now go south to Tarbes. If we had an automobile, it would be a quick journey, but by cart it will take hours. Do you have an identity card?"

Mitchell nodded. "I should tell you also that I have twenty thousand francs."

"Good. It may be that the money will come in handy as your escape is prepared. I have almost nothing except what change there is in my cash box. Come, let us go." He locked the front door, pulled down the shade in the front window, and led Mitchell through a back room filled with clocks in various stages of repair, through the back door into the street.

Etienne held the reins of the horse lightly in his hands. In the back of the cart a grandfather's clock was wrapped snugly in burlap, but not so tightly that its face could not be seen. "If we are stopped," Georges said, "we are delivering merchandise to a firm in Tarbes."

They climbed into the front, Etienne strapped the old horse on the flanks, and the journey was begun. Later they stopped by a stream and ate bread and soft cheese and shared a small bottle of wine. And as the long golden twilight descended on the countryside, they took a little-used dirt path off the main thoroughfare, just wide enough to accommodate the cart, and stopped before an old building.

"This is your new home, Michel Bayard." Georges

fished in the back of the cart for a package, which he handed to Mitchell. "Here is a change of clothing." He removed an official-looking document from his coat. "This is your transfer paper. You will work here in the old furniture factory for Jacques Beaufils, the foreman. He is one of us." He held out his hand. "Good luck, *mon cher*."

Mitchell shook his hand formally. "Thank you for all you've done, Georges. Until we meet again, then." They embraced, and he took the package and opened the back door to the old building. The familiar smell of sawdust filled his nostrils with nostalgia. Suddenly he felt as if he were ten years old and back in Angel in his father's cabinet shop.

# 13

## Born-Before-Sunrise

*It was a blustery, rainy day; January 12, 1944*

Sam went out on the balcony of the small suite at the Shoreham Hotel and took a long breath, trying to expel the cigarette fumes from the party inside. He was tired, and Washington was only the first stop on an exhausting train tour that would take him from Philadelphia to New York, Denver, Seattle, and Los Angeles. When he had complained to the publicity girl, she had retorted that he'd be going to forty cities if it was peacetime. He would be appearing on as many as seven radio shows a day, plus enduring at least two newspaper interviews in each city. The air shows would be the most difficult, because the publicity girl had told him not to expect the hosts to have read his book, *Born-Before-Sunrise*. He hoped that he would not be expected to discuss his famous patients. It would be difficult to get across to his interviewers the fact that a case of whooping cough afflicting the son of the Mayor of New York City would not differ consequentially from the same malady contracted by a Negro youth in Harlem, or the fact that one of the fathers being a professional politician and

236

the other an experienced hod-carrier did not lessen or increase the virulence of the bacillus.

Sam continued his breathing exercises, brushed the raindrops from his turban, then came back into the suite and turned with a smile to the vacuous blond female hostess of Washington's most popular radio show, who was to interview him later in the afternoon. She was no more than twenty-two or -three, he judged. He knew that she had not even glanced at either the dust jacket of the book or the press kit that had accompanied it, when she looked at him with wide blue eyes and asked sweetly, "What part of India do you call home?"

"I have never been to India," he replied quietly.

"Oh, really?" Her mouth stayed open a moment in surprise, and he noticed, from her extremely even upper row of central incisors, lateral incisors, and canines, that she had at some time or another undergone extensive orthodontia. As he continued to examine the contours of her mouth, it was evident that she had suffered from excessive malocclusion—an attitude that she probably still mentally maintained.

"Then why are you wearing a turban?"

"It is the ancient headgear of my people."

"You were born in *this* country?"

"Yes, in Tahlequah," he announced with the same conviction as if he had told her that he was a native of New York or Philadelphia. In a small way, he was enjoying his perversity. He was not going to make it easy for her, he decided.

"I've never heard of Tahlequah. The name has a foreign connotation."

"Not at all," he replied quietly. "It was formerly the headquarters of the Cherokee Indian Nation. It is now part of the state of Oklahoma."

"Oh," she said with relief. "That, of course, explains everything. The mystery has been solved. You're a *red* Indian."

"No," he corrected her suavely, "an *American* Indian."

She looked at him levelly, holding her ground, not willing to give an inch. "But I thought all red men wore feathers."

"Many tribal members did—and still do, when they don regalia for ceremonial dances or other official appearances," he replied gravely in his high-pitched voice. "But many Cherokees also wore turbans in the eighteen hundreds—fashioned of cottons and silks, some even multicolored. You see," he explained in the same tone that he used for preschool patients, "feathers were not as plentiful in Georgia or other Southern climes occupied by my ancestors. Turbans protected the head from cold during severe winters, and kept away the rays of the sun in summer."

"If your people came from the South, what did they do during the Civil War?" Although she kept her voice down, her erect back and high head told him that she was seething inside. He set her up. "We fought on the side of the Confederacy, because many of my people worked plantations."

"Slaves?"

"No, lady, they *owned* the plantations."

"Then they kept slaves themselves?" She was incredulous. He could see that it was difficult for her to mentally picture red men overseeing black men.

"Yes."

She shook her head. "I'm afraid my listeners would have difficulty understanding that." Then she added as an afterthought, "My grandfather, of course, fought on the side of the North." She peered at him. "Are you an anthropologist?"

"No," he replied gently, "I am a pediatrician."

"Oh, well, this being the nation's capital, my listeners are naturally more familiar with the political scene."

He looked at this woman with the vacuous stare,

238

with a sad smile on his lips. His voice was very soft. "Then let us deal with the politicos who ordered General Scott to march my people from Georgia to the prairie wastelands of Indian Territory."

"March, Doctor, *march*?"

"Perhaps," he replied, 'pushed' or 'drove' would be a better description. Many were on foot, some on litters, others rode horses—in the sun, in snow, over mountains, through valleys; and during this incredible journey our tribe was decimated by one-fourth."

"I don't really understand—"

"I am saying," he replied, his voice a bare whisper, "that when the Governor of Georgia found that gold had been discovered on the Cherokee plantations, he confiscated the property for the state and, with Congress behind him, exiled my people to 'lands beyond the Mississippi.'" He paused thoughtfully. "If a political discussion is what you want, I have dossiers filled with such interesting data."

She stiffened. "That is all quite historic, I'm sure," she said, glancing over the room, looking for an avenue of escape, "but perhaps it might be best to go into more recent history of—your people."

"That is perfectly all right with me," he replied quietly. "Many Cherokees have bettered their lot by attending universities and now earn good money through white-collar professions. But many families, because of inadequate educations and opportunities for advancement, also sharecrop land that was once their own. We can discuss this more fully, if you like."

"Excuse me," she said, "I can see my producer has just arrived."

As Sam watched her wend her way quickly through the crowd, there was a touch on his elbow, and he turned and looked into the face of an attractive middle-aged blond woman who seemed familiar, but he could not place her face.

239

"I haven't seen you, Sam, since I was a little girl. I'm John and Fontine Dice's daughter, Charlotte."

He flushed with pleasure and took her hand. "You look like your mother," he said at last, "especially around the eyes. How is she?"

"Fine. I don't get back to Angel as often as I should, but we talk on the telephone."

"And your father?"

"The same. Still keeps regular hours at the bank." She paused and took his hand. "Before I go, please autograph a book for me?"

"Of course." Charlotte, Sam thought, had had an ingratiating personality as a little girl, and as a middle-aged woman she seemed to be very much in command of herself. Obviously she was confident, mentally secure, and certainly poised. He had a feeling that she was also a realist. He liked her very much. "I saw your parents last at the Herons' family reunion. That was a strange experience, seeing all those people that I had known as a young man. We had all known each other for half a century."

Charlotte took a sip of her champagne cocktail. "Angel's not for me, Sam, and never has been since I went away to college. I don't have anything in common with those people anymore. They haven't had a new thought in years. They use the same old-time expressions, their outlook is still narrow. Of course, Letty and Bosley are more sophisticated because they've traveled all over the world. Dad and Mother have also remained unspoiled. Luke Heron's all right, and we speak when we see each other, but, let's say, we don't fraternize. His wife's an iceberg." She grew thoughtful. "I have a good job in the Department of Justice, a safe position not affected by political shenanigans. Maybe I'm the peculiar one, but I've never wanted ties—perhaps because I'm so critical of others, and I shouldn't be."

"We have that in common," Sam agreed.

Charlotte glanced over the group of people crowded into the small suite. "I don't want to keep you from your guests, Sam. After all, this is a publicity party for you. How long are you going to be in Washington?"

"I leave tomorrow. This afternoon I have a radio show with that blond young lady over there—the one who is gesticulating to that plump little man."

"Deborah Wassell? How do you get along?"

"Not very well, I'm afraid." He was apologetic.

"She's not one of my favorite people," Charlotte admitted.

"She thought I was from India."

"Oh, then she hadn't read the book. I'm not really surprised." Charlotte laughed, and the lines deepened around her eyes. "Deb performs five times a week, and I think they probably have to lead her to the microphone."

A blond young man came through the crowd and joined Charlotte, who took his arm. "Myron Driscoll, I'd like you to meet my favorite doctor, Sam, Born-Before-Sunrise."

The men shook hands, and Charlotte said, "You know, Sam, I've known you all my life, and I don't know your last name."

"It is Korda. I took the name of my foster parents." He smiled knowingly. "When they died, as you know, I inherited enough money to go to Harvard."

"I'm looking forward to reading your book, Doctor," Myron said quietly.

He was so good-looking that it was disconcerting to the other males in the room, Sam noticed with amusement. "Thank you. Frankly, writing was good therapy for me. I dispensed with many old ghosts."

Charlotte looked at her watch. "Myron, perhaps you'd better try to find a taxi."

"Yes," he agreed, "at this hour there may be a wait." He faced Sam. "It was a pleasure meeting you, sir."

They shook hands again, and the moment he was gone Sam murmured, "It's a pleasure to meet such a polite young man. You should be a very proud mother, Charlotte. Obviously you've raised him exceptionally well."

She blanched. "Sam," she said quietly, "that's not my son. I've never married." She paused and then went on carefully, "Myron Driscoll is my lover."

Sam had not blushed in years; he blushed now. "I am terribly sorry, Charlotte. I hasten to apologize for my gaffe."

She rather enjoyed his discomfort and continued warmly. "As a matter of fact, Sam," she said understandingly, "He *is* young enough to be my son." She held her head up, as if to defy the room as she looked over the crowd. "I suppose the fact that I like younger men would scandalize Angel, but in Washington no one turns a hair." She faced him frankly. "In certain quarters, I'm sure, I'm thought to be eccentric, but the Dice name does come in handy. If one has status here, and I do—after all, Dad *was* a Senator, and the oil money helps—then one can do almost what one wants." She paused and then added quickly, "Now don't get me wrong. I don't flaunt my lovers. If I'm invited to anything political, I have suitable men in my own age group to escort me." She smiled wryly. "One isn't interested in women, and the other's impotent, so it works out all the way around."

He nodded. "You're very sensible, Charlotte."

"Do you think so?" She sighed. "I suppose I'm frozen in time somewhere back in the Twenties when I was Myron's age. I never got to liking older men." She glanced at him appraisingly. "There's a catch to it, Sam. I keep wondering how long I can go on attracting the young ones. It's not that I'm falling apart *yet*, but it does cross my mind occasionally that one of these days I'm apt to be out in the cold." She paused, then whispered, "Hold onto your turban. Here comes Deborah." She turned swiftly and held out her hand to the woman. "How nice to see you, my dear."

"Charlotte, what a surprise! You look ravishing. Is that a Cassini?"

Charlotte held out the skirt of her dress. "What else? No one works with crepe de chine like Oleg."

Deborah smiled knowingly. "I just saw your latest young man. I understand he's received his draft notice. We must have a wake."

Charlotte swallowed quickly and retorted, "It will be the fourth one this year, if we do. Fortunately there's always a replacement in the wings." She turned blithely to Sam. "It's been a pleasure seeing you after all these years. I hope your book sells a million copies. See you around, Deb."

Sam and Deborah Wassell faced each other over the small table and shared the same microphone. After a musical introduction that sounded suspiciously like Handel's "Water Music," the director in the control room signaled Deborah, and she read from her notes.

"This evening, on *One on One,* we are most fortunate to have with us a distinguished doctor, Sam Korda, who has written a book that is on several best-seller lists across the country." Her voice was intimate, warm, and ingratiating—everything she was not in person. "His book is called *Born-Before-Sunrise.* Welcome to Washington. May I call you Sam?"

"Of course, Deborah, please do," he replied smoothly. "I'm only a doctor in my clinic on Barbados."

"I was there just before the war. It's a lovely island."

"Yes, and I'm proud to say that we have almost eliminated such diseases as ringworm by instituting strict hygienic measures."

"That is very worthwhile, I'm sure, Sam. Your book truly fascinated me. I recommend it. Of course, aside from being autobiographical, it works on several levels and in its way is rather shocking. I was especially intrigued by the fact that you're a full-blood Cherokee Indian. I know that your people were one of the Five Civilized Tribes. Could you tell us about those early days, when the Cherokee Strip, in what was to become the state of Oklahoma, was first opened?"

Charlotte Dice lay in Myron's arms after making love and listened to the interview on the radio and marveled at the smooth flow of questions and answers. Sam was acquitting himself superbly. He came over as the slightly reserved, kindly man that he was, while Deborah Wassell was everything expected of a good interviewer. She was quick on the uptake, never interrupted or cut him off in midsentence, and her questions were designed to bring out the right answers without touching controversy.

At the end of the program, Charlotte reached over the side of the bed and shut off the set. "Well," she said languidly, "once again that miserable bitch was saved by her staff." She paused thoughtfully. "Poor Sam."

"Why 'poor Sam'?" Myron roused. "I thought the interview went over very smoothly."

"That's not what I meant." She reached under the coverlet. "He doesn't have any of these," she said softly. "Just think what that means."

"My God!" Myron exclaimed, and his scrotum drew up tightly in her hand.

"He was only a boy," she explained, "when a drunken group of Indians attacked his house and emasculated him."

Myron drew away from her. "Jesus! That poor guy!

244

I wonder if he ever wants to go to bed with a woman."

"My Dad asked him that once when I was a little girl. I was playing hide-and-seek with Mitchell Heron behind the haystack, and I overheard the conversation. Of course, what they were saying didn't make sense then. I remember Dad asked him if he ever got the "urge," and Sam replied that, thank God, that wasn't one of the things that plagued him. The only thing that really bothered him, he said, was the fact that he would never have any children of his own." She paused meaningfully, "Yet the strangest part of it all is that he chose a profession where all of his patients—thousands, over the years—are children. So his paternal instinct was turned outward. He has become a humanitarian."

Myron turned to her. "Do you want a baby?" he asked playfully, placing a hand over her breast.

She laughed. "No, thank you. And besides, I'm one of those women that my mother would call 'barren.' I'm sure, even at my age, she thinks I'm a virgin." She turned and caressed his cheek. "I'm a disgrace to the family, because they wanted grandchildren. When I didn't accept Clement Story's proposal, Mother almost had apoplexy. . . ."

Myron sat up in bed. "*The* Clement Story?" he asked incredulously.

"The one and the same. We grew up together."

"He's my favorite orchestra leader. I've been a fan of his ever since high school. His 'Red Sails in the Sunset' is so great! I have a big collection of his records." He regarded her with new interest. "You know, Charlotte, I've never known anyone who has so many famous friends." He ran his hand over her stomach. "I'm going to miss you like hell," he continued, slowly becoming aroused again.

"Because of my famous friends?"

He laughed, showing all of his perfect teeth. "No, be-

245

cause I've never known a woman who would have sex as often as I want it, and I've got to make up for when I go in service and won't get any at all."

She swung over him and looked down into his blue eyes and drew in her breath at his fresh male beauty. "Just lie still," she whispered, "and this time let Mama do all the work."


Letty settled down with Sam's book, opened the first page, and read:

The first thing I remembered was a bloodcurdling scream, which I finally realized came from my mother, who was still in the house. The darkness covered me. I lay stone-still, wrapped in a blanket, under the china-berry tree, the straw mattress at my back. I shook myself because I thought surely that I must be dreaming. But the stars above still sparkled, the wind still caressed the branches of the tree, loaded with its hard, transparent fruit. Then I heard the scream again. I was awake. I knew in my nine-year-old mind that something horrible was happening in the dark house. Creeping toward a window, I saw three strange horses teth-ered in the barnyard—mustangs that were sniffing the air suspiciously and raising their nostrils, and pawing the earth and whining. It came to me that the animals had caught the smell of blood.

I crept along the side of the house, my newly beaded deerskin moccasins making a small, silent wind. I crouched beside the open door. My father lay in a widening red pool, his face turned away from me as if in false modesty—as if he did not want me to see him surprised by death. I did not pause as I passed him, but I went to the bedroom, drawn by the low moans of my mother. The room was filled with the acrid smell of corn whisky. The window curtains had been drawn, so that no moonlight filtered into the room; yet, because my eyes were accustomed to the dark, I saw one black form, clothed in buckskin, rise up from the low bed, and another take its place.

Mother was sobbing hysterically now, and I knew, and yet did not know, what was taking place. With all of my strength I flew at the man who was lying over my mother, and clawed at his back. The other man picked me up and threw me into the corner of the room. There was the sound of raucous laughter, punctuated by Mother's screams. Then I heard a soft thud, and she cried out no more. Positive that she was dead, I got up on my knees and shouted at the men. The one who was not busy on the bed picked me up again and threw me into the living room, then staggered drunkenly after me. I smelled the liquor on his breath and looked up into his red face—the most evil face that I had ever seen. Like a demon out of an old Indian myth, he focused his bloodshot eyes on my face. He was like a wild man. Suddenly a new burst of fury enveloped him with an inner fire. I was terrified. He was joined by the other man, who lumbered into the room, tugging his bloody buckskins up around his waist. I half rose up, the pain in my back spreading down my legs. Searching their faces, I realized that they were from a strange, unrecognizable tribe. As I mustered strength for a new attack, I saw a blade flash in the moonlight. One of the men grabbed me roughly and pulled at my trousers, exposing me. He clutched my waist with one hand and held me while the knife slashed my bare flesh. The pain that I had experienced up to that time, was as infinitestimal as the farthest star in the heavens compared to what I then felt. The blood gushed down from my groin and ran down my legs. Thankfully, then, I lost consciousness.

When I awakened a day later, I was wrapped in a white sheet. Through the haze, I saw my mother's face, blackened and bloated almost beyond recognition, and I thought: *Thank God, she's alive.* When I opened my eyes fully, I saw that she was crying—she, who had never cried in my presence before. She was moaning over, over and over and over again, "Oh my boy, my poor squaw boy. . . ."

Letty could read no more; tears filled her eyes. She sighed gently and let the book slide to the floor. She had known Sam's story—as who had not in those early years of the territory? But to read about his torture in his own words was the most horrifying experience she had ever known.


Fontine Dice finished the third chapter of *Born-Before-Sunrise* and giggled. Sam's experiences at The Widows were absolutely delicious. Being what was essentially a major domo at what was once called a fancy house—she had used the term herself—was not nearly as titillating as she had supposed at the time when she herself had been young. Leona Barrett had closed The Widows after Oklahoma Statehood in 1907. Fontine was never very good at figures, but this was 1944. Had that all happened thirty-seven years ago?

"My stars!" she exclaimed aloud and turned the page to Chapter Four. Her face flamed. Sam had written:

Dear people were John Dice, who had come up from San Antonio to The Territory to make The Run, along with his father, a crusty old man called Poppa Dice. "Jaundice" and "Fourteen"— John's wife, Fontine—as the old fellow called them, had been dirt farmers in "Santone." But as ignorant and as unsophisticated as they were, educationwise, the family soon prospered. Poppa Dice, when he went to work as Faro keeper at The Widows, asked me to teach him how to read and write, and he in turn taught Jaundice and Fourteen their ABC's.

Fontine colored, and her hands shook. She got up unsteadily and, with blood pounding in her temples, picked up the telephone. "Nellie, is that you? Please get me John at the bank. . . . Jaundice," she began to fume, "the devil take him, that Sam. . . ." She lapsed back into her old speech patterns. She was so angry, she shook, spilling her platinum curls around her head. "He's a yellow-livered bastid, that's what he is!" She stopped suddenly. "We gotta sue, Jaundice, we gotta sue. Wait'll you read what he says about you."

John Dice's voice was very low and very patient. "I've read the book," he said simply. "I don't know why you're so upset, Fourteen, it's all true."

"But with you bein' a former Senator and a banker and—"

"Just calm down. If you'll finish the book, dear one, he tells all about that too. I'm proud—and you should be too—that we have come such a long way. It's easy to forget now—with what we have and what we've become—that it was so terrible in the beginning."

Fontine paused a moment, and her composure came back. "Is our story really so *extraordinary*?" she asked, somewhat placated.

He chuckled. "Yes indeedy. Wait until you get to the part where he tells about you throwing all of our furniture into the creek when we got that first oil check for five thousand dollars."

"But I *never*!"

"Fourteen, your memory is very, very short."

She paused. "Well, maybe I did and maybe I didn't." She drew in her breath. "But everything was so *old*—"

"If you'd saved all those old pieces, why, they'd be worth a fortune today. You threw away genuine antiques, Fourteen."

She cleared her throat and changed the subject. "Anyway, Bosley and Letty are coming for supper," she

249

said. "They just flew in from Washington, so come home a little early."

She hung up the telephone and picked up the book again. Through the pages, she saw herself again—the young, naive yellow-haired girl with wide eyes. She glanced at herself in the mirror in the living room and was startled to see a plump, rather shapeless face staring back at her. Of course, the hair was still yellow—golden, really—but the color now came from mixing a bottle of peroxide with a bottle of ammonia. She glanced at the apparition in the glass again. No—and she puffed up with pride—she did not look at all like she was sixty-six years of age. She went back to the book, and was just at the point where Letty and George Story's Discovery Well had come in in 1903, when the doorbell rang.

It took a moment to come back to reality; then she frowned and looked at her diamond wristwatch. It was five-thirty! In a panic, she went into the kitchen, where the new cook, Betty Lou, was making biscuits. "I forgot to tell you, w-we're having company for dinner," she stammered, her face beet red. "Is there any food in the ice chest?"

The pale, gaunt woman looked up as her hands worked the dough. "There's nothing in there except a mite of beef stew left from last night, and I only bought two small pieces of liver for tonight. With you being on a diet and all—"

"We'll have the stew," Fontine said quickly. "Add a can of peas, a can of hominy, make some butter gravy, and throw the biscuits on top." The doorbell rang insistently. Fontine rushed out of the room, then turned back. "And make some tapioca for dessert."

She walked to the front door as fast as her short legs could carry her, patted her golden curls in place, and breathlessly opened the door. "You'll never believe this, Letty," she said, eyes fluttering, "but I got so caught up

250

in Sam's book that time just slipped away, and the upshot is we're having leftovers—we're doctoring the stew—for supper, I mean dinner."

Letty laughed. "Stew is always better the second day anyway." She sympathized. "Isn't it strange to go back to the beginning?"

Bosley nodded. "I think that *Born-Before-Sunrise* is a classic book."

Fontine sighed. "I'm half a mind about it now." She paused. "Please do come in and sit in the parlor." She led them through the hall. "I don't know whether it's good to stir up all that again or not. It all happened such a long time ago. It's funny, seeing us all through Sam's eyes—but it's also an invasion of privacy in a way."

Bosley smoothed back his white hair. "It gave me a pause, too. I didn't realize that we were all so *green*."

Fontine laughed. *"Dumb*—a better word, Bos." She gave him a long, penetrating look. "I was mad as a wet hen at first, I don't mind telling you; then, as I went along, I began to look at it differently." She paused. "But if I had it to do all over again, I wouldn't. I'd have stayed in Santone where I belonged."

"No, you wouldn't have missed any of this for the world!" Letty exclaimed. "None of us would." She gathered her skirts and sat down on the sofa. "You have to look at it like—well—"

"Like the all-American success story that it is," Bosley put in gently.

At that moment Betty Lou came in from the kitchen. "You'll never believe this, Mrs. Dice, but I just scorched the stew," she said apologetically. "I'm sorry. I don't know what's got into me today."

Fontine grinned and then said calmly, "In the old days that we were just talking about I would have thrown a tizzy, fired you, run out in the barnyard, wrung a chicken's neck, and ended up fixing a meal in no time flat that would knock your eye out." She looked at Letty and Bosley with a resigned expression. "But tonight the Stevens Hotel dining room will be serving four more people than they'd planned."

# 14

## The Slip-Up

*H. L. Leary threw the telephone into its cradle and clenched his fists.*

He went to the bar and poured himself a straight finger of scotch, which he downed in one gulp. "Do you want a drink?" He turned to Pierre Darlan, who shook his head.

"What has upset you so much that you take a drink in the middle of the day?" Pierre asked.

"They can't bring him back!" Leary exclaimed.

"Who?"

"Michel Bayard or Mitchell Heron or whatever in the hell his name is."

"But I do not understand." Pierre said, working his mustaches.

"The whole network has been exposed. The last was a watchmaker, Georges, who no one knew was on our team."

"What of Lise?" Pierre leaned forward, trying not to show his nervousness.

"Thank God, she got away, which means the contents of the tube are safe, at least. But apparently all hell has broken loose over there. It will take time to set up new people."

Pierre shrugged. "I would not worry about our man. He can take care of himself. He has a safe job; the foreman at the plant is a friend. He knows his work. He will pull it off well. He can be trusted."

Leary glared at him. "Of course he's physically all right; that is the least of my worries. But he has a business to run, and he can't stay on vacation forever. Already we have run out of those postcards and letters that he wrote for us before he left."

Pierre took a deep breath. "We must get a message to him, but it must be carefully and succinctly composed, informing him that we will get him out eventually and that we have used our 'writing expert' to continue his messages to his company and family. With everything else on his mind, we do not want him to worry about his affairs at home." He paused meaningfully. "As long as he is there, H.R., you could use him for another mission. Had you thought about that?"

"Of course," Leary snapped. "But I don't want to tempt the gods. He has completed the job he was sent over to do, and it's too difficult and involved to use him again, unless . . ."

"Lise?"

He nodded. "She must get her report back some way." He pursed his lips and paced back and forth in front of the bar. Then he poured himself another finger of scotch, which he sipped slowly. "Yes," he said, more to himself than to Pierre. "Yes, we shall have her contact him. She can be reached by short wave." He downed the rest of the drink. "Yes, that is the way to do it. The boys in the South will be very pleased indeed."

Mitchell Heron lay on the bed in his small attic room and read the French-language newspaper. The news—

heavily censored, he was certain—told very little, but looking over the sheet was one more way that he could pass time. Each evening the family gathered below and listened to the BBC, where the news, however brief, was at least concrete. The French were apt to mix their metaphors, and while the phrases might be quite descriptive, the English news seemed to have a better information factor. Of course—he grinned to himself—he was prejudiced.

He had become a familiar figure in the few streets that bordered the factory and the little cottage situated in the rear of a small garden. He took care to look and behave exactly as his neighbors did. He performed his job well, balancing the gunstocks automatically, so that his mind was free. When old Beaufils had informed him that the network had been dissolved, and that it would take a few weeks to become reestablished, he had become morose and uncommunicative for a day or so; then he realized that he could do nothing except wait. He was a pawn on a chessboard that included almost all of Europe.

He realized, with a fair amount of pride, that he could stay in Tarbes the rest of his life because he had fitted himself so well into the existing pattern. Yet he was growing weary of living a lie; the early excitement of a new adventure was wearing exceedingly thin. Enid now seemed to be a marvelous, remote haven. Although he thought a great deal about his return, he knew very well that circumstances could intervene; there was the distinct possibility that he might never see America again. He found that he had become a realist; he did not daydream anymore.

Weeks passed, and then, late one morning, as he and old Beaufils shared a lunch of bread and cheese in the misty courtyard of the old factory, one of the journeymen stopped by, ostensibly to pass the time of day, but when a few men nearby finished eating and sauntered into the street for a short stroll before going back to the assembly line, the man whispered, "A message came via short wave this morning: "Don José meet Carmen, noon Saturday bicycle south Château Latte.' "

Michell awaited Saturday by performing odd chores about the cottage. He did not even go to the café.

A knapsack that contained bread and cheese on his back, Mitchell made certain that the bicycle tires were inflated and took care to look like a workman on a tour of the countryside. At five minutes to twelve he started south toward the château, which had been converted into a small outpatient clinic.

He reached the fork in the road, where he had to make a decision to continue up the cobblestone driveway to the hospital or turn in the direction of Vic, which was located twenty-five kilometers north. At that moment a peasant girl on a bicycle pedaled down the drive from the château, and he waited a moment and lighted a pipe. When she was a few feet away, he recognized Lise. "Good afternoon," he said casually, his heart thumping, and tipped his cap. So this was Carmen!

"Good afternoon," she replied. Her brown eyes took in his apparel, and she nodded with approval. "Shall we proceed?" Surprisingly, she took the road back toward Tarbes, and soon they were pedaling side by side, giving the appearance of two lovers seeking the seclusion of the hills and valleys of southern France.

"I brought some wine," she said, "since it is an occasion of sorts."

He threw her an amused glance. " I have food."

"There is a path leading to an abandoned farmhouse near that oak," she said. "We can hide the bicycles in the underbrush."

A few moments later, when they had made their way down the overgrown path to a small hill concealed from the road by holly bushes, she removed her head scarf and shook out her hair, then sat down on the brown grass. "A message has finally come through for you," she said with a smile. "It has been most difficult these last few weeks to communicate with the outside." She passed a hand over her brow. "So much has happened that I cannot even touch upon. The original plan of your escape has been scuttled because the southern network is in great trouble. The route that you were to take is no longer safe. You are to stay at the factory. Does your job go well?"

He nodded. "Yes. Some of my inward nervousness has disappeared, but I am still anxious to leave. I have business elsewhere."

"Yes, I do too, but I made the journey back because no one knows you by sight since Paul and Madeleine and Georges were captured."

"Not Georges too?" He felt an odd churning in his stomach. "And what of Etienne?"

"He was the first to go—shot in the cart on the way back from delivering you to Tarbes."

"Oh, no!" He turned away a moment, and the import of his mission threw cold chills up and down his spine. "Murdering children . . ."

Her mouth was set in a hard line. "You were most fortunate, Michel, to escape with your life. We know the collaborator." Her eyes blazed. "After the war— perhaps before, if it can be arranged—we will get him. It is only a matter of time. It is ironic, in a way, that they killed Etienne. Being just a boy, he could have been made to talk, and you would have been captured. Georges was more resourceful. He had a capsule."

Mitchell shivered. "It is such a strange feeling, Lise, that these people died because of me. I hope my mission was important enough to make up, in some small way, for these senseless deaths. It is a big responsibility on my shoulders."

She ignored his entreaty and went on brusquely, the skin over her cheekbones very taut. Her mouth became a thin line once more. With words tumbling out, her lips barely moved. "I was told to inform you not to worry about your business affairs. Your absence has been explained."

"Thank God for that!" he exclaimed. "That was my biggest worry."

"Should the factory become unsafe—and conditions are such that it may—you will again be transferred. The password, in that case will be 'Otter,' which is your code name. Now," she finished, "shall we eat?"

After they had consumed the bread and cheese, and the small bottle of red wine that she had brought along, Mitchell examined her lovely face. "It is sad that you and I cannot really talk about the things that interest us most. You know nothing about me except that I was dropped out of the sky. I know nothing about you except that you are a metallurgist."

"Who told you that?" she demanded, her face a mask.

"Paul."

"The fool!" she spat out. "Well, he deserved to die."

"I don't understand you."

"He should have known better. In this work one never gives unnecessary information that could be passed on. He was a stupid old man who had grown complacent—which is the most dangerous attitude of all." She questioned harshly, "What else did he tell you?"

"Nothing."

She placed the empty bottle back in the large pocket of her peasant skirt. "We will not meet again, Michel," she said, and handed him the familiar silver tube. "This you must take with you."

"Then my mission is not over?"

"You must return this flask to the person who gave it to you in the first place."

He looked at the container for a long moment, barely breathing. "If it is discovered—do I also have a capsule?"

She shook her head. "We will get you out safely," she replied softly. "It may take time, but you will be returned." She glanced up at the sun. "I must get back to the hospital. I have a long journey ahead tonight." She was about to continue, thought better of it, and buckled his knapsack, which she handed to him with a little ceremony. "Sometime in the future," she said quietly, "you may know more about"—she made a gesture—"all of this—but then again, you may not. Shall we proceed?"

"Thank you for all you have done," he said lamely.

She held out her hand, and he kissed her cheek instead. "Until we meet again," he said and looked directly into her eyes.

She nodded, and they walked down the small incline hand in hand. They retrieved the bicycles, and she headed back toward the Château Latte, and he proceeded toward Tarbes. They did not look back.


Mitchell was more restless than he had ever been; not even in the days during the depression, when he was drifting from town to town, never knowing where his next meal was coming from, had he been at such odds with himself. But there was no more news filtering in from the Underground, and he spent the night tossing and turning in his attic bed. Scenes from his childhood in Angel kept crowding out other memories, some

259

as recent as his encounter with the young man in the bistro whose face held the unmistakable Heron look.

He awakened at three in the morning, tense with sexual excitement, and he thought of the few women who had meant anything to him in his life. One? Two? He had never had a long affair, and he did not consider those once-a-week appearances in Belle Trune's bedroom an affair. That was, more correctly, a release. Finally he turned over and went fitfully back to sleep.

Jacques knocked softly on the door.

Mitchell was instantly awake. "*Oui?*"

A moment later Jacques was kneeling beside his bed. "It is time," he said. "You are to go, *now*."

"What shall I take?"

"Only what you came with."

Mitchell put on his tweed coat and pants. "Wooden shoes?"

Jacques grinned. "*Non, mon cher*, you will not walk very far in those. Regular shoes, please. Hurry, Michel, your guide is waiting."

On first sight, Mitchell thought that the boy standing by the side of the road was Etienne, returned miraculously from the dead; then he saw that the lad was more robust.

"My name is Joffre," he piped, "but everyone calls me Sparrow. Come, Monsieur, we must hurry."

Mitchell shook hands with Jacques, and they kissed in countrystyle, one peck on each cheek. "Go, for the liberation of France," Jacques said emotionally.

Mitchell nodded. "I will never forget you, Jacques." He turned to the boy, and they started down the road together.

When they had gone, Jacques printed a message on a scrap of paper to be later read over the short wave to be monitored by the BBC Home Service. The message read: SPARROW LEADS OTTER.

\* \* \*

They walked all night, occasionally bypassing a soldiered barricade, and at dawn the Sparrow stopped before a small cottage surrounded by goats, and pushed the door open.

"The place is empty!" Mitchell exclaimed.

"By design," The boy answered, and Mitchell looked at him as the sky grew brighter. Under his green cap he was dark-haired and gray-eyed and, although he could not have been thirteen, wore the most solemn expression that Mitchell had ever seen on a child. It was as if he had never smiled.

A knapsack containing food had been left on a table. They consumed some bad, moldy cheese and a piece of hard black bread. Then the boy disappeared for a few moments and came back with a small jug of goat's milk, frothy and warm. In his present frame of mind, it was the most delicious beverage that Mitchell had ever tasted.

They slept in the corner on a pile of straw, covered by an old German army blanket, and at nightfall started out again. From time to time Mitchell was forced to stop to rub his swollen feet. The Sparrow had brought along some soothing unguent, which anesthetized his toes, allowing them to proceed.

The second night was spent in the stable attached to a grand residence where German soldiers were billeted. They ate scraps of food from the table: cheese, wheat bread, washed down with terrible watered wine.

The third night they were picked up by a cart at a prearranged crossroads, and at dawn a hospital dispensary played host. Stretched out on two long operating tables, covered with white prewar blankets, they slept exceptionally well and awakened to a delicious, plentiful dinner of hot gruel, scraps of rye muffins, and lukewarm tea. But the biggest treat of all lay at the bottom of the bread basket: a single piece of black German chocolate.

The fourth night, a full moon, they spent in a foul-smelling hay mound, and, since there was no food conveniently left for them, Mitchell could see that the Sparrow was worried. Had there been a slip-up that meant their contact had been captured? "What is wrong?" he asked quietly.

The boy shrugged his thin shoulders. "It is my fault that we do not eat tonight," he said at last. "I am almost certain that I have the wrong mound." And he could not understand why Mitchell laughed. "What is so funny, Monsieur?"

"We will not die of starvation, Sparrow. Do not be so concerned. An error is understandable."

The boy shook his head violently. "No, Monsieur, an error is never permissible."

"Then it may be the other contact's fault," Mitchell replied gently. "You may have the right hay mound."

"I counted very carefully, Monsieur, the third one from the road, sixth one from the west."

"Then," Mitchell replied softly, "the moon must have blinded your eyes. The next one over is the sixth."

"Mon Dieu!" the boy exclaimed, and when they moved, there was a loaf of fresh bread and some strawberries wrapped in a damp cloth.

Since the boy would not talk, even of inconsequential matters, Mitchell had not asked him where they were going, but eventually a peeling sign by the side of the road read: Privas. An arrow pointed south. He had never heard of the place. Once in a while they would have to wait outside a village for the sun to set before they could proceed, but the lad was very clever, and he seemed to sense the lay of a road the same way that Sam sought hidden animal trails through the woods in the old days. Mitchell wondered how often the lad had made the trip, and how many he had led to safety.

The fifth night a mechanized lorry picked them up near an old ruin of a château, and, although they were traveling on rough country roads, successfully avoiding barricades, a distance of some three hundred kilometers was covered. The silent driver evidently knew the route like the back of his big freckled hand. They spent the day in an ancient boathouse on the river Rhone, a ramshackle building that had once been the mooring place for skiffs that entered regattas long before the war, when Hitler was only just coming into power in Germany.

The sixth night, as a low fog crept over the ground, Mitchell and the Sparrow packed their knapsacks with provisions left in the boathouse, and when a low whistle was heard, the boy held up his hand for complete silence. He froze, waiting for the signal again, then, lifting his fingers to his lips, he gave an identical answer.

A moment later a small, compact little man dressed in black came into the room. He flashed a smile. "I am Anatole. The plans have changed again," he said with a heavy Alsatian accent. "We are to take my boat." He smiled widely again. "Luck is with us; the fog stretches all the way to Culoz, and the currents are swift." He placed his hands on the boy's shoulders. "I will deliver him," he said kindly. "You are to go to the safe house in Romans. Can you find it in the dark?"

The boy nodded. "*Oui.* I know it well." He turned on his heel and held out his hand to Mitchell. "Good luck, Monsieur Bayard. Go, for the liberation of France."

Mitchell's throat constricted. He had grown close to this strange lad; their silences during the long night treks had brought about a peculiar camaraderie. "You have done well, and I thank you."

Suddenly the Sparrow smiled, and his face lighted up momentarily. "It was a very great honor, Monsieur." Then he became serious once more. It occurred to Mitchell that the fleeting smile had been a relieved reaction that he had accomplished his mission, rather

263

than a genuine expression of friendship. So it must be with these courageous boys of the Underground, he reflected, who risked their young lives for their country. How many more boys, filled with a terrible responsibility that made them old before their time, were involved in the network?

Mitchell held out a bit of chocolate, which he had secreted from their third night at the dispensary. The boy shook his head, but Mitchell insisted. Then a smile lighted up the Sparrow's face once more, and he took the candy, which he did not pop into his mouth, as Mitchell expected, but carefully wrapped the morsel in a bit of cloth and placed it in his pocket.

Five minutes later Anatole had guided the boat to the center of the river. Occasionally a fish could be heard plopping out of the water in some moon dance, and Anatole whispered, "The Germans have forbidden fishing, but on nights like tonight we still set our seines, as I am doing now. When we reach our destination, there will be a breakfast of good perch."

At midnight Anatole offered a piece of coarse black bread spread with chicken fat, and a jar of clabbered goat's milk, and the *pièce de résistance,* a small cake made of ground raisins, flavored with cinnamon.

The fog grew more dense toward morning. The boat sped on silently through the mist, and they did not even encounter a patrol.

At dawn Anatole took to the oars, and the tiny craft slipped into a mass of reeds. "We will rest here on the banks," he said, helping Mitchell out of the boat. They walked up and down by the river's edge, stretching their legs and limbering their backs. Then Mitchell accepted a big piece of chewing tobacco, and Anatole and he sat by the river—each engaged in his own thoughts—and chewed and became close in companionship.

"The place where we go today is not a usual safe house, but arrangements were made last night when the plans changed and we took to the river. These ladies are genteel and, although not French, are nevertheless good patriots." He chewed thoughtfully for a moment, then spat into the reeds. "You must be very careful. It is a large house, but there are two officials billeted there at the moment. Let us hope they are on duty and away for the day. Are you tired?"

Mitchell nodded. "Very. All the walking is catching up with me now. I am not used to so much exercise."

"Then wrap yourself in a blanket under that tree, and I will awaken you when it is time to go. If God is good, the fog will keep covering us." He paused. "You have papers, in case we are stopped by *les Boches*?"

Mitchell patted his breast pocket. "Safe and sound."

As ten o'clock approached, with the fog thicker than ever, Anatole grinned as he made a packet of the fish. "Come, I know the way by heart," he said, "but take hold of my coattail. After your long journey, I do not wish to lose you."

At last, after they had stumbled through the mists for another hour, through the side streets of Culoz, they were again in an open space. Soon a large house surrounded with spacious grounds loomed out of the fog, and Anatole knocked softly at the side door, which was opened by a tall, thin woman with a rather pronounced mustache that perfectly matched her dark hair.

"My name is Alice. Welcome. Do come in out of the wet."

Mitchell had difficulty believing his ears. Her impeccable French was delivered with a strong American accent. She held out a bony, fragile hand that was slightly cool.

"I am Michel Bayard," Mitchell said, bowed, and kissed her hand.

265

They were in a kind of sitting room, with several large paintings on the cluttered walls. Out of the shadows of the hall came a heavy-set, large-boned woman with gray hair cropped close to her head. She held out two strong hands in a gesture of welcome, and she and Mitchell kissed each other's cheeks. Her skin gave off the faint smell of tuberoses, a scent he had forgotten existed. Belle Trune, during the time between the wars, had used such a perfume.

"I am Gertrude," she said in a low voice. "You must be very tired, Monsieur." Her accent was wholly American.

Very carefully, because he was exhausted and wanted to speak pure French, Mitchell replied, "Call me Michel." There was no reaction. He had passed the test.

Anatole held out the packet of fish to Alice, and she laughed. "Is this what I think it is?" And he nodded. "Bless you," she said. "Is it perch? I shall prepare them now." She looked up quizzically, like a hovering bird. "Shall I set the table for four?"

Anatole shook his head. "No, I must go back." He waved, shook hands with Mitchell, waved to the ladies, and left through the side entrance.

"I will prepare tea," Alice said, "which you can sip before we eat." She went into the kitchen, and he heard words spoken—obviously to the cook.

Gertrude examined his face, and he found himself smoothing his mustache. "I am certain that you would like a bath, Michel. When we moved here from Bilignin, we brought a water heater, a bathtub, a stove, and a refrigerator—all electric. In the time that it will take for Clothilde to scrape the fish, you shall enjoy a bath."

Once ensconced in the tub, Mitchell relaxed completely. He had forgotten what it was like to luxuriate in warm water, and as he spread a fine lather over his skin he was very much at home in his environment. Gertrude had said the soap was the last of a cache. The two American ladies, living so incongruously in wartime France, were a puzzle that stayed unsolved in the back of his mind. They were at once familiar and unknown. He closed his eyes, memories fighting with each other. He went back to his years in Lyon. Ah, yes, now it came to him—the women, writer-poet Gertrude Stein and her companion, Alice B. Toklas, had lived in Paris.

Of all his dealings since he had been dropped in France, this was the most bizarre. He had fooled Frenchman into believing he was French, but could he carry on his masquerade with his own countrywomen? He broke out in a cold sweat.

There was a knock on the door. "Food is on the table," came Alice's reedy voice.

With his second bite of the fish, which the cook had prepared with a delicate sauce, Mitchell began to feel more at ease, and he confidently decided to start a conversation, plunging into dangerous waters, and choosing his words very carefully. "I have noticed your American accents"—he used classic phrases—"and I am pleased to be in your house, Mademoisselle Stein and Mademoiselle Toklas."

Gertrude laughed, her presence filling the room. "I was wondering if you knew us, Monsieur Bayard, because we live very quietly here, not at all the way we lived in Paris before the Occupation, which sent so many Americans back to the United States, but we stay on through it all because we belong here, Alice and I, and the war goes on and we go on and the food is not the way it used to be before, but then again what country is the same?"

Mitchell nodded, sopping a piece of excellent white bread into the sauce and savoring the flavor.

"We are billeting two Italian officers now, but that is better than the Germans that we had to take in before, but they were so involved with their work, which was very hard, I gather, that fortunately they paid little attention to us and so it worked out very well, although the villagers were very frightened that we would somehow give ourselves away. When we first came from our *manoir* in Bilignin, our friend the former *sour-préfet* of Belley told us that we must embark for Switzerland or be sent to a concentration camp, but neither Alice nor myself cares much for the mountains." Her large eyes were very penetrating. "And the customs there are so different and because we have lived in France for so many years, we decided not to go but to stay and see what would happen to us and so we are still here. It was all rather funny." She paused. "Now that you have finished the fish, would you like to go to bed?"

It was then that Mitchell remembered that Gertrude Stein had many famous paintings. "I would like to see your collection of art before I rest," he said formally, pronouncing his words carefully.

Gertrude Stein shook her head sadly, and her whole body took on a tragic look. "Most of them are still in Paris in the apartment in the rue Christine, but we brought a few with us, one or two of which we have had to sell to keep going, because, of course, we have been unable to take any money from the United States for a very long time. Friends have been very kind, but we cannot keep expecting them to give us everything." At that moment a white ball bounded into the room and landed in its mistress's lap, licking her hand in a kind of joyful dance. "This is Basket," Gertrude said. "She has sustained us and you may not be able to see it, but she is a poodle. We are not going to have her trimmed until the war is over, and on Liberation Day she will have a new cut and will look like her old self again."

Then she led Mitchell into the drawing room, where a number of paintings were displayed, and she told a story about a green landscape and an anecdote about the man who painted a portrait of Alice B. Toklas, but

Mitchell was very tired, and the names that she bandied about so carelessly meant nothing to him.

Alice had placed fresh-smelling but almost threadbare sheets on a daybed in a room at the back of the house, and as soon as Mitchell's head touched the pillow, he was asleep. When he awakened, it was late afternoon and Basket was curled up at his thigh. It seemed that the small dog was offering protection. His eyes smarted. It was difficult to believe that he was the guest of two of the most famous ladies on the Continent. It was as if the war had never existed. Then he heard conversation in Italian and realized that the two officers had come back to the house.

Mitchell picked up a small volume beside the bed and discovered to his pleasure that it was printed in English: *Rebecca* by Daphne du Maurier. He opened the book to the first page and read: "Last night I dreamt I went to Manderley again. It seemed to me I stood by the iron gate leading to the drive, and for a while I could not enter for the way was barred to me."

He had become so engrossed in reading the English text that he did not hear the small knock on the door, and when he was conscious of a presence in the room and looked up, he saw that Gertrude Stein was standing on the threshold. "A man called Claude is waiting outside with a car," she said, "so you must hurry. Alice is fixing a small package of food, all we can spare at the moment, but you must hurry because it is getting late and there is a long way to go." His heart was beating very fast, but she had not noticed the book in his hands.

He dressed quickly, picked up his knapsack, and accepted the small parcel that Alice thrust into his hands. He kissed the ladies properly on their cheeks and was out the door before Gertrude caught up with him again. "May you safely get home." She pressed his arm. "These are such strange times."

He turned on his heel, ran down the steps, and

climbed into the front seat of the small car, startled at the driver in a German uniform.

The man held up his hands. "I am Claude, do not be frightened, this is a disguise." He headed the automobile down the drive and turned onto the road that ran by the house. "The frontier is closed again," he announced, "so our plans have changed once more. Additional guards have been brought in at the Swiss border. This time, if the fog is heavy again tonight near the Rhone, you will be taken by boat to Lake Geneva, which is also fraught with danger. If it is clear, then we will keep you a day or so longer in a safe house in Bellegarde. How did you like the crazy ladies?"

Mitchell smiled. "They are very nice for Americans."

Claude pursed his lips. "They are also very brave to stay in France."

"Do they help much?"

Claude shook his head. "It is too dangerous for them to be involved in our work. But they agreed to put you up for a night because we do favors for them, and we also had no place else to hide you."

"What will I do in Switzerland?" Mitchell asked quietly, as if he did not expect a reply.

Claude laughed. "That is not my concern, Monsieur Bayard, and I say this with relief. The Swiss are not a happy people, surrounded as they are by fighting, but that is a better route than over the Pyrenees into Fascist Spain, at the moment. If you have to hide"—he gestured vaguely—"then, Monsieur, you will have to hide!" He looked about him as the fog rolled in and nodded. "We will shortly be coming to a barricade in the road. It is manned by only two men, who know my uniform and will recognize my credentials. There is no other way, or I would spare you this ordeal. You must do me a favor." He stopped the car at the side of the road. "Hold up your hands, please. I must handcuff you for the moment."

He slipped the rough iron bracelets over Mitchell's wrists and clamped them shut. "The favor is this: quite out of character, I am certain, you must act very frightened." He ran his hand over Mitchell's smooth hair, giving him the look of a wild man. He then reached under the seat and picked up some grease on his fingers and smeared some of the black stuff on Mitchell's cheek, thrust open his shirt, and tore a rip in his lapel. "I have just captured you, *mon cher*; please be appropriately stunned."

He put the car in gear and three minutes later stopped at the wooden fence that stretched over the road. Two sentries, one on each side of the barricade, stood guard. "Halt!" they cried simultaneously, and, as if they had carefully rehearsed their actions, came forward, one on either side of the car.

Claude flashed a light into Mitchell's face. Mitchell opened his mouth and rolled his eyes. Claude whispered, "Don't overdo it! . . . I found this one stealing cabbages."

"A thief in these times is worse than a child-molester, Oberleutnant," one of the guards said, and the other laughed ruefully. "Take him to headquarters; he may have been stealing much more than cabbages."

"Yes," Claude replied, "I'm on my way. It is my night off, but I wanted to perform a service for the Fatherland."

The guards said nothing, and it occurred to Mitchell that they might or might not have agreed with Claude. "Pass," they said in unison, and the car sped down the road at an unhurried, leisurely pace. Rounding a curve, Claude picked up speed.

The car was stopped twice more during the night, and both times the men acted out the previous scenario. After the last encounter with the German patrols, Mitchell felt that he was giving an award-winning portrayal of a frightened, captured Frenchman. But he was becoming more and more uncomfortable riding the rough roads of France in the vibrating little Citroën; flesh was swelling around the tube that he was accommodating, and when they reached their destination the next morning, Mitchell found blood on the seat of the car.

The next two days he spent alone in the upper rooms of an old monastery that overlooked the mists of Lake Geneva. He ate prepared sandwiches of thin slices of tinned corned beef and tiny fancy cakes of preserved orange peel that Alice had fixed for him, and he howled with glee when he reached the bottom of the packet and discovered a handful of popped corn. Only Americans would think of such an oddity; so Gertrude and Alice knew his nationality. How? He searched back over his visit with them and could find nothing amiss; then he thought of the book. Of course, *Rebecca* had given him away.

The next morning Claude showed up very early and drove him up a winding mountain road, where a short runway had been cut into a high plateau. Mitchell's throat caught, and tears filled his eyes. He clutched his St. Christopher medal. Under a green netting rested a gray camouflaged plane! The journey was far from over, but freedom lay ahead.


Pierre Darlan stood stiffly beside the old battered Chevrolet and watched the military plane land on the semi-dark field. He relaxed somewhat against the hood and lighted a cigarette. He was filled with an inner excitement that he could not show. He always felt a certain surge of elation when one of his boys had made it home again. So many had been lost, swallowed up in Nazi prisons or burned in concentration camps.

Two military policemen were escorting the tall, slightly bent figure across the airstrip, and when Pierre

272

waved the men stopped and Mitchell came forward awkwardly. The two men looked each other in the eyes, and Mitchell said soberly, "There were times, Pierre, when I didn't think I'd ever see you again." He took the small, rather frail hand in his and held it for a long moment.

The Frenchman grinned and replied confidently, "I must apologize for the delay in bringing you back, but all hell broke loose. The planned route was closed at the last moment." He broke into a slight laugh. "But that's not important now. I'm certain that you would like a good supper. I'll take you to the National for a good meal, but first we must make one stop at a little house on Connecticut Avenue, where you will be relieved of that irritating little tube."

Mitchell sighed gently. "Yes, I will be glad to get rid of it." He got into the car. "I suppose that all those convicts who use this unsanitary method of concealing personal property develop a certain cavalier attitude about wearing them, but I never got used to the discomfort."

Pierre turned out of the main gate and headed toward Washington. He laughed softly. "I suppose you want a medal?" He glanced at Mitchell. "Where should it be pinned—on your breast or on your ass?"

Mitchell grinned. "*Very* funny!" He paused and sobered. "How long will the debriefing take? I'm anxious to get back to Enid."

"There will be no debriefing. I've made a reservation for you at a hotel. You can leave tomorrow, if you like."

"You mean you don't want to ask any questions?" Mitchell asked incredulously.

"No, all we're interested in is the *package*."

"But I naturally thought you'd want to know all about my. . . ."

Pierre nodded. "I understand, and I don't mean to be

273

impolite, but we have full reports of all your activities in *triplicate*—and, you see, Monsieur Bayard"—and he switched to French—"I won't be able to answer any of your questions."

"You mean I still won't be able to learn anything about what I've just been through?" Mitchell's eyes were dark and troubled.

Pierre shook his head and continued in French. "I know only slightly more than you do. Someday, after the war, we'll get together—God willing—and exchange experiences, but for now . . ."

Mitchell smiled bitterly. "You mean, now that I'm back, it's all over?"

Pierre inclined his head. "Yes, my dear Monsieur Bayard, it is finished."


Mitchell took the small suitcase of clothing that Pierre had kept for him, and checked into the Statler Hotel, where a room lay ready for him. It seemed so strange, this modern building jutting up into the sky, and the well-dressed, well-groomed crowd in the lobby and the smiling elevator girls and servicemen out for a night on the town. It was difficult to believe that the war still raged, and his adventures of the last weeks seemed remote—the stuff of which movies were made, played out against a French countryside.

He looked down at his rumpled tweed suit, which still smelled musty, and suddenly he was pedaling down the streets of Plaisance-du-Gers, his wooden shoes strung over the handlebars of his bicycle.

He snapped back to reality as the elevator opened. Life was moving too fast, and he was suddenly depressed, and he was feeling old, and the sweet-faced elevator girl reminded him of . . . Lise. He shook his head and moved to the back of the lift. He was still back in France, where elevators were called lifts and rye flour was mixed into bread dough and the people had no eggs and ate turnips and the Germans set up barricades in the middle of roads and friends turned against friends—

"It's Mitchell Heron, isn't it?" The soft voice came from behind.

Swiftly he masked his face and turned.

"Don't tell me you've forgotton Charlotte Dice."

He managed a smile. "Of course not," he replied with a forced warmth. "How very nice to see you!" She was very carefully made up, but there were lines under her eyes and mouth; she had not aged well. "It's been a long time," he continued, trying to be cordial. "Let's see, it must be all of fifteen years."

"Yes, I don't go back to Angel anymore, Mitch; there's nothing there for me." She glanced at his unpressed suit, and he could see that she was shocked by his appearance. If there was anyone in the whole wide world that he did not wish to see, it was someone that he knew from the old days.

"I've just been on a . . . fishing trip into Maryland," he remarked casually. "Actually, this is my first vacation in years, and I've just been sort of seeing the country—no real destination, just going where my nose leads me."

He saw that she was relieved. It was as if she were afraid that he was going to ask for a handout.

"Are you staying in the hotel?" she asked.

"Yes, for tonight. I'm going back to Angel tomorrow."

"That's too bad. I would have liked to talk over old times." Her tone was warm, and yet he had the feeling that she was glad that he would not be in town longer and she would have to entertain him.

"This is my floor," Mitchell said, and turned and kissed her on the cheek. "Would you like to have a drink with me later?"

275

"Thank you, but I'm meeting some friends. Give my love to the folks when you see them."

"I will. Good-bye, Charlotte."

"Good-bye, Mitchell."

He got out of the elevator and found his room. He was more depressed than ever. Poor old Charlotte Dice! He smiled to himself. Poor she was not, at least in the financial sense. Fancy running into her in an elevator? Life was very strange, very unpredictable, and he did not want to think anymore about anything. All those months in France, not letting down for one moment, living with the fear that he would be captured, always frightened that he would make a fatal mistake, that some mannerism, some slip of the tongue, would betray him. Now he was back in a real world, where he was not required to be watchful—yet he would always be on guard, because he could never tell anyone about his experiences.

After a hot, luxurious bath, he called room service and ordered a bottle of Kentucky bourbon and allowed himself the privilege of getting drunk for the first time since the war had started. If he babbled in his sleep, there was no one to hear him, no one to jot down his meanderings.

Mitchell arrived in Enid on the night train. He could have easily taken a taxi, but he wanted to walk down the streets and savor the feeling of being home again. He turned up Broadway at the square and looked at the courthouse, and then he came to the building that housed the Heron Furniture Company. The showcase windows were lighted, and the display in the center, a bird's-eye maple bedroom set, was beautifully arranged. Lights in the back of the store threw interesting shadows over the furniture on view. Pride welled up in his breast. The place looked almost more inviting than when he left.

He opened the door with his key and went back to his office, which was spotlessly dusted. He reached in his pocket and took out the St. Christopher medal, which he hung above his desk, over a picture of the Heron clan taken at the family reunion. He picked up the telephone and asked for the Trenton number in Angel, but the line was busy; a few moments later he heard a female voice. "Hold on, they've just hung up."

"Nellie, is that you?" he asked. "This is Mitchell Heron."

"Well, it's about time you got back, young man," she admonished. "I suppose you've had a good time seeing all the sights from Biloxi to Miami!"

He laughed. "Yes, thank you. It was very illuminating."

"I'm sure it was," she said disapprovingly. "Now, if you'll hold on, I'll connect you." . . .

"Aunt Letty? It's Mitch."

"Well, welcome back," Letty said. "I got your card, saying you were on your way. My, you must have seen a lot of the country! Bosley and I were just saying that it's a pity more folk can't travel, but with it being wartime and all . . ." She paused. "When are you coming for a meal? Soon, I hope."

"I'm in the mood for some good Oklahoma cooking." He paused, feeling like a boy again. "Can I come out Sunday for dinner?"

"We'd be disappointed if you didn't."

They said good-bye, and he went into the old storeroom and twirled the dial on the safe. He placed the accounting books on his desk and became immersed in figures. While he was gone, business had improved three percent. He shook his head, thinking of his adventures in France. It almost seemed as if he had

277

emerged from a long dream. Then, glancing at the reunion photograph, he saw Luke's face and he thought of that man in the bistro in Plaisance-du-Gers. The face came up before him, and he felt a pang of deep regret. If conditions had been different, he would have tried to find him. Perhaps, after the war—when, as the lyrics of the song proclaimed, "the lights go on again all over the world"—he would take a trip back to France to find him.

Six weeks later, when Luke had flown in from Tulsa, Mitchell drove over to Angel for supper, and just before they sat down to eat, he asked Luke to go for a walk. As they strolled down by The Widows' Pond, Mitchell inquired, "Do you ever think about World War One?"

Luke looked at him quizzically. "No. What brought that on?"

"The other day I was thinking about how we met at Château-Thierry. If I remember, you were going with a local girl."

Luke shook his head. "No, I patronized the local *estaminet,* which I think I recommended to you. I didn't have a regular."

"You mean you never screwed one of those gals that used to hang around the railroad station?"

"No, our C.O. put the fear of death into us. He said they were all diseased and to not have anything to do with them." He laughed suddenly. "So we all went to the *estaminet,* because the girls were supposed to be examined regularly by a doctor. Of course, that was no sign that they were clean, considering the fact that right after the doctor left they could pick up something, and if you were next in line, you'd get it. I was lucky, though, for all of my fucking around; I never did get anything. How about you?"

"Me neither. Of course, I didn't play around very much."

"Don't I remember you telling me about some chit in Paris?"

"Well, there was one girl that I did see quite a bit, but outside of that . . . Are you sure there wasn't one gal that you went with beside those at the *estaminet*?"

Luke looked at him strangely. "No, I just told you," he replied irritably. "Why are you so curious at this stage of the game?"

Mitchell shrugged his shoulders. "Oh, I don't know, it was all just coming back."

"Well," Luke replied quietly, "I don't like the past. I was young, and a fool, and I carried on in ways that I wouldn't now."

"Of course you did." Mitchell threw him a long, meaningful look. "We all did; there's no crime being hot and horny. In fact, I'd do a lot more today if my age wasn't in the way."

Luke turned by the maple tree. "Mitch, look at the old house from this angle. Don't you think it could do with a new coat of paint?"

"You're right," Mitchell replied quietly, "it could." Luke had changed the subject. The past was gone. Well, if Luke was so certain that he had only played around with the girls at the *estaminet,* then that boy in the bistro must be his, or some kind of a weird family throwback, because everyone knew that whores didn't have babies.

# 15

## *The Dark Part of the Sea*

*The DC-6 neatly cleared the foggy runway after a refueling stop at Bangor, Maine.*

Clement leaned back in his seat and tried to relax. He still did not like to fly, although he had logged tens of thousands of air miles during 1942 and 1943. An old Air Force colonel who had flown in the European Theater had once told him that most airplane accidents occurred during takeoffs and landings.

Clement waited patiently until the plane was fully airborne, then looked about the cabin. There was a full complement of V.I.P.'s aboard: Pentagon officials, a British diplomat whom he had once met casually, and several officers like himself—one was an R.A.F. major. Then, of course, there was the old admiral, who had arrived in such a drunken condition that he had to be strapped into his seat by the steward, a burly sergeant. He became docile at once and had immediately passed into an alcoholic stupor.

Clement patted his coat pocket, in which rested the familiar envelope—ostensibly a harmless letter from Sarah, actually coded and composed by a handwriting expert. He had read the innocuous letter, filled with newsy items and terms of love. The contents must be very special indeed, because his commitment to film a short subject with the orchestra at Universal Studios, to be shown to servicemen overseas, had been canceled at the last moment. He had quickly been booked to appear at a May Day war orphans' benefit in the London suburbs, and the boys in the band had been flown over the pond the previous day.

Leary never interfered with Clement's professional schedules unless it was crucial. If the old man could have transported the information to London any other way, Clement was certain he would have done so; the spying business must be in a bad way if they had to summon a courier all the way from California.

Since he had worked steadily for the last twelve months, making as many as three appearances a day, he was physically and emotionally depleted. His mother had written that they were having a heat wave and students were swimming in The Widows' Pond.

The plane was scheduled for a touchdown in Newfoundland to pick up passengers, and Clement was aware that the runway was icy from the way the plane skidded sideways upon touchdown. He smiled at the familiar Heron logo emblazoned in dull blue on the side of the tank car on the railroad siding by a hangar. Nowhere in the world could he escape that bird. It was omnipresent.

The gruff sergeant, who looked nothing at all like a steward, served icy ham sandwiches and lukewarm coffee once they were airborne. Then Clement stretched out his long, lean legs and dozed. Twelve hours more remained before touchdown in Scotland.

Sleet hitting against the window awakened Clement from a troubled sleep. He roused and looked about the cabin; with lights out, all was serene. Only the old admiral snored. Clement sighed and curled up as best he could, seeking a comfortable position. Thoughts of Angel came back again. Childhood scenes washed over the years. His father, George Story, was lifting him up over the crowds during the first day of the Ringling Brothers and Barnum and Bailey Circus on the old North Broadway lot in Enid, so that he could obtain an unobstructed view of the multicolored clowns leapfrogging over girls in pink tights. The strong, handsome face of his father came up before his eyes, only to be replaced by his shrunken body lying in the upstairs bedroom, being consumed by the cancer that killed him.

His first public appearance, at twelve, at the concert hall in Oklahoma City, where he had played Grieg's "Wedding at Trodhaugen" for an encore showpiece, came back with alarming clarity. He remembered the initial thrill as the audience rose up en masse, giving him his first standing ovation. The scene was replaced with another that had taken place years later; it was just before the war, when the orchestra was playing a gig somewhere in the Midwest. Suddenly the dancers, seemingly mesmerized by his music, had drifted around the old bandstand, concentrating solely on the sounds emanating from the best band in the swing field. The dancers then had sat on the dance floor in a wide, thick circle and looked up with such appreciation and delight on their faces that he again felt his eyes smart and go out of focus. This tribute always made him feel humble, no matter how often it was later repeated.

In the cockpit, the pilot flexed his fingers, yawned, and asked the navigator where in the hell were they anyway? A Texas drawl assured him, that, as far as he could determine, they would be sighting the Scottish coast in about fifteen minutes.

The copilot grinned and rubbed his groin, describing in exquisite detail what he would be doing to whom in what hotel room in about an hour and a half. He had just finished the part where he was washing up for the second bout in bed, when through the fog he saw a familiar shape. "Hey," he shouted, "isn't that a Heinkel 219?"

The pilot peered through the haze. "Damned if it isn't!" Cold perspiration broke out on his forehead. The Heinkel 219 was rumored to be the Nazis' best night fighter. He had been briefed about its specifications: two 30mm cannons, mounted in the fuselage, could be fired both backward and forward, which allowed the pilot to position the cannon to take advantage of an enemy bomber's blind spots. For this reason, the adroit firing mechanisms, with their distinctive *ruty, tuty, tut tut* sounds, were called *schräge Musik*, or, in English, jazz music."

The pilot swallowed hard as he peered through the mists on the right side of the plane, where a second shape came out of the cloud shadows. It was as if they were being escorted. Then, from the far left and above, in a comparative stretch of purple sky, he glimpsed two Junker 88G-1's, extraordinarily versatile aircraft that could be utilized as bombers, reconnaissance, or day or night fighters.

"Holy shit!" he shouted to the copilot. "They're out to get us!"

He knew then, as perspiration poured from his armpits, dampening his beautifully hand-tailored O.D.'s, that their only salvation was to head for the heavy cloud bank to the left, which he had planned to avoid because of the resultant turbulent air. He accelerated suddenly, throwing the occupants in the cabin backward. The old admiral roused. "What the fuck?" he mumbled.

Clement's head snapped back painfully; he rubbed his neck and peered out of the window, then sucked in his breath. A strange-looking aircraft was approaching so fast that he could see the goggled pilot maneuvering the cannon. There was a rapid burst of flame, and the DC-6 shuddered, quieted, shuddered again, and then leaped up only to fall back, seemingly as leisurely as a skiff on an ocean swell.

Clement watched in horror as a burst of *ruty, tuty, tut tut* sound, accompanied by tongues of flame, knocked out the right engine. It was as if the occupants of the plane were suspended somewhere, watching a graphic, pictorial war-training film that was slowly turning into reality. The DC-6 swerved to the left in a cockeyed slow-motion movement. There was the sound of metal twisting, and pieces of the blackened smoke-filled sky above could be discerned, as if they were all gazing through a giant sieve. It occurred to Clement that the aircraft was literally disintegrating before his eyes. He was helpless.

In that last incredible, terrifying moment while the monstrous rush of air hissed about him, before the final free-fall—as blood gushed from his eyes—he saw the Chenovick's peach trees in full bloom. From far away, as if through the smooth, serpentine depths of a tunnel, he faintly heard the last strains of Torgo's violin playing "The Old Chisholm Trail."


"I don't give a good goddamn what you think!" H. L. Leary shouted. "Send out *more* search planes. Clement Story was on board."

"I know that," the young major was saying over the wire, "but so was Admiral Leonard."

"That old drunk!"

"I beg your pardon, sir?" The major's voice dripped ice.

Leary was about to give a heated reply, then thought better of it. "Now, give me the details again," he said patiently, "to be sure I've got it right."

The major sighed audibly. "Apparently the plane was shot down at about eight hundred hours, sir. Heinkel 219 fighters were seen in the air—*schräge Musik*."

"That's strange. Any other Allied planes in the air at the same time?"

"One, but apparently they were *after* that plane."

"Ah," Leary replied, "I see." He paused a moment, collecting his thoughts. "No debris anywhere?"

"The seas were very choppy. An hour or so later a storm blew up, and any traces were wiped away." He paused. "By the way, I didn't know you were a fan of Story's."

"I'm not," Leary replied angrily and hung up; then he reached for his direct-line phone. "I suppose you've heard the news," he said to his superior. "Rotten luck. I liked that man. I told the major to see that additional planes were sent out, and I'd appreciate it if you'd also put on some pressure."

"Luke Heron is sure to put the needle on some of his Pentagon buddies to launch an investigation," his superior replied. "We've got to have our flanks covered."

Leary lighted a cigarette and blew the smoke out all at once. "At least, if they got Story, our other man got through. Have you heard from him?" There was a pause, and Leary's face fell. "Oh, no! Damn! That's pure, unadulterated carelessness. If he missed the fucking plane, why wasn't someone else sent? What? Yes. Very well." He hung up and snubbed out the cigarette in the tray and went into the chart room, where Pierre Darlan was bending over a map of the Low Countries. "Clement Story," he announced sadly, "has just been lost at sea."

"Oh, *non!*" Pierre's mustaches quivered, and he turned to the window and looked out over the grounds at Langley, Virginia. "*Merde!*" he exclaimed.

"My sentiments exactly," Leary retorted. "The other courier didn't get through either—missed his plane or some such amateur thing. It's impossible to believe, sometimes, that we're a bunch of professionals, when an incident like this happens. My God, missing a plane!" He paused. "Well, at least Operation Overlord—D-Day in Europe—has been set. It's the sixth of

June—at Normandy." He smiled ruefully. "The Allied Command has gone poetic. The starting signal is to be a line of Paul Verlaine's about the changing of the seasons. The BBC, in broadcasting its usual coded messages to the Resistance, will announce, '*Les sanglots longs des violons de l'automne.*' "

"Ah, yes," Pierre replied, translating, " 'The long sobs of the violins of autumn.' "

"Yes; then the Resistance will know to listen in for the second line, which will indicate invasion within forty-eight hours."

"I know the line," Pierre said. '*Blessent mon coeur d'une langueur monotone*'—which is, of course, 'Wound my heart with a monotonous languor.' " He shrugged his shoulders. "I wonder who came up with those lines? Eisenhower? Highly unlikely; he's a capable general, but I am certain his knowledge of the French classics is limited. De Gaulle? He's out of it, so who could it be?"

"Admiral Sir Bertram Ramsay?"

"He's too stiff."

"Field Marshal Montgomery?"

Pierre laughed. "Who knows? There may be a poetic streak lurking in some of these men that only a patient wife or an understanding mistress would ever know about. Who knows what happens in a bedchamber or what poems are quoted in a passionate embrace?"

Leary laughed. "You're impossible, Pierre."

"Perhaps." He grew silent. "All I can really think about is the world being deprived of that wonderful musicianship, and all because of—what? A set of plans that did not get through anyway. A senseless death."

"No," Leary replied softly, "no deaths in war are senseless."

Pierre threw him a long, searching look. "Have you been in the business so long that you have lost touch with the humanities?" He sighed. "No," he went on sadly, "we will go on decimating ourselves in war after war until, in the end, there will be a great deal of technology and a handful of people. Will they be yellow or black or white? Somehow I do not think there will be much of a mixture. Most of the countries will go up in smoke, *mon cher*."

Leary frowned. "It's not like you to be so pessimistic, Pierre. Your concept of the future is very dark indeed."

Pierre nodded. "Yes, it is, at the moment. I may feel differently tomorrow, but now I feel like getting very drunk. Let us repair to a good restaurant and have a good dinner, then have some cognac—in memory of that boy who came down in the sea."

Leary got up stiffly and rubbed his back. "That sounds excellent. But before I go I must do something that is very difficult for me to do, yet it must come from me and not his commanding officer. I must send telegrams to both Letty Trenton and Sarah Story. Damn the war, Pierre, damn the war!"

Letty's arm was tired and wet with perspiration; her fingers numb. She looked down at the dark, reddish devil's food batter in the round bowl and rested her hands a moment. Fontine's Santone recipe stipulated fifty strokes. "And don't do any less or it won't turn out right," she had cautioned. "Also, the liquid has to be genuine Coca-Cola, not that other stuff you get at soda fountains these days."

Letty thought of her dear friend, whom she had known for fifty years, and smiled softly. There was no one in the whole wide world quite like Fontine Dice. She completed the last fourteen strokes, rubbed her aching arm, and poured the rich, dark cherry-colored batter into two pans, which she placed on the middle rack in the oven. On the hottest day of the year, she would bake! The doorbell rang. She wiped her hands on her apron and, since it was Hattie's day off, answered the door herself.

The Baker boy, one of the few lads in town under draft age, stood on the porch. She recognized him from the large nose and the red hair that ran in his family. She had known his grandfather, Eben, who had opened the first general store in Angel in 1893. She smiled pleasantly at the lad, who stood throwing his weight from one foot to the other. "Stanley, isn't it?" she asked.

"Yessim." He fidgeted nervously.

"Well, do come in, it's too hot to stand out there on the porch," she said. "I'll get some iced cocoa."

"Can't stay," he muttered, but made no move to leave.

"Well, what can I do for you, Stanley?" she asked kindly, thinking about her own boys when they were in that awkward, adolescent age and didn't know what to do with their hands.

Apprehensively, he thrust a telegram in her face, wheeled around, and ran down the path as if pursued by demons. She stood a long moment looking down at the yellow envelope, feeling slightly faint. She did not feel the hot blast that blew in from the street. She sat down on the warm bottom step of the porch, holding her breath for a moment, gathering courage, then with trembling fingers opened the envelope and unfolded the yellow square. She read, then reread the telegram until she knew it by heart:

TERRIBLY DISTRESSED TO INFORM YOU THAT CLEMENT'S PLANE WAS SHOT DOWN WITH NO SURVIVORS STOP DETAILS YET TO COME STOP WILL INFORM YOU PARTICULARS WHEN AVAILABLE STOP KNOW THAT HE DIED IN SERVICE TO HIS COUNTRY.

H. L. LEARY

Strangely, the tears would not come. Letty got up slowly, and went back into the house, her footfalls resounding hollowly in the quiet hall. Thank heavens she was alone with her grief. She could not have borne Bosley's sympathy. She went up the stairs slowly and down the hall, into Clement's old room, which had somehow retained some of his personality. From the top of the chiffonier, his irregular features stared out from a photograph that had been taken during his jazz-band days. On the wall was a recent picture of him standing with his baton, surrounded by his uniformed orchestra.

Letty went to the window and raised the blind. Angel was asleep in the afternoon sun. Few people were about. Old Mrs. Stevens, holding a loaded shopping bag, was emerging from the grocery store, and Stanley Baker was trudging along the dusty side street that led by God's Acre.

She went downstairs, and let herself out the front door. How strange it was, the way that the town had sprung up around her very doorstep, she thought. In the old days she had only been able to see the general store and the blacksmith shop from her upstairs window. A few moments later she opened the new, fancy wrought-iron gate to God's Acre and went to the plot, where George Story was buried.

Letty swept away parched, yellow leaves from the side of the impressively-carved granite stone that had cost fifteen hundred depression dollars, collected a mound of reddish earth, then placed the telegram on the uncovered humus. She methodically piled dirt and brown grass over the yellow envelope. "This is where you belong, Clement," she whispered, "next to your father." Then, still dry-eyed, she made her way back to the clapboard, her stooped figure shuffling along the warm sidewalk that was sending heat waves into the atmosphere.

Before reaching the porch, she saw that the hired

man had swept a path through the dried leaves to the meadow down to the stile that spanned the fence to the Dice place. The air was cooler now and seemed peculiarly refreshing to her lungs. She decided to walk further. She was less short of breath now as she made her way carefully down the cleared path. She paused by the old maple tree that stretched heavy laden branches to the sky—Clement's favorite spot as a little boy. She leaned against the tree as his sweet treble voice seemed to echo eerily through the woods:

*. . . With my knees in the saddle and my seat in the sky, I'll quit punching cows in the sweet by and by.*

It was then, hearing the memory of his tiny, bell-like voice, telescoping the years, that she began to weep. She leaned on the old tree trunk, her face pressed into the rough bark, and sobbed as if her heart would break. Then, after a while, she stood up straight and in the gathering dusk found her way back down the path to the clapboard. Now that she was composed, she must call Sarah.

Sarah's thin voice came strongly over the wire. "I don't care what they say, Mother, Clement is *not* dead." Letty knew her pose; she would be standing defiantly, feet wide apart. "I would know. There was a closeness between us, Mother. I always knew when he was in trouble or sick on the road. If he was dead, I'd feel a terrible sense of loss. I don't."

Letty sighed softly. "Oh, Sarah, we must face life as it really is," she pleaded. "We can't go on hoping against hope; it's not fair to his memory."

"They've not found his body."

"They haven't found *any* of the bodies, Sarah. The currents around Lands End are fierce, and . . ." Her voice was faint. She had cried until she could cry no more, and she had not called Sarah until she was certain that she would not break down. Now it was as if she had run into a blank wall. "No wreckage has been discovered."

"Isn't there a possibility that the plane was captured, Mother?"

Letty sat down on the sofa. "They say not. Apparently there was another plane fairly near that reported enemy fighters and a flash of light, an explosion, as Clement's plane came down. It's certain there are no survivors."

"Mother," Sarah said quietly, "I know he's alive."

"Oh, my dear, my very dear," Letty said compassionately.

"Oh, don't console me! I can't bear that. After all, he's your own son."

"We must face reality, Sarah." She paused and then asked gently, "You know they're going to award him, and the others who were lost, gold medals?"

"I don't want a piece of worthless brass."

"Very well, my dear." Letty paused. "When can you come to the farm?"

"Not for a while. I'm busy at the Red Cross in the morning, and I join the Gray Ladies in the afternoon at the railroad station, passing out doughnuts and coffee to the troops going through. Then, in the evening, it's the U.S.O."

"I understand," Letty replied slowly.

"Pray for Clement to come home, Mother."

Letty's eyes filled with tears. "Let's talk again soon, Sarah."

Letty was about to hang up, when Nellie came on the line. "Poor dear," she sympathized. "I had a sister who lost her husband and never admitted that he was dead, even when they sent back his ashes."

Suddenly Letty could take no more. "Would you

please mind your own business for once, Nellie!" And she threw the instrument into the cradle.

Luke Three, red-eyed and pale, appeared at the station for work at eight o'clock in the morning, but Jerrard was already engaged in cleaning the latrines. "Hi," he said, his face pinched. "Sure sorry to hear about your uncle." He pushed the mop back and forth, not looking up. "You didn't have to come in; I can handle the business." He leaned on the mop handle. "Why don't you go back home?"

Luke Three shook his head. "No, I want to keep busy. I'll hose down the front. The family's in an uproar, and I'd rather be down here anyway." He straightened his back and puffed out his chest. "Jerrard, how old do you think I could pass for?"

Jerrard grinned. "Oh, I dunno. You've sure popped up this summer. I'm six two and a half, and you're almost up to me. You're skinnier, of course, and you've still got to fill out some, but I'd say you could pass for nineteen—that is, if you'd keep that silly grin off your face. Why?"

Luke Three removed a miniature file from his key chain and sought to remove the grime under his nails. "Do you still have that refugee friend in Pond Creek?" he went on conversationally. "You know, the guy that fixes fake driver's licenses and such?"

"Sure. His price has gone up, though. I think he charges fifteen dollars now. Why?"

"I want him to make up a phony birth certificate for me, showing that I'll be eighteen in a couple of weeks. Can he do that?"

"I don't see why not." Jerrard paused and sucked his teeth for a moment. "Why do you need it?"

Luke Three's eyes smarted, and he turned away. "I can't stay here in Angel." Under control, he looked at

292

Jerrard. "I know you won't give me away if I tell you I want to enlist in the Marines."

"Why do you want to go and do that for?" Jerrard looked at Luke Three as if he had suddenly lost his reason. "My God, going over there and maybe getting killed when you don't have to? Look, it's possible the war will be over before you have to sign up. Then, let Uncle Sam draft you."

"Naw, Jerrard," Luke Three replied softly. "I want to go in. Somebody has to take Uncle Clem's place. There isn't anybody left in the family to represent the Herons or the Storys or the Trentons." He clenched his fists. "It's my place to go."

"Your *place*! My God, it's nobody's place to *go*! Thank the good Lord I have a punctured eardrum. If I hadn't, I'd have been a conscientious objector. I don't believe in taking up arms against my fellow man."

"That's horseshit, and you know it!" Luke Three shouted, his face a mottled red. "Where did you read that crap? Just because you're yellow, don't be handing out any advice. I've got to go, and that's that, and if you won't put me in touch with that guy in Pond Creek, I'll find someone else."

Jerrard wrung out the mop in the hand wringer. "Well, Luke Three"—his voice was very low—"I suppose if you gotta go, you gotta go." He looked up. "Just think it over real carefully. You have to think about the future. You're in line for the presidency of Heron Oil when your old man retires, and the way he's burning the candle at both ends, that won't be long. What's going to happen to the company if you're killed, or, worse yet, come back without an arm or a leg or end up a vegetable in an institution?"

Luke Three nonchalantly stuck his hands in his pockets. "All of this won't matter if we lose the war. In that case, Heron's president will be some goddamned Jap or Nazi, and our Heron logo will be replaced with

293

the Rising Sun or the Swastika. I've got to fight that, Jerrard. I can't stay here pumping gas for the duration."

"Okay, tell me what information you want on the certificate, and I'll have my friend do his duty, but because of your name it's a bad risk, and he'll probably charge you double, or even triple. If it ever became known that he forged your birth certificate, he'd probably be deported."

"I don't care what it costs—get me that paper!"

"Hold on a minute!" Jerrard exclaimed. "Something just hit me. If you're inducted, your old man is going to move heaven and earth. Within hours the phones will be ringing off their hooks between Tulsa and Washington, and you'll be right back here where you started— or, even worse, in military school in Tulsa. He knows the right people to call."

"Hell!" Luke Three exclaimed. "Of course you're right. I hadn't thought about that."

Jerrard laughed wryly. "If you're bound and determined to do this fool thing, as long as my friend is forging your birth certificate he might as well give you a new name too."

"That's a great idea. But what am I going to call myself?" He looked idly around the station and saw the movie card for the June coming attractions at the Blue Moon Theater:

*Deanna Durbin*
*in*
CHRISTMAS HOLIDAY
*with*
*Gene Kelly*

He whirled around. "How about Gene Holiday?" He was fired with enthusiasm, "And the address?" He looked up at the numbers on the station. "Yes, that's it,

294

Gene Holiday, three-seventy two Main Street, Angel, Oklahoma." He paused. "Do you think I can get away with it?"

Jerrard shrugged his shoulders. "Why not?" He jerked his thumb at the hoist. "They can string me up there by my pecker, and I wouldn't give you away."

Luke Three, being a realist, highly doubted that statement, but he nodded his head. "Thanks, friend," he said, keeping his grin inside.

The telephone rang, and when Luke Three answered, he heard his grandmother's excited voice. "It's happened, my boy, the troops have landed at Normandy. This is D-Day!"

Three days later, Luke Three took the morning train to Enid and filled out all of the forms at the recruiting station, where young men like himself had stood in line since early morning. On the train, he had thought that he would be nervous and doubted that he could look the sergeant in the eye, but once in the huge center, looking into frightened faces of the older men, he knew that he would have no trouble with keeping his composure. Also, he felt extremely good about his age; some of the boys in line had not even begun to shave on a regular basis, while his own beard was heavy and dark. He was surprised to find that he was one of the tallest of the group.

When he handed in his papers and the long test, the weary sergeant did not give him a second glance. "You'll be hearin'," he said casually. "Next, please."

# 16

## The Runaway

*Luke Three met Darlene at the Sugar Bowl immediately after work, for Dr. Peppers "with a squirt of cherry flavoring."*

"I've got something important to tell you," he said gravely, once they were ensconced in the back booth.

She had never seen him so composed, and she regarded him thoughtfully. Suddenly it struck her that he was a man. Of course she was aware of his new growth in height; it seemed that every time she saw him he was taller, and he was now wearing his hair slicked back in a smooth ducktail, which made him look older. His face had taken on more character, too, and he was sporting a vague five-o'clock shadow. But it was his manner, more than anything else, that had changed and matured.

When they were sipping their drinks, he looked her in the eye. "Now, Darlene, I'm going to tell you something, but you've got to promise that you won't tell a soul. Can you keep a secret?"

"Of course. You know that I don't have a loose mouth."

He grinned. "You sure don't." And he noted for the

hundredth time that her lips were perfectly formed in a wide bud shape, perfectly outlined by the fire-engine-red lipstick that she always wore. With the late-afternoon sun pouring in over the booth, she looked like a china figurine in the Bon Marché shop across the street.

"Now, Luke Three, tell me your secret."

"If you ever tell," he said intensely, "I'll come back and haunt you."

"Is that it? Are your parents forcing you to go back to Tulsa for the new school term?"

"They aren't forcing me to do anything." He paused, and then blurted, "I joined the Marine Corps today!"

Her mouth dropped open. "You *didn't*!"

"I sure did," he replied proudly. "I can't wait to go; it's getting so that I hate Angel and everyone in it—except you, of course, Darlene."

She took his hand. "Luke, how can you go? You're not old enough."

"I'm almost eighteen. I didn't lie very much."

"But I know your mom and dad didn't sign a paper for you, and that's the only way. . . ."

He shook his head. "I can't tell you how I did it, but I did." He looked at his watch. "I've got to get home for supper. Will you go with me to the picture show tonight?"

"What's playing?"

*"Hail the Conquering Hero."*

She laughed. "It's kind of apropros, I suppose."

He grinned. "I didn't think of it that way, but I suppose it is. I hear that it's a swell comedy. Let's go to the second show. It starts at eight-thirty."

"Okay."

"Pick you up at your house about eight? We can walk downtown together."

"No," she put in quickly, thinking about her mother. "No, I'll meet you in front of the Blue Moon."

Luke Three and Darlene were in a good mood as they left the theater. "I don't know when I've enjoyed myself more, Luke Three," she said.

"It was a comic picture, all right." He paused. "I don't feel like going home, do you?"

"Not really, the night is too pretty."

"Tell you what, why can't we go for a drive?"

"I'm low on gas."

He grinned. "Hell, don't worry about that." He stole a look at her. "Didn't you know that 'gas pump' is my middle name?"

She giggled, then gave him the keys. "You drive, I just want to look at the moon."

He headed the roadster out toward McClain Road to an incline behind God's Acre, and parked at the end of the lane. Then he hurriedly took her in his arms.

She pulled herself free. "Luke Three!" she gasped. "I said I wanted to look at the moon. I didn't say anything about being pawed."

"I'm not pawing you."

"Keep your hands to yourself," she said, cuddling against his shoulder and looking through the windshield at the round disk.

"Will you miss me?" he asked quietly.

"Yes, I won't get any more free gas," she teased.

"Be serious. I am."

She looked up at him. "Of course I'll miss you." She opened her lips, anticipating a kiss.

He lowered his mouth to hers. The kiss grew deeper and deeper, and the electricity built up for them both. She wanted to break away, but he held her strongly, bringing his hands up on either side of her face, holding her like a vise, while he explored her mouth with his tongue. He released her gently, then. "I do love to smooch with you," he said breathlessly.

She moved her fingers over his lips. "You're a sweet,

sweet boy, Luke Three." she said as she moved down into his arms, feeling the pounding in his groin, which felt good against her thigh. They kissed again—a more daring position this time, with him assuming an aggressive pose over her half-reclining body.

It was wonderful, she decided, to be held so strongly by someone that she truly cared a great deal about. It was not like the senior quarterback whom she had dated the summer before. He had been clumsy and had not given her time to respond properly to his kisses before he had stretched himself over her on the blanket beside the car. And it had done absolutely no good to plead with him, because he was so overpoweringly muscular. She had cried a good deal afterward, too, especially when he had not spoken to her all the way home. But what hurt the most was that he never called her again.

When she had first kissed Luke Three, when he had first come to Angel, it had been fun because he didn't know what to do with his hands. He was so sweet and awkward, but he was an easy pupil, and the thrill of his lips could be very overwhelming. He had been fun because he was like an erotic younger brother, but now he had changed and taken command. He was gentle and caring, and she realized suddenly that she liked him more than she had admitted to herself in the past. And, oh, she loved the feel of his lips on her own!

He held her tightly and wondered what move he should make next. She was wearing a soft angora sweater and a plaid skirt, and the pearls around her neck were pressing into his chin. She was responding so well to his kisses that he placed his tongue in her mouth again, and she pressed up against him even more closely.

He freed his hands and brought them up to her breasts. "Hey, cut that out," she said—but not very convincingly, he felt. He tried to change his position, but the front seat of the roadster was so small that he could barely fold his six-foot-two frame at an angle to accommodate Darlene, and she was not a tiny person. Besides, his right foot was asleep, which took away some of his ardor.

"I've got to get out and walk a little," he said. "My foot's as dead as a doornail." She giggled and unwound herself from his embrace.

He staggered out of the car and limped up and down, while she doubled up with laughter. "You look like an old man!" she exclaimed. "All you need is a cane."

The opportunity was too great to pass up, and with the feel of pins and needles piercing his foot, he placed his hand on his hip and limped even more badly, while she shouted with glee. He knew at that moment what Uncle Clem must have felt like when he was entertaining a large group of people; there must be an enormous amount of appreciation that flowed between the audience and him, if *he* could feel the forceful pull that Darlene was exerting as she tuned in to his performance. He pointed to the moon. "Look," he said.

While the feeling was returning to his foot, Darlene leaned up against the front fender and looked up at the sky. "There's Ursa Major!" she exclaimed. "It's so very clear tonight."

He came up beside her. "I don't see it," he said.

She took his hand and raised it to the northwest. "There."

"Ah," he replied, "it is beautiful." Then, instinctively, he turned to her. "But not as beautiful as you are now," he said, and took her in his arms again.

She had not meant to lean back on the fender, had not intended for him to be so close, but that time with the quarterback in high school suddenly paled compared to what she was experiencing now. Before, there had been only a fleeting emotional moment, but, encased in a warmth that was surprisingly intense, she

300

knew that she wanted to feel Luke Three near, nearer, *nearest*.

He bent her slightly back over the fender and found that he had positioned himself between her saddle shoes. While he pressed up against her, he began to kiss her neck and her ears and then her mouth. Then he raised her skirt, exerting more pressure on her lips, and then, somehow in the heat of the moment, he was free of his trousers and suddenly he felt a marvelous warmth. She moved slightly, uttering little cries, and then all of his awkwardness vanished as he raised himself up slightly. At once they were partially together. She was breathing very fast and she began to shudder as she moved slowly and carefully upon him, and he knew one pure moment of delight. They shuddered deliciously together, discovering the wonderful warmth of the aftermath. Then she began to move slowly until she felt him deep inside. The moment that they were completely together, they shuddered once more; then they kissed again and again.

The moon was covered for a moment with a cloud, and while the area was in darkness they became themselves once more.

Later he got behind the wheel, and she snuggled down into his arms. "When will you go?" she asked.

He shook his head. "Soon." He cupped her face in his hands, suddenly feeling powerful and strong and very much a man, while she was soft and feminine and very small in his arms.

His heart gradually returned to normal, and he was filled with inner peace. Jerrard, in all of his tales about making love, recounted a hundred times, had never told him about the feeling of contentment that he was experiencing now. Or was he feeling something that was totally unique with Darlene and himself? "I almost don't want to go now," he said, at last, "and leave you here."

She looked up at his face, which was suffused with a

new expression that she had never seen before. "I won't hold you, Luke Three. I don't think any woman should hold a man when he knows what he wants to do. I know how important it is for you to go. If you stayed here, it wouldn't be the same."

"You're right," he replied, "it wouldn't. Now, one thing, Darlene, I promise I'll write to you, but you won't be able to write back right away, because I've got to get so much straightened out. There are things I can't rightly tell you."

She placed her fingers over his lips. "I know that." She paused. "Don't you know that I trust you?"

He looked at her with growing appreciation. "And— why, Darlene, I trust you too." He smiled. "Yes, I do." And it was the first time in his life that he had come out in the open and made a statement like that, and suddenly he felt very proud. He started the engine. "I best get you home," he said, placing the car in gear.

She laughed. "Stop in front of your house, Luke Three; then I'll take the wheel. No use you driving me home and then walking back. That's not fair."

He kissed her cheek. "You know that I love you, don't you?" he said lightly.

She shook her head. "No."

"How do you feel about me? I mean, now that we've. . . ." He could not finish the sentence, because he was red from embarrassment.

"I've loved you for a long time, Luke Three, only I didn't know it until tonight."

"Will you wait for me?" he asked slowly.

She nodded. "Yes."

"I'll get you a ring to seal the bargain."

She shook her head. "That's not necessary, Luke Three. A ring wouldn't make it right if it wasn't right already."

He looked at her with new appreciation. "I like the

302

way you're able to say things, put your thoughts in order, Darlene. I feel the same way, but I don't think I could have said it so well."

"Do you really think that I need a reminder, Luke Three?"

"I hope not, but I want to give you something."

She smiled softly. "I'll have the memory of you. That's all I need, Luke Three."

He was to remember those words often in the months ahead.

July 8, 1944, the induction papers arrived at the Heron station. Luke Three stood in line at the armory in Enid with other men in mufti, carrying only a shaving kit. At one-thirty, along with thirty other men, he was standing naked before a harried doctor, while holding a blue duffel bag containing his clothing. Two older men in front of him were laughing, their heads together. One of them pointed at Luke Three. "My God, look at the piece of meat on the kid!" Luke Three blushed and turned away, yet he was pleased and complimented. He threw back his shoulders.

At two-thirty he was admitted to a tiny cubicle, where a psychiatrist looked up and snarled, "Do you like girls?"

Luke thought how soft Darlene Trune had felt in his arms, and nodded numbly. "Next," came the retort.

Luke Three found himself in a line that led by another doctor, seated in a chair, who clasped his testicles and barked, "Turn to left and cough." Luke complied with the order, and the doctor shouted, "Next!"

He was in turn X-rayed, poked, probed, tested, and bled, and at four-fifteen was dressed and herded with forty other men into the back of a truck and transported across town to the railway station; and at six-thirty he was in a smoky turn-of-the-century Pullman that sported gas lights, on his way to Camp Pendleton Marine Base in California.

At seven o'clock Stanley Baker trudged up to the Trenton clapboard with a letter. Letty opened the envelope and started to cry. Wordlessly she handed the message to Bosley, who read:

Dear Grandma and Grandpa:


I don't want to hurt you and I don't want to hurt Mom and Dad, but I just had to join. Don't try to find me, because you can't. I'm taking Uncle Clem's place.

Love
Luke T.


Bosley placed the letter on the table and took Letty in his arms. "He doesn't know what he said, does he?"

She dried her tear-drenched face. "It's like history is repeating itself," she said slowly. "What a turn that gave me! It was as if I was reading Clement's letter when he ran away and enlisted in the First World War." She turned to Bosley. "Call Luke and see what he wants to do. I can't talk right now."

She went out on the porch and sat down in the old rocker. Any other time, she would have enjoyed the long, golden sunset that turned the landscape orange. She idly watched a bevy of quail cross the road in front of the house, and she thought: *Her family is safe in her protection.* What had she done to protect Luke Three?

"Nellie, is that you? Get me Tulsa, the Heron home number, please."

"The circuits are all tied up, Bos," came the high-pitched voice.

"Damn the circuits. Get those old hens off the line. This is an emergency!"

She hung up with such a clatter that the noise reverberated in his ear, but the connection came through clearly. A moment later Luke came on the line. "Yes, Uncle Bos?"

"I don't know how to tell you this, so I'll come straight out with it. Luke Three has run away and joined the service."

There was a long, shocked pause, then Luke exclaimed, "Damn him! Give me the particulars."

"We got his note this very minute. He went to work as usual at eight this morning. It was his day off, I guess. I get his hours mixed up sometimes."

"He must be still over in Enid. Hang up, and I'll make a call. I know one of the colonels."

"What are you going to do?"

"Bring the stupid kid back—what else? He's only seventeen—"

"—and a half."

"Don't be sarcastic."

"Clement was only fifteen when he joined."

"Yes, but he was mature and responsible. Luke Three is a kid."

"He's a sensible boy. He's grown up a lot lately, if you haven't noticed."

"Don't try to defend him," Luke put in. "He's coming home, and that's that!" He was becoming angry. The line went dead in his ear. Luke placed a person-to-person call to Jim Patterson at the armory in Enid, but the colonel was busy, said an aide, and would return the call.

Luke paced up and down in front of his desk for the fifteen minutes that it took before the call came in from Enid. "Jim, I've just learned that my son, who's not eighteen yet, paid you a visit today."

The colonel laughed. "Well, he didn't get anywhere, Luke. The recruiting station won't take him without parental consent, so don't worry. We get boys like that in here every day, and we usually stall them until their parents come after them. Don't worry, I'll do a little checking."

A half-hour later, he called back. "We didn't have one underage kid today. Then, in case of a snafu, I went over the roster of inductees, in the event he somehow got as far as receiving his greetings, but no Heron was listed."

Luke paused a long moment. "Could he have gone to Oklahoma City?"

Jim Patterson shook his head. "No, any notice would have had to have been mailed from here. Let's see if anyone's come in from Angel." His finger went down the list. "He's not among the batch that we're processing now. Three other carloads have already been run through today, but I can't check those manifests, dammit, because all the papers have been sent along with the inductees. Most young guys want the Air Force."

Luke searched his brain. "I don't think it's ever come up in conversation, Jim."

"Then he could be in any group that went out today, if there's been a foul-up. If he's passed his physical, we'll have to wait a day or so until I can get someone to run through the cards. I wish I could be of more immediate help, but we're really swamped over here. A job like this is something for the birds. If my kid pulled a stunt like this, I'd murder him."

Luke's voice was weary. "Thanks, Jim. Call me as soon as you find out any leads. I'll pay whatever expense is entailed in bringing him back home."


Luke Three had folded himself into the cramped, ancient upper Pullman berth at lights-out the night before, and now at five o'clock in the morning he tried to find a comfortable position. Every bone in his body ached. He wondered where the armed services had found such relics of another era. He also had a classic case of indigestion, caused by either the supper of corned beef and

306

black cabbage served in a mess kit or the unaccustomed vibration of the train traveling over rusty tracks—or perhaps, he reflected, by both.

Breakfast consisted of a yellow, watery concoction that did and did not resemble eggs, and bacon as salty and bitter as brine, served along with a piece of burned toast. Some joker had commented that they were now in New Mexico, and he would have liked to see the landscape, but due to wartime rules the train blinds had been lowered, and with the gas lights flickering, the ninety-degree heat, three poker games going simultaneously, and a strange assortment of bodies and accents, Luke Three felt as if he were on some strange, primitive camping trip.

At Fort Sumner, New Mexico, population 508, the train was placed on a siding, and thankfully the area was sufficiently remote that the men were permitted to disembark. Lines formed in front of the local drugstore for ice-cream cones and wartime cola served in paper cups. Luke Three queued up at one of the pay telephones and after forty minutes finally placed his call to the office in Tulsa.

"Bernice, is Dad in?"

"Luke Three?" Her voice sounded relieved. "I'll put you right through." He could hear her excited voice: "Mr. Heron, it's *him*!"

"Where in the hell are you, anyway?" Luke's voice was so loud it hurt Luke Three's ear.

He was nervous because he had never stood up to his father before. "Now, just simmer down, Dad. I can't tell you where I am, or you'd send the militia after me."

"You're godamned right I would."

"If you have me tracked down, I'll enlist again."

"Are you trying to tell me that you've already been accepted? How did you pull that off?"

"A lot of guys are waiting to make calls, Dad, and I've got to hang up." His voice broke, and he thought

307

for a moment that he was going to cry. He swallowed hard. "You won't be able to write to me, but I promise that I'll keep in touch. Look after Murdock."

"Tell me where you are!"

"I can't, Dad."

"But why are you doing this to your mother and me?"

"I'm not doing anything to anybody." His voice held new conviction. "It's my life, and I'm going to do what I have to do. You don't really need me around, Dad, you never did, and besides, I'm doing this for Uncle Clem. I gotta go, Dad; if these guys don't get to make their calls, I'll probably get knocked in the head. Give my love to Mom, Grandma and Grandpa, and Murdock. Don't worry about me, Dad. I'll be okay."

The line went dead. Luke stared at the receiver for a long time. Suddenly he was back in France at Château-Thierry, where he had encountered Clement. He saw him standing there in the dusty little square in his private's uniform, and saw how flushed and happy he was, and once more he experienced the thrill of camaraderie that they shared on that occasion. He had admired Clement for running away from home and enlisting at the age of fifteen. What had the years done to him? Why hadn't he been close to Luke Three, so that the boy could confide in him? Somewhere along the line he had forgotten what it was like to be young. In France, it had been Clement and he against the world. Was that the way Luke Three felt—alone, abandoned, forced to make his way in an alien place?

Luke called Bosley in Angel. "Uncle Bos," he said brokenly, "I've just spoken to Luke Three. . . . Yes, he's fine. . . . I've been thinking, if going into the service is so important to him, I don't think we should use extraordinary means to bring him back. I've failed the kid in probably more ways than I even know about. If he feels he's got to be on his own to be a man, then I think we've got to let him find out what it's all about."

"Whatever made you change your mind, Luke? Why, just last evening you were going to move heaven and earth—"

"I know, I know. But I got to thinking about Clement and me in France. I don't remember whether I told you about that or not. Anyway, the scene came back, and the most startling thing about my attitude was that when I met my little brother on the battlefield, I didn't feel at all protective or apprehensive. I was there, he was there, and that was that—an accepted fact. I suppose if I was Luke Three's age right now, I'd probably feel the same way he does. I mean, the kid's bright, he's no fool. He knew that if he waited until he was eighteen, I'd have arranged a commission for him and he'd have it a lot easier. Now he's on his own with very little money, I'm sure. Out there, somewhere, without any illusions . . ."

"I think what you've just said is . . . very wise, Luke," Bosley replied softly. "As time passes, our memory starts to rust, and we forget what it's like to be young and full of piss and vinegar." He paused meaningfully. "You know what our biggest problem's going to be?"

"Convincing the women?"

"Right you are. It's not going to easy, you know."

"No, Uncle Bos—in fact, it's going to be hell—but at least Jeanette has Murdock to worry about, and he's temperamental as hell. In fact, he has all the Heron characteristics. At a year and a half, he's walking without help. He looks up at me with such an intelligent expression on his face, I expect him to start speaking."

Bosley chuckled. "I wish I could say that he's a chip off the old block, but your mother tells me that you were three and a half before you spoke a word."

"My God, was I *that* dumb?"

"Not exactly. When you did start, you spoke in entire sentences. Your first words were 'I want a candy bar.' "

Luke laughed. "Even then, I was always thinking about something to eat." Then he looked down at his desk, and the past was pushed away as he saw the paperwork in front of him. "Uncle Bos," he continued seriously, "could you come into the office next week? I need your advice." He picked up a report from Calgary, Canada. "What do you know about tar sands?"

There was a long pause at the other end of the line. "For a moment you threw me, Luke. But it's just what the term indicates: tar embedded in sand. There's lots of it around, but the problem is it can't be pumped because it's congealed—solid matter."

"How far is it *down*, usually?"

"I've seen some that's practically on the surface. Why do you ask?"

"I've got a report from Calgary."

"Oh, there's a good deal of tar sand up there. But it would have to be heated some way to separate the bitumen, which would then have to be cracked and refined into oil. It would cost a fortune. We don't have any technology to cope with it. I think we better stick to our usual recovery methods."

"How about more research?"

"It would cost more than it's worth. Most future oil will come from the Middle East. Better put your money into Saudi Arabia, where the oil pours out of the ground spontaneously, rather than try to filter tar sand."

"Thanks, Uncle Bos."

"Now, it wouldn't hurt to get other opinions."

Luke shook his head, "No, you've yet to steer me wrong. I'll take your word for it." He paused. "I'm still upset about Luke Three. Emotionally I understand, but intellectually—"

310

"You know, that's the first time in years I've heard you use that word?"

" 'Intellectually'?"

"No, 'emotionally.' Good-bye, Luke."

" 'Bye, Uncle Bos."

He puzzled for a long time over his uncle's question.

# 17

## The Return

*Bosley parked the pink Cadillac in front of the train depot.*

Letty was pleased to note that even in wartime the *Silver Streak* was exactly on schedule. Flashing in the sun, the long, sleek train sped into the station, paused briefly to disgorge five passengers, then started up smoothly again on its way toward Enid.

Sam was dressed in a gray double-breasted suit and wore a soft pearl-colored Stetson, and, without his familiar turban, looked like a businessman. He waved, picked up his small case, and with back erect, as always, walked the short distance to the car.

"Welcome home!" Bosley said.

Sam shook his hand through the open window. "It is good to be back," he replied in the high-pitched voice that they knew so well. He went around to the passenger side and shook Letty's hand. "Thank you both for coming to fetch me." He blinked at the car, then broke into a wide smile. "You've brought a touch of Hollywood to Angel."

Bosley laughed. "I've always called it Letty's Folly. It's shaken up everybody in town, including Fontine Dice. Personally, I like it!"

Letty smiled crookedly. "It's not like the old days, when we had Hans and Clara. No one wants to be a domestic now. If a 4-F can get a well-paying job in the war factory, why not? Why should he drive someone around? And everyone laughs about Rosie the Riveter, but why should a woman clean house for a living when she can make four times as much money in the aircraft industry?" She turned to Sam in the back seat. "How come you decided to move back to Angel, Sam?"

"Barbados is not home to me anymore. The island has changed, and then, too, at my time of life, I wanted to be around people who mean something to me."

Bosley drove slowly down Main Street. "How long has it been since you've had a good milkshake?" he asked.

Sam laughed. "Years, I am certain."

"Let's stop by the drugstore," Letty suggested. "Angel has come up in the world. Do you know we now have curb service?"

Bosley parked diagonally in front of the building, which sported a new facade of black glass.

"This is very elegant, lady," Sam said.

"Yes, isn't it?" Letty replied. "War money has come into the town since we've reopened the refinery."

A young girl, incongruously wearing bobby socks, brown-and-white saddle shoes, a red-and-blue paper hat, and a dress that looked suspiciously like a nurse's uniform, answered the automobile horn. "What'll it be?" she asked, her mouth moving in rhythm as she chewed a mountainous lump of pink bubble gum.

"I'll have a chocolate milkshake," Letty said.

"Ditto," Bosley added. "What would you like, Sam?"

"Strawberry." And as soon as the girl left, Sam sighed gently, looking up one side of the street, then the other. "It is good to be home. Do you know that I am going to purchase the Heron homestead from Mitchell?"

313

"Oh," Letty cried jubilantly, "then we'll be neighbors!" In the pause that followed, she grew pensive. "Sam?"

"Yes?"

"Won't it be strange to look out the upstairs window and see—well, the place where you used to work—"

"As a houseboy?" he finished for her. "Actually, The Widows, as we knew it, has been closed since nineteen seven. It has been the Barrett Conservatory of Music for thirty-seven years. My memories are happy." He paused and then went on gently. "You see, lady, my book was excellent therapy. I exorcised many ghosts, not the least of which was that boy that I once was."

The girl with the bobby socks placed a metal tray on the outside of the front passenger window and pocketed her tip with a tight, bored smile and departed, her saddle shoes making little *plip-plop* noises on the sidewalk.

"Remember, Sam, that's the way the old pumps on the oil wells used to sound," Bosley remarked, handing the tall glass with two straws to Sam in the back seat.

"Yes," Sam replied with a little laugh. "I hated that noise when the wells were first spudded; then I got so used to the sound, I was not even conscious of it." He took a sip of the pink concoction. "I'd forgotten how good Oklahoma milkshakes were."

Letty nodded. "Just milk and ice and flavorings. When ice cream is used, it's just not the same. When do you take over the Heron property, Sam?"

"The deal has been concluded when I sign the final papers at the Dice Bank. I should be settled soon."

"I'm surprised in a way," Letty said, "that Mitchell would sell the farm."

"He is not sentimental," Sam replied. "He wrote that he has a new home on the outskirts of Enid, near the Garber mansion."

Letty nodded. "His furniture store is so successful that he takes vacations lasting months on end. Anyway,

I'm happy that you bought the place, because you'll be just next door, so to speak."

Sam finished the last of the strawberry milkshake and chuckled. "I must say that I did consider that arrangement when I made the purchase."


Sam left the *Angel Wing* office, where he had taken a subscription, and was walking down Main Street toward home when he noticed Lars Hanson's shingle. On impulse, he entered the office and paused before the sweet-faced nurse at the desk. "I'd like to make an appointment with Dr. Hanson."

"It is wonderful to see you again, Doctor. I read your book. It's so wise and so beautiful."

He flushed with pleasure. "Why, thank you, Nurse Stevens."

"When you told about bringing my father, Reginald, into the world, I cried. He said you hadn't left out a thing."

Sam nodded. "Reggie was the second baby I birthed in the Territory. Is he well?"

Lorraine Stevens nodded. "Fit as a fiddle. He still runs the Stevens Hotel."

"I must drop by and see him one day." Sam paused. "About that appointment . . ."

"Oh, of course. Forgive me, Doctor." She laughed. "It's just not every day that we have a celebrity." She ran her finger down the appointment book. "If you have an immediate problem, the doctor's free now." She explained apologetically, "We've had two cancellations this afternoon."

He nodded. "And they both waited to call until they were almost due?"

She gave him a knowing look. "Naturally. Excuse me, I'll tell Doctor that you're here."

A moment later Lars Hanson came out of his office,

hand outstretched. "It's a very great pleasure to see you again, Doctor." He pumped Sam's delicate hand up and down. "Won't you come into my office?"

When they were seated, Sam folded his hands on his lap. "I haven't had a checkup for over a year. At my age"—he smiled—"I should not want to tempt fate."

Lars Hanson was suddenly all business. "We can do a preliminary now, if you like." He paused. "Do you want the works? An upper and lower G.I. and—"

Sam waved his hand. "Only the usual run of blood tests, urine, cardiogram, lung X ray. Blood pressure is normal. I check that myself. You might run a basal metabolism."

Lars Hanson smiled. "You could check into the hospital and order all this yourself."

"Yes, but I am retired, and I think it is wise to give my business to a fellow professional. By the by, how is Luke Three progressing?"

Lars broke into a chuckle. "I gave him four shots, and he's now six feet two inches."

Sam nodded. "I am very pleased. I felt something should be done." He looked around the pleasant room with its cheerful wicker furniture. "Shall we get on with it?"

In the middle of the tests, when Lars Hanson was examining his ears, Sam reached up and removed his false gray mustache, laughing gently. "I forget about this appendage," he said, "I've worn it for many years. I was always conscious of the fact that I had no beard."

"Is this a Cherokee characteristic?" Lars asked.

Sam sighed. "Not at all!" He paused, "I take it, you've not read my book?"

"Nurse Stevens has a copy, which I've been meaning to borrow, but . . ." Lars was embarrassed.

"I was quizzing you only for medical purposes, Doctor, not because I'm trying to increase my readership." Sam grinned. "The reason that I do not have a beard or

316

other body hair, is because of an accident that I suffered when I was about nine years old. I tell about it in the book." He paused meaningfully. "I've always been delicate, but I was fortunate to have had strong forebears, so although I'm not developed well physically, and my muscles have been weak, I've always exercised and taken care of my body." He sighed gently. "Then, I've also been involved in somewhat controversial hormone therapy. Someday, perhaps in the not-too-distant future, there will be greater hope for men like me. It is possible that gonads one day may be implanted, and while certain moral restrictions might be imposed, it would allow normal growth and functions."

"This has always intrigued me, Doctor. If I had the time and the money, I would devote my life to research." Lars looked up quizzically. "You have studied this area a great deal?"

Sam drew in his breath. "Yes, we must talk about this one day, when your appointment book is not quite so full."

After the series of tests was concluded and evaluated, Lars Hanson telephoned Sam. "For a seventy-two-year-old man, you're in remarkable health. The only thing that should concern you is nutrition. You're slightly underweight."

Sam laughed softly. "I always have been. I will dry up gradually, and someday blow away in the wind."

Lars Hanson chuckled. "I will probably grow old and fat. I've a weight problem already."

"Yes," Sam said, "I know."

"Oh," Lars Hanson replied, "I keep forgetting that you're a doctor too."

Letty went down the familiar path to the Victorian Heron clapboard, but hesitated as she turned at the maple tree. She had known, of course, that Sam was restoring the place, but she had not realized the extent of the work until she saw the facade of the house. Her mind flew back to 1896. It was as if she were standing on the same spot, looking at the finished house for the first time. She could hear Edward Heron say distinctly, "There she be, and she'll outlast all of us."

The exterior, which had gone through several color changes over the years—including green in the late Twenties, and yellow in the early Thirties—was now back to its original pristine white. Even the roof had been newly shingled. The porch, which had sagged, its posts rotted away, had been rebuilt, as had portions of the cupola, which had been infested with termites. The privet hedges surrounding the house had been trimmed back to a size more in keeping with the height of the structure; even the flower beds were arranged in the same triangular shape that Priscilla had designed. As Letty came up the new brick walk, she was pleased to note that the old smokehouse and barn had been repainted white, and gleaming new tin roofs reflected the sun.

Sam came down the front steps, wearing his familiar white turban. "Good morning, lady," he said in his high-pitched voice. He extended his hands.

"Sam, I've got tears in my eyes!" Letty exclaimed. "It's just like it used to be, except . . ."

"Yes?"

"Except for the sound of the children."

He nodded. "And the noise of the oil-well pumps."

"It *is* silent, Sam. Do you suppose there're any spirits around?"

"I am quite sure that there are." He grew thoughtful. "But they have good feelings." He frowned momentarily. "I thought I might be disturbed that Priscilla died so badly in this house."

"Yes," Letty agreed. "She was a tortured soul."

"Death is only a transition, anyway. We were not friends, as you know, but we have made our peace. The first day that I came into the house, I said out loud, 'Priscilla, if you will forgive me, I will forgive you.'"
He went on sadly, "If I had not been so young, I would have handled the matter of her prejudice more intelligently. In a way, I fed on her antagonism." He paused. "It was a mental clash of wills."

"When you and I speak together, Sam, I see the world in a different light. We've always had this sympathy between us."

"Yes, I know," he replied. "Now come and see the house."

The living room was newly papered in a blue-design pattern, almost identical, Letty thought, to the original. The woodwork, the mantel, and the ornate balustrade, all of which Edward Heron had carved and fashioned by hand, had been sanded smooth and a light birch stain applied, with an overcoat of clear lacquer.

The prisms on the gas chandelier, ordered from Sears and Roebuck in 1897, which had cost seventy dollars, had been replaced, and the ugly electrical wiring was gone. "Why, Sam, you're using gas lights again!"

He smiled. "The original fixtures were still on the walls. Only in my study upstairs did I leave electricity to read by."

As Letty toured the rooms rehabilitated to their original beauty, she was very moved. Sam had had the original furniture repaired and reupholstered.

"Mitchell," he said proudly, "did the restoration work." He opened the door to the upstairs bathroom. "Look!"

"Why, you've had a new coat of porcelain applied to the Japanned plunge! That's a real antique nowadays. I'd forgotten that Priscilla never had it replaced with a modern bathtub."

"Come down the hall, lady, and see what Priscilla's

sewing room has become," Sam said, opening a door to reveal a large walk-in closet. To the right, large racks held suits, and to the left, shoes were carefully arranged on a long bench. Her eyes were drawn to a pair of tattered, beaded deerskin moccasins. She recognized them at once. "Why, Sam, you've saved them!"

His eyes gleamed. "Actually, they are my only Cherokee relic left from the old days. These were the shoes I wore that day when my mother brought me to Leona Barrett's back door."

Letty sighed. "Oh, Sam, the past is very near, very near!"

"I know. That's why I'm so content here. I chose this house as my place of transition. It will bridge what is here now and what is yet to come."

She looked at him out of the corner of her eye and smiled crookedly. His face, dark skin drawn tightly over high cheekbones, and brilliant dark eyes and white, majestic turban, gave him the look of a seer, a man of incredible wisdom.

"You're my good, good friend," she said quietly.

He waved his hands in front of his face in an old Indian gesture that George Story had often used. "And you were my first true friend in the Territory, lady," he replied slowly.

"Why, Sam—" She was about to continue when a cheery voice was heard from below.

"Doctor, Doctor, are you home?"

"Yes," he replied; then he turned to Letty. "Come, you must meet my housekeeper, Rebecca. Her mother was part Cherokee, but she grew up in Colorado and knows nothing of our ways. I sometimes think that she is more American than some of the white people I know."

"But we are *all* Americans, Sam."

"Of course," he answered lightly, "but you know what I mean."

Rebecca, a large woman with dark hair swirled on top of her head with the aid of a tortoise-shell comb, was tying a Mother Hubbard around her waist as they came into the kitchen. After the introductions, she turned to the new electric stove. "Mrs. Trenton, going back to the turn of the century was fine with me, because I don't really mind the inconvenience of gas jets, although replacing those mantles can be a chore, but I told the doctor that I couldn't manage an old wood cookstove, nor would I wash clothes with a scrub board. Those times are long past." She laughed. "Take a peek on the back porch, and you'll find a prewar washer and dryer."

Sam raised his eyes to Letty. "Rebecca is just as entitled to a modern kitchen as I was to my brand-new hospital facilities in Barbados."

Rebecca laughed. "Now the doctor is happy with his old antiques and I'm happy with my new appliances." She patted the electric mixer and eyed Letty. "By the way, Mrs. Dice said that you'd give me the recipe for angel cake."

"Well, Rebecca, you take the whites of twenty-two eggs—"

Sam held his hands up before his face, once more in an Indian gesture. "When you finish," he said gravely, "you'll find me sunning myself in the garden."


The last of July, Bosley was invited to attend a series of meetings in Washington, and Letty decided to open up the Connecticut Avenue house. "We won't even bother with the upstairs," she explained, when he protested that the operation would be too strenuous to attempt. "After all, we might as well use the downstairs. Getting reservations at a hotel is impossible these days, and truthfully, I won't mind cooking and cleaning." She thought wistfully of Hans and Clara, and how she had taken them for granted in the old days when domestic help had been easy to obtain.

On August 1st, a letter arrived that caught Letty completely offguard. She gave a little cry of joy. "Bos," she cried, "what do you think? We have a most extraordinary invitation."

He ambled in from the garden, his old gray sweater buttoned crookedly down the front, and, taking the letter, read aloud:

July 31, 1944
Val-Kill Cottage

Dear Letty Trenton:

I wonder if you and your husband would come by the cottage for a picnic this Sunday, August 6, about two in the afternoon? There will only be a handful of Hyde Park friends. Of course, it will be very informal. Take Albany Post Road (U.S. 9) four miles north of Poughkeepsie. We're not difficult to find.

Eleanor

Bosley whistled. "My God, Letty, I didn't realize that you and Mrs. Roosevelt were *that* close."

She shrugged. "Neither did I. Of course, she's always been cordial to me, and I did help her out on that committee for the National Conference on Negro Youth, but that was some time ago."

"It will be very interesting to see why we have been summoned to Valhalla."

"It must be a different sort of world."

"I would like to know what Mrs. Roosevelt's reaction would have been"—he grinned—"had we invited her all the way to Washington from Hyde Park for an afternoon picnic."

"Well, dear," Letty replied softly, "she could hardly invite us to stay the night. Val-Kill Cottage is rather small, I gather, and since we're essentially *her* guests and not the President's, we couldn't be formally invited to Hyde Park, so what else was she to do?"

Bosley snorted and turned away. "I should think," he groused, "that if she wanted a favor—which she obviously does—she could have found a vacant bedroom somewhere."

Letty and Bosley took the train from Washington to New York on Saturday. The train was crowded to the bursting point, although additional cars had been added. Most of the standees were members of the armed forces. Bosley took care of the luggage, then came back with a resigned air. "I still think, Letty, that we should have driven."

Letty raised her eyebrows. "If we're going to visit the President's lady," she said, "it just won't do to be chauffeured. Just because we own the Heron Oil Company, we shouldn't give the impression that we waste gasoline—especially to someone as politically involved as Mrs. R. Don't you agree?"

He nodded resolutely. "I suppose you're right, Letty. We want her to know that we abide by the Heron austerity program."

"Occasionally," she added, following him into the compartment, "it's necessary to show that we Republicans are an integral part of the war effort too." She paused. "Besides, it's rather exciting traveling this way." She looked out the window. "It's been a long, long time since we've taken the train."

At the first call for luncheon, Bosley escorted Letty down the crowded aisle. As they wended their way through dozens of soldiers and sailors with duffel bags in tow—some in a happy mood because of furloughs or shore leaves, and others with grave faces because they were reporting to battle stations—a kind of sadness overcame Letty, which was also mixed with pride.

She looked at the bright-eyed lads with caps at a

jaunty angle and shoulders straightened by snug tunics, and she thought of that other war in 1914 and how she had watched the boys leaving Angel for Enid. The despair she had felt when she had learned that Clement, at the age of fifteen, had joined the Army wafted over her briefly again.

They were escorted to a table for two at the rear of the car by an old Negro waiter. She looked down at the hands folded in her lap. Were those wrinkled, spotted, thin-skinned fingers hers? There was no point in tearing out one's hair because of something as silly as age, especially when she felt no more than thirty inside, she thought, and it was really only when she got up from a chair, or sat down again, that her body did not respond as well as her mind thought it should.

At Penn Station they collected their luggage and, not being able to find a taxi, hailed a hansom cab.

"How long has it been since we've made use of a hay-burner?" Bosley chided, and Letty laughed, seating herself in the shiny leather seat.

"Let's see, George bought our first motor car, a Model T in nineteen nine." She laughed. "It used to regularly break down twice when we went to Enid— once going, and once coming back."

The clattering hansom headed up Sixth Avenue; its old horse, with its head down, paid no attention to the cabby's entreaties to go faster. Outside of a few taxis, only half a dozen automobiles were in view. But the foot traffic was very heavy, and the clatter of thousands of shoes of all shapes and sizes, hitting the cement in unison, rose in a roar that eventually became only another part of the myriad sounds of the city.

At the Plaza Hotel, the Trentons were soon ensconced in a sixth-story suite, placed at their disposal by a friend of Charlotte Dice's. Tired, they decided to take a nap. Lying side by side on the quilt, with a light blanket covering their bodies, Bosley took Letty's hand. "You know," he said quietly, "it's been a long time since I told you I love you."

She smiled in the partially darkened room. "Just yesterday morning, Bos."

"I try to remember every day, but sometimes it slips my mind."

"Oh," she scoffed, "you never forget *anything*!" She paused. "Now snooze a bit, because I want you to take me downstairs to the Edwardian Room for dinner. Thank God it's not meatless Tuesday!"


Letty and Bosley took the 12:05 to Poughkeepsie. Crowding into the train, they were soon swallowed up among the other commuters: businessmen in dark suits, hats, and ties; working women with shopping bags full of groceries; and the usual smattering of military personnel. No one paid any attention to the elderly couple, who managed to find seats at the rear of the coach. "This is a far cry from Angel," Letty whispered to Bosley.

He grunted. "Damned inconvenient, if you ask me."

Letty waved her hand. "After all, we're fortunate to be invited—particularly in view of the fact that you've never been especially kind to the President in any of your little speeches here and there."

"No," he agreed. "Yet I've never come out publicly against him, nor, for that matter, has Luke." He paused. "I don't believe in airing dirty linen in public. Besides, if a Chief of State, whether Democrat or Republican, ever needs cooperation it's during a war. What's fair is fair."

Only about thirty people got off at Poughkeepsie.

325

Bosley managed to signal the one taxicab before another couple, who were waving frantically, had even amassed their luggage.

"Val-Kill Cottage at Hyde Park," Bosley told the cabby, an old man who turned to ascertain whether his fares had famous faces before starting the automobile.

The drive was pleasant. Leaves were blue-green, although the old maples sported a few yellow patches here and there. The countryside was deserted, but the old cabby drove at a steady pace of forty miles an hour down Albany Post Road, then dropped to twenty near the entrance to Hyde Park. At an old pumphouse, the cab stopped.

"What's your names?" the cabby asked without turning around.

"Bosley and Letty Trenton," Bosley replied, feeling somehow like he was in Sunday school on the first day of a new semester.

At the gate, a man in plain clothes came forward, exchanged a few words with the cabby, then stepped lightly onto the running board of the car. As they came into the main drive of the estate, Letty took Bosley's arm. "If that is the rose garden on the right," she said, "the big house must be back there somewhere." She was filled with awe.

The cab continued on for two miles over a winding packed-dirt road that was protected by flowering shrubs, bushes, and tall stands of trees. At last a modest two-story fieldstone-and-stucco house came into view.

The Secret Service man alighted from the running board and knocked at the door. A moment later a tall figure in a white blouse, brown skirt, and white brogues came down the steps. The cabby opened the door and helped Letty, and then Bosley out of the taxi, before pocketing his tip. They stood rather awkwardly on the gravel driveway.

Eleanor Roosevelt came forward with outstretched hands. "So good of you to come," she said warmly. It struck Letty that Mrs. Roosevelt, with soft brown hair pulled back from her forehead—usually half covered by an unflattering hat—was far more attractive than the newspaper photographs would lead one to believe. When encountered before, she had always been swathed in furs and worn hats with veils.

Mrs. Roosevelt waved to the Secret Service man, who joined the cabby in the front seat. As the car sped away quickly, Mrs. Roosevelt took Letty's arm. "You must forgive me," she said quietly. "I would have met the train if I'd known you were coming by rail. I naturally assumed that you'd be driving."

"It's quite all right," Letty replied.

"We enjoyed the ride through Dutchess County," Bosley said as graciously as he could.

Letty looked up apologetically. "We're rather sensitive about making trips by car because so many people who really need a priority gasoline sticker can't qualify."

Bosley admired the house and grounds. "I must say that everything looks homey. Rather reminds me of some of the houses in our little town."

Mrs. Roosevelt smiled, and he wondered how she enjoyed her food, since her occlusion was almost nonexistent. Leading them up the steps into the house, she related an apparently familiar story. "Franklin built Val-Kill for me in nineteen twenty-seven—a retreat from the big house. This was a furniture factory for a time, but we've added rooms now and again, until it's rather a hodgepodge." She opened the door. "Please come in and rest a bit. Our picnic things will be ready shortly."

They followed her into a small paneled sitting room that Letty liked at once. There were several chairs covered with flowered prints, along with a collection of comfortable sofas and footstools, but the fireplace was surrounded with rather badly arranged family photographs.

"Please sit down." Mrs. Roosevelt indicated a sofa. "Would you like some ice-cold lemonade?"

"Thank you, yes," Letty replied, and at that moment a dark-haired woman entered, who was introduced as Mrs. Thompson.

"The President's on his way," she said. "Will he be joining us?"

Mrs. Roosevelt glanced at her wristwatch. "No, Tommy, he's already had lunch, he's just taking his afternoon turn." She addressed Letty and Bosley. "The President drives about the grounds every afternoon. He's surrounded by people so much of the time," she explained, "that it's a pleasure for him to be by himself." She added with a knowing look, "He doesn't have much privacy, you know."

"Public life must be very painful," Bosley said.

She nodded. "But he's really never known anything else. For me it was more difficult, because I was brought up very strictly, and I was rather shy, to boot." She smiled. "I still am sometimes." She paused. "I think I hear his car. Shall we go outside?"

They had assembled on the steps as a small blue Ford coupe drove into view, with the President, wearing an old hat, at the wheel. He maneuvered the hand controls, stopped in the driveway, and opened his mouth in his familiar crooked smile. Mrs. Roosevelt made the introductions.

The President, Bosley thought, looked old and very tired. "I've got to go back to Washington this afternoon," he said apologetically. He glanced up at his wife. "Babs, why don't you bring the Trentons over later? They might like to look at the horses." He glanced at Bosley. "I've a new stallion that I'm very proud of, a gift from Haile Selassie. He's a beauty!"

"Thank you, Mr. President," Bosley replied. "We'd very much like to see him."

The President gunned the Ford's motor with his hand control. "You should know, Mr. Trenton"—he looked up with a twinkle—"that I never use anything other than Heron gasoline." He laughed. "Now I've got to get back. So glad to have met you both." He touched his forefinger to the brim of his hat, smiled again, turned the car around carefully, and left the way he had come, over the winding dirt road.

They watched until the car was out of sight, then Mrs. Roosevelt guided Letty and Bosley across the road, where a white tablecloth had been spread on a grassy knoll. They sat in camp chairs, and Mrs. Thompson brought out several couples, who were introduced as Hyde Park neighbors. Mrs. Roosevelt personally offered frankfurters, potato salad, and beer, along with pickles and a variety of condiments. Coffee and small pastries were placed on the tablecloth after the paper plates had been collected.

Letty, looking over the pastoral scene, was struck again by the unpretentious air of her famous hostess. *Why*, she thought nostalgically, *it's just like a picnic at home*. But of course a picnic in Oklahoma was not complete without cold fried chicken, missing from this modest spread.

The other guests left early, and after a second cup of coffee in her sitting room, Eleanor Roosevelt put down her cup. "I've wanted to meet you both for a very long time," she said earnestly, her voice rising in her peculiar manner of speaking. "And I'd like to say something about your son Clement."

She paused thoughtfully, and went on carefully. "Franklin and I had always been fond of his music—in fact, followed his career with interest." She lowered her voice. "What I have to tell you now is classified material, Top Secret, and, of course, must go no further than this room. In about a month, I will personally call Sarah Story and give her the information, but until then it must remain secret, because some of the events have not yet come to pass. I will try to make this as simple as possible." She paused, her homely face grave, and her large, beautiful eyes wide and knowing. "When Clement Story joined the Armed Services to certain the troops, he very often carried confidential papers to be passed on to important contacts. When he was first conscripted as a courier, he was told that he might occasionally be in danger and for that reason could refuse an assignment." Her voice was low and melodious now. "He never turned down one job, because he believed, as his superior did, that because of his celebrity status he would be above suspicion."

She leaned forward, face soft, eyes shining. "For three years he performed extraordinary service for his country. Two months, ago, when the Allies were preparing for D-Day, and while the Germans were planning an important offensive, certain strategic blueprints came into our hands. Clement and his orchestra were immediately booked to play a war orphans benefit in the London suburbs, and he was to carry a set of those plans for the British." She paused thoughtfully; when she continued, her voice was touching in its intensity. "After the plane was airborne, apparently it became known to the Germans that someone aboard the aircraft had the documents. The High Command knew that identical sets of plans would be on their way within hours if the original contact was prevented from delivering the drawings to the British."

She went on slowly, emphasizing certain words here and there in her speech. "But timing was of the essence, because a certain surprise attack had been scheduled and the secret fortifications would become known as soon as the first shot was fired. A few hours' lead time was all that was required. The Germans sent out fighter planes to shoot down Clement's plane." She looked out the window and sighed. "We hope his passing won't seem like a fluke, now that you know the truth. The President wanted to know that Clement Story provided a very great service to his country and also to his Indian heritage."

Letty wiped her eyes. "Thank you for telling us, Mrs. Roosevelt."

The President's wife looked up with a soft, sad smile. "Please call me Eleanor," she said gently; then she got up slowly. "With four sons of my own in the service, I never know when word will come that one of them has been taken." She glanced at her wristwatch, and her mood changed. "Now, if you like, I'll show you the big house—and, of course, the horses. My favorite is Old Dot, but, like me at this moment, she's feeling her age."

Mrs. Roosevelt slid behind the wheel of the big, roomy station wagon, and as she maneuvered the car dexterously down the old road, Letty was struck anew with the particular ambience of the afternoon. How strange, she thought, to be in the company of the First Lady of the land—that much praised and much maligned woman—and treated to a special part of her private life! Mrs. Roosevelt was sharing her world, devoting an afternoon to what must, even at best, seem to her to be a public duty. As Bosley settled himself comfortably in the back seat for the short drive, Letty knew that he too felt at home. She seemed like a distant relative whom they liked but knew only casually.

Mrs. Roosevelt turned up the drive to the house. "We've tried to keep the grounds as countrified as possible," she remarked, "but this part of the estate has to be manicured. Fortunately the wild animals stay pretty much in the brush and seldom venture close to the big house." She glanced at Letty, who was sitting in the

331

front seat next to her. "I've made friends with a blue heron who lives in the marsh. In flight, he looks rather like your Heron logo."

Letty smiled. "Do you know, my son Luke dreamed up that symbol when he was fourteen." She paused. "I haven't really *seen* it in years, because it's such a part of our lives that I don't even think about it. At first it was rather disconcerting, having a name that was synonymous with a bird."

Mrs. Roosevelt nodded. "I know what you mean. It's the same thing when I travel—especially abroad. People look at me not as a woman, but as an extension of my husband. It took a very long time before I became accustomed to that. Now, of course, it doesn't bother me at all."

She braked the car in front of the sweeping balustrade of the long front terrace, then, escorting Letty and Bosley up the steps to the colonnaded portico, she led them into the large main hall, down the left steps to the living room and library. The furnishings—neither masculine nor feminine, Letty noted—while old, were very comfortable-looking: brocaded overstuffed chairs, Aubusson carpets, and paneled wood.

"Hyde Park was actually Franklin's mother's home," Mrs. Roosevelt revealed, "and she ran the household until her death at eighty-seven, three years ago." She pointed to a portrait over the mantel. "That was how Gilbert Stuart saw Franklin's great-great-grandfather Isaac Roosevelt. The original family name was Van Rosenvelt, you know, and I think they came over from Holland in the sixteen forties." She led them back into the hall and pointed into a nice-sized room. "This is the Snuggery; Franklin's mother always opened her mail and wrote letters here."

"It looks very inviting," Letty replied, looking around the spacious room.

Mrs. Roosevelt smiled. "It was the most used room

332

in the house when the children were home." She led them once more into the hall and into another large room. "This is the Dresden Room," she explained, "so named because Franklin's great-grandfather, James Roosevelt, brought back the Dresden mantel and chandelier from Germany in eighteen sixty-six." She went into the adjoining dining room. "You'll appreciate the oak table, Letty," she continued. "It can be let out for twenty people." She paused. "Wasn't a relative of yours in the furniture business?"

"Yes, my former brother-in-law, Edward."

"I thought so. I have a nineteen-eight Heron footstool at the cottage that I should have shown you. It's quite lovely. When we made furniture at Val-Kill Industries, we tried to copy the stain but couldn't."

"Edward was a master craftsman," Bosley put in. "Up until about nineteen fourteen he finished all of his pieces himself, and he always concocted his own stains and varnishes."

Mrs. Roosevelt nodded. "The old way of working is, unfortunately, going by the wayside. We couldn't make a profit on our furniture. We closed up the shop because we didn't want to go into a cheap line." She paused. "Now, I won't show you the kitchen or the servants' quarters, but there are several rooms upstairs that have certain interest."

She led them up the narrow stairs into the upper hall and indicated a bedroom on the left. "This is Franklin's boyhood room," she said quietly, "and it's never been changed." Then she showed them the Blue Room, the Morning Room, the Pink Room, and the Chintz Room—all comfortably but Spartanly furnished. She pointed to the wing on the right. "Our bedroom and sitting room are located there." At that moment the grandfather clock downstairs intoned four o'clock, and she guided them down the hall to the stairs. "May I offer you some coffee?"

Letty shook her head. "No, thank you . . . Eleanor."

"We had best be getting back, then."

Every room contained an ordinary kitchen chair with diminutive wheels, Letty noted, so that when the President was seated he would not give the impression of being in a wheelchair. It was these homey touches that Letty loved most of all about Hyde Park.

As they came into the downstairs hall, Mrs. Roosevelt looked tired, although she was smiling graciously. "I'll have you driven back to the station," she said, "and again, you must forgive me for not meeting you."

On the outside terrace, Letty held out her hand. "Thank you so much, Eleanor, for inviting us." She paused. "I do have time now and then, and if you need someone my age to help with one of your committees, please let me know."

Mrs. Roosevelt nodded. "What do you mean, 'your age'? You're very vital."

"Thank you, but at seventy-two I'm slowing down."

"I was sixty this year," Mrs. Roosevelt admitted. "Thank heavens I've always been full of energy, but travel is more tiring than it used to be." She paused. "I'm really looking forward to retiring. There's so much to do and so little time left to do it."

"Does that mean," Bosley interjected gently, "that the President will not run for a fourth term?"

Mrs. Roosevelt stepped back, and it seemed as if her whole mind and body withdrew. "I don't know, I'm sure," she replied, and it seemed to him that she was trying to be warm but was not quite succeeding. "He seldom gives me advance notice. We often have rather different views." She looked up. "Ah, I see the car is here." She held out her hand.

"Thank you for your hospitality, Eleanor," Letty said.

They were helped into the car by the young driver,

who Letty was certain was a Secret Service man, and her last view of Mrs. Roosevelt was a tall figure waving good-bye from the steps of the big house at Hyde Park.

For some reason, Letty felt her throat catch, and she wondered if she would ever see the First Lady in person again. She liked her very much.

Robert Desmond placed the receiver back in its cradle and called Jorja in from the outer office. "There is the most delicious story making the rounds on the Washington cocktail circuit. It seems the Trentons were invited to Hyde Park; the reason is not quite clear, but apparently it was Eleanor Roosevelt's idea. They took the train, and then a *taxi* to the estate." He placed his head in his hands and laughed. "It must have been pathetic—this elderly little couple, without even a valet or a maid, using *public* transportation. They could have been robbed or kidnapped or trampled under foot. Going out alone, with their name and all that money? Mrs. Roosevelt almost fainted when she saw the taxi."

"I think it's rather sweet," Jorja replied softly. "They live very simply, according to Luke—and he does too, for that matter."

His eyes narrowed. "Why are you so defensive?"

"I'm not; it's just that I don't know why these things should bother you."

His eyes were dark. "They don't *bother* me, it's just incomprehensible to me that these famous people are so unsophisticated."

" 'Uncomplicated' is a better word, I think," Jorja replied. "Could it be that you're just a wee mite jealous?"

"Of course I'm jealous! But the company will be handled differently when I take over. There's a way of gracious living—" He answered his private line. "You have?" A wide smile broke over his face. "You did?" His smile became wider. "Yes, a celebration is certainly in order."

335

He hung up and, placing his hands behind his head, whirled around in his swivel chair. "It's done!" he exclaimed, stopping in front of his desk. "I've just found out who owns the last big block of Heron stock—the Barrett Conservatory of Music in Angel." He pursed his lips. "The school was once a whorehouse run by one Leona Barrett, and somehow—it's not quite clear—she ended up with a fabulous amount of the company. The trustee of that stock is a banker, John Dice." He examined his fingernails very carefully. "If I have to offer him the world, I've got to have that stock. Thank God, Mother left me some personal money that Daddy didn't know anything about. Will you help me with a plan, Jorja dear?"

She smiled slowly. "Don't I always? Incidentally, I'm seeing Luke this evening. I've often thought of how to break off with him. I think I'll say that I have found someone else. I think that will play better—"

"I don't want you to end the affair. You can't be tied to me, outside of a business relationship. Stay where you are, funneling information to me—at least until I officially take over Heron."

She shook her head. "I'd rather end the business."

He interrupted angrily. "Don't you see, you'll be more valuable to me than ever! I'll need certain data that only you can provide."

"Don't make me do this, Robert. Leave me some self-respect. If our relationship ever came out—I mean, I couldn't look him in the eye."

"I can't believe that you're turning into a softie, Jorja. This is not like you at all. Could be that you *do care* for him?"

"No, not the way you mean. It's just that I understand him."

"And I suppose you don't understand *me*?"

"Oh, I know you inside and out. You're not a terri-

336

bly complicated man—ambitious and uncompromising, yes; complicated, no. Luke has many sides."

"In other words, my dear Jorja, you don't want a confrontation?"

She paused. "Yes, you can say that. Allow me to bow out now, and the future will take care of itself."

"Afraid that you'll end up in an alley with your throat cut?" he smiled softly.

"Be realistic, Robert. Luke isn't a violent man."

"But he could have you 'taken care of.' He has power."

She faced him. "Robert, I think we're finally coming down to it. It isn't the Heron money you're after; it's the Heron *power*. Well, for your information, it would never occur to Luke to use his power in that way." She gestured vaguely. "If you were in his position, you'd be pulling all kinds of tricks."

"Yes," he admitted, "I would use everything in the book if I wanted something badly enough. That's why the whole damned family are failures. They never use their influence in the right way. They have so many irons in the fire, and they don't have the sense to fuel the furnace. Here we are in the mist of war, and they haven't done anything about developing the oil field in Saudi Arabia, for instance, or trying new drilling techniques in the Maracaibo district in Venezuela."

"But, according to Luke, they will be able to introduce new dynamics after the war is over."

"Which may be ten years from now—who knows? They are spending hundreds of thousands of dollars laying pipeline all over the Midwest that will fall into disuse in peacetime. Those old men on the Heron board can't see beyond their noses."

"Well," she retorted, "I don't see that you've done so much in the areas you're talking about. You've not been terribly imaginative about management."

337

He stood up and took a glass of water from the cooler, then opened his desk and removed a half-empty bottle of bourbon. He measured out a finger very carefully, replaced the bottle, and took a sip of the drink. "My dear Jorja," he said at last, "during the next few months you will see an operator at work who really knows his business. I have been working very quietly, but when I have the power—"

"We're back to that word 'power' again, Robert. The moment you take over Heron, do you think that you'll be crowned king? Do you believe for one moment that all Heron employees are going to kowtow, or that you'll be giving earth-shaking orders?" She shook her head. "I never realized before that you have such a high opinion of your abilities. The petroleum world is not going to be turned upside down when you take over as president of Heron." She smiled suddenly. "The Seven Sisters will see to that. Now if you were taking over Standard Oil—"

"You're being funny, Jorja, and I don't like that. Why aren't you on my side?"

"I *am* on your side. My God, what more can I do? Do you think that going to bed with someone you don't like that way is *fun*? Pretending to be something that you aren't?"

He paused. "Of course I'm appreciative of all your efforts."

"Efforts!" she exclaimed incredulously. "My God, what more could a woman do?"

"I know," he soothed. "Suddenly today we're involved with semantics. I've been using all the wrong words. I suppose it's because so much rests on how I go about acquiring the Barrett Conservatory stock." He paced back and forth in front of his glass-topped desk. He paused before the mirror and straightened his necktie and studied his handsome face, grimacing and making faces at himself.

"Oh, *really*!" Jorja cried. "There are times when you behave exactly like a little boy." She laughed tonelessly. "A little boy with a candied apple—that could turn into a time bomb!"

# 18

## The Tide Runs Out

*Sam stood up straight and stretched his back.*

The hot, August sun beat down on the line of runner beans that curled luxuriantly around the four-foot posts. A half-dozen cabbage heads clustered, like a family, around a small asparagus bed, and lacy carrot tops made a sea of light green near the fence. Tufts of butter lettuce grew snugly among a few orange marigolds that had been planted to add a dash of color to the garden. He would pick some lettuce for Letty and Bosley's dinner. They had complained about the lack of fresh vegetables in Washington.

Looking over what Fontine would call his "spread," Sam sighed with contentment and went up two steps to the back porch. Rebecca, in her usual Mother Hubbard, was bending over a linen cloth on which had been sprinkled a light coating of flour. She made a small well in a pile of flour and mixed in equal amounts of lard and cold water with her hands. He watched the operation silently, appreciating the dexterity with which she moved her fingers. "You should have been a surgeon," he said.

She threw back her head and laughed. "Not me,

Doctor. You got your profession, and I got mine. A lot of young newly married girls nowadays use vegetable shortening in their pie dough and wonder why it don't come out right." She shook her head. "It's pure lard that makes the difference."

"That's what Audrey used to say," he replied.

"Who was that, your wife?"

He smiled softly. "No, I've never been married. Audrey was a woman who used to keep house for—for—people I used to know." He glanced out of the kitchen window at the spires of the Barrett Conservatory of Music and allowed his gaze to wander over the cupola of the old main house, barely visible over the treetops. "Right over there." He pointed. "It used to be called The Widows."

Rebecca flushed and without thinking said, "Some old-timer told me it used to be"—she fought for the right word—"a fancy house."

Sam was suddenly very grave as his mind went back to his youth. "It was a house, but it was not very *fancy*," he said at last.

"Well, Doctor," Rebecca retorted, "you know what I mean."

"Yes," he replied evenly, "I know what you mean. Long before I got my medical license, I worked there."

Rebecca stopped mixing the pie dough. "But what did you *do*?" She colored and continued. "I'm sorry, I'm forgetting my place." She bent her head and began to smooth out a handful of dough with a rolling pin.

"I do not mind talking about those days, Rebecca. Everyone over the age of forty here in Angel certainly knows the story by rote. Someone later very kindly called me a major domo, but that is not quite the truth. I was a sort of lackey." He leaned on the countertop. "Is there any coffee? I feel a bit tired."

"I shouldn't wonder, Doctor," Rebecca retorted good-naturedly, pouring a mug from the pot on the back of the stove. "You've been working out there for a good two hours."

Sam sat down on the wooden stool that Edward Heron had made, and grasped the mug between his thumb and forefinger. He was about to take a sip when all feeling went out of his arm. The mug crashed to the floor.

Rebecca smiled. "Butterfingers! It's a good thing it wasn't Dresden. Here, let me get you another."

Very calmly, Sam pressed his left hand against his leg. He felt nothing. He leaned back on the sink, his face drained of color. "Rebecca," he said quietly, "telephone Dr. Hanson at once. Tell him to come immediately. Then come back and help me to the settee in the living room."

"But Doctor—"

"Do as I say," he said slowly. "Do as I say."


Bosley answered the telephone, paused a long moment, and replied, "Thanks for calling, John." He frowned and replaced the instrument, then went into the solarium, where Letty, surrounded by greenery, was crocheting white edges on a blue handkerchief.

"Who was that, dear?" she asked, not looking up.

Bosley cleared his throat. "It was John. Fontine just called him. Sam had a stroke this afternoon, and Doc Hanson's put him in intensive care."

Letty dropped her hands into her lap. "Poor dear Sam! Is it bad?"

"Apparently he's paralyzed all over."

"Oh, my God!" All energy went out of her body. "Bos, do you ever pray?"

He was surprised at her question. "Why—yes, occasionally. Why?"

"If anyone in this world needs our prayers, it's Sam."

\* \* \*

342

Sam lay immobile in the white bed, flat on his back, staring up at the ceiling. Letty moved into his line of vision, and as he recognized her a slow smile spread over his lips. "Hello, lady," he said softly.

"Hello, Sam."

"Where is Bosley?"

"Doctor Hanson said that we could both see you, but one at a time."

Sam moved his head. "He's overcompensating. I told him yesterday that I should be allowed to be taken for a drive, but he laughed and said that was a long way off." He hesitated. "He hasn't been out of medical school very long and he's still frightened about severe cases. I believe I am his first stroke patient."

"What is your own prognosis, Sam?"

"I would shrug my shoulders if I could, lady." And she understood that he was making a private joke. "Sometimes the paralysis extends also to the head. I am fortunate that my mind is not affected and that I can speak and that my face is not distorted. But it will indeed be a miracle if I ever regain use of my body again."

"Are you positive, Sam?" Letty asked, her heart going out to him.

"That is why, after a few more tests are completed, I will ask to be taken home." His breathing had become somewhat labored, and he rested with his eyes closed, then glanced up at her again. "Will you come back and see me tomorrow?"

"Of course, Sam." She reached out and touched his cheek.

"Thank you, lady."

Letty walked to the door, back erect, and somehow managed to get into the hall. Bosley made a move to comfort her, but she gently shook him away. "He wants to see you." She sat down in the corner by the window, removed the blue handkerchief from her purse, and began to crochet quietly. She was still working the lace when Bella Chenovick came into the waiting room and sat down beside her.

"How is he, Letty?"

"Remarkable, as far as his mind goes. But there isn't anything else."

"I thought as much," Bella replied. "And, knowing how hospital food is—even as good a dietitian as Mabel Baker is—I brought a jar of my spiced peaches. I gather he's not on a special diet."

"When he gets home, we must all bring him food. That's about the only thing that he can enjoy now. Where's Torgo?"

"Out in the car." She smoothed her dress over her knees. "He was afraid that he would break down. You see, Letty, Sam was his first friend in the Territory. I suppose it was because we were from Bohemia, and he felt foreign too. To most of the settlers, we were Bohunks and he was Indian, and that was that."

Letty colored. "Why, Bella—"

Bella laughed. "Oh, Letty, all of that is ancient history! Torgo and I have never minded what people called us." There was no rancor in her voice. "Fontine Dice called me a Bohunk to my face once in front of Baker's Mercantile Store. I'll never forget it." She sighed. "Anyway, Sam taught Torgo to hunt rabbits and trap game and recognize the tracks and signs of animals. Lord knows, we were poor in those days, but we always had wild meat on the table. When everyone else had mush and beans."

Bosley came down the hall and greeted Bella. "Are you sure you want to go in? Remember, he can't move his body at all, so it won't do any good to hold his hand."

"Just touch his cheek," Letty said.

Bella gathered up her courage. She held up a pint of plump fruit, which still had a blue ribbon affixed to the

344

brass lid. "I thought this would amuse him. I won first prize again for my spiced peaches at the County Fair."

Letty smiled crookedly. "How many years have you won now? I've lost count."

Bella laughed until her jowls shook. "The first County Fair was got up in nineteen eight; this is nineteen forty-four." She calculated quickly in her head and then declared. "Thirty-five years! I didn't enter in nineteen twenty-five because Torgo was sick and couldn't drive to the fairgrounds in Enid."

Letty stopped crocheting. "How does it feel to be an institution, Bella?"

Bella grinned. "At this point, a little lonely." She grew serious. "I'm not going to enter my spiced peaches anymore, Letty. I've got so many ribbons I don't know what to do with them, and besides, it's high time I let some of the younger women win." She smoothed her black bombazine skirt over her wide hips and looked Letty straight in the eye. "That's one of the things with the older generation—we hang on too long."

A week later, Sam came home. He had purchased a hospital bed that could be raised or lowered at will, and engaged the services of two nurses: Louise, a plumper, raven-haired version of Fontine Dice, who worked the morning shift; and Tammy, a young R.N. who resembled a blond Jane Russell and worked the night shift. They were relieved by Rebecca, who looked after him in the late afternoon.

Earlier that week John Dice had come to the hospital, bringing along two witnesses to certify power of attorney, so that he could look after Sam's investments and pay bills.

Installed in the upstairs bedroom that had originally belonged to Edward and Priscilla Heron, Sam would sit in bed and read, with whoever was on duty turning the pages for him. When his eyes grew tired, the women would read to him or turn on the radio to his favorite programs. He mourned that he would never hear Captain Clement Story broadcast again. He loved his music.

One morning he awakened earlier than usual. The room was black, and the open window magnified sounds of various barnyard fowl in the neighborhood giving a disjointed morning welcome. Then, from far away, he heard the noise of vehicular traffic on Main Street. Could it be that another dust storm had obliterated the sun? But no, the dust would have filtered into the room, and the air was still clean. Then from below he heard the rattle of dishes, and finally a step on the stair. Were the nurses changing shifts? If so, it was eight in the morning. Why was the room still dark? He held his breath and fought to keep from crying out. He heard the nurse open the door to his room. Very evenly, he said, "Louise, I don't feel like breakfast yet. Would you leave me alone and come back in half an hour, please?"

"Yes, Doctor," she said cheerfully, and when the door closed he forced himself to breathe evenly. A few moments later he was in control.

During the night, he reasoned, he had suffered a small stroke that had cost him his eyesight. There was no turning back. He smiled at the irony of the moment. One massive stroke had robbed him of his body; another had taken his sight; the next might kill him altogether—or paralyze his voice or the movement of his head, but not his brain. To be alive inside of a dead body was no life at all. In the days that he had lain in the hospital, philosophically reviewing his case, he had thought that, if he had lost his body, at least he had his eyes and his brain, but now . . .

When Louise brought his breakfast tray into the room at eight-thirty, Sam said calmly, "Nurse, you must help me eat. I have lost my eyesight."

"Oh, no!" she exclaimed. "I'll call Doctor Larson at once."

He shook his head. "No. Give me breakfast, put on the radio, and telephone Mrs. Trenton to come visit me; then I want you to go to the grocery store." He paused. "When you call Mrs. Trenton, I want you to give her this exact message. Tell her: 'I need her.' Repeat the phrase, please."

"Very well, Doctor," she frowned, "I will say: 'You need her.'"

"I hope the eggs are exactly three minutes," Sam said.

"On the dot. I made them fresh. The toast is hot, too." She tied a napkin around his neck. "Open your mouth, Doctor."

He smiled feebly. "What comes first, the egg or the toast?"

Louise answered Letty's knock. "Go on up, Mrs. Trenton." She waved the grocery list. "I'll be back in an hour or so." Tears came into her eyes. "Honestly, Mrs. Trenton, I've been on all kinds of cases, but I've never met a more courageous human being than that man in all my life. In his profession, he knows exactly what's happening. This morning when he told me he was blind, well, I . . ."

She turned her head away, and suddenly Letty was holding her close. At last Letty broke away and wiped her eyes. "Sam would never forgive me if I broke down in his presence." She shook her head. "Our friendship goes back so many years, Nurse. You see, the Cherokees in the old days believed in certain rules that were ritualistic. One held in one's emotions, because if the *body* could be controlled, so could the *mind*. And they were right. People who can't control their own emotions can never control their own lives."

Louise nodded. "I'm inclined to agree."

Upstairs, Letty knocked softly on the door, but there was no answer. "Sam," she called. "Sam!" She heard nothing. She pushed the door inward and turned toward the bed. Sam was sitting up very stiffly, his hands resting outside the coverlet, in the exact position that Louise had left him moments before. Instinctively Letty took his warm hand, then touched his face. A gurgling sound came from his throat. She knew a moment of pure, ghastly horror. Now Sam, she realized, could not move his head; he was totally paralyzed. She forcibly held her mouth closed, stifling a sob, and repeated over and over in her mind, *I must not cry! I must not cry!* She placed her fingers over his Adam's apple. Sounds vibrated into her hand.

"Sam," she said slowly and distinctly, "can you hear me?"

He uttered a low sound. She paused, controlling her voice again. "The nurse gave me your message that 'You needed me.' I thought the wording very strange until I remembered that was the exact phrase that George Story used when he asked me to summon you all those years ago." She paused and then went on very gently, "Sam, my dear, dear Sam. Do you want me to *help* you?"

Again her fingers picked up the signal he made with his throat.

"Where are the capsules hidden? Now, don't use your strength. I will enumerate the places where they might be kept. Don't make a sound until I'm getting close." She went on slowly, "The medicine cabinet . . . the kitchen cupboard . . . the buffet . . ." She sighed and began to collect her thoughts. Obviously she could not name every possible receptacle in a house she did not know. She must think, *think*. To a doctor, the capsules would be classified as medicine—but Sam was not a doctor yet when he first knew of the Indian remedy. As a Cherokee, where . . . "Sam!" she exclaimed. "Are they hidden in an Indian artifact?"

He emitted a faint, very weak sob.

"Ah." She closed her eyes, trying to think over that first morning when he had showed her his newly furnished home. She knit her brows together. She could remember not even one relic; in fact, there was nothing that she recalled as being particularly Indian. Then, in the back of her mind, came a picture: she was looking at something very briefly. She closed her eyes tightly, conjuring up the scene again. They were coming out of his room, and she heard him say distinctly, "See what Priscilla's sewing room has become." He had turned the small area into a walk-in closet. His suits were hung neatly on the right. On the left, on a ledge . . . "Sam," she said, excitement raising her voice an octave, "the moccasins?"

A cry of joy escaped his throat. She rushed down the hall into the closet and, without even turning on the light, knelt, brushing her hand along the smooth ledge to the beaded deerskin. Her hand came out of the toe clutching a small bottle. Then, her heart beating a strange new rhythm, she returned to Sam's bedroom, poured a glass of water from the old pewter pitcher, and sat on the edge of Sam's bed. She gathered her thoughts, looking tenderly into his face. His normally dark-brown skin was now transparent, which contrasted with his snowy white hair. His eyes were closed, and she noticed for the first time that his eyelashes were coal black. "Sam," she said gently, "let me know how many. One?"

There was no answer.

"Two?"

There was no answer.

"Three?"

He made a soft sound, so deep in his throat that she was not sure that she had heard it at all. "Three?" she repeated.

A greater effort forced out a small sigh. Very gently she opened his lips with her fingers, and suddenly she panicked inside. What if he could not take the capsules? "Sam," she asked, "can you swallow?"

Again there was a slight noise, as soft and breathy as the wind.

She placed a capsule on his tongue, then, holding his head tenderly in her right hand, she poured a little water in his mouth. He swallowed slowly. Twice more she repeated the ritual. Something was missing. "Do you want your turban?" she asked.

He stopped breathing for a moment, as if summoning strength, and then he let out a low sound. She unfolded the piece of shiny white cloth, which had lain on top of the chiffonier. She sat down on the edge of the bed and held his head so that he would not pitch forward. She had seen him wrap the material so many times that she knew the draping by heart. Very slowly she brought the material around his head again and again, until the cloth was piled high and tucked in at the side. She held him in her arms a long moment, then rested his head back on the pillow.

It seemed then, attired as he was, that he looked almost the same as when she had first seen him in the meadow gathering white and beige mushrooms. He had said, after her inquiry, "Certain ones contain a powerful medicine that must only occasionally be used."

She must start him properly on his voyage with an expression of love. "Sam, of all the people that I have known over the years, I think that your accomplishments tower above all of them. You have become a great man, but, more than that, you have become a great leader and teacher and humanitarian. Your own people, too, are justly proud of you." She paused. "You are loved very much." She took his hand in hers; his pulse was still strong. She placed her fingers at his throat, hoping that he could feel her presence. "You are going on a long journey, my dear friend. Ahead, there is a brilliant light. . . ."

As her voice rose and fell in the room, Sam felt that he was moving in time and space. While he was still encased in darkness, up ahead there was a powerful brilliance, to which he was drawing closer and closer. He was conscious of several stationary figures, with headgear like his own, far in the background. Were they statues or human figures posed in some ancient tableau? As the light became brighter, he felt himself smiling. The figures were familiar now as he moved forward. He could walk. His arms and legs moved freely. He could talk, and his voice was very low and more melodious than ever before. There was a new fullness in his groin, and he knew a moment of pure delight: he was whole again! Suddenly his people were surrounding him, protecting him with their great and powerful knowledge, and they began to travel together—forward, always forward, toward the very essence of that magnificent ambience in the distance. . . .

Letty still held Sam's throat in a loose embrace when Louise returned. She closed his eyes with her palm and looked down at Letty.

"Look, Mrs. Trenton," Louise said softly. "He's smiling."

After Lars Hanson brought Sam's body to the hospital for an autopsy, Letty walked up the incline toward home; the old path, which had been so well worn in the days when she and Priscilla had visited back and forth, disappeared now here and there, overgrown with wild grass and nettles. An early prairie fog was rolling in softly, obliterating everything outside. She went in the

351

back door and poured a cup of coffee from the pot on the back of the stove, then sat down at the kitchen table. The house was strangely silent—an eerie quiet, matched by the white mist that seemed to enclose the old clapboard in a sort of vacuum. Mentally, she was devastated and welcomed the solitude. She only roused from the reverie when she heard Bosley stirring in the living room.

"Letty, are you back?" he called.

"Yes, I'm here in the kitchen."

He leaned back against the doorjamb. "How is Sam?"

Her voice was a bare whisper. "He's gone."

"Oh, how sad!" Bosley turned away, then went on brokenly, "An extraordinary man—a true free spirit and a remarkable friend. Always there when we needed him."

Letty sighed. "I feel so lost, Bos, it's as if one of my own flesh-and-blood children had left for good. Sam was almost as old as I am, yet isn't it peculiar? I've always thought of him as—a boy."

In control of his emotions, Bosley turned back to her. "Were you there when it happened?"

"Yes."

"I hope there was no pain."

"None at all. He just slipped into afterlife—or transition, as he always called it—like George did, so calmly. It was, I suppose, a peaceful journey filled with light."

"Light?" Bosley asked. "What do you mean?"

Letty gestured vaguely. "The end, the journey—the discovery . . ."

"You're not making sense, my dear."

"Sam had prepared the capsules many years ago." Her voice grew faint. "I remember George's last afternoon so well." She turned to him. "Didn't I ever tell you about that, Bos?"

"No."

"Strange. I thought I had. Anyway, George knew that he was dying, the same way that Sam did. It was a Sunday. The children came up to his bedroom, one by one, and said their good-byes." Her voice was flat, devoid of emotion. "I remember very distinctly that there were no tears. When everyone left, Sam gave George the capsules and started him on the journey."

Bosley sat down at the table beside Letty. "None of this is making any sense at all, Letty. What was in the capsules?"

Letty looked at him helplessly. "Why, the powdered mushrooms from the glen, of course! Folk medicine, I suppose you'd call it. George was dying, Bos," she explained gently, "and there was so much pain, he was going out of his mind. Even the morphine injections weren't helping anymore. The medicine separated the pain, Sam said. I told George that I loved him, and Sam spoke about the long tunnel ahead and the bright, white light that was at the end of it." She paused. "I repeated as much of the ritual as I could remember."

Bosley frowned. "The medicine, then, had some mesmerizing property?"

Letty's eyes opened wide. "Of course—that's what I've been telling you, Bos! The medicine gave George a pleasant passing."

"And," Bosley said increduously, "Sam took the capsules too?"

"Of course. I gave them to him. He was dying. The paralysis had crept slowly up to his vocal cords—"

"But Letty, that's called *euthanasia!*"

"Well," she replied quietly, "whatever it is, it's marvelous."

"You call it marvelous to help someone die!" Agitated, he went to the window, moving his shoulders up and down, then turned angrily. "Letty, do you know what you've done?"

"Why are you so upset, Bos?" Her strained face

showed every line. Nervously, she smoothed back a strand of gray hair from her forehead.

"That's *killing*," he shouted.

She stood up and faced him. "No. Both George and Sam were *dying*; the medicine gave them a smooth transition."

Bosley shook his head. "Transition! Death! It's all the same thing. What you did was wrong, Letty, wrong!"

"To ease pain is wrong?"

"Oh, my God, Letty," he replied in an anguished voice. "Oh, my God!"

Letty paced up and down the hospital corridor while Bosley sat, stone-faced, in front of the nurses' station.

At last Lars Hanson came out of the autopsy room, face grave, eyes weary. "Sam had instructed us to be very thorough," he said. "He hoped that we could discover something that would be helpful to medical science, because we know so very little about the causes of creeping paralysis. I sent for Dr. Borden, a specialist who practices in Enid. It was Sam's theory that strokes of this sort might be the result of sudden hormone imbalance or a malfunction of the endocrines." He paused and pursed his lips. "There have been some new findings concerning servicemen who've suffered severe cerebral hemorrhages in battle. There's also a possibility that shrapnel, embedded in sensitive tissues, may cause an overproduction of certain antibodies."

"What was the cause of . . . death?" Letty's voice was a whisper.

"The paralysis finally reached his brain."

Letty brought out a handkerchief tied in a knot. "Doctor, this is Sam's medicine. Would you have it analyzed, please?" She went on softly, "He made these up himself." Her heart pounded erratically. "It's very important for me to know."

Lars Hanson untied the handkerchief and examined one of the red capsules. "I'll send these to the lab," he said. "By the way, did you know Sam wanted to be cremated?"

Letty shook her head. "No, that's strange." She paused. "But I suppose it has something to do with his Indian ways."

The doctor nodded. "I didn't know anything about it, but John Dice called and said also that there was to be no service of any kind and that the ashes were to be spread over The Widows' Pond—wherever that is."

Letty, who had held in her emotions all afternoon, now felt her eyes smart and fill with tears. "The pond is still there, but they call it something else now." She held her eyes open very wide to contain the tears, so that her cheeks would remain dry. She had not cried for George, and she would not cry for Sam.

Two days later, while Hattie was washing the supper dishes, a car was heard in the driveway, and Letty, looking out of the window, saw Lars Hanson's Chevrolet coupe at the door. "Good evening, Doctor," she said. "Do come in and make yourself at home."

He smiled at the old-fashioned expression and replied in kind. "Don't mind if I do." The moment he was seated, he looked from Bosley to Letty with wonder. "I've just run into the most extraordinary situation," he cried, as excited as a young boy. "Those capsules you gave me contain, I think, an extraordinary drug. The lab technicians had never encountered anything quite so phenomenal!"

"It's poison, then?" Bosley asked, his hands shaking.

Lars Hanson shrugged his big shoulders. "No—at

355

least nothing of the sort that they're ever encountered before. They've sent samples to a famous pathologist in Oklahoma City for further analysis." He paused. "I hope that he's able to isolate the substance." He looked at Letty. "Sam didn't give any information as to the nature of the drug?"

She exchanged glances with Bosley, who shook his head faintly, but went on very quietly. "The only thing I know is that it's a certain type of mushroom."

"Mushroom!"

She nodded. "Years and years ago, even before Oklahoma became a state and this was known as Indian Territory, I came upon Sam gathering mushrooms in the glen." Her mind went back in memory. "I believe— yes, I remember now—the mushrooms were kind of brownish speckled with scarlet. I think they grew . . . under oak trees."

Lars Hanson hit his palms together. "How unusual!" He went on quickly, as if he could not wait for her answer. "Did he have other medicines?"

"Oh, many! He gave me something while I was in labor with Luke, that eased my pain, and yet I was conscious all the while. He used to prepare a cough syrup out of petroleum and other ingredients that was the best cure for croup that I ever came across. He had a wonderful curative for colic that was made out of catnip, peppermint, fennel, and lobelia. He used mullein-flower oil for earaches."

Lars Hanson sat down in the big chair and looked at the ceiling. Perfectly calm now, he was filled with a grave responsibility. "John Dice told me that Sam willed all of his filing cabinets to me." He leaned forward, his boyish face filled with wonderment. "If those papers contain his life's research, there may be a new world." He shook his head. "If I had only known that he knew these things, I'd have asked to study with him.

356

I assumed that his main study had been hormones of the estrogen and testosterone types."

Bosley nodded. "Of course you have no way of knowing if he continued his Indian folkways after he became a medical doctor."

"That's true," Letty agreed. "I only remember the curatives that he used as a boy."

Lars sighed. "I shouldn't get my hopes up, then, because he may very well have discarded his home remedies after he got his degree." He paused, and then looked up earnestly. "Are there other Cherokees who practice old medicine, Mr. Trenton?"

"I don't know. Letty?"

"George used to say that his people took on the ways of the white man very early on. Sam's mother must have taught him the use of herbs. He helped her birth babies, so she must have been a kind of native doctor, which she combined with midwifery. I know that she was illiterate, hadn't even learned the Cherokee written language. I imagine that her knowledge had been passed down in her family." She grew irritated. "Why didn't we ask Sam these things when he was still living? We were fools."

"I wish I'd known him better. I haven't even read *Born-Before-Sunrise*."

Letty went to the bookcase and removed a volume, which she handed to him. "Return this the moment you've finished, because it's very precious. It's personally autographed to Bos and me. I think, Doctor, you'll understand Sam and his philosophy after you've read this book. You'll most certainly look at Angel differently. It's all here, you know, the history of the town." She turned toward the kitchen. "I got up very early this morning, before daylight, like I do sometimes, and when I'm bored, I always bake. Today it's a triple chocolate cake. Would you like a piece with some home-made vanilla ice cream, Doctor?"

357

He brightened. "Nutritionally, I certainly don't need it"—he patted his waist—"but emotionally, I'm all for it!" He grinned. "I need more calories like a hole in the head, but I love chocolate cake."

"I thought you might," Letty said as she waved the men into the dining room. "Can you cook?"

"Not very well," he conceded. "Batching was all right in med school, and even during residency, but not now. I eat most of my meals at the Red Bird Café."

"Belle Trune's a good cook," Letty replied evenly, "and I can't, to this day, top her butter beans and ham."

"I understand from Lorraine that Sam told all about the old families in this book. I suppose I'll learn all about Belle, too. She has such an interesting face—as though she's lived."

"She has that," Bosley conceded with a tight smile, "but she's not in the book."

"Oh, but she *is*," Letty cried from the kitchen, "only Sam didn't use her real name. He called her—"

"Remember yourself!" Bosley called reproachfully.

Letty came in with two plates of cake and ice cream. "You've right, Bos. Sam was discreet, and I almost wasn't. No, Belle has turned out all right, and, as I said before, she's a darned good cook."

After the doctor left, and the rest of the house was dark, Letty looked up at Bosley, who was on his way up the stairs. "I'm going to sit down here for a bit. I'm not at all tired. In fact, I may stay up to listen to *Amos and Andy*."

"Very well," he said, "just don't forget to turn out the lights. We've got to conserve energy."

"Yes, dear."

Letty looked down at her hands, the same hands that had found the capsules in Sam's moccasins, and she examined her palms. Was she guilty of what Bosley said—what was the word, that strange word? Euthanasia? It sounded like the name of a woman, or a place, or a thing. What is your name? *Euthanasia!* Where do you live? *Euthanasia!* What is that flower? *Euthanasia!*

Letty smiled crookedly. She had been thinking a good deal about George lately. She saw him as he was when he had asked her to marry him: big, olive-skinned, flashing teeth, shiny black hair, aquamarine eyes. . . . Was cancer the true cause of death, or was it the capsule? She tried to remember what the autopsy report showed. Doctor Schaeffer had scribbled something unreadable, she was certain; he always did.

The clock in the hall chimed nine. *Amos and Andy* was off the air. She shook the past away, tuned in the Blue Network, and leaned back in the easy chair, waiting for soft music to lull her into a sleeping mood before she went upstairs to bed. Then, as if from a distance, she heard the opening bars of "Lady Luck." Were her ears deceiving her? Why would they be playing Clement's theme song?

Then the soft, honeyed voice of the announcer came over the airwaves. "Ladies and gentlemen, our regularly scheduled broadcast has been postponed because of technical difficulties, so we are taking this opportunity to pay a tribute to the late Clement Story, whose plane was so tragically shot down off the coast of England. We will replay his last recorded radio show."

"Lady Luck" segued into a brief salute to the Army, Navy, and Marine Corps, making adroit use of their theme songs. Through wet eyes, Letty beamed in the darkness as Sousa's battle march floated into the room. Clement, she thought proudly, had accomplished what he had set out to do: add harmony to the ancient war-horses, modernizing the old pieces. Soon Clement's new signoff, "I'll Be Seeing You," added a last note, and Letty switched off the radio and, with the house in total darkness, found her way slowly up the stairs to the bedroom. It was as if—hearing Clement's voice again—he had returned from the dead.

Now, without Clement's music providing a melodic background, she was suddenly afraid again. Had she violated God's law when she had helped Sam find peace?

# 19

## The Decision

*Bosley came into Heron headquarters straight from the airport.*

Luke was checking figures from a new Wall Street report on his desk. "How was Washington?" he asked in a bored tone of voice that suggested he did not really want to know.

"It rained for three days," Bosley replied darkly. "I had a hell of a takeoff, and you know Currier and Ives are tops. I swear National Airport should be condemned—such short runways. But that will change when we get into jet air travel. They'll be building an airfield out in the open country where those big birds can land and take off safely." He slouched down into the leather chair opposite Luke's desk. "Another thing—my back hurts. It's hell getting old. Then, too, your mother's been overdoing again. She dragged me to four fund-raisers this last week."

Luke lighted a cigarette and blew the smoke out in a perfect oval. "I've never heard you complain so much, Uncle Bos. You're supposed to be the incurable optimist in the family. What's bothering you?"

Bosley fidgeted in the chair, clasping and unclasping

his hands. "I'm worried, Luke, very worried. I saw President Roosevelt recently"—he paused, frowning—"and he looks like death warmed over. His skin has that awful gray color." He shook his head. "I think at this point that he's acting a role. He's like a shadow."

"But if he's so sick, why is he going to run for a fourth term?"

Bosley shook his head. "He's overestimating himself. He does, you know—always did.—And there's nothing wrong with that; optimism, as you've suggested, was always my forte, and I've been overestimating myself for years. But when a man can't recognize when he's on his way out . . ."

Luke leaned forward, puffing languidly on his cigarette. "What is it that you're trying to say, Uncle Bos? You've never been much involved in politics."

"The only reason is that the damned Democrats have been in power for twelve years! Heron Oil greatly benefited from the Hoover administration. Remember, your mother and George Story were entertained regularly at the White House. Their friendship with Herbert and Lou went back to World War One."

Luke snubbed out his cigarette in the oversized ashtray on his desk. "I still don't know what you're trying to say."

"Just this: There are stories going around the Hill that Senator Harry Truman may be tapped as Roosevelt's running mate in November. He's a far better man, in my estimation, than Vice President Henry Wallace, whom I've always thought was an ass." He folded his hands across his chest. "Do you know Harry?"

Luke shrugged. "Scrappy man. I met him once about a year ago, when he was investigating the inefficiency of Army bases and munitions plants. He did a good job there, saving the taxpayers millions of dollars." He paused. "Why do you ask?"

"Well," Bosley replied, "you can bet the Republicans

will get behind Tom Dewey, and, as you know, I don't get along with him, nor did I admire Wendell Willkie." He became excited and his eyes flashed and he looked ten years younger than when he had come into the room. "You see, Little Luke—"

"Hold on! You haven't called me 'Little Luke' since I was a boy." Luke laughed out loud.

Bosley colored. "Sorry about that; it's just that I'm nervous, and I've got to present this in the right way or you'll think I'm daft, as the English say."

Luke replied softly, "Just because I'm president of Heron Oil now, Uncle Bos, and you really think of me as a boy, don't be patronizing, just tell me what's on your mind."

"I'm trying, Luke, I'm trying. But I've got to show you my point of view." He sighed. "We've never been able to work with the present administration because Roosevelt's always been a son of a bitch. Oh, he's always cheerful and pleasant and polite on the rare occasions when we've met, but frankly, I don't think we Republicans have a chance in hell winning this election."

"Frankly, neither do I."

"But the point is, I think we can deal with Truman. He's a Midwestern fellow, plain, conservative, and Bess isn't an uppity wife. She's not going to run Washington society the way her family ruled Independence." He paused and fought for the right words, then blurted, "What it all boils down to, Luke, is that I think we'd better switch over to the Democratic ticket and vote for Roosevelt, but *only* if he chooses Truman over Wallace as Vice President. I'm firmly convinced that Roosevelt's going to die in office."

Luke leaned on his desk and ran his fingers through his crew-cut hair. "We've really got to think this out, Uncle Bos. Off the top of my head, I'd have to say no. There's too much involved. All my life—"

"I know, I know," Bosley interrupted. "I feel the

same way. We've always voted Republican, but I think it's time to look beyond political beliefs. If we expect Heron to grow in the next decade, we've got to have more influence in high places. The Seven Sisters are more powerful now than ever before, and other oil companies are springing up here and there, and our stock situation is still critical—too much being sold. It took a war to get us out of the depression, and Lord knows what'll happen after the fighting stops. We've got to invest in researching the Labrador Sea. Oil cartels are going to be coming out of our ears, and the Middle East is going to be crucial. The government will be monetarily assisting Saudi Arabia, and, thank God, we already have a friend in Sheik Muhammad Abn. We've got to be very wise about the future, Luke, and open—"

"I know, Uncle Bos, I know. Although it goes against my grain to vote for—"

"Mine too, Luke, mine too, and I don't know what your mother's going to say, for instance."

"Or any of our other Oklahoma friends. Let's research a little more before we decide one way or another, Uncle Bos."


John Dice threw down the copy of the *Enid Morning News* with such force he knocked over a cream pitcher. "That does it! That does it!" He took off his cowboy boots and threw them against the wall.

Fontine ran in from the kitchen. "Jaundice, what's got into you?" She had not seen him so mad since he had lost his seat in the Senate.

"Never thought I'd see the day that a Heron would turn traitor. Luke has just announced that the Heron Oil Company is supporting Roosevelt for a fourth term, and I bet dollars to doughnuts that senile old Bosley

364

Trenton put him up to it." He lapsed back into his old Texas way of speaking. "Bastids, that's what they are, bastids!" he shouted, red-faced, hands clenched. "And the devil take them!"

Fontine put her arm around his broad shoulders, but he broke away angrily and went to the window. "Leave me alone, Fourteen! I've got to cogitate."

Fontine sighed softly. "Oh, Jaundice, don't make so much out of this. I know you're campaigning for Dewey, but—"

"Stabbed in the back, that's what I am," he shouted without turning around. "My best friends turning against me." He turned back slowly and gazed directly into her eyes. "From this day forward," he said intensely, his jaw set, "Fourteen, we no longer speak to the Herons."

"But Letty and I are going to Enid shopping this afternoon."

"Call her up and cancel."

"But Jaundice, I *can't*." Fontine shook her head until her platinum curls danced.

John Dice removed the receiver from the hook. "Nellie, is that you?" Then he asked for the Heron number. He handed the instrument to Fontine.

Tears gathered in her eyes, and as she looked up beseechingly into his face; he turned away. "Letty," she said in a small voice, "I can't go to Enid with you." Then, before there was a reply, she hung up the telephone and burst into tears.

Letty stared at the receiver in her hand. "That's strange," she said to Bosley. "Fontine just canceled the trip today."

"So?" he said over the top of the paper, then took a sip of coffee. "It's probably her arthritis."

Letty shook her head. "No, there's more to it than that, Bos. I've never heard her use that tone of voice

365

before. You know Fontine, she always goes on and on; even when she was busy in Washington, our conversations always lasted fifteen or twenty minutes."

Bosley folded the paper, then glanced at the front page. "Oh," he said, "I'm beginning to see the light." He pointed to the headline: HERON OIL BACKS DEMO- CRATIC FOURTH TERM. He reached for the telephone. "Nellie, is that you? Get me the Dice connection, please." He paused. "Hello. This is Bosley Trenton. I'd like to speak to Mr. Dice, please."

There was a muffled sound at the other end of the line as the maid placed her hand over the mouthpiece. A moment later her shocked voice came clearly over the line. "I'm sorry, Mr. Trenton, but Mr. Dice says to tell you that he's not home." There was an embarrassed pause. "He also says, sir, that."—her voice had fallen to a whisper—"that he'd be much obliged if you'd not call again."

The receiver clicked in Bosley's ear, and he sighed gently and stood beside Letty. "He's mad," he said gently, "and I don't blame him." He paused. "I guess, my dear, we've lost our dearest friends."

She nodded helplessly. "How many more, Bos, how many more?"


Robert Desmond headed his long black 1940 Cadillac convertible down the country road northwest of Perry. Although he had a map spread out on the seat, he had been lost twice. Finally he saw a sign: ANGEL, 13 MI.

He was not accustomed to driving such a long way, but he had decided to give the chauffeur a day off. It was best that he appear by himself. The right psychological impression was important.

From seven miles away, he saw the town, laid out flat against the prairie, a water tower silhouetted against the buttermilk sky. Here and there, a few oil wells pumped, but the countryside was mainly dotted with small clapboard farmhouses, huge barns, and a clutter of outhouses, chicken coops, and occasional silos.

The road led directly into Main Street. Many of the old wooden facades had been freshly painted, and some of the brick buildings had been covered with black mirrored tile, but the most striking feature were the trees that lined the small thoroughfare, which added a picturesque quality to the scene.

In spite of himself, Desmond warmed to the place. The town had a prosperous, spacious feeling that he had not expected; he had envisioned a Western cowtown look.

He parked diagonally in front of the Dice Bank and, before getting out of the car, wiped the red dust from his shiny black shoes. He checked the immaculate navy-blue serge suit that fitted his slight, slender frame like a piece of dark cellophane.

Desmond handed his card to the young, open-faced girl at a desk, who wore a red peasant blouse and flowered skirt and looked more like a pompom girl in a high-school band than a receptionist at a bank. He was not at all surprised when she loped to the rear office in anklets and brown-and-white saddle shoes.

She returned a moment later with a wide, friendly smile. "Mr. Dice says for you to come on in." She pointed to the back of the bank. The tellers smiled and nodded as his leather shoes made a clicking sound over the white parquet flooring, a sound that reverberated in the cavernous old building with the tin ceiling.

As a boy in Tulsa, Desmond remembered seeing pictures of the famous old Senator from Oklahoma in his ten-gallon hat and a wide, toothy smile, and he expected to be greeted at the door marked PRESIDENT by an older version of the same man. Instead, through the

367

glass pane, he glimpsed a pair of long legs encased in cowboy boots, resting on a polished mahogany desk. Behind the legs, a blue-checked suit led eventually up to a rosy face and rumpled gray hair. A huge hand bade him enter.

The form unwound itself and stood up. "Howdy," John Dice said. "Come on in, Mr. Desmond, and rest your bones." He indicated a straight-backed chair by the side of the desk. "We're informal here."

"It's refreshing, sir," was all that Robert Desmond could think to reply, and his Oxford accent hung in the air as if a foreign element had been introduced. They shook hands. He placed his alligator briefcase on the polished hardwood floor and tried to find a comfortable position in the hard seat.

"Nice spell of weather we're having," John Dice remarked conversationally, arranging his big frame in the swivel chair. "Hope you had a pleasant drive from Tulsa."

"Yes, thank you. I only lost my way twice," Desmond replied.

"That's not surprising. When I had a little say in state affairs a while back, I tried to do something about the roads being paved and graveled, but during the depression there wasn't very much extra money to play with, and I got turned down." He looked at his visitor quizzically. "Are you going to be with us long?"

Desmond shook his head and smiled inwardly, almost retorting, "A number of years, I hope." Instead he said soberly, "I just drove down for the day."

"Pity," John Dice replied. "I was going to invite you to stay for the fifty-first Cherokee Strip celebration in Enid." He smiled widely, then looked up. "Of course, only those who actually made The Run are encouraged to take part in the ceremonies, but it's a lot of fun, anyway."

"It does sound . . . fascinating," Desmond replied,

wondering when the small talk would lead into serious discussion.

John Dice cleared his throat. "What brings you to Angel, Mr. Desmond? Oil?"

He kept his face blank. "Yes. As you may know, I'm president of my own company."

John Dice nodded. "Yes," he replied dryly, "your firm was founded in nineteen thirty-seven, when your dad took over the Macauley leases near Drumright. Since then, you've accumulated some wells that Harry Sinclair thought were unproductive, and your field men have done a good job in redrilling with the new rotary, and your natural gas spread in Pennsylvania is reported to be a goody." He lighted a cigar and puffed energetically. "Wasn't your papa mixed up in the Teapot Dome oil scandal?"

Desmond picked a piece of lint from his coat. "He was cleared."

John Dice nodded. "I was acquainted with some of those boys." He placed his cigar on a large tray. "What can I do for you, Mr. Desmond?"

"I understand that you're Trustee for the Barrett Conservatory of Music?"

"Yes, that has been one of my main pleasures over the years." John Dice grinned. "Do you know that some very famous musicians have graduated from Barrett, and a couple of up-and-coming composers too? We're very proud."

"The place has an excellent reputation."

"Are you—musical?" John Dice examined Desmond's face carefully, and then his hands, which were folded in his lap.

"No, unfortunately not, but of course I'm very appreciative."

There was a pause. "I like chamber music myself."

Desmond raised his eyebrows. "Me also." He drew a breath and then went on leisurely. "I understand that when Leona Barrett Elder passed away several years ago, she left several large blocks of Heron Oil Company stock to the university."

John Dice puffed on the cigar. "Yes, that's true, but it's not generally known—the part about Leona Barrett, I mean. It must have taken a long time to ferret out that information, Mr. Desmond."

Desmond smiled. "I'm interested in acquiring that stock," he said simply.

John Dice looked at him coolly. "The terms of her will are very restrictive. I don't know that it would be possible to transact such business, even if the board of directors would be amenable. What's the stock selling for now?"

"As of yesterday, eighty-six dollars a share."

"Overpriced."

"True, but even so, I would offer somewhat more."

"Oh? Tell me, Mr. Desmond, why do you want that stock?" The question slipped out as easily as if he had asked his guest to have luncheon with him.

Desmond kept his composure and replied in the same tone of voice, "Because, very simply, I want to acquire control of the Heron Oil Company. The Barrett blocks of stock are the only thing standing in the way."

"What's your offer?"

"Five dollars per share beyond market price."

John Dice raised his eyebrows. "That's a good price."

"Yes, and for a struggling Conservatory . . ."

John Dice smiled. "I wouldn't say that the place is exactly struggling, but taking the cash out now and reinvesting might be a smart idea." He got up from his chair and held out his hand. "I'll let you know, Mr. Desmond." He paused. "Incidentally, didn't your papa vote for me?"

Desmond shrugged. "I imagine so; the family has always been Republican."

John Dice broke into a wide smile. "Aft'noon." He nodded.

Desmond nodded back. "Good afternoon, Mr. Dice."

He walked out of the bank, head held high. He was experiencing a certain elation mixed with fear: he was elated because he felt the meeting had gone well; he was fearful because he had a feeling that, under all that air of cordiality, John Dice was a bastard.

As soon as Robert Desmond had backed out his Cadillac convertible and headed toward Main Street, John Dice performed a little jig and shouted, "Whoopee!"

The tellers and the receptionist looked up, but he impatiently motioned them to return to work. He rubbed his palms together. He finally had the upper hand with the Trentons and the Herons! He could easily convince the board members to dispose of the Heron stock, which had initially cost five thousand dollars and, with doubling and tripling several times in the last forty years, was easily worth in the neighborhood of fifteen million dollars. He could not wait to see the expression on Bosley Trenton's face when he heard the news that the Barrett Conservatory had disposed of its stock. He would teach that slimy son of a bitch to back that cripple in the White House!

Luke cast a brief look down the long conference table at the twelve men who comprised the Heron Oil Company board of directors, and he drew in his breath almost inaudibly. He was conducting the meeting for chairman of the board, Bosley, who was ill with the flu. Mel Jasper, vice president and treasurer, was a fat fifty-five; Hardson Mallory, vice president in charge of marketing, a thin, ascetic-faced man of sixty; James Hightower, the comptroller, looked rather like a ferret—a middle-aged man with a waist as thick as his shoulders; Harold Timberlake, vice president of research and development, resembled a pear that had lain too long in the larder. There was not one member of the Board under fifty years of age. Luke glanced down at his own reflection in the highly polished mahogany table and drew back. Every one of his fifty years was etched indelibly on his face. It suddenly occurred to him that he, also, was an old man.

The meeting began. Each board member gave reports: production of hundred-octane gasoline up twenty-five percent to twenty-five thousand barrels a day . . . military oils and greases used in planes with six-mile-high altitudes reevaluated and improved . . . Navy fuel and regular-grade gasoline increased ten percent . . . one tanker out of the fleet of eight sunk by the Germans . . .

Luke listened with half an ear, knowing full well that the data would be reprinted in the annual pamphlet sent to stockholders, and he had suddenly had his fill. He stood up. "I am well aware of what we are doing for the war effort, but, gentlemen, what are we doing for peace?"

There was a stunned silence; Jasper looked at Mallory; Mallory looked at Hightower, and Hightower looked at Timberlake; and Timberlake looked at . . . Luke closed his weary eyes a moment and then opened them very wide, looking, he well knew, rather like a gray owl. "Gentlemen, what would happen to Heron Oil if an armistice was declared tomorrow?"

The men looked at one another blankly a moment, digesting his question, and Luke pointed his finger at Hardson. "What percentage of our current business can be attributed to the war effort?"

The vice president of marketing blinked quickly. "Fifty-five percent was my last figure, I believe."

"So if the war ends tomorrow, within weeks over half of our business is kaput." He paused dramatically.

"Mel, how much profit do we have this year?"

The treasurer shrugged. "Looks good, at least on paper. Earnings will be about one-sixty per share of common stock, as compared to one-seventy-five last year."

"I shouldn't think our stockholders will be shouting for joy at a fifteen-cent reduction," Luke replied sarcastically.

Mel Jasper did not flinch. "But we had to close seven hundred fifty retail outlets that weren't paying off."

Luke nodded coldly. "Yes, and one of them was in Angel, which hardly endears me to my home town." He turned to Harold Timberlake. "What does R and D look like if the war ends?"

Timberlake nodded his speckled face, looking more than ever like an overripe pear. "Home oil burners will account for an upswing, airplanes will be converting to jet propulsion, railroads will be using Diesel engines, and more recreational vehicles will be manufactured. Boats will be bigger and need more fuel, thousands of tractors will be built that require—"

Luke drummed his fingers on the tabletop and smiled coldly. "In other words, gentlemen, we're in the wrong business. The home office should be relocated to Detroit." He pushed out his lower lip. "It appears to me that peacetime is going to benefit the automobile, tractor, boat, and locomotive industries. Perhaps"—his head throbbing with fatigue—"we should sell Heron Oil and invest in General Motors, John Deere, Chris-Craft or Pullman."

He carefully evened out a stack of papers on the table, which he transferred to his briefcase. "I want each and every one of you men," he said, still busy with his task and without looking up, "to go home and compose a very fanciful, imaginative plan on how we can survive after the war. Be creative for a change. Go out on a limb. Explore." He looked up. "I'll call a special board of directors meeting in about six weeks. Also, let's try to find out who is purchasing so much of our stock. We've got to plan for the future, because if the war ends—"

Jasper held up his hand. "Luke, with all of your talk about peace, do you know something that we don't?"

Luke swept the room in a glance. "We didn't turn from Republican to Democrat for nothing," he said quietly, and left the room.


*Later that evening, Luke telephoned Bosley.*

The old man sighed and asked, "Did you shake the board of directors up a bit?"

"I sure did, Uncle Bos, and I must say, it was electrifying. I think I got them off their duffs and back to thinking positively again." He paused. "They've got to come up with some answers in about six weeks. We still don't know who is buying up Heron stock. It's got to be some mastermind. I put the fear of God into the old boys."

Bosley grunted. "If they don't produce?"

There was an immediate response. "They'll be out on their asses."

"Now you're talking, boy."

Luke smiled to himself. "Boy, Uncle Bos? Boy?"

"Just because you've turned fifty, Luke, don't think you're not still a boy in many ways. I was your age in nineteen twenty, and the good life was really just starting. Hell, you've still got your life before you."

Luke laughed self-consciously. "Thank you for that,

374

Uncle Bos; you don't know how lousy I feel at the moment."

They said good-bye, and then Luke dialed Jorja's number. "Hi," he said. "Are you free this evening?"

"I've got to be at the U.S.O. until eight, but I'll go right home after that."

"Can't wait to see you," he blurted, and then felt foolish. He was sounding like a depraved middle-aged man, when he felt nineteen.

She laughed again. "In that case, I'll get off a little early. See you at seven-thirty."

He was mixing a scotch and water when he heard Jorja's key in the door. She came in quickly and kissed him on the cheek. "Mix me one too. All that jitterbugging wore me out. There was this one Marine who had two left feet, and he *fell* on the dance floor *twice*. He was clever, though, and improvised a little bit while he was down there. The crowd thought it was part of the dance."

She went into the bedroom and started to undress, then, in panties and bra, came back into the kitchen for her drink. He brought his hands up to her breasts. "You are very sexy tonight," he said, kissing her on the lips.

"So are you," she replied, then stood back and took a sip of scotch. "Go on in and get ready for bed. I've got to take a shower to wash this paint off my legs." She looked heavenward. "What I'd give for a pair of nylons. Don't you have any contacts on the black market?"

He shook his head. "I can get almost anything under the counter in Washington, *except* stockings. With all of those thousands of unattached women in the nation's capital, screwing every man in kingdom come for nylons, all the black marketeers are having a field day. Even Charlotte Dice, with all her connections, can't get stockings."

"Is she still sleeping with all those boys?"

He smiled. "Yes, but one at a time. Jackson, the last, wasn't eighteen yet. I swear he'd barely begun to shave."

Luke followed Jorja into the bedroom and removed his clothing, then stepped into the shower with her. "Here, let me soap your back." He ran the rough sponge over her arms and then knelt down and rubbed her legs gently. The beige paint ran down in rivulets over her ankles into the drain. Then he rose up and took her in his arms while the spray from the shower head beat a pulsing rhythm over their bodies. "Hey," he said, "you're slippery!"

She snuggled into his arms, her hair now wet and dripping over his neck. "Yes, and I love it." She ran her hands up and down his thighs, a gesture that never failed to produce the expected response, but this evening he was completely flaccid. "What's happened to Robert Taylor?" she asked in wonderment.

"Robert Taylor isn't Tayloring anymore," he quipped.

"Too much action in Washington?"

"You know better than that." He kissed her lips and then wiped his mouth with his hand. "Your lipstick tastes like pine needles."

"That's the soap, silly!" She laughed and turned off the shower. They dried each other's bodies with soft, furry towels, then, flushed and warm, lay down on the bed. He took her lightly in his arms, kissed and caressed her face, neck, and then the wide circle of brown around the nipples of her pink breasts. Soon she was warm and moist, yet he remained cool and detached.

"What's wrong, darling?" she asked, concerned at his detachment.

"Oh, nothing. It's the mood I'm in, that's all."

She ran her fingertips lightly down his hairy chest to his stomach, where she made light circular motions with

376

her nails, then darted below, and he sighed. With her hand moving, she kissed his chin and mouth, and he moved his arms around her and held her tightly.

"Dammit," he complained, "I'm tense everywhere except where I want to be."

She increased the pressure of her body and kissed him deeply again. When there was still no response, she murmured, "Let's rest a little, darling."

He brought a comforter over their bodies, and they snuggled down into the warmth. Soon he was breathing evenly. She held him more loosely now, and examined his careworn face before she too fell asleep.

They both awakened as the clock in the hall chimed ten. "Hey," he said, "I'm hungry."

"How's Robert Taylor?"

He shook his head. "Nothing."

She smiled and patted his groin. "Maybe he's hungry too."

Ten minutes later they were eating scrambled eggs and toast, and fifteen minutes after that they were back in bed. He was very tender with her, but the more he increased his foreplay, the more aroused she became, the more he physically withdrew. Finally he turned on his back. "Jorja," he said quietly, "nothing is going to work. It's just one of those—"

"Well, why don't you fire the board so you can think of something else besides those worn-out old men?" The moment that she had made the statement, she realized that she had made a mistake, but before she could soften her remark, he came back quickly. "Most of them are my age, Jorja. Do you think I should be put out to pasture too?"

"You're putting words in my mouth, darling," she said gently, covering her tracks.

"Oh," he replied irritably, "Don't call me 'darling.' My name is Luke."

She got up very quietly and went into the bathroom.

A few moments later he heard the shower running again and felt guilty. Why was he thinking about Jeanette?"

He lay back in bed and tried to relax, tried to think of an erotic episode that would stir his imagination, tried to arouse himself—all to no avail. Those twelve old men around the conference table still haunted him.

When he heard the shower cut off, he went into the dressing room, where she was drying her back. He came up behind her and placed his arms over her breasts. "I'm sorry, Jorja, I'm as crotchety as an old bear."

"You'll get all wet," she answered.

"I don't care." He paused. "You have to put up with a lot because of me."

She turned in his arms. "Let's get one thing straight, Luke," she said soberly. "I am not one of the ten neediest cases. I happen to like my life. I have a good job that suits me to a T; I have a boyfriend who means a good deal to me."

He sighed. "Yet there must be so much that's missing."

She shook her head. "No, Luke, I wouldn't trade places with anyone in the world just now." She smiled inwardly. Indeed she wouldn't! In the next few months she would become the most important link between two men, Robert Desmond and Luke Heron, but only one of them would know what she was doing. In her way, she had power in her hands and was not about to let go of it.

She turned defensive. She regarded him earnestly. "You know, Luke, no one ever stands up for the 'other woman.' We're always someone like Ray Schmidt, the heroine of Fannie Hurst's *Back Street*, a mistress who leads a 'shadowed existence' out of the limelight. Many of us aren't that way at all. We like our lives. People think we're lonely because we can't 'be seen' with our men. Well, there are other things about life than going to restaurants and the theater and being seen in public with our men. We're always categorized as pathetic examples of womanhood. Actually, we're very happy to come home at night and not worry about fixing an elaborate dinner or being beautiful all the time. If we want to go to bed with cold cream on our faces, we don't have second thoughts. When our men see us, it's because they want to be with us, and we want to be with them."

"I hadn't thought of it that way," he replied quietly.

"I know, Luke, I know." She slipped away from him and finished toweling her legs. "Now, go stretch out on the bed and think about something sexy, because I'm going to come in to see you in a minute and make love to you." She grinned, suddenly looking very beautiful and very desirable.

He picked her up in his arms, and she giggled. "I feel exactly like a kept woman," she said, "and I love it." She paused. "Don't you feel wicked?"

He laughed and bit her lightly on the ear. "Yes," he said, "and Robert Taylor does too!"

Letty and Bosley were taking their usual afternoon stroll down Main Street to the post office, when Lorraine Stevens called out from the doctor's office, "Do come in, the doctor's free for a moment."

They followed her into the cheerful, sunlit waiting room, then into the small consultation office at the back of the hall, where Dr. Schaeffer had once kept his files. The room was painted a soft yellow color; the wicker furniture looked like it had been ordered from *House Beautiful*. In the old days, Letty reflected, the office had been painted dark green, so that Schaeffer's patients often referred to it as "the jungle." Letty was highly appreciative of the changes.

Lars Hanson, his blondish hair slicked back with Brilliantine, came in the side door with a sandwich wrapped in waxed paper and a mug of steaming coffee. "Hi!" he said. "Glad that Lorraine caught you. Saves me a trip to your house." He sat down at the wicker desk. "Excuse me for eating, but I didn't have dinner last night, breakfast, nor lunch." He took a sip of coffee. "I've been going over Sam's papers." He was elated, and looked like a small boy who had been handed a gross of peppermint sticks. "It's the most extraordinary thing, this world of holistic medicine! Sam *did* use native herbs after he became a medical doctor. It's all there, written in his fine Spencerian hand."

"Have you received the lab report from Oklahoma City?" Letty asked, keeping her voice steady.

"Oh, yes," he replied casually, "in this morning's mail." He took another sip of coffee. "Please excuse me, I'm not quite myself—being up all night, reading." He spread the contents of a manila folder over his desk. "Dr. Swain, who's the most famous medical chemist in the Midwest, did the analysis. It turns out that the compound is purely vegetable—which we knew—but is not poisonous per se." His voice rose an octave in his excitement. "At least, not in the amounts packed in the capsules." His enthusiasm grew. "Oh, it's the most exciting thing! The compound has very peculiar properties. It's a hallucinogen." He sat back in his chair and waited for their reaction.

Letty and Bosley looked at each other blankly. "What else was in the lab report?" Bosley asked.

"Further experiments are continuing, involving experiments with lab animals, which may take some time, but the answer, I feel, is in Sam's papers. That's where I found the term 'hallucinogen,' a derivation from the word "hallucination.' "

"Ah," Bosley said, understanding at once. "Then

both George and Sam were in a state of delusion at death."

"No, no," Lars Hanson corrected him. "There's a great difference. 'Delusion' means to cheat or delude; 'hallucination' means a *wandering of the mind*. According to Sam's studies, carried on for over forty years, certain substances—like those contained in the mushrooms—*alter* the state of mind. Indian medicine men apparently knew where to obtain these drugs. Oh, they probably didn't know *what* they were, but they were very famliar with the results produced. During an agonizing death, the drugs eased the torture by separating the pain from the body."

"That's what Sam said," Letty put in, "but none of us knew what he meant."

"But how is that possible?" Bosley asked.

"We don't know how the compound works in the bloodstream," Lars Hanson expounded. "Sam's research, in case after case, supports the theory that, when given the dosage, the patient is no longer conscious of the *quality* of pain. In other words, he doesn't *hurt* any more in the conventional sense. The pain is no longer connected to the body. Pain apparently takes its place with everything else that's going on in the room— like sunlight coming in the window, a nurse reading a book, a doctor feeling the pulse, a relative conversing. Pain, per se, no longer commands the patient's complete attention the way that it did before."

Letty nodded. "Yes, I can see that. Neither George nor Sam suffered, I'm sure of that. With George especially, he was shaking with unbearable agony, but upon taking the capsules he relaxed, and shortly thereafter started the journey." She looked up at Lars Hanson questioningly. "What about the tunnel and the light? Was the . . . hallucination brought on by the drug?"

The doctor took a deep breath and expelled the air

from his lungs all at once. "Sam thought not; he believed that was what death was." He took a sip of the now cold coffee and grimaced. "I'm only getting into the papers, just scratched the surface of the mountainous research." He leaned forward. "You see, this all began when Sam was on vacation in England after his residency. He was in a small seaside resort when an epidemic of smallpox broke out. Having already had the measles, he was immune—"

Letty nodded. "Ah, yes, I remember. He helped out the time that we lost little Betsy in an epidemic of the pox in Angel."

"He saw many of the stricken children die," the doctor continued soberly, "and they all seemed to see a tunnel with a bright light at the end. Now, Sam already knew, more or less, a bit about this journey that he called 'transition.' He spoke to the children in a soothing voice, and they answered his questions, supporting what he already had suspected was true. He didn't have any of the compound with him—although he tried to obtain some, but it was winter and there were no mushrooms—so he could not aid the children in their journey." He paused. "He must have spoken to George Story about this experience, because when George was dying, he asked for Sam to come. Right?"

Letty nodded. "He trained all the way from New York. We didn't have many airplanes then. It was October twenty-nine, nineteen twenty-nine, just after the great crash."

"If Sam finished his residency in nineteen eleven," the doctor calculated, "and went to England, by the time that George needed him, he must have had some eighteen years of research behind him. He was well versed in what he had to do."

"But," Letty exclaimed, "Why didn't he publish his findings?"

Lars Hanson held up his hands in a helpless gesture.

"I can only speculate. The American Medical Association had not progressed to the point where such proposals would be accepted. In fact, even today they are greatly skeptical of any new drug. I suppose that Sam didn't want to endanger his own standing in the community, or his practice. After all, he was a very famous pediatrician by this time, and he probably couldn't devote as much time to research as he would have liked."

He put the folder together and filed it in a drawer. "I suppose, too, that if he broached the subject to colleagues, there was probably a great deal of poohpoohing. Also, he would have had to experiment with the drug in ways that he probably refused to do. He makes the statement somewhere in the papers that these mind-altering drugs can be extremely dangerous if not used in the correct amounts. He further speculated about possible unwanted side effects that might be produced. Sam only knew that the drug was invaluable in cases of an extremely painful death, when side effects were unimportant. He theorized that the drugs worked in coordination with other substances manufactured by the body that possibly changed certain types of insanity, namely schizophrenia—"

There was a knock on the door. "Mrs. Chenovick is here, Doctor."

"Very well," he answered, turning to Letty and Bosley. "I'll talk to you more about this later, when I digest more of Sam's material. By the way, why don't you go out the side door? Unless, of course, you want to see Bella?"

"Thank you," Letty said gratefully. "I love her very much, but I couldn't think of a thing to say after what you've been telling us. I've got to go home and *think*!"

"And," Lars Hanson replied, "I've got to treat Bella's sprained back. You'd think that at her age she'd hire a man to prune the peach trees, instead of getting up on the ladder herself."

Letty smiled softly. "I'm certain that when it's time for Bella to make her 'transition,' Doctor, there'll be acres and acres of peach trees in bloom at the end of the tunnel."

# 20

## *Middle East Meets Middle West*

*"We'd better run over this list again, Luke, to be sure you have the phrases down right," Jeanette said.*

They were sitting in the living room of Bosley and Letty's Connecticut Avenue house and, although it was early November, there was a thick blanket of snow on the smoothly landscaped grounds.

"Yes, let's practice some more. I want to show Sheik Muhammad Abn that we are courteous people." He closed his eyes. "I greet him with *is-salaam 'alaykum,* which means 'Peace be upon you.' "

"Yes," Jeanette said, "and he replies, *wa-'alaykum is-salaam,* which is, 'And upon you be peace.' "

He looked at her blankly. "I've forgotten the phrase for 'Good afternoon.' "

"It's *masaa' il-khayr.*"

"Oh, yes." He closed his eyes again and repeated the words.

Jeanette leaned forward. "Now he will reply, *masaa' in-nuwr,* which means 'Evening of light.' " She paused. "I wonder why there's so much repetition?"

"The Arabs apparently never rush anything." He grinned. "When Bos and I visited the Sheik in nineteen thirty-eight, it took an interminable time for everything.

There's so much ritual. And in those days we didn't know any Arabic, and we must have made fools of ourselves. I'm afraid we were impatient about everything. Now I want to show the old boy that I've picked up a bit of class since then." He laughed. "Of course, he's accustomed to Anglo ways. He graduated from Cambridge *cum laude*. Let's try to improve my terrible accent. I'll try to go through the farewells again with a little feeling. I say, *fiy amaan illah,* which means, 'Go in the care of God.' "

"And," Jeanette replied quickly, "he replies, *fiy amaan il-kariym*—'Go in the care of the Generous One.' They must be very religious because they mention God so much."

"Muslims are followers of Islam, which means submission to the will of God. All Arabs are supposed to have descended from Ishmael—who was Abraham's firstborn, if I remember my scriptures. Their bible is the Koran."

"Do they have a leader, like the Pope?" Jeanette asked.

"No, and they don't have preachers like we do, either, or congregations to hold the people together. Holy men called *imams* call the populace to prayer. Islam, I suppose, could be called the religion of the individual. Incidentally, their holy day is Friday, not Sunday." He smiled. "That wouldn't work with Christianity, would it?"

"Oh, I don't know, Luke. We haven't been to church lately, but I don't feel like an outcast, and I hope you don't either."

"Well, I'm sure, Jeanette, that the same God, or Allah, that the Muslims worship is ours too. And I'm also not so sure that we Christians wouldn't be better off if we had the sort of civil administration like the rules and regulations described in their *Shari'ah*, which is the law."

386

"Well, we *do* have the Ten Commandments."

He smiled softly. "Of course, but they differ considerably from the Constitution of the United States. Islam religious and civil laws incorporate *both*, and that's what seems so foreign to us. But when you think about it, it's logical." He picked up the list again. "And what does it really matter who brought down the principles of God, whether it was Christ or Buddah or Muhammad?" He took a deep breath. "Now, cue me again, will you? This time, as I pronounce the words, I'll try to think about what I'm saying and use a little expression."

Jeanette threw him a long look. "Remember the time that Fontine Dice went to that dramatic teacher in Enid to take elocution lessons to eliminate her Texas drawl? As time went on, she began making the most ridiculous faces as she tried to emphasize every other word. John Dice finally had enough of it and said, "Fourteen, you're never going to sound like Katharine Hepburn, no matter how you try. So just forget it and stop trying to put on the dog.' " Jeanette laughed until tears came into her eyes.

Luke nodded. "I remember John Dice telling me that one of the joys of living with Fontine was that she was never boring. I suppose he's had to put up with a lot over the years, yet they're perfectly suited to each other." He went to the window. "There are so many really funny stories about the Dices. To me, growing up, they were just friends, but to Mama and Bos they're like family—they grew up together." He shook his head. "It's too bad that they can't enjoy each other's company in their old age. But I guess John can't forgive us for going Democratic. A foolish thing to keep friends apart."

Jeanette took his hand. "Yet *we* almost separated."

Luke nodded. "Yes, but that was caused by something we could not control."

"God bless Sam," Jeanette said quietly. "He saved my life, really." She pressed his hand tightly. "I almost ruined our marriage, and I knew—and didn't know—what I was doing."

"But you weren't yourself. Sam explained all of that so carefully." And Luke almost went on to say that Sam had also contributed to the decline in his relationship with Jorja, but Sam's words came back: "Do not, in a moment of weakness, start confessing all your sins to Jeanette. You have made peace, keep it that way."

The reception for Muhammad Abn was small, according to State Department standards for foreign dignitaries, but the two dozen people already assembled when Luke Heron's name was announced were Washington's most select. The group included a Senator, two Congressmen, a man from the State Department, a cabinet minister, an ambassador, a British diplomat, a five-star general, and several industrial giants, as well as a few businessmen who had dealings in the Middle East. Luke was pleased to see that Heron was the only petroleum concern represented.

Muhammad Abn stood in the center of the room, surrounded by a handful of men and members of his entourage. Muhammad had changed little in the seven years since they had first met, Luke noted. His dark mustache and beard were somewhat longer and more luxuriant, and, without his head wrappings and dressed in a dark blue Western suit, he appeared more animated.

A sterling silver tea and coffee service was laid out on the elaborately set table decorated with a row of American and Arabian flags, presided over by a dark man in Western attire who was obviously an aide-de-camp. It was the first State Department affair that Luke had ever attended at which liquor was not served.

Muhammad Abn nodded, a moment later excused himself from his group, and came forward, holding out his hand, which Luke shook. "Mr. Heron," he said formally, his Cambridge accent snapping off consonants.

"*is-salaam 'alaykum,*" Luke said.

"*wa-'alaykum is-salaam,*" Muhammed Abn replied, smiling.

"*masaa' il-khayr.*"

"*masaa' in-nuwr.*"

Luke searched his face. "How *are* you?"

Muhammad Abn nodded. "Fine, praise be to Allah!" And Luke sensed that the Sheik was surprised and pleased to be greeted in his native tongue.

"I trust that King 'Abd-al-'Aziz ibn-'Abd-al-Rahman al-Faisal ibn-Sa'ud is well?" Thank heavens he had been able to pronounce the long name with some fluency; he mentally thanked Jeanette for insisting that he go over the words again and again.

"Very well indeed." Muhammad Abn inclined his head. "He hopes to visit the United States soon. In the meantime Prince Faisal brings greetings in his name to this country." His dark eyes became more expressive. "You are president of the Heron Oil Company?"

"Yes, my stepfather, Bosley, is the chairman of the board. He would be here today, but oil business kept him in Tulsa. The war plays havoc with much."

Muhammad Abn nodded sympathetically. "There has been much discussion about our joining the war on the side of the Allies. We are in accord."

"Your country is in a very difficult position—the gateway to the Middle East."

"What Prince Faisal would like to accomplish is to set up a legation here in Washington."

Luke drew his breath. "The next logical step would be for the legation to be turned into a Saudi Arabian embassy."

"That is our thinking. Step-by-step is the only way to

proceed." Muhammad Abn raised his brows. "There have been some changes since you were in my country—not as many, perhaps, as we would like, but, for one of the oldest civilizations in the world, we are still a comparatively new country. Events progress slowly. When can I expect you to visit me again?"

"The war, as you know, is very intense just now, and my plans will be difficult to arrange."

"Then I shall state it this way," Muhammad Abn replied warmly. "Each month I shall send you an invitation—with the exception of the holy month of Ramadan, which is devoted to fasting from dawn to sunset each day. When you can accept my invitation, please reply." He paused, and a cloud came over his face. "There are certain areas that I would like you to explain about. Would it also be possible to bring your stepfather with you? I do not know as much about geology as I should."

Luke shook his hand. "We would be pleased to accept your invitation." "He paused." I do not want to keep you from other guests, Muhammad Abn."

"I, too, do not want to start a controversy. I have spoken with you for five minutes. I will now spend five minutes with each of the others." He smiled. "Go in the care of Allah."

*"fiy amaan il-kariym."*

Luke watched the Sheik striding slowly to a cluster of guests, moving with such grace that one could almost see robes flowing across the room with him. He liked the man immensely. There was both trust and warmth to his personality. It had been a long time since Luke had conversed with a person whose motivations were not nurtured and spurred on by greed or avarice. He would accept the second invitation. Above all, he did not wish to seem eager, but on the other hand, neither did he want to insult Sheik Muhammad Abn.

Jeanette was curled up on the divan in the library, reading, when Luke came back from the reception at the State Department, He bent over and kissed her forehead.

"How did it go?"

He laughed. "Very well, I think. Muhammad Abn is a remarkable man. Without his usual regalia, he is, of course, not quite as flamboyant as I remember, but there is still a good bit of drama about him. I like him."

"Is the feeling mutual?"

"I think so."

She sighed softly. "Someday we may be able to meet. He sounds fascinating." She looked up. "Look, I've been reading *The Arabian Nights*."

"But Jeanette, that's all fantasy, like our *Grimms' Fairy Tales*."

"But it's great fun!" She was excited and suddenly looked like a young girl again. "Do you remember when we were kids and used to admire Rudolph Valentino so much? I'll never forget *The Sheik*."

"Another fairy tale!" He frowned. "Jeanette, all of those films about Persia and Arabia set back that country a hundred years. All that mystery and romance and adventure never existed. It's unfair to paint an entire culture that way. Look, it's the same idea that so many Europeans have about America being overrun with cowboys and Indians. To this day—even if there wasn't a war on—many foreigners wouldn't think of visiting the United States because they firmly believe they'd be shot with bows and arrows or kidnapped and held for ransom. They'd expect cattle drives and rustlers and outlaws holding up trains."

"Oh," Jeanette scoffed, "I'm sure it isn't as bad as all that."

"No?" Luke took the book from her lap. "This is going in the trash right now."

391

She stood up defiantly. "You're treating me like a child, Luke." Her voice quavered furiously. "Giving impossible orders!"

"What's so impossible about *not* reading a book?" he asked calmly.

"It goes far beyond that, Luke, and you know it!"

"Why can't you take a simple suggestion in the spirit it is given?"

"You *grabbed* the book out of my hands."

He looked at her and suddenly burst out laughing. "Oh, Jeanette, look at us—at our age—behaving like newly married twenty-year-olds, fighting over . . ."

Her anger vanished, and she smiled self-consciously. "It *is* kind of funny, isn't it, Luke?" She sighed gently. "I guess, if the truth be known," she went on slowly, "I was a bit jealous of you going to the State Department without me—and I'm afraid that's the truth."

He took her in his arms. "Jeanette, I couldn't take you along, or I would have, of course." He turned to the mantel and then turned to face her. "Let's study Arabic together. I'll get some really good books. I don't want to make many mistakes over there."

"Are you going," she asked incredulously, "even with the war?"

"Yes, the country is at peace—at present." He paused. "I want to go before they join the Allied cause. Groundwork about petroleum research must be done before they enter the war."

"Then you think they will definitely go in?"

"Yes, my dear Jeanette," he replied gently, "it's only a matter of time."

Charlotte answered on the first ring. "Jackson?"

"No, this isn't Jackson!" Fontine exclaimed indignantly.

"Oh, hello, Mother," Charlotte replied, trying to get out of her garter belt. "How's everything in Angel?"

"I didn't call to chitchat."

Charlotte stripped off her nylons and checked her rather full figure in the pier mirror in her bedroom. She unsnapped her brassiere. "When are you and Dad coming? You'll have to make early reservations at a hotel, because I know there'll be a shortage of rooms. My new apartment doesn't have an extra bedroom, you know."

"Is that what the war means to you—a shortage of hotel rooms?"

"No, of course not, Mother," Charlotte said placatingly, running a hand over her freshly combed upsweep. "Don't be absurd. Oh, excuse me, someone's at the door." She placed the receiver on the nightstand and opened the double-locked door in the hall. She smiled at the tall young man. "Come in, Jackson honey, I'm on the telephone."

When she picked up the receiver, the line was dead. "It was just Mother," Charlotte said. "Eventually she'll call back." She placed her arms around Jackson's neck and kissed his closely shaven cheek. "Take everything off."

"Socks too?" He grinned, looking five years younger than his twenty-five years.

"Socks too." She looked at herself in the half-mirror in the lavatory, which conveniently cut her image off at the waist. She smiled wryly. The mirror was doing her a favor; her hips and legs were not quite as nice as her bosom. She had inherited her mother's rather heavy figure, and her legs were quite short. She didn't have as many lines in her face as some of her women friends who also worked in the Department of Justice. She smoothed her lips with her tongue and marched into the bedroom.

Jackson, in a state of obvious arousal, was lying on his back, smoking a cigarette. She looked at his midsection obliquely, and a moment later he was kissing her rather violently and with a good deal of passion, which she hoped was not feigned. No matter what one said, in the last analysis it was *youth* that really made the difference; young men could dash away for hours and hours, and that feeling of being a willing receptacle for eons was what she loved most of all. Older men were more mentally stimulating, could order passable dinners in French, had better taste in clothing, and could usually dance better, but when it came to making love, they often went directly to sleep after the first bout. Not so the golden boys, narcissistic to the core; they were still too involved with the wonder of their own bodies to go directly to sleep afterward. Oh, they might doze a bit, but their abilities for reconstitution were phenomenal.

Then a fearful thought came to her. She stopped moving under him. "Jackson, dear, what is your draft status?"

"One-A," he panted, pumping away.

She began to move under him once more, this time taking greater pleasure in his gyrations. It was obvious that sooner or later she would have to find another body to take Jackson's place, just as he had slid into Myron's empty bed. With every young man being conscripted, she might have to settle for a service reject, a 4-F. She would have to be very careful to select a body with flat feet or a broken eardrum rather than one afflicted with a glandular problem that might impede bedtime performances.

Charlotte Dice awakened with a start, and, as an almost sexual spasm shook her body again, she realized that she had been dreaming. She glanced quickly to her right, but the tousled golden head on the pillow did not move. Jackson was still asleep.

Suddenly, she felt nauseated. Was it the dream that had turned her stomach or the late drinks at the Fairfield Supper Club? Truthfully, the long pub crawl was rather hazy. She remembered vaguely that they had started out at Napoleon's, a little French place above a pastry shop on Connecticut Avenue, where the pianist and violinist had serenaded them with sentimental numbers made popular during the late Thirties. Then they had moved on to a great many other hideaways, finally floating into her apartment after midnight. Jackson had made frantic love to her on the living-room sofa, and then again in bed. She was always amazed at how he could be so magnificently tumescent after drinking. Her thighs ached—but it was a good ache.

She slipped carefully out of bed, put on a warm magenta wool dressing gown, and prepared scrambled eggs, holding her breath so that she would not be ill while she ladled the soft yellow mass onto a plate. The odor of eggs always reminded her of the large henhouse at home on the farm. Her mother still gathered the eggs herself each afternoon. "Gives me exercise," Charlotte could hear her say. "Also, it reminds me that for weeks on end, during the depression, all we had to eat were hen fruits." Hen fruits! Charlotte swallowed quickly and prepared the bed tray with a glass of orange juice that she always squeezed fresh for Jackson. She also hated orange juice—the same color as egg yolks.

"Sweetheart, it's time to get up," she called, coming into the bedroom.

He roused, shaking his head covered with a mass of yellow curls, and opening up that lovable mouth in a wide yawn. He liked to have breakfast first thing in the morning; sex was always second.

"Morning," he said, wide awake now.

It always surprised her that anyone could be so cheerful in the morning. She placed the tray over his lap with a smile, kissed his cheek, and slyly reached under the sheet. He, like other young men of his age, was always delightfully erect in the morning. She caressed him languidly.

"Didn't you get enough last night?" he asked play-fully.

She giggled. "Yes, but that was"—she checked her wristwatch—"nine hours ago. As usual, we've over-slept." She looked at the watch again. Yes, it was eleven-thirty. "Oh, my God!" she exclaimed, looking dismayed. "I'd forgotten. I'm due at National Airport at twelve-thirty. "I'd better june."

"*June*?"

"Oh, just an old Oklahoma expression. It means 'hurry.' "

He grinned and finished the orange juice. "What's so important on a Sunday?"

She turned on the tap in the bathtub, then came back into the bedroom. "Mother and Dad are coming in. I told you about the trip yesterday—but you never lis-ten!"

"Can I come along?" He grinned boyishly, and she paused a moment to enjoy his fresh young beauty. He was twenty-five. It was sad, she reflected, that he could not remain twenty-five for eternity. He should be frozen in time.

"Be back in a moment." When she returned, still toweling her back, he was lounging on top of the coun-terpane, listlessly caressing his chest and nipples, his body in the same turgid condition as upon awakening. "That looks awfully inviting," she said with a small smile, "but there's no time now. I should be back about two-thirty. I'll rush back even sooner, if you'll stay."

"I just might do that. I won't say I will and I won't say I won't, but I might," he replied playfully, stretch-ing his back so that his bronze, muscular body and his golden head were highlighted by the sun from the open window.

She slipped the navy-blue crepe-de-chine dress over her head and shoulders. She sat down at the dressing table and removed her last pair of nylons from the drawer and sighed. Should she save them for a more momentous occasion? No, she decided, she supposed she owed it to her folks. She smiled wryly. Glancing in the mirror, she saw that her hair looked like a rat's nest. She ran a comb through the bangs on her forehead and encased the rest of her hair in a snood, then selected a pair of small diamond earrings. Diamonds in the daytime? Why not throw caution to the winds?

Jackson came in from the dressing room in the new gray suit that she had given him last week. He fiddled with his tie, then, as an afterthought, threw a rumpled yellow piece of paper on the bed. "I got my 'greetings' yesterday."

She whired around. "Why didn't you tell me?"

He shrugged. "Well, you knew I'd be getting it sooner or later. I'm One-A."

"Damn the war!" she said peevishly. "When do you have to report?"

"I've still got two weeks. I'm putting in for the Air Force, but, with my usual luck, I'll end up in the infantry."

She put her arms around him and pressed her body against his. "I suppose we've got to be philosophical, Jackson. You won't be the only soldier in the world, and I won't be the only woman without a man." She paused, then murmured, "Will you remember that you loved me a little?"

"Hell, no." He laughed. "I'll remember that I loved you *a lot*." He held her tightly in his arms. "Come back and we'll make love all afternoon." He paused. "Shall I get the car gassed up for you?"

"Please, it would save me time."

"I'll need some money for gas."

She rummaged in her purse. "I haven't anything but a fifty. Will they accept that?"

Probably not, but I will." He took the money. "Could you spare another fifty?"

She colored, reached into the secret pocket, and brought out a twin bill. "Here," she said, "but try to make this last." Then she felt contrite. After all, he would be going away soon, and what was fifty dollars— or a hundred, for that matter? "At least a couple of days," she added lamely.

He was looking at her critically now, and she was glad to be completely dressed. She glanced casually in the mirror. She did look chic; the snood added a youthful touch, and the knee-length dress showed her good legs to advantage while hiding her rather heavy derriere. Wartime fashions suited her, she decided.

"I'll see you downstairs in five minutes," he said, turning serious but not looking at her. "By the way, I'd like the car for a couple of days this week. I want to visit my family in Baltimore."

"Very well," she said, "but I thought you just visited them *last* week?"

"I did," he replied too quickly, "but with going into the service . . ."

"Of course you may have the car," she said, "but in that case I'd better taxi to the airport, and you'll need gas for your trip."

He arranged his lips in an attractive pout. "Aren't your folks in the oil business?"

She gave him a long look. "It's not like they run a bakery, Jackson, and can take home an extra loaf of bread whenever they want to." She patted his chin, making a circle around his Cary Grant–type dimple. "Anyway, there'll be plenty of gas to get you to Baltimore and back."

He kissed her suddenly on the cheek. "You're a sweetheart," he said, unable to hide his glee. And it was then that she knew for certain that he had no intention of visiting his parents. Somewhere, perhaps not too far away, there was a girl—a young girl with a small waist and firm pointed breasts and a smooth, unlined body.

A girl who, if she caused such joy as he had just exhibited, was definitely not a virgin.

The taxi made its way slowly into the line of traffic at National Airport. Charlotte told the cabby to wait, which was against regulations, but a crisp ten-dollar bill placed a smile on his face.

Flight 18 brought only a planeful of servicemen. Mr. and Mrs. John Dice of Angel, Oklahoma, had been bumped!

She fished in her purse for the number of that attractive young man, Dorian Locke, whom she had met in a malt shop, and heaven smiled, because he was home. Yes, he would have dinner with her at seven o'clock at her apartment.

Fontine and John Dice got out of the cab and were greeted by the new doorman, who tipped his hat politely.

"Where might we find Miss Charlotte Dice?" John asked.

"Four-BB." The doorman smiled. "I remember you, Senator, good to see you again. I used to work at the Shoreham."

John held out his hand. "Of course, how are you, Tim?"

The man broke into a wide smile. "Thank you for remembering."

Once in the elevator, Fontine took John's arm. She was awestricken. "How on earth did you remember him?"

He shrugged his shoulders. "Damnedest thing. It came back to me just like that." And John snapped his fingers.

They knocked on 4-BB twice. "Dorian!" Charlotte exclaimed and thrust open the door. Her face turned red, but she recovered immediately and adjusted the neck of the wine-colored floor-length lounging pajamas that hugged her rather generous body like a wet piece of chiffon. "Oh—hi, do come in."

"We finally got a late flight," John said, "after we got bumped."

"I know, I went to the airport."

"Who," Fontine asked, "is Dorian?"

"My new boyfriend." She hugged her mother and kissed her father. "Please come in."

Fontine looked about the living room, where a small table had been set for two. "I hope we're not interrupting," she said.

"Oh, no," Charlotte replied as courteously as possible, "but I thought you'd call when you got to the hotel and we could arrange to meet later." She paused. "Would you like a drink?"

"Some water with ice, please," Fontine said, then turned to John. "Want a beer?"

"Yes, thanks."

"I'm afraid I haven't any beer, Dad. My boyfriends drink cocktails."

"Boy*friends*?" John echoed.

Charlotte looked at them with something like amusement. "Well, after all, just because I live alone is no sign that I don't date occasionally. It's nice to have an escort." She went into the kitchen and returned a moment later. "Here's your water, Mother. I brought you a tiny tumbler of whiskey, Dad—Kentucky bourbon, just like they used to serve at The Widows."

John laughed. "I guess you read Sam's book."

Charlotte nodded. "It was just wonderful, especially about the part where you came up from San Antonio. Also it was marvelous when the first wells came in and brought all of that money."

John smacked his lips after taking a sip of the whiskey. "That is *smooth*."

400

Fontine gave him a long look, and her curls danced. "Don't you be getting a taste for booze at this stage of the game, Jaundice!"

He grinned. "It's just pure D good!" he exclaimed.

"Well, please do sit down," Charlotte said, indicating a large brocade sofa. "I'd ask you how things are going in Angel, but those people don't interest me anymore."

Fontine sighed audibly. "I've never understood why you've just abandoned everyone. We raised you to appreciate good things."

Charlotte laughed. "I know. That's why I love Washington. Every time I drive down Pennsylvania Avenue, I get such a good feeling. It's a far cry from Main Street in Angel. I love the White House, too—although of course I'm not invited there—and I like my job, which isn't at all demanding. I think you could call me a happy woman, Mother."

"I don't understand your way of life, but apparently it suits you."

"To a T, Mother, to a T."

John looked about the beautifully decorated room and glanced at his well-groomed daughter, who was at once very dear to him and yet foreign, and it occurred to him that he did not know her at all. "I've been thinking," he said, "that maybe we didn't do right by you, Charlotte. We should have insisted that you to go Phillips University instead of sending you off to William and Mary. I don't like the airs that your Eastern education gave you."

She turned to him in surprise. "Dad, what's got into you suddenly? You were so proud that I wasn't going to stay in Enid. And, as for airs, I don't know what you mean." She examined her long polished fingernails. "I'm going to be forty, Dad; you've never had any misgivings about me before. I think it's very strange that you're talking this way at this stage of the game." She peered nearsightedly at him. "Has it suddenly occurred

401

to you, that you've had a daughter all this time and not paid very much attention to her?"

Fontine looked on in shocked silence. "Charlotte, I think—"

"Let him answer, Mother."

John's cowboy boot toed the carpet. "Maybe. I was busy all those years at the bank, and then later in the Senate. Weren't we all closer when we lived here in Washington?"

"Nearer," Charlotte replied quietly, "but not closer."

"We've always loved you, dear," Fontine put in quickly.

"Of course, you have, Mother, and I've loved both of you. She ran nervous fingers through her chic gray coiffure. "Loving from afar is just as wonderful as loving next door." She paused, "I don't know why we're engaging in this peculiar conversation. I've always thought that our relationship was very special. No ties."

John lighted a cigar and puffed energetically a few moments. "Maybe that's what's eating me. Now that I've got more time on my hands, I'm looking back, I'm picking holes in my life, looking at things differently."

Charlotte got up slowly and opened the door to the terrace. "Yes," she said quietly, without turning around, "like selling all of Leona Barrett's Heron Oil stock, just to get even for Bosley and Luke turning Democrat!"

"Now, hold on a darn minute, Charlotte!" he replied angrily. "You don't know what you're talking about."

Charlotte turned from the window, the sunlight throwing an aura around her entire figure. "I've just found out from a very confidential source that you're going to sell the Barrett Heron stock. And the only firm that could have been a worse choice than Desmond Oil would have been Standard." She paused. "I suppose that you're going to keep your own Heron stock, hoping that you'll be appointed to the Desmond board?"

John was speechless. He puffed on the cigar, his face red and mottled. At last he stood up. "Fourteen, it's time we left."

Fontine glared at him. "I don't want to go. Now that the subject has come up, I think we should have it out."

He turned to her in amazement. "Keep out of this, Fourteen!"

She stood up and placed her hands on her hips, her platinum sausage curls dancing around her face. "I've been 'keeping out of it,' as you say, for far too long, to my way of thinking. I've sat by, like an old setting hen, and let you make a shambles of the greatest friendship we've ever had. I should have stood up to you before. I should have a say in our affairs, Jaundice. After all, it's my money, too!"

Charlotte applauded. "If nothing else happens here in Washington, Mother, it's the fact that you're finally standing up for your rights."

"You don't have any rights, Fourteen!" John spat out.

"Oh, yes I do! There's never been a divorce in this family, but if I left you right now don't you think I'd get a fair share of our holdings and our money?"

He stared at her as if seeing her for the first time. "Remember yourself! I don't know why all of a sudden you're carrying on so. Did you and Charlotte have this all cooked up beforehand?"

Charlotte coolly lighted a long cigarette. "No, of course not, but what we've been talking about today probably should have come up a long time ago. Why on earth you want to back Desmond is a mystery. He's a slimy little man, and that dreadful Jorja is really a piranha."

"What's that?" Fontine asked.

"One of those fish that consumes everything in sight—including their own flesh and blood. She's going to become head of consumer affairs."

John grimaced. "Well, why not? You're all for these so-called women's rights!"

"Not with that bitch!"

"Charlotte!" Fontine admonished. "Really!"

Charlotte snubbed out her cigarette angrily. "Well, Dad, if you think that you've licked the Herons, you've got another think coming"—she lapsed back into her Oklahoma mode of speech—"because if they maneuver it properly, they'll turn Heron into a private company."

"How's that possible?"

"Heron Oil, as you very well know, is made of many divisions. The Wildcat Bit is a separate manufacturing entity; so are the trucking firms that transport oil. The service stations are operated by another division, new exploration is still another, and then the refineries and the cracking plants . . . They can make private the main section of the company—oil production—then allow Desmond to absorb the other divisions that may not be profitable. All Luke has to do is buy up more stock, which I understand they're doing as quietly as possible, just like Desmond acquired his." She smiled suddenly. "For instance, I'm selling them the blocks you gave me when I reached my majority."

"Why, you can't do that!" he cried. "That's not yours to sell, that's income for your old age."

"I can do what I like with the stock, Dad; it's in my name." She smiled wryly. "And as for my old age, who can say it isn't here now? How does anyone know how long they'll last? Look at poor Clem Story, killed in the prime of life." Her voice broke, and she began to cry.

Fontine put her arms around her, but Charlotte broke away and went to the door of the terrace. "I'm sorry, I don't know what's wrong with me today." She turned back a moment later, under control.

"You . . . really loved him, didn't you?" Fontine said at last.

Charlotte wiped her eyes with a dimity handkerchief.

404

"I didn't realize it until I heard of his death, then I knew that I really loved him all those years ago."

John frowned. "Well, why didn't you get married that time? It was all planned."

"Do you want to know the truth, Dad?" Her face was white, and the wrinkles at the corners of her mouth deepened. "He found out that he didn't love me. He said just because we grew up together, we took each other for granted. Truthfully, I wasn't too upset at the time, if you remember. But, now, like you, Dad, I'm beginning to see a lot of things differently." She turned to him. "If my stock means that Luke can keep control of the company," she said evenly, "you can bet your bottom dollar that he can have it all!"

John sat down and placed his head in his hands. "I'm glad I came to Washington. Being away from Angel always gives me a different perspective."

There was a double knock on the door. Charlotte stood up very straight. "That's Dorian," she said evenly, "and, since today is a day of revelations, you might as well have one more."

"What kind of work is he in, dear—oil?" Fontine asked.

Charlotte shook her head. "No, he's never had a job. In fact, he's up for service. I imagine he'll be drafted any day now."

"But if he's about to receive his 'greetings,'" John said, "he must be . . . quite a bit younger than you."

Charlotte looked her father in the eyes. "I believe he will be nineteen on his next birthday."

"*Nineteen?*"

"A perfectly good age. We were all nineteen once." And before her parents could reply, she opened the door to the tall blond-haired young man in a smartly tailored suit, the young man who resembled all the others—Greek gods with empty pockets.

She turned and smiled sweetly. "Dorian, I'd like you to meet my mother and father, Fontine and John Dice from Angel, Oklahoma."

John caught Fontine as she fainted.

# 21

## *A Basket of Bitter Apples*

Christmas, 1944 was solemnly celebrated at the farm in Angel. Luke and Jeanette, along with twenty-eight-month-old Murdock, flew in from Tulsa, Sarah trained in from Kansas City, joining Letty, Bosley, Mitchell, and Patricia Anne, who Lars Hanson had picked up in Enid in his old roadster.

A six-foot evergreen tree, cut from the back forty acres, was decorated the evening of the twenty-fourth with ornaments that had been in the family for forty years. Fragile little drummers, jolly Santas with angel-hair beards, and assorted colored balls of all sizes—some of which had lost their luster—were hung among strings of popped corn, festoons of speared cranberries, and miniature homemade candy canes.

Yet it was a Christmas like none that had gone before. After a prayer of thanks for the food, when the turkey had been carefully carved, Bosley stood at the head of the table and held up his glass of sweet cider. "Let us toast those who are not with us," he said simply, raising his glass.

As Letty took a sip of the amber liquid, she glanced

at Sarah, who also stood up and raised her glass. "May God send Clement home soon," she said quietly.

There was a shocked silence, and as the dishes were passed back and forth, Letty thought, *Heavenly Father, give Sarah the courage to face her tragedy*. It was heartbreaking, the way that she worked from early morning to late at night at the Red Cross and the U.S.O. and the Gray Ladies, carrying out a hopeless mission, counting the days on the calendar to when Clement would return.

Over coffee and mince pie, Sarah turned to Luke. "I have a problem and I need advice. You talk to lawyers every day and are up on legal matters." She pursed her lips. "Clement's agent, Max, is very disturbed. He's been getting some inquiries from certain musicians who would like to carry on the Clement Story civilian orchestra and perpetuate the sound that he made famous. Of course, I won't allow it, but now that the government has so stupidly officially declared him missing, how can I protect his work?"

Luke considered her question for a long moment. "Did he have a will?"

"Yes. Everything was left to me. Of course I haven't done anything about it yet, because I know that he'll be found."

"Isn't Tracy Newcomb continuing the Army band?"

"Yes."

"Then I don't think you have anything to worry about. There can only be *one* Clement Story orchestra. I'd just wait, Sarah. Certainly money is still coming in from his recordings."

She nodded gravely. "Now more than ever, since he's been declared missing. The ghouls are buying his old records." She smiled wanly. "When he gets home, he'll have a good laugh to think that he's become more popular dead than alive."

Luke looked into his teacup to hide his shock at her

408

words. "Yes," he replied, and he wondered how long she could go on believing that Clem was alive.

Patricia Anne and Lars Hanson, bundled in coats and hats and sweaters, took a short walk by The Widows' Pond. Once out of sight of the occupants of the house, he took her mittened hand, through which he could feel the glow of her body warmth. "Have you told them that I've asked you to marry me?" he asked.

She shook her head. "No, Lars, I haven't said a word."

"Why?"

"Because I'm not sure yet that I really want to become involved."

He dropped her hand as if he had been holding a burning hot coal. "Involved—is that what you call it?" He was hurt and turned away, but she followed him.

"It's not like it sounds," she said gently.

"We've been going steady for over two years." He laughed ruefully. "I sound like a high-school kid—'going steady.' That usually means a commitment."

"I am committed to you, Lars. I'm not going with anyone else. But what's the rush?"

"The rush is that I'm twenty-nine years old," he replied seriously. "The sexual peak of the male is somewhere between sixteen and eighteen."

She burst out laughing. "Oh, Lars, you're so *clinical*."

"And I suppose you're so *experienced*!"

"That's not what I mean, and you know it!" She paused. "It's just that I don't think we should be talking about—well, about sex."

"My God, Patricia Anne, this isn't the Dark Ages, this is nineteen forty-four."

"I can count."

"So what do you want to do?"

409

"About *us*! Why do we have to do anything?" she cried.

"Then you don't love me?"

"It isn't a matter of love," she answered quickly. "It's that I don't want to think that far ahead just now. My studies are very difficult. I have to work very hard for my grades; I'm not very clever, really, and I didn't inherit very good brains. I don't want to think about marriage, and I don't think you should keep on hounding me."

He whirled her around. "I'm not hounding you; I just want some kind of answer."

"I can't give you an answer, Lars. I only know that I don't want to get married while I'm in college."

"And I suppose," he said darkly, "that you don't want to marry a small-town doctor, either!"

"Oh, Lars, I'm proud that you're a doctor, a *good* doctor, but living in Angel . . . I don't know yet."

He nodded gravely. "So it's out at last! I suppose you want to go to New York or Washington and have a big career."

"Not necessarily. But you must remember, Lars, that I'm the first woman in my family to ever go to college, and it's a big responsibility. I want to *finish*. I don't want to drop out to marry you."

He took her in his arms and kissed her quickly, and the touch of his lips caused her to draw in her breath. "Oh, Lars, I do love you, I guess."

"You *guess*." He stood back as if he had been struck. She was immediately contrite. "I *know*."

"That's better. So you love me—that's out in the open now. What am I to do? Wait two more years until you get that precious sheepskin? I'll be thirty-one years old."

"And I'll be twenty." She paused and looked into his eyes. "We're *young*, Lars. It's not as if old age was creeping up, for heaven's sake!"

410

"But the thought of us having to wait just burns me up!"

"You're acting like a teenage boy, Lars. The next thing, you'll be pouting."

He looked heavenward. "Why, oh why did I have to fall in love with a practical, headstrong woman?"

"Instead of a clinging vine?" She took his gloved hand. "I do love you and I do want to marry you, and if in two years you still feel the way about me that you do right now, I'll say yes. How's that?"

He shook his head. "Waiting—it's the waiting that's killing me."

"Is . . . that part of your life so important?" She was embarrassed but had to go on, "Have there been . . . many girls?"

He shook his head again. "Only one, while I was in college, and we weren't right for each other." He turned away from her. "You were asking a moment ago, I assume, about my sex life. I might as well be blunt. That's what you meant, wasn't it?"

Her face flamed, but she said nothing, looking down at her mittens.

"Well, you might as well know the truth, since all sorts of interesting things are turning up today." He paused, and then blurted, "I've never been to bed with anyone."

She looked up quickly into his red face, and then she threw her arms around him. "Oh, Lars, I think that's—beautiful!"

"Well, I don't, and me a doctor, too! It's disgraceful, and I've never told that to anyone in all my whole life."

"Then," she said tenderly, "we'll save ourselves for each other." She stood back and looked him directly in the eyes. "If I can wait, so can you."

The man in the wheelchair looked blankly down the wide expanse of lawn in front of the old mansion, his eyes lingering on white-garbed figures and other figures in assorted attire. It was a familiar sight that he had witnessed every day for the last eight months. He pulled at his beard, soft and silky; it felt good in his hand, but the touch was somehow foreign. He knew vaguely that he did not belong in this place, yet he was comfortable and looked after well. He looked down at his feet in the red house slippers, as if they did not belong to him; they too were unfamiliar. He knew that they should not be red.

White figures scurried across the lawn. The dark, gathering sky meant that rain would soon fall. He hated the feeling of dampness on his wool bathrobe; yet he could not move his chair. Soon he felt the first wet drops on his hair; then there was a deep rumble and the heavens blackened suddenly and his face was hit with a blast of icy rain. He hunched forward as the precipitation gathered on his hair in big droplets, then ran down his neck. He shivered.

From one of the porches came a female cry. "My God, the goof's out there! Someone get him."

He felt his chair being wheeled quickly around, and soon he was being propelled over the lawn to the dry comfort of the awning. The same voice scolded, "He's wet clear through. Better get him changed and fed. Lord knows how long he's been out there."

He knew the voice; it belonged to the large woman with the fancy apron. A scene from the past emerged from the gloomy confusion in his brain: he was very small, and a large woman in a fancy apron was holding him in her arms and playing a game with his fingers—pulling them gently apart and stretching them as wide as she could. For a moment he could feel the muscles tightening and then relaxing, tightening and then relaxing. Then the images were gone, replaced by dark shadows.

412

In the back of the room, the familiar voice of the white figure called out, "Are you going to put the goof to bed or take him to the big hall?"

"It's too early to put him down for the night," another familiar voice replied. "I'll take him. He won't be any trouble in the back of the room. I don't want to miss the gala."

The man was conscious of a great deal of noise, which he wished would go away. The sounds hurt his eardrums, and the reverberation inside his head increased. Somehow he had to stop that terrible barrage of thunder. There was no one near to help him—or, if there were, how would they know what he wanted? The clamor continued unabated. He looked down at his hands on either side of the armrest, and, with the resounding tumult still going on in his brain, with great effort he separated his fingers and raised his arms slowly from his elbows. At last there was peace and quiet as he placed his fingers firmly in his ears.

A long time afterward, when the lights had gone up in the big hall, they found him hunched over in his wheelchair, his hands still holding the sides of his head.

The man was conscious of a passage of time; light and dark shadows were crossing and recrossing in front of him. There was great activity. Along with the others in the ward, he was propped up in bed with his hands placed outside the white sheet. His hair and beard had been combed, and he had been fed some dark liquid which warmed his stomach. There was a hubbub of a vague, remembered sound which he could not identify, yet knew that it was connected to that part of his past that he could not recollect. A great deal of noise again hurt his eardrums. There was an unfamiliar blond figure standing before him in a dress the color of . . . blood. Behind her stood another figure, holding a big box in his arms, a big box that moved to and fro. The

413

noise was deafening now, and as he looked at the red figure, the sounds gradually sorted themselves out into bars of music. He heard a clear voice sing melodiously:

> *And I've seen toasts to Tangerine*
> *Raised in every bar across the Argentine.*
> *Yes, she has them all on the run,*
> *But her heart belongs to just one.*
> *Her heart belongs to Tan-ge-rine.*

The blond woman in red held out her hand. "How do you do," she said sweetly. "My name is Betty Grable."

"How do you do," he replied in a strange guttural voice. "My name is Clement Story."


Bosley answered the telephone on the third ring. "What?" he said, looking at his watch. It was seven o'clock in the morning. "We seem to have a bad connection. Nellie, will you kindly get off the line?" He listened for a long moment.

Letty roused from the other side of the bed. "Who is it, dear?"

Bosley's voice shook. "Would you please repeat that, sir? Here's my wife." Wordlessly, he handed the receiver to her.

"Yes?"

"Hello, Mrs. Trenton," H.R. Leary said slowly. "Listen carefully. I have wonderful news. Your son has been just discovered in a soldiers' nursing home in Cornwall. He's been in a state of shock all these months, but he's well again and in command of his senses. He'll be flown back to the States today for extensive tests at Walter Reed Hospital." He paused, and laughed. "Yes, Mrs. Trenton, he's *fine*. . . . What? Oh, yes, no broken bones, and his fingers are all right, too; already he's playing the piano. I'm sorry to get you up early, but the news will be going out on the wire services and will be announced on the radio this morning. I wanted you to hear the news from us first. Do you have his wife's number in Kansas City?"

"I'll call her," Letty said as the tears coursed down her face. "Thank you for calling." She hung up, and suddenly Bosley was holding her, and he too was crying.

"It's a miracle!" she said at last, and then picked up the phone. . . . "Yes, Nellie, it *is* wonderful; now will you get me Sarah's number in Kansas City?"

"Mother?" Sarah said jubilantly. "I know from the tone of your voice. Clement's been found, hasn't he?"

Letty and Bosley flew to Washington and opened the big house on Connecticut Avenue. "We've been putting it off for so long," Letty said. "Clement's homecoming is excuse enough." And, walking through the big, spacious rooms, with a staff hired from the best agency in town to remove the dust covers from the furniture and clean the rooms, she thought of how beautiful the house looked—and perhaps how foolish it was not to have opened it earlier.

Sarah helped decorate the ornate balustrade in red, white, and blue material, with huge bows that dipped to the carpet. "Doesn't this seem grand after the farm, Mother?" she asked, excitement building under her voice.

Letty nodded happily. "You and Clement were married under the arbor outside in the middle of summer. Such a lovely wedding."

"Yes," Sarah agreed, "but Jeanette and Luke's wedding was just as beautiful, in here with Christmas poinsettias."

"What time is it, my dear?" Letty asked.

"One-fiftteen."

"Then I must call Bosley in from the garden. It's time to dress."

"Dress?"

"We're going to a concert this afternoon."

"But, Mother, Clement is due at two-thirty!"

Letty took her arm. "I know; that's why we're going to the concert."


Sarah was waiting on the front porch as the cab stopped in front of the house, and a moment later a uniformed figure was running up the walk.

"Clem, oh, Clem!" He held her tight, and she could not keep the tears back. She looked at his face. "I thought, somehow, you'd be old," she said, "and you look like a cherub!"

He grinned. "I've had the first rest in all those years on the road. Apparently I was fed extremely well." He studied her face and figure. "You look delicious!" he exclaimed. "Absolutely smashing, as the English would say." He held her around the waist and kissed her again, and they went up the steps into the house. He looked around the great hall with wonder. "It's just like I remembered," he said, "so grand, and so clean—and so quiet."

"The servants are gone. No one's home but us."

For an answer he kissed her again, then lifted her up into his arms. She laughed. "Aren't we sort of . . . mature for this kind of thing?"

He shook his head. "Remember what Clark Gable did to Scarlett O'Hara when he carried her up those stairs? That's what's going to happen to you."

She giggled like a young girl. "Oh, I hope so!" She paused and turned serious. "I'm a bit heavy for you."

"After eight months of rest and relaxation? No, you're as light as a feather." He carried her up the curving staircase to his old room at the back of the house.

Later, when the shades had been pulled down and the room was reflecting the golden autumn without, they lay unclothed on the white sheets and caressed each other. He kissed her ankles, twisting the slave bracelet around and around. "You've not taken it off," he said with wonder.

"Why should I?" she asked softly. "You placed it there yourself. You see, Clem, it was all I had left of you."

"It must have been awful, waiting," he said quietly.

"It was, but you see, Clem, I never gave up hope, because I knew that you weren't dead. And when they awarded you that posthumous medal, I scandalized everyone by not showing up at the ceremony."

"I didn't know where I was," he replied. "It was like being out of my mind, I suppose. I knew that I was being cared for, but that was about all. When they fished me out of the sea, I apparently only had on a pair of G.I. drawers—nothing else."

"But why didn't someone recognize you or connect you with the plane that had been shot down?"

"Because," he explained patiently, "you'd have to be over there to understand. Several planes had been lost, and I was only one of several men washed ashore. The nursing home was very remote." He paused. "Let's face it"—he grinned—"there were no Clement Story fans around who knew what I looked like. When I recovered, let me tell you, *that* bothered me!" He laughed and touched the little heart on the gold chain; then he kissed her knees, the outside of her thighs, her stomach, her breasts, and finally her chin. Then he held her so tightly that she almost cried out, but she kept her equilibrium, because she understood that he wanted to know that she was still there and was not some wraith conjured up out of the night.

They made love a very long time, melded together; the first time was very brief, but then, still joined, he started agonizingly slow movements again, and when at last she rose up to meet him, her body hungered for his touch and the feel of him inside. He, in turn, took delight in her warmth, which was fiery in its intensity, and in that final supreme moment of desire and passion they labored together for a long, sweet, tender, and consuming release. "Oh, Clem," she murmured, "how wonderful! How exquisite!"

He sighed. "Yes, my darling." And as he drowsed she held him close, and it was only then that she realized that the window shades had darkened and that dusk was falling over the house on Connecticut Avenue.

Lars Hanson and Patricia Anne had returned to his apartment, in the rear of his office building, after the Saturday midnight showing of *Arsenic and Old Lace* at the Blue Moon Theater, still laughing about those old ladies who dispatched their roomers with deathly potions of elderberry wine. He opened Cokes, and they sat on the sofa, recounting their favorite bits of dialogue from the picture.

Then he placed his arm around her shoulders, drew her to him, and kissed her on the mouth. "I love you, Patricia Anne," he said, "and I want to make love to you."

"Well, you can't," she said, breaking away from him. "I don't think it's right to keep pressuring me all the time."

For a reply, he kissed her deeply, and she returned his caresses with an ardor that surprised him. As they cuddled down on the couch, she became more and more breathless, and he was beginning to think that she had changed her mind, when the telephone rang.

418

With difficulty, he got to his feet. "Doctor Hanson speaking," he panted, then paused, obviously listening to a long diatribe. "I would suggest, Mrs. Blake," he said patiently, "put Gretchen back to bed, give her two aspirins, and keep her covered. The chill will go away. I'm certain that she's just coming down with another cold." He paused. "Well, yes, if you feel . . ." He flung the instrument onto its cradle. "Damn, those people from California have more colds than the rest of the town put together. Cissie Blake is sure that Gretchen has a fever of a hundred and four, although she has misplaced the thermometer." He sighed. "Well, I've got to go. One thing, at least they pay their bills." He touched her face with his hand. "Will you be here when I get back?"

She shook her head. "No, better drop me off at Grandma's. We've got to get up early in the morning for church. Will you come with us?"

He looked heavenward. "I'd prefer to sleep in, because I'll probably be up half the night as it is, but I suppose I must. It's good for business."

She placed her hands on her hips. "Is there anything that's *not* good for business, Lars Hanson?"

"Yes," he kidded, "being in love with *you*. And taking care of Gretch the Wretch!"

The next evening, Lars pulled out the last long drawer of Sam's file cabinet and picked up the first manila folder. He stretched out on the sofa, took a sip of hot spiced tea—one of his triumphs of the culinary arts—and opened the file. To his astonishment, there was a fat envelope addressed to himself. He read the letter:

Dear Dr. Hanson:

If you have progressed thus far into my files, I know that you are truly interested in my work, otherwise you would have given up long before this. I observed you most carefully, both from a respectful distance and closer, as a patient. I tested you when I brought up my hormone theories in conversation, and I could see the fascination you felt for the topics we discussed. Your work with Luke Three was carried out in a most painstaking, careful way, as were your consultations with Jeanette, and again I could see that you were interested in pursuing your studies. I know what it is to start with nothing and work for a career, and I know that you feel tied down in Angel in general practice. Therefore, in the packet in this envelope, please find the money to carry on my work. I hope that you will not stop with my research, but that the file material will only inspire you to proceed of your own volition. Good luck. Make yourself proud of yourself.

Sam

Lars opened the packet, and fifteen one-thousand-dollar bills slipped to the floor. His eyes stung as he went to the mantel and took down the volume of *Born-Before-Sunrise*. He looked directly at the color portrait of Sam for a long moment. Mentally, he said: *Thank you, my friend*. And in that space in time he could hear Sam's light voice repeating, "Make yourself proud of yourself."

Letty stood at the top of the stairs at the house on Connecticut Avenue and glanced at the guests in their wedding finery milling below. It was February 14, 1945. The house had been decorated in silver and white for Patricia Anne's wedding, and crystal and silver gleamed on the dining-room table, closed off for the guests until after the ceremony. She surveyed her pale lavender dress and looked in the oval mirror at the top of the stairs and smiled at her reflection. She wore a coral cameo pin at her throat, and she thought that she looked rather like Whistler's Mother. All she needed, she speculated with a crooked smile, was a little lace cap. She might be ready for that one day, but not yet, she decided.

Bosley came in from the bedroom and asked for help with his cummerbund. "I hate these things worse than death," he said. "It's too tight."

"All right," Letty replied with a sigh. "Let me loosen the back a bit. The material is stiff, that's all. It surely couldn't be that you have gained weight?"

"Of course not." Then he kissed her cheek. "You're just as pretty today as when I married you thirteen years ago!"

She laughed. "Thank you, Bos, but I was an old woman even then!" She checked his tuxedo, and smoothed her dress, then went on hurriedly. "Come on we don't want to keep our guests waiting."

At two minutes to two o'clock, Bella Chenovick sat at the small rented organ and started the first few bars of the Wedding March. Patricia Anne, dressed in white lace, with a veil that Fontine Dice described as at least as long as the drive up to the front of the White House, came down the ballroom aisle, holding her bouquet of white lilies of the valley close to her waist to steady her trembling hands. Clement—grayer than Letty remembered, proudly walked by her side, and she was amused. He had been in show business so long, that he gave the impression that Patricia Anne was escorting him!

Letty caught her breath and remembered the other weddings in the house. Clement and Sarah had been married in the rose garden outside on a hot summer day, and Luke and Jeanette had taken their vows at

Christmastime with poinsettias gracing the ballroom. She glanced at Lars Hanson, standing so tall and proud, waiting to join Patricia Anne at the altar, and she was pleased; he would be a welcome addition to the family.

She looked around at the family members gathered: Mitchell, filled out more in the face, was becoming quite good-looking in middle age; and Luke, dear Luke, tall, commanding, looking less weary than in several weeks. She thought of Sam, and how he would have been pleased to be present.

Appearance-wise, the women actually seemed to fare better than the men. Sarah, trim and fit, looked at her husband with adoring eyes as if to say, "I believed in you when no one else did; I knew you were alive." And Jeanette, hair upswept, had lost weight so that her figure did not look at all matronly, and she held Murdock, aged two and one-half years, on her lap. For once the child was behaving; what appeared to interest him most were the festoons of white and pink roses on the huge chandeliers. This change-of-life baby had brought new happiness into all of their lives.

To the side, Torgo sat stiffly in his wheelchair; crippled with arthritis, he had still insisted on coming to Washington. Charlotte, dressed in blue brocade, was surely accompanied by the son of a wealthy friend, a handsome blond youth in a superbly tailored gray pinstriped suit with a white shirt with diamond cufflinks.

In the front row sat a special guest: Nellie had taken her vacation to coincide with the wedding, and she wore a dusky rose suit that set off her ruddy complexion.

Letty sighed and wiped a tear from her eye, noting that when the minister asked Patricia Anne if she would become Lars Hanson's bride, her clear voice, responding "I do," let the gathering know that their marriage was to be a partnership, not an "I serve you, Master" relationship.

422

The only missing ingredient was Clement's orchestra, which he had re-formed with Cherokee-blood musicians after being mustered out of the Army. "It's not right for the bride's father to conduct the orchestra at the reception," he had said, and so a local band had been hired, a band that Letty thought decidedly inferior. She thought of those who could not be with them. The Dice's should have been invited; it was sad that John had broken off their relationship, yet, what could Bos have expected when he threw Heron Oil support behind Roosevelt's fourth term? And, Luke Three, somewhere in the South Pacific, wrote occasionally, but there was never an address on the envelope. They didn't even know his A.P.O. number. It was a Valentine's Day wedding, she reflected, and yet, the ghosts of those not present in the ballroom, created a strange air of uncertainty. Personally, she could not wait to return to Angel.

At nine o'clock in the morning, on April 12, 1945, Lars Hanson turned over the keys to his office to Dr. William Platt, who had recently finished his residency at the University of Kansas Medical Center. "Remember, Bill," he said jovially, "if I get bored with my research at Walter Reed, I just might decide to return, if those army doctors throw me out!"

The young red-headed doctor smiled, his brown eyes lighting up, "I doubt that. After all, you've been *invited* to study there. But with Angel growing like it is, if it gets too miserable, come back and be my *assistant*."

"Fat chance!" Lars replied, then paused, "Oh, I almost forgot to give you this. . . ." He turned to the bookcase and removed a slim volume. "Even before you see one patient, you must read this book. It's called *Born-Before-Sunrise*. It's all about Angel, but the most important thing, it's about the *people*."

423

They shook hands; then William Platt drove Lars out to the landing field. The Heron Company plane, which had been stripped of its wartime gray-and-green camouflage, had been painted a pale ivory color that contrasted with the big blue Heron logo stenciled on the tail.

Half a world away, the Battle of the East China Sea concluded, the weary Marines of the Sixth Division had reached Cape Hedo on Okinawa, when word came that President Roosevelt had died. Luke Three's platoon was on the march, and the heavy artillery could be heard near Kanna, where a small pocket of Japanese Thirty-second Army was still holding out.

The platoon was given a five-minute rest, and as the men collapsed near a newly dug slit trench, the sergeant gave the news: . . . massive stroke. . . . Warm Springs, Georgia. . . . Harry S. Truman sworn in . . . Still, all the happenings seemed so remote, somehow, and the exhausted Marines lighted cigerettes; a couple made the sign of the cross. Luke Three watched the ritual and thought of Bella and Torgo Chenovick. Then Darlene's elfin face came up before his eyes. Suddenly, he felt a burning in his groin.

The sergeant shouted, "On your feet," and the men shouldered their weapons and started on the march again. Luke Three, rubbing his stubbled cheeks, dreamed of a warm bath in a pure white tub with dozens of bars of soap, of acres of soft, white toweling. . . .

He had only trudged a few feet, when the pain engulfed him. *Oh, my God,* he thought, *I've been hit.* . . .

Luke Three lay on the hospital cot in the green tent, and read an old copy of *Time* magazine that some thoughtful wife had sent to her surgeon husband. He shifted his weight and turned a page. A twinge of pain engulfed his side, and he grimaced, more in anger than discomfort.

Four other marines of the Sixth Division lay on cots near him, in various positions; all had been seriously wounded. He shook his head at the ironic situation and tentatively looked at the black sutures of his appendix operation. He was certain to have a nasty-looking scar; well, it was better than getting his ass blown off! Besides, no one would probably be aware of the incision for a very long time.

Would Darlene Trune ever run her fingertips back and forth over the ridged skin? He shook his head. He had been thinking a great deal about Darlene the last few days, and he had come to the conclusion that he did not love her. It wasn't that she was older than he, but, as he looked back, he knew that she had been with other guys, and that bothered him. He had been to bed with four women since he had enlisted, and while each was different from the others, they were *all* good— much better than Darlene. So if any woman could give him sexual pleasure, why should he settle for a girl he didn't love? He decided that he would sleep with as many women as he could, because that was what being a man was really all about—but when he married, he would marry for love, and he had the feeling that love, somehow, was a very long way off into the future.

He turned another page of the old *Time* magazine and was suddenly staring into the face of Uncle Clement! His eyes focused on the caption to the photograph: "Captain Clement Story, whose plane was shot down by the Germans, May 1, 1944 has been found in a rehabilitation unit . . ."

Luke Three's eyes filled with tears, which he quickly brushed away; then he read the rest of the article, and pride swelled through his chest. He wanted to turn to the private in the next cot and tell him that his famous

425

Uncle Clem had been found, but he couldn't, because his name was Gene Holiday and he was fighting the war under false pretenses.

He shook his head angrily. Of all the stupid acts to commit in the whole wide world! Why in the hell had he enlisted in the first place? Getting himself involved, having those papers forged! What had seemed like a clever move at the time now appeared sophomoric. So what if he had pulled it off like a professional? Suddenly he wanted to be back in Angel, even back at that stupid school in Tulsa. He could confess that his real name was Luke Heron III—but where would that get him? The Marine Corps was famous for red tape, and by the time his case would be unraveled, he might very well be an old man with gray hair. He sighed. Well, he would stick it out somehow, if he didn't get killed when he went back on the firing line.

The colonel, still dressed in the gray-green fatigues used in the operating tent, pulled back the flap of the makeshift ward. He did not look more than thirty, although his face was lined with utter exhaustion. "Thought you men would like to know that there has been another big landing of troops at Sarangani Bay on Mindanao."

His statement was met with complete silence. He shrugged and placed the tent flap back in position.

A sergeant in the last bed grunted. "Hurray for our side," he said unemotionally and rubbed the stump where his right leg used to be, then turned over on his stomach.

A week later, evacuation began at the tent-hospital. The same colonel wearily conducted the mass exodus; he was going home to be mustered out, yet he was still in a state of shock. Luke Three looked into his eyes, and all he saw was a blank look of despair. He understood, because he had seen the same tortured expression in men returning from the battlefield. The surgeon

426

and his team of doctors did not see the front-line firing; all they saw, day after day, was a parade of mangled bodies, only a fraction of which could be saved.

Luke Three paused when he reached the ship, and looked back at the beachhead. It was as if he were watching a war movie filmed on the shores of California, a war movie with anti-aircraft flak in the sky, but without bombs exploding and sending a ton of sand up into the air, a war movie where all that was left were the wounded and the dying.

He blocked out the journey home; he was only one of a steaming mass of humanity aboard the troopship, waiting to be fed, waiting to use the head, waiting for that glimpse of the Golden Gate Bridge.

The day that the troopships lay at anchor outside the three-mile limit, waiting for other ships to discharge their human cargo, was at first sunny and bright, but by the late afternoon, when the anchor was drawn up, fog washed over the decks. The men in uniform stayed where they fere, shrouded in mist, hoping for a look at the San Francisco skyline, but it was not to be. As the ship began to move in the thick mist, Luke Three hugged the rail. The prodigal had returned, but there was no homecoming; that came the next day, May 7th, when General Eisenhower signed the papers that made possible the surrender of Nazi Germany. Luke Three celebrated by drinking a beer; he and his buddies were restricted to base.

# 22

## The Return

"On August sixth, nineteen forty-five, an atomic bomb weighing four hundred pounds, equal to twenty thousand tons of TNT, was dropped on Hiroshima, Japan."

Mitchell Heron switched off the radio in his office, and his hand was shaking so badly that he could scarcely finish writing up the order for a twelve-foot cherrywood china cabinet. He looked out over the showroom, which was closed for inventory, and he was glad that there were no employees to gather in little clusters and discuss the war situation. He was, truthfully feeling numb, and the magnitude of what he had just heard over the radio had not really penetrated his consciousness. An atomic bomb—made of what? Air, water, and what else? He shivered. Would this mean the end of war as he knew it? Suddenly he could no longer bear being shut up in the office. He would drive over to Angel and have a meal with Aunt Letty and Uncle Bos. He wanted to feel as if he belonged to a family unit; he wanted to feel loved and protected. It was as if he were a little boy again, going home.

* * *

The next morning, a hot wind skimmed over the prairie and disturbed the dried leaves piled up along the curbs at Enid. Mitchell, busy with bookwork that he hated, smoked cigarette after cigarette and downed what he thought must have been three gallons of coffee. He stretched his back and looked out over the showroom, which was empty of customers.

He was about to turn back to his account books, when a familiar figure blocked the doorway. Backlighted by the hazy sun, the man seemed larger than Mitchell had remembered. He watched in a daze as the form came toward him, still not sure that he was not dreaming.

The man was real, he decided at last. He got up from his desk and came forward, unconsciously lapsing into French. "Monsieur Darlan!" he cried. "How good it is to see you, especially today. It looks like the war will be over very soon."

Pierre's mustaches twitched, and Mitchell thought he looked rather like a rabbit. The resemblance became more pronounced as he ambled forward; he had aged, and his back was hunched. "I did not plan to make my appearance to coincide with the atomic bomb." He said gravely, "Believe me."

"Come into the office," Mitchell said cordially, "where we can converse privately—and in English."

Once seated, the little man looked appreciatively around the small room with its golfing trophies, Chamber of Commerce citations, and a blue F.F.A. ribbon awarded to a Heron employee for a prize-winning Brahman bull. He grinned. "So you are successfully settled in," he remarked. "Do you ever think of the old days, Monsieur Bayard?" He noticed the St. Christopher medal hanging over the desk.

Mitchell smiled at the mention of his old cover name. "Not much. Oh, once in a while I read something in the newspapers about the southern part of France, and I wonder whatever became of Lise and Beaufils and the others, but I'm not one to dwell on the past. And you? Are you still part of the game?"

"I don't suppose I'll ever retire," Pierre confided. "Our work has another name now, and there are new people in charge, but the work proceeds as usual."

"What brings you to Enid?" Mitchell asked as conversationally as he could, trying to quiet the beating in his breast.

Pierre ignored the inquiry by asking another question. "How is business? Good?"

Mitchell nodded. "Business has improved about thirty percent, and with the war over, it'll get better!"

"You have, then, been working very hard?"

"Yes. I haven't had a vacation—since I got back from France, actually."

"Then you could, conceivably, take a bit of time away from your work?"

Mitchell looked at Pierre directly, examining his face with care; his expression had not changed, only his eyes held an amused, faraway look. "It would depend, I suppose, on the assignment." He grinned. "My fondness for parachutes has not increased."

Pierre held up his hand. "*Non, non.* Nothing like that. Before, you were a peasant; this mission requires a grand gentleman who speaks German."

"How long would I be away?"

"Oh, perhaps six weeks."

Mitchell laughed wryly. "Six weeks have been known to turn into six months."

"Ah, yes, I remember, but that was because we experienced difficulties in bringing you back. That could not happen this time, I assure you."

"Your assurances do not always work out, Pierre."

He was amused. "You can be certain—this time."

Mitchell leaned forward, his elbows on the desk. "Before I answer, can you tell anything about my former mission, or is it still secret?" He paused. "Just what did I accomplish—or not accomplish?"

Pierre smoothed his mustaches. "I suppose it will do no harm to tell you now. Much has become public knowledge. Your mission had to do with a formula that had to be checked. Lise was a prize pupil of a very famous but modest physicist by the name of Enrico Fermi, who left Fascist Italy for the United States after winning the Nobel Prize in 1938. Eventually he was appointed associate director of the Manhattan Project at Los Alamos Laboratory in New Mexico."

Mitchell's mouth dropped open. "But wasn't that where the atom bomb was perfected?"

Pierre shrugged his shoulders. "Wrong word, 'perfected'; 'developed' is a better term. Fermi had left Italy rather hurriedly, and some of his notebooks had been left with Lise, who was going back to France to live with her family. He had forgotten all about the material, but in 1943 a formula he had earlier developed needed to be confirmed. Word went through the network, and it was found that Lise still had the files in her possession. Because it was known that the Germans were also working on atomic fission, information could not be given over short wave. Broadcasts were carefully monitored by the Nazis, and we did not know which of our codes had been broken. We had tried unsuccessfully to get the information to Lise before you were conscripted. A woman was sent through a safe passage through Spain, the formula worked into the lace of her chemise. But she never got through."

"Captured?"

"*Non.* It was a fluke. She and a small child that she was using as a decoy were run over by an omnibus. At first it was thought, naturally, that the accident had been arranged, but it was nothing more than a civilian error. To be certain, we asked that all of her clothing be turned over to an operative who would then pass the collection along to Lise, who would take the formula from the chemise."

Mitchell shook his head. "But if, dead or alive, the woman accomplished her mission, why was I called into the affair?"

Pierre smiled sadly. "Because the undertaker, thinking that, because of the clothing shortage, her family would only be interested in the outer garments to pass along to another relative, burned the underwear, which was bloodied. The undertaker was a member of the French Underground, and his word was as good as gold."

"So my flask, then, contained the formula?"

"Yes, plus a small sample of a certain type of bromide, which had to be checked out by Lise."

Mitchell leaned back in his chair. "So that was why she was so disturbed when I inadvertently found out that she was a metallurgist. She must have supposed I knew what I was carrying in the tube."

"Possibly. At any rate, she checked the formula against Fermi's files, corrected a small technical error, and placed her findings back in the tube."

"What happened to her? She was so lovely," Mitchell asked.

"You did not know?" Pierre paused and ran a hand over his jaw. "Of course—how could you have found out?" He smoothed his mustaches. "She was captured at Château Latte shortly after you left France. Again, an unfortunate fluke. She was arrested along with some other nurses suspected of harboring operatives. It was ironic, in that the château was a legitimate hospital. Lise just happened to be working there, awaiting transfer."

"Did she escape?"

Pierre shook his head. "*Non*. If she had only known that the questioning was routine—they eventually let

432

the other nurses go—she would be alive today." He sighed gently. "She bit into a capsule."

"Then, of course, they knew——"

Pierre shrugged. "*Non!* Thankfully, the idiot who was interrogating her assumed that she had been so frightened by the arrest that she had suffered a heart attack; the symptoms are identical." He paused dramatically, and then went on, "Monsieur Bayard, you *did* perform a great service for your country."

"Which no one will ever know about—no more than there will ever be a plaque erected to honor Lise."

"Aha, but *you* know, and we know, and that is all that is important!" Pierre exclaimed.

"But Lise didn't. She died not knowing whether an atomic bomb would ever be developed or not."

"She was a brilliant woman. The Manhattan Project was very close to success. Fermi felt that she knew that they were in the last stages of development when she saw the formula."

"Now, saying that I would be available, Pierre, when do you want me? Today? Tomorrow?"

"Timing is not crucial. Eight weeks, we think."

Mitchell felt adrenalin course through his veins. "It will be *fun* to be active," he said at last. "Truthfully, I was becoming bored."

"In the meantime," Pierre suggested, "go to the best tailor in Enid and order a half-dozen very good tweed suits, a cashmere overcoat, and some excellent accessories. Also, a couple of homburgs would not be out of place; then you will be ready when we need you."

"What do I do with the bill? You must realize that I'm a very conservative dresser."

"You will be reimbursed."

"I must say that's very white of you." Mitchell considered his question and then went on lightly. "There is one thing you can do for me, Pierre."

433

Pierre opened his eyes wide. "*You* want a *favor?*" He made the query sound like an impossible quest.

"Since I have performed a service for my country, I think it's time that my country performs a service for me."

"With an epigram like that, I assume"—Pierre chuckled—"that the favor is quite immense."

"Not really. It's a family matter. Someone has been purchasing huge amounts of stock in the Heron Oil Company. I would like very much to know who it is."

Pierre got up very quickly. "I don't think that I can help you," he replied coldly; he was so angry that his mustaches almost bristled. "There are rules and regulations—"

"Which, you once told me, were meant to be broken," Mitchell retorted. "You may use my telephone."

Pierre whirled around furiously. "Stupidity! Even if I could get this impossible information for you, I could not find out immediately. Have you lost your reason? Have you forgotten all that you were taught?"

"I have forgotten nothing," Mitchell replied quietly. "You are making this whole episode sound subversive." His voice was low and conversational. "Either you find out the information, or you can forget about using me on whatever mission that you've in mind." His face was hard, his mouth a straight line. "Our little game can be played both ways."

Pierre appraised him. "At last I get to see the real Michel Bayard in action, and in a way that is new to me." He paused and picked up his hat. "I shall see what I can do, but even if I come up with an answer, how are you going to tell your family without giving away secrets?"

Mitchell smiled slowly. "One of my rich oil customers passed along the word. These things can happen."

"Very well, Monsieur Bayard, *adieu*." Pierre tipped

434

his hat at the door. "You may—or may not—hear from me."

The next morning Mitchell, who was on duty in the showroom, answered the telephone; his excitement built as he recognized Pierre's voice. The message contained only two words: "Robert Desmond."

That same night, Luke was waiting for Jorja at the apartment when she returned from work at five-thirty.

"Hi," she said lightly. "Mix me a drink. I've had an improbable day." She took off her coat and baby-doll shoes and rubbed her feet. "I'd go to bed with any man who offered me a pair of nylons. I'm absolutely ruining my feet," she joked.

He glared at her. "I dare say you've gone to bed for less."

She looked up in surprise. "You're in a nasty mood, Luke Heron!"

"Does that shock you, Jorja?" He walked toward the center of the room, his eyes blazing. "It's not every day of the week that I find a traitor in the bushes."

"Traitor? Bushes?" she scoffed. "Really! What *are* you talking about?"

"I'm talking about Robert Desmond trying to take over Heron Oil—as if you didn't know. You really are a bitch!"

Her heart began to beat rapidly as she dug her toes down into the carpet, trying to make her face an expressionless mask. "If he's trying to take over your company, I certainly don't know anything about it." She tried to make her voice sound convincing in the face of his fury.

"Don't give me that." He grabbed her by the shoulders and shook her violently back and forth. "You were in on this from the beginning. You knew exactly what

435

you were doing. Apparently you'd do anything for money! Everyone knows that Robert Desmond is a womanizer. Were you sleeping with him too? With both of us? Answer me!" he demanded, clutching her shoulders until the pain spread down into her arms. "Answer me!"

"Let me go," she said evenly. "You're hurting me."

"Hurt! See what it's like to be hurt! Do you know what you've cost me?"

"What *I've* cost *you*?" she answered furiously. "What do you think that you've cost me? What do you think it's been like going to bed with a man who can't even get it up anymore?" Her eyes were thin slits. "Do you think that's been *fun*? Letting you slobber over me until I thought I'd lose my mind? When your wet lips were on my breasts, I could hardly endure it."

Color drained from his face. "And I suppose Robert Desmond is a better lover?"

She laughed, throwing her face back in a wild grimace. "He's not my lover, you silly ass, he's my *brother*."

"Your brother?" he asked incredulously.

"And together we're going to take you for every nickel you've got!"

Before he knew what he was doing, he had slapped her hard across the mouth, and she staggered backward until she fell on the carpet by the door.

"If you don't get out of here, I'll kill you!" he shouted.

She got to her knees, her mouth dripping blood onto her white silk blouse. She held the doorjamb for support and, still barefoot, ran down the hall and stood at the elevator door, frantically pushing the button.

Dizzily, Luke clutched the hall table for support and, breathing heavily, looked up unexpectedly to find his reflection in the oval mirror. What he saw shocked him

436

almost as much as Jorja's revelation. He was looking at a pudgy, bloated face with a slack mouth and bloodshot eyes. Suddenly, then, he was crying—sobbing for his youth and for the peaceful life that had eluded him, and a wife whom he loved but who no longer loved him—and growing old and impotent.

After the stinging, boiling tears stopped, he looked up again at his reflection, and somehow he was suffused with new hope. "You're not licked yet, Luke Heron!" he exclaimed, and he suddenly thought of a way out of his dilemma.

Letty knew that it was Fontine's custom to walk to the top of the incline above the pecan grove every afternoon about three o'clock. It was a "set of exercises," she had often said in the old days, that kept her mobile. Letty waited by the maple tree until she saw the small, stocky figure reach the top of the hill, and then, as Fontine surveyed the old orchard from her perch, called out her name very softly.

Fontine turned around, a guilty expression on her plump face, then looked quickly to the right and to the left and, seeing no one was near, came forward with her hands outstretched. "Oh, Letty, it's so good to see you!"

The two women embraced. "I miss you so much," Letty replied gently.

Fontine broke away and touched Letty's face with her hand. "Menfolk are supposed to know best, it's said"—she sighed gently—"but when Jaundice broke off our friendship, it just broke my heart—and over something so silly as politics."

Letty nodded. "Yes, but from John's point of view . . ." She paused. "Fontine," she went on seriously, "I greatly need your help."

"Why, Letty, you know I'd do anything—that is, if I

can." Her wide blue eyes were very wide, two aquamarine gemstones in a pie-plate face.

Letty waved to an old log. "Come, let's sit awhile." She arranged her skirts about her and then took Fontine's hand. "We're in terrible trouble. There is a man called Robert Desmond—"

Fontine nodded. "Yes, Jaundice knows him. He's a young fella from Tulsa."

"He's been buying up the Heron stock for years, a little bit at a time, and now he wants to take over the entire company."

"Can he really do that?"

"Yes, if John sells him the stock from the Barrett Conservatory. We always thought, from what Leona told us, that she had the will written so that it could never be sold. But the lawyer who made up her will in New York didn't quite put it that way—which we knew, but we always thought that with John having power of attorney and being conservator of the estate, and all, that we'd have no problems in that department. But now, with the bad blood that's between us—"

Fontine began to wring her hands. "Oh, Letty, I wish I could help, but Jaundice has forbidden me to even mention the name of Heron, and you know what he's like when he's mad."

Letty sighed, "I know you'd help if you could, Fontine. It was just a thought." She looked over the nut trees and thought of herself as that young girl who had stood with George Story under the trees, catching pecans in her apron as he knocked the branches with a stick. "Let's meet up here again, Fontine," she said slowly. "The hourglass is running out now, and we're just two old ladies. How long can we go on?"

For once in her life, Fontine Dice did not have a ready reply.

\* \* \*

438

The headline in the *Tulsa World*, August 8, 1945, shocked the petroleum industry: DESMOND SEEKS TO BUY HERON.

And the accompanying article stated:

The acquisition-minded Desmond Oil Company, which has purchased two trucking companies last year, is dickering to buy the huge block of Heron stock owned by the Barrett Conservatory of Music at Angel. The Heron Oil Company's president, Luke Heron, confirmed reports of the negotiations in a brief announcement. John Dice, president of the Dice Bank, conservator of the Barrett holdings, and former U.S. Señator (R) from Oklahoma, has been discussing a 'possible sale' of the stock, worth eighty million, which totals twenty-five percent of Heron, to the Desmond interests. If the transaction is consummated, Desmond, with current holdings, will own sixty percent of Heron. . . . Robert Desmond, thirty-two, would presumably, from reports from within the industry, take over as president, retire chairman of the board Bosley Trenton, and replace various other board members with hand-picked appointees, including sister Jorja Desmond Porter as president of consumer affairs. . . .

After the Heron company plane landed at National Airport, Letty and Bosley took the limousine to the Connecticut Avenue house where a Heron board of directors meeting had been called for one o'clock. It was August 9, 1945.

Luke had worked all morning assembling the reports, and as he stood up before the group of men gathered around the long dining room table, it seemed that he was more in command than ever, yet there was also a relaxed air about him that was new. "Before I turn the proceedings over to Bosley," he said clearly, "I will tell you in detail about the rulings our lawyers have given on forming a private company. Heron will retain our petroleum holdings, which have significantly increased during the war. Our other divisions—"

Letty appeared in the doorway. "Excuse me, gentlemen, but we have a caller."

Luke snapped the folder shut. "Mama, this is a board of directors meeting, not a social—"

"I know," she replied apologetically, "but this is one man I'm certain that you all want to see: Mr. John Dice."

The men around the table looked at one another with wonder as the big man came into the room, his cowboy boots making a clicking sound—not unlike oil-well pumps—as he strode over the hardwood floor.

He stood behind Bosley's chair at the head of the long table. "Excuse me for butting in like this," he said, his soft Texas drawl sounding very strange in the formal dining room. "I suppose my coming here today in the light of my past actions may not exactly be cricket, but whether it's proper to barge in isn't important, but what I have to say is . . ." He paused and took a deep breath. "I've been fighting all of you tooth and nail." He ran his tongue over dry lips. "But I'm now taking my hat off. I'm not going to sell the Barrett blocks of stock to Desmond."

The men at the table broke into smiles, and there was a hubbub of talk and laughter and a prolonged round of applause. John kept his head lowered. "I don't deserve any hand-clapping," he said quietly. "The only thing I'm entitled to is a kick in the butt."

"But what made you change your mind?" Bosley said, turning around and looking up into the face of the man he had known for so many years.

"A lot of things, mostly personal, but it came home to me a while ago that I was being a small man. In all my life, no matter what people said of me—and there was quite a lot of controversy when I was on the floor

440

of the Senate—no one ever called me *small*. Now, with the second Atom bomb going off over Nagasaki, the war will really be over. I feel insignificant." He looked at the stunned expressions on the faces of the men. "You mean you hadn't heard?"

Luke shook his head. "No one's been listening to the radio."

Bosley sighed gently. "So Truman will really be stuck with rehabilitating the Orient." He stood up and hit the table with his gavel. "Gentlemen, this meeting is adjourned."

Robert Desmond stood erect, his back toward the Tulsa skyline. He turned over the painting, and surveyed the map on the other side. The Heron empire, marked with tiny blue flags, seemed to mock him, and he grimaced.

Jorja, seated on the leather sofa in front of the fireplace, lighted a small cigarillo. "It's not all that bad, brother dear," she said. "When you get all the stock signed over in your name, you'll still have enough to warrant a position on the Heron board of directors."

"Of course!" he exclaimed. "But that's not what I want. All of those men are boring old-timers who don't have sense enough to come out of the rain."

"With Bosley Trenton retiring at last, you might eventually end up chairman of the board."

"A most unlikely prospect, I assure you. I would have to become president of the company before that—"

She smiled sweetly. "That's what I was thinking. You're twenty years younger than Luke. Think about it; you have time. If you have the executive ability that I think you have, you can get through on sheer brilliance alone."

"Are you being sarcastic?"

"Not especially. I'm just saying that you can become

441

a real moving *force* in the petroleum industry, but you won't do it by being a demi-god."

"That's a nasty word, Jorja." He took a cloth out of his desk and started to polish the glass top. "But you're right. I've got to set my sights on something a bit more lofty." He frowned. "Damned old John Dice! He must be senile."

"Just because he decided not to sell the Barrett stock? Hardly. He was right, but for the wrong reasons. With the war over, the public is going to buy cars like there's no tomorrow, and the oil industry will flourish as never before—you've said that yourself. Heron stock will continue to rise, particularly if you're able to put over some of your ideas about new explorations in Calgary, Canada. Offshore drilling, for one thing, and development in the Middle East. Something should also be done about the North Sea." She paused. "Luke is a reasonable man; he'll listen."

Desmond grimaced again. "To a man who's used every trick in the book—including using his sister as bait?" He shook his head. "No, I don't think so, Jorja."

"You're wrong. He'll pay attention, as long as you deliver." She paused and smoothed her hair back from her face and adjusted the chignon at her nape. "He's statistically minded, so at least you have *that* in common. And, as far as me—well, I went into the affair with both eyes open, and I left the same way. I'm a realist, and I suppose I got what I deserved. Like you, I was working for a bigger slice of the pie. I lost, but it was a good game, a chancy turn of the wheel of fortune. I don't regret those years with Luke. I'm still young, and frankly, I learned far more from him about business than I did from you. That's why I want to be appointed your assistant."

His polishing cloth stopped in midair. "You know that's impossible. They'll insist on a man."

"Of course they will. That is when you insist that I'd

be much more capable than some stooge they'll foist on you! I don't care if I start out as a glorified secretary." She laughed, showing all of her very white teeth. "After all, we're on the same side of the fence: 'I'm *for* the Heron interests, not *against*."

He glared at her. "I'm coming to the conclusion, Jorja, that deep down inside you're not a very nice person."

She raised her eyebrows. "Whatever gave you that idea?" She sniffed. "We had the same mother and father."

The private line rang, and Desmond answered. He paused, listened intently a few moments, biting his fingernails, then he reddened. "I'll think it over, Mr. Heron," he replied and hung up.

"*Luke?*" Jorja asked unbelievingly.

He nodded. "The most startling thing is, he welcomed me to the company. He actually asked if I'd be interested in *selling* Desmond Oil."

Jorja threw back her head and laughed again. "You should be able to appreciate the irony of that offer more than anyone else in the whole wide world. Of course, selling out would be the farthest thing from your mind."

He thrust out his lower lip. "Not necessarily."

"But Daddy would turn over in his grave."

"True, but I never liked him very much anyway. He had his public funeral and a solid-bronze casket and a thirty-thousand-dollar tomb—what more could he have hoped for in this world?" He placed the cloth in the drawer, which he closed softly. "I've never believed in the motto 'If you can't lick 'em, join 'em' until this very moment, but if Heron did buy Desmond, I would have *more* power, a real say, and the important thing would be—"

"It's legitimate," she finished for him. "I see what you mean."

"Exactly. I'd have prestige right from the beginning. I'd have to be consulted on every project up and down the line." He hit the desk for emphasis. "Sometimes it pays to be flexible. Who said this wasn't a good day?"

# 23

## A Fateful Hand

*The clapboard glistened with a new coat of white
paint.*

Letty and Bosley, standing back by God's Acre and
looking at the old house, nodded in unison. "You'd
never know we added two bedrooms and a bath on the
lower floor, would you?" Bosley said.

Letty smiled. "It's high time we did it, too, considering the fact that a new generation will be springing up,
now that Patricia Anne and Lars Hanson are expecting
a baby."

"Surely looks good," Luke Three shouted, coming up
the sidewalk in back of the wrought-iron gate that surrounded God's Acre. He wore overalls, on which was
pinned his ruptured-duck service pin. He wiped greasy
hands on a blue cloth, which he waved in the air. "One
of my ideas," he said proudly. "Dirt don't show on
blue, so why should Heron service stations use white?"

"How's the training program going?" Letty asked,
looking at her handsome grandson with a maternal
smile, glad that the station was open again.

"Fine. At least I can tell a carburetor from differen-
tial. Jerrard is a darned good teacher. When Dad comes

445

in this weekend from Tulsa, I'm going to suggest he put him in charge of a new training program for service-station mechanics. Now that a lot of the guys who worked on equipment will be filtering back into civilian life, we're going to have a lot of people with mechanical knowledge, but they've got to be taught the Heron way."

"Good thinking," Bosley replied. "When are you going to Tulsa and really knuckle down to work?"

"When I complete the course. Then Dad's going to take me around to the field offices." He started to clean his fingernails with a small file attached to his key chain. "I'm anxious to meet Robert Desmond; they say the guy is a real firecracker."

Bosley raised his brows. "That he is—not a bad sort, really, smart as a whip; a little on the sissified side, I think, as fastidious as an old maid."

"A rotten apple if I ever saw one!" Letty exclaimed.

Bosley held up his hand. "Don't jump to conclusions, dear; he's full of spice and vinegar and he's shaking up the board of directors, which is good. He'll be an asset to the company, once we remove his fangs."

"What about his sister, Jorja?" Letty sniffed.

Bosley broke into a wide smile. "Oh, she's teaching a course in economics—that was her major in college. I think she's living in Boston or one of those New England suburbs."

At that moment an airplane was heard overhead. "Oh, my Lord, there must have been a tailwind; he wasn't supposed to arrive for another hour." Letty said, looking down at her apron. "I'll change while you go over to the field, Bos."

"I better clean up, too," Luke Three said.

Letty nodded. "Yes, as the heir apparent, you don't want to look like an ordinary grease monkey."

"I want to look good, I hope, I hope, I hope," Luke Three cracked, rolling his eyes and laughing.

The shiny new DC-6 came out of the sky like a giant roc and made a perfect landing. A moment later Currier and Ives deplaned and stood on either side of the stairway, standing at attention. Bosley smiled. The boys were taking on an air of class befitting the occasion. He only hoped they didn't overdo it.

Sheik Muhammad Abn, dressed in a severely tailored English-cut gray suit and wearing a gray homburg, came down the steps, followed by an aide-decamp who was also in Western attire. Bosley walked forward to shake his hand.

John and Fontine Dice stood back under an evergreen tree on the side of the field and watched the deplaning. "Which one's the Sheik?" she asked. "The one in back?"

"I don't think so, Fourteen. The one up front that looks like a college professor, I think he's the one."

Bosley nodded. "*is-salaam 'alaykum,*" he said soberly.

"*wa-'alaykum is-salaam,*" Muhammad Abn replied. "*masaa' il-khayr.*"

"*masaa' in-nuwr.*" Then, the greeting ritual over, Muhammad Abn shook Bosley's hand. "A wonderful trip!" he exclaimed. "I did not realize that your country was so beautiful. Everything looks so very fertile." He glanced over the terrain. "I am so pleased that you invited me to your home."

"We are truly honored," Bosley replied. "We live very simply here in Angel. There is no show."

Muhammad Abn nodded. "Simplicity is best always, this I believe. It will be interesting to see what happens to my own country, when we deprive the earth of its petroleum riches." He paused thoughtfully. "I sometimes wonder if it is a good plan."

"I feel the same way; yet progress is progress, my friend."

\* \* \*

447

Muhammad Abn and the aide-de-camp were es-conced in the two new rooms on the back of the house, along with twenty pieces of luggage.

While Hattie added the finishing touches to a dinner of minted lamb with a variety of seven vegetables, Letty iced the angel cake. "I'm so nervous," she confided to Hattie. "Women in his country aren't liberated like we are, and I don't want to be forward. Of course, the Sheik was educated in England and is familiar with Western ways. Still, I don't want him to feel uncomfortable in my presence."

"Oh, I don't know," Hattie replied, sucking her false teeth. "Men are men, no matter whether they come from a jungle or live in a tent in the desert. I know, I once met a nice man from Ireland, and he was just as regular as—"

"Yes, I've heard the story, Hattie." Letty smiled, having no intention of hearing about the one spark of romance that had lighted up Hattie's youth. She, as well as everyone in Angel, knew the details of the aborted love afair.

At dusk, a half-hour before supper was to be served, Letty and Hattie watched the Sheik and his aide leave the house through the new back entrance to the bedrooms and walk up the incline toward the glen. "Bos says they have found a quiet place to pray."

"You mean they carry on like that every evening?" Hattie was incredulous.

"They pray five times a day."

"They must be awfully religious, then. I don't know if I could even get down on my knees five times every day or not, let alone have strength enough left to pray!"

Muhammad Abn came into the dining room in a pearl-gray cashmere suit; his eyes danced as he looked at the magnificently appointed table.

Bosley came forward. "I would like you to meet my wife, Letty Story Trenton."

Letty inclined her head. "Welcome to our home," she said as demurely as a young girl.

Muhammad Abn bowed slightly. "Thank you for inviting me." And he flashed a brilliant smile that reminded Letty of Sam. There was a warm, friendly air about the Sheik that she appreciated very much. All fear left her at once. She liked the man immensely.

The meal progressed smoothly. The meat was deliciously pink, the vegetables crisp and not overcooked as Hattie's dishes sometimes were, and the Sally Lunn rolls were especially relished by the guests. But it was the angel cake that was the hit of the evening, and after Muhammad Abn finished the dessert, she saw the look of longing in his eyes and took another piece of cake herself. He was pleased to follow suit, she noticed with amusement. It appeared that it did not matter in what part of the world men originated; they all had a sweet tooth. Muhammad Abn was no longer on a pedestal.


Luke Three closed the station just as Darlene Trune drove into the driveway. "Fill me up, please?"

"How much do you have in your tank?" he asked.

"A couple of gallons."

"Going anywhere special?"

"No."

He leaned over the windshield. "Then can you wait until tomorrow? I've just closed up the cash drawer."

She smiled softly. "I was hoping we could go to the picture show tonight," she said, arranging her skirts around her upper thighs so that he could get a good look at her legs.

"Sorry, but we have house guests, and if I'm going to make points I've got to be there. Dad says I can go to Saudi Arabia if I can establish a good rapport with the Sheik."

"What's he like?" she asked, wide-eyed. "Fontine Dice said he was very handsome—of course, she's near-sighted."

"He's kind of dark, looks a little like Sam did when he was young, I guess." He looked down at her legs and sighed, pressing himself against the fender of the car. "I wish I could go with you." He paused. "Could I meet you later?"

She shook her head. "No, not just for *that*!" She paused. "If I have to go to the movie alone, then I go home alone and crawl into my little white bed by myself."

He sighed and stood back so that she could see the evidence of his arousal very plainly through his uniform. "Why don't we drive out into the country right now?" he asked, looking intently at her face.

She colored. "Oh, I don't know." She looked at his trousers again, and he saw that she was weakening. "Maybe—but I'll need more gas."

Very quickly he unlocked the pump and filled the tank to the brim, slipped the lock together again, and jumped into the front seat. "It's on the house," he explained.

She drove to a quiet section road a half-mile from the Chenovick peach orchard, and parked under a weeping willow tree. He took her in his arms and kissed her deeply, with his hand inside her low-cut blouse.

She drew back. "Just a moment, Luke Three, we've got to have a little talk."

"I brought protection along," he said. "Don't worry about that."

"I'm not worried about anything right now, except, if I'm going to be your steady girlfriend, I should know what your plans are."

"What do you mean, Darlene?" He brushed his hair out of his eyes, and she thought he looked very handsome indeed.

"Before you went into the Marines, you asked me to wait for you. Well, I waited. I didn't date anyone. You've been back for months, and you haven't said anything about marriage."

"*Marriage?*"

She looked out of the window, and her face was very strained. "Don't you remember the promises that last night before you went away?"

"I don't recall much about that," he said slowly. "I've been through so much since then, with Okinawa and all."

"I've read all about understanding what you boys endured overseas, and rehabilitation and all. That's why I've been very patient. But now I think you're back in the swing of being a civilian, and I have my rights." She adjusted her blouse. "I don't want to see you anymore, unless you ask me to marry you."

Embarrassed, he looked down at his hands, which still had traces of grease under the nails. "I wasn't the first," he said at last, "so you can't say I took your virginity."

She slapped him hard across the mouth. "How dare you say that to me!"

His face flaming, he got out of the car and slammed the door. "It's been nice knowing you," he shouted, and then climbed the fence and started to run down the Chenovick pasture toward home.

Darlene looked after the sprinting figure disappearing in the dusk, and she placed her head on the steering wheel and cried as if her heart would break. She had lost him, just as her mother had lost his Uncle Mitchell.

Banners festooned Angel's Main Street, and the crowds had begun to gather early in the day from nearby towns—Enid, Covington, Garber, Billings, and as far away as Pond Creek, Medford, and Blackwell. It was April 18, 1946. Farmers had set up stalls, displaying jars of bright spiced fruit and green and yellow vegetables, while ladies of the various churches had buried their religious differences long enough to preside over one enormous table of pastries. The Odd Fellows and Rebekahs served coffee and tea, while the Boy Scouts manned brooms to keep litter out of the street.

Precisely at twelve o'clock noon, the first float, decorated with red and white crepe paper, started down Main Street from the depot, and the crowd went wild as Clement and his orchestra, displayed in the decorated flatbed Mack truck, struck up "Lady Luck," followed by "The Battle Hymn of the Republic."

The next float in a long lineup was made up of members of the newly formed Junior League, wearing evening dresses and an assortment of sequinned jackets, intermixed here and there with fur stoles. They were followed by buckboards, carriages, and traps driven by the original settlers who had made the Cherokee Strip Run in 1893. The ladies wore calico dresses and poke bonnets, and the men wore everything from cowboy hats to chaps, and many of the old-timers sported newly sprouted beards.

After the settlers, came a new Cadillac containing Cherokee Indians from Tahlequah who had come down for the festivities. Only one very old chief wore a feathered headdress; the other members of the fourth generation were dressed in suits, ties, and pork-pie hats with one long plume.

The last float, a huge mockup of the front page of *The Angel Wing*, had been put together by George Starger, and the headline read: NEW LIBRARY DEDICATED AT ANGEL.

The new building, designed in Early Federal style by a team of architects from Enid, was situated next to the Heron farmhouse, which was now open to the public at fifty cents a head. The columns of the new library, with forty steps that led up to the enormous double entry doors, gleamed in the sun, standing out on the prairie and resembling, Clement thought, one of those facades built on the backlot of Universal Studios in North Hollywood.

The band gathered on the top steps of the building and played "America the Beautiful," while the crowd gathered around the property. Letty looked over the gathering, and tears welled in her eyes. The people that meant most to her had come from the four corners of the land. Luke and Jeanette held hands on the sidelines, and Murdock, aged four, sat on a little camp stool with his hands folded sedately in his lap. She had observed a new closeness between Luke and Jeanette, and, seeing them together, she realized that something had come between them during the war. They had not confided in her, but she was certain that whatever problems had existed between them had somehow been dissolved.

On the opposite steps, Mitchell Heron, his gray hair gleaming in the sun, sported a new English-cut suit and square-cut brogues, and he had told them earlier that he was going to Europe on yet another vacation. She was aware of a change of fortunes when he had opened his second furniture store in Guthrie last January, but she had not realized how successful the operation evidently was turning out to be. Trips to Europe were very expensive.

Beside Mitchell stood Patricia Anne and Lars Hanson, along with Dr. Platt. Patricia Anne carried her baby very low, and the smock that she wore hid her figure expertly; she appeared to be a fashionable model who had chosen a billowing afternoon frock.

Luke Three stood in back of the crowd and did not acknowledge either Belle Trune or her daughter as they made their way to the head of the line. He had changed while in service. Of course, he was grown up now, and ambitious like his father and his father's father. He would bear watching, she thought. He was joined by Robert Desmond, smart as always in a pale ice-cream-colored suit and a matching stetson, and they were soon engaged in an antimated conversation.

Torgo Chenovick, in his wheelchair, was presided over by both the new nurse and Bella, who was dressed in her old native Bohemian costume. John and Fontine Dice had brought along folding chairs, and they sat on the front steps. The moment the band stopped playing, as if on cue, a slight wind blew over the prairie, ruffling the women's dresses and adding a touch of drama to the scene.

John Dice stood up, doffed his ten-gallon hat, and addressed the throng, which now numbered over a thousand. "Angel was formed by Letty Trenton in eighteen ninety-three, as all of you people know. I was there, and so were many settlers gathered here today. Our town has prospered and also had its setbacks, but with all the tribulations, we have come through in grand style. We are fortunate to have a great conservatory here and what will be a great airport, and we hope to attract some of the subdivision construction companies. We feel—and I know that you will all agree—that Angel is on the brink of greater prosperity. We have a new Territorial Museum, left to us by our great friend Sam, Born-Before-Sunrise. And now, with the dedication ceremonies of the new Angel Library, we have added one more cultural footnote to our town."

He paused and wiped his forehead with a white handkerchief. "Now, all of you who are interested in Oklahoma Indian lore will make good use of Sam's research room. The children will be more interested in the Dice wing, with its new record collection. For those drawn to folk arts, we have the Chenovick wing, and the main reading room was contributed by the Trentons, the Storys, and the Herons." He walked up to the huge double front doors, flourishing a large key. He turned back to the crowd. "Would Letty Trenton please come forward?"

The crowd made way for her as she slowly climbed the steps, one by one to the new building. She placed the key in the lock, and the doors swung open. Cheers and applause greeted her as she faced the crowd. She waited until the tumult died down, then she raised her hands in little motioning gestures and said very clearly, "Come in, everybody, and we'll open a keg of cider."

The festivities continued the rest of the afternoon, and while the populace was drinking cider and examining the interior of the library, the Ladies' Aid set up a huge forty-foot buffet of fried chicken, potato salad, and other delicacies contributed by the townspeople. The Trentons and the Storys, joined the Herons at the dance held in the newly refurbished ballroom of the Stevens Hotel, where Clement and his Cherokee Swing Band kept everyone dancing.

At ten o'clock, the lights were lowered, and Clement raised his baton once more and the band played, "Goodnight, Sweetheart."

Bosley took Letty by the hand, and they danced to the slow beat of the music. "Well," he whispered, "we did it, my dear, the library is a reality."

She nodded. "Yes, this is a great occasion for Angel." She smiled crookedly. "But you and I, Bos, are not the important ones here tonight. We've had our day. It's the younger generation that's important now, because they've got to carry on after we've gone. What do you suppose the future will be like, Bos?"

He smiled and held her close. "I don't know, my dear, but I plan to stick around awhile and find out."